EARTH YELL

BOOK 5 IN THE EARTH SONG SERIES

NICK COOK

ABOUT THE AUTHOR

Somewhere back in the mists of time, Nick was born in the great sprawling metropolis of London. He grew up in a family where art was always a huge influence. Tapping into this, Nick finished college with a fine art degree tucked into his back pocket. Faced with the prospect of actually trying to make a living from his talents, he plunged into the emerging video game industry back in the eighties. It was the start of a long career and he produced graphics for many of the top-selling games on the early home computers, including *Aliens* and *Enduro Racer*. Those pioneering games may look crude now, but back then they were considered to be cutting edge. As the industry exploded into the one we know today, Nick's career went supernova. He worked on titles such as *X-Com*, and set up two studios, which produced

Warzone 2100 and the *Conflict: Desert Storm* series. He has around forty published titles to his name.

As great as the video game industry is, a little voice kept nagging inside Nick's head, and at the end of 2006 he was finally ready to pursue his other passion as a full-time career: writing. Many years later, he completed his first trilogy, *Cloud Riders*. And the rest, as they say, is history.

Nick has many interests, from space exploration and astronomy to travelling the world. He has flown light aircraft and microlights, an experience he used as research for *Cloud Riders*. He's always loved to cook, but then you'd expect it with his surname. His writing in many ways reflects his own curiosity about the world around him. He loves to let his imagination run riot to pose the question: *What if?*

Copyright 2021 © Nicholas P Cook

All rights reserved. This book or any portion thereof may not be reproduced or used in any manner whatsoever without the express written permission of the publisher except for the use of brief quotations in a book review.

Published worldwide by Voice from the Clouds Ltd.

www.voicefromtheclouds.com

For dreamers everywhere who imagine how this world can be a better place and do everything they can to make it happen.

CHAPTER ONE

I FELT like an island in the sea of people gathered together for the launch party. I gazed towards the curved sickle blade of a new moon, lost in the drumbeat of my own thoughts as the murmur of a summer breeze caressed my face. The glowing crescent hung in a bright dusting of stars stretching away over the eastern mountain range.

Perfect. But in reality it was a perfect illusion.

That was because all of this was conjured up on the screens that lined the curving ceiling. Even the wind on my face was the product of air circulation ducts discretely built into the walls. All this effort was designed to fool the senses into believing it was all real, but the reality was that we were actually standing in the middle of a cavern at least a thousand metres underground.

The party was in full swing now round Alice's log cabin style mansion. Streams of festival lights had been strung up and Leroy and his team were working their usual magic with dozens of large green barbecues. The air was filled with woodsmoke and cooking meat, two of my favourite scents in the whole world. Normally that would have been enough to make me feel ravenous, but I was feeling too wound up to even think about eating at that precise moment.

There were hundreds of us on the select guest list for tonight's event. A number of knots of people had grown around three dozen men and women, who were all wearing red jumpsuits with an Osprey squadron logo emblazoned on the sleeves. Those people were the VIPs of today's celebration and would be heading out on one of the three Pangolins that were due to launch the following day, craft that had been fitted with additional shielding to protect their crews from any solar radiation spikes.

Ruby stood nearby with one of the crew, Jane, a pretty redhead with her hair tied back in a scrunchie. Jane was somebody that Ruby was finding every excuse to spend time with every chance she got. She had even noticeably mellowed out a fraction as she'd got serious about the blossoming relationship. Quite how the pair were going to work a long-distance relationship when she was millions of miles away after Jane joined Troy and the others on 16 Psyche, a three hundred and seventy million kilometre distant asteroid, I had no idea.

Everyone else here tonight, including Ruby, might already be celebrating, but as I looked at all the happy faces around me, I knew that the knot of apprehension that had taken up residence in my stomach wouldn't be going anywhere until this was all over.

'Hey, what's with the long face, Lauren?' Jack said as he approached me with a fresh glass of champagne, Tom in tow just behind him.

'Sorry, I just won't have the headspace for this party until we hear back from Troy about how the landing on 16 Psyche has gone.'

'Well you won't have much longer to wait,' Tom said, gesturing towards the countdown timer on the ceiling, which was reaching the last couple of minutes. An expectant buzz was already building in the crowd and a lot of gazes kept flicking up towards it.

An image unhelpfully smashed into my mind of freshly smouldering impact craters from where three Pangolins of Falcon squadron had slammed into the surface of the asteroid.

I pulled a face at Tom. 'But you do all realise that because of the time delay, whatever has happened on 16 Psyche actually happened twelve minutes ago and it could have already gone spectacularly wrong?'

Tom crossed his arms. 'I have utter faith in Troy's ability to cope with anything that is thrown at him and his crew, including dealing with last second hitches, and so should you.'

'Yes, yes, I know, but still...' I took a sip of champagne to try and distract me from my growing anxiety attack as I caught Jack and Tom raising their eyebrows at each other. They needed to try living in my headspace sometime, where my brain always rushed to the worst-case scenario.

The swing jazz that had been playing from the speaker system around the house was suddenly muted.

Alice appeared on the veranda in her wheelchair, holding a wireless microphone in her hand. 'Okay, everyone, the big moment is nearly with us,' she said, her voice amplified by the speakers.

A hush fell over the audience as all our gazes turned up towards the time on the virtual display – now down to the last ten seconds.

Then the crowd began joining in like this was a New Year's Day celebration ticking down towards midnight.

'Five, four, three, two, one,' they called out, but I couldn't join in and instead just chewed my lip.

There was a moment of absolute silence that felt like it lasted several lifetimes, but in reality was probably only a split second.

Then a crackle of static echoed around the cavern and a large video window opened up on the virtual sky dome just over the mountain range. Troy's face was suddenly gazing out at us from the bridge of his Pangolin, his crew busy at their work stations behind him.

'Eden, this is Falcon One, we are in the final descent stage,' he said, his voice all professional, steel-forged calm. 'And you should see what we're seeing because it's quite the view.'

My pulse sped up as the camera changed to an external one facing down towards the asteroid's surface. An overlaid altitude indicator counted down past a thousand feet. Short puffs of plasma came from the craft's manoeuvring jets as the Pangolin descended towards a massive crater directly below it. Mountain ranges stretched away to either side, the landscape a pale monochrome palette of greys and blacks.

This was 16 Psyche in all its glory, an M-type asteroid. Two hundred kilometres wide, it was a protoplanet rich in metals that sat between the orbits of Mars and Jupiter. And if this mission was the success that everyone was praying it would be, then Troy would establish Serenity Base on it. This would be the start of an automated factory, planned to manufacture a large fleet of X-craft from the abundance of raw materials mined directly from the asteroid's surface.

Of course all of this was necessary for our ever-developing plan to help defend the Earth from the coming Kimprak invasion. Even now, the mechanised alien scavenger race was hurtling through the interstellar expanse between the stars towards our solar system to harvest all of its useful materials and wipe out all life in the process.

'Landing legs have been lowered, radar computer has detected a valid landing solution and all systems are still showing nominal,' Troy's voice said over the video feed.

An absolute silence had now descended over the crowd; the

tension that I'd been holding inside now visible in so many faces around me. Then despite his reassuring tone of a moment before, Jack's hand sought mine out.

'Slight lateral drift detected and compensating,' Troy's voice said calmly, as though the fate of the whole world wasn't potentially resting on his Falcon squadron pulling this off.

The altitude indicator ticked down past two hundred feet, close enough to the ground to now make out individual boulders casting stark shadows across the asteroid's surface.

'Increasing REV drive lift to slow our rate of descent,' Troy's voice said.

The indicator dropped past a hundred feet and the giant flying saucer extended its four large hydraulic landing legs.

'Eden, we are go for an attempted landing,' Troy said.

I swear that in that moment not a person in the cavern was even daring to breathe, especially me. And Jack was now squeezing my hand so hard that I was sure I was going to be left with a few bruises. Tom looked just as pensive, standing next to us as he watched.

A smooth area among the rocks was opening up on the video as Falcon One dropped towards it. A circular shadow cast by the enormous craft was growing larger fast as its manoeuvring plasma jets started to kick up little swirls of dust on the surface.

'Twenty feet...' Troy said, still totally calm.

The X104's shadow grew to fill the screen. Then there was a slight shudder as the view went black.

My heart crunched into a ball...

'Eden, I can confirm that Falcon One has successfully just touched down,' Troy said.

I let out a huge gasp, my legs turning to jelly as everyone whooped and cheered around me.

Jack drew me into a tight hug and then held my face between

his hands to make me look at him. 'You see, we all told you it would be okay.'

I managed a vague nod as he let me go, finally daring to believe his optimism now that the landing had actually happened.

Everyone's attention returned to the feed as it switched from the cockpit to an external view of the other two Pangolins in the Falcon Squadron. They touched down one after the other in a choreographed dance of expanding dust clouds.

'And the whole Falcon squadron team has just made a home run,' Troy said. 'So to paraphrase my namesake's most famous speech, this is one small step for Eden, one giant leap towards mining this huge lump of space metal to help defend our own precious world.'

At last I felt the weeks of tension starting to drain away as my neck muscles started to loosen. Troy and his squadron had actually done it – although now the really hard work would begin for them.

Tom gazed at me with a told you so expression on his face. 'You see, that mission was always in good hands.'

'It always was,' I replied, now able to smile at him. Then much to his and even to my own surprise, I leant in and hugged him. Tom managed a few gentle taps on my back with his palms before I pulled away. Any show of affection so wasn't his thing.

Troy's face, now grinning, appeared on the video feed again. 'So this is a message for the Osprey squadron, who'll be joining us shortly. Haul your asses out here, because the space weather is mighty fine and the view of the stars is to die for.' He held up a thumb and everyone burst out cheering again, especially the Pangolin flight crews scattered across the crowd. Then the video finished with Troy snapping a salute to the camera.

My gaze flicked across to Jane and Ruby, who were also hugging each other. I just hoped that Ruby, ever the party girl, wouldn't keep the engineer up too late tonight celebrating. Jane really needed to be bright-eyed and bushy-tailed for her ride to the stars tomorrow.

Alice picked up her mic again. 'Okay everyone, we better get our reply ready to send because it will be another twelve minutes until they receive it. So I'd like you all to raise a glass to Commander Troy and his intrepid team further out in the solar system than any human being has ever travelled before. I'd also like to toast the incredible men and women of the Osprey squadron who are here with us tonight, who will be heading out to join Commander Troy and his team at this new frontier for our species.' She raised her champagne glass. 'We salute all of you.'

Everyone in the cavern raised their glasses, including the flight team members, who were beaming at each other.

'We salute you,' we all echoed.

Then Alice gestured towards the barbeque. 'And with that message recorded and now winging its way back to Troy and the rest of Osprey squadron, let's get eating.'

Leroy nodded and his team started opening up the smokers. As soon as the rich scents of cooked meat hit my nostrils my appetite rushed back in with a vengeance.

We grabbed one of the picnic tables with Tom and before long I was tucking into the most succulent ribs that I swear I'd ever eaten in my life. Next to me, Jack had a completely blissed out expression as he devoured some smoked brisket with a side of sweetcorn and red slaw.

Jack wiped the back of his hand across his mouth as Leroy headed in our direction. 'Damn this is some of best barbeque I've had in a long time,' he said, raising a glass of champagne to the great man himself.

Leroy winked at him. 'It's all down to my grandmother's secret rub. It makes all the difference.'

I raised my own glass. 'Then here's to her too.'

He grinned at us and headed past with his tray of sliders to the raucous table next door, filled with Niki and several members of his security team.

But then Jack's expression tensed as he looked at them.

'Oh great, here we go again,' he said.

I turned to see a young blonde woman and a guy with spiky gelled hair squeezing their way through the crowd straight towards our table. Both were wearing white flight suits, identifying them as some of the latest pilots to graduate from the flight training programme.

'Just remember to be polite,' Tom said, giving me a pointed look.

Before I could reply, they arrived and the young woman snapped a salute towards me. 'We just wanted to introduce ourselves to you, ma'am.'

I pulled a face at her. 'Ma'am? You do realise that you just made me feel like a hundred and eighty.'

A slightly terrified look filled the woman's face as Jack laughed.

She lowered her hand. 'Sorry, I didn't mean—'

The guy shook his head at his companion, followed by a bit of an eye roll. 'Hush now before you put your foot in there too, Erin,' he said. Then he stuck out a hand to shake mine. 'The name's Daryl and it's good to meet you all. But please excuse my pilot. She has a bit of a fangirl crush on you, Captain Stelleck.'

Erin's cheeks were now flaming. She pulled away from Daryl and gently punched him in the arm. 'I do not!' Then she turned back to me and took a deep breath. 'Okay maybe a little bit. But I just wanted to say that you and the rest of your team have been a real inspiration to all of the cadets. Thank you for everything that you've done.'

'Um, thanks,' I said, feeling my own face heat up. I so hated this sort of attention. Then I caught the amused look that Jack was giving me and had to resist the temptation to punch him in the arm a lot harder than Erin had just done to Daryl.

Cadet school was one of the new programmes that Alice had set up to make sure we had enough skilled pilots to fly our ever-expanding fleet of X103s and Pangolins. But this wasn't the first time that some of them had sought us out; they looked up to us, especially me for some reason.

Daryl gave me a far more relaxed salute. 'Sorry to disturb you, Captain. We'll let you enjoy your food in peace.' Then he hooked his hand under Erin's arm and steered her away as quickly as he could before she could begin to protest.

'Give me strength,' I muttered.

'You all deserve the attention you're getting round here,' Tom said.

I grimaced. 'Not so sure about that. That aside, is it just me or did those two look incredibly young to be a flight crew?'

'I believe that both of them are in their very early twenties and are at the top of their class,' Tom said. 'According to her instructors, Erin Connor is an exceptional pilot and her weapons officer, Daryl White has even threatened some of Ruby's high scores recently on the target range.'

'Oh he's that guy,' Jack said, giving the retreating back of the man's head a respectful nod.

'It's great the training programme is working out so well, but I do wish they wouldn't idolise us like this,' I said.

Tom raised his eyebrows at me. 'You'll have to soak it up, Lauren. I'm afraid that fame within the walls of Eden is all part of your celebrity lifestyle now.'

'I don't remember seeing that in the small print when I signed up to all of this,' I replied.

Tom chuckled softly and raised his glass to mine; I clinked it.

Jack glanced around us. 'Has anyone seen Mike and Jodie? I thought they would have wanted to be here for the big moment.'

'They are trying to retrofit a QEC radio to the Osprey squadron's X104s,' Tom replied. 'And you both know what they're like when they get a new science project under their belts.'

'What's a QEC radio when it's at home?' Jack asked.

'A quantum entanglement radio designed to instantly communicate between devices, however far apart they are,' I said.

Jack peered at me. 'Are you saying we'll have a way to instantly keep contact with the Osprey squadron with no communication lags as they head out towards the 16 Psyche?'

'Precisely. No more waiting for over twelve minutes to be able to hear a reply to a message to Serenity Base when they establish it,' I replied.

A flurry of movement at the doorway to the lab caught my eye and I turned to see Jodie running into the cavern, scanning the crowd. Spotting us, she rushed over.

'Hey, where's the fire?' Jack asked as she reached our table.

'Fire? There's no fire, but Delphi has just had a positive hit trawling a Reddit message board. She's found possible evidence of a micro mind waking up. Lucy is scanning the data right now for any more clues.'

I sat up straighter because this was all about our plan A to defend our world. Despite the enormous fleet that we were planning to build, our best hope was still to track down every one of the Angelus micro minds. Contained within them was some secret plan by their creators to defeat the Kimprak threat to Earth.

'And has the TREENO network detected a neutrino burst to go with it?' I asked.

'No, nothing yet, but that aside it still sounds like a promising lead.'

'Which is pointing to where exactly?' Jack asked, putting his champagne flute down on the table.

'In the middle of the ocean, just off the coast of Cuba. Anyway, I need to scoop up Alice. I'll see you guys in the briefing room.' Jodie bounded away through the crowd.

Tom scratched the back of his neck. 'If this turns out to be a real lead, you do realise what that means?'

'That there may be a micro mind at the bottom of the ocean?' I said. 'But can you begin to imagine the logistical nightmare that's going to give us trying to retrieve it?'

'If so, this is going to be a real doozy,' Jack said, scraping his hand through his mane of blond hair.

CHAPTER TWO

WE ALL SAT in the briefing room, the walls lined with screens filled with video and social media feeds from across the Internet. Nearly everyone waited with expectant expressions about what we were about to learn, although Ruby looked distinctly pissed off thanks to being pulled away from the party and more specifically, Jane.

Lucy, an Angelus AI that I'd grown close enough to to view as a best friend, was also in attendance utilising her new proxy, namely a rendered avatar of herself. This way she could project onto any of Eden's screens, allowing her to move beyond the constraints of the holographic Cage in the lab, where the micro mind that powered her was actually situated.

Lucy's face, modelled on a younger version of my aunt, now peered out at us in a overlaid window on the large viewing monitor at the far end of the room. Thanks to the fact that she'd chosen her study in Christchurch College as the background, her video feed bore more than a striking resemblance to a regular Zoom call. Just to add to her, *you need to take me seriously credentials*, she was also wearing a pair of half-moon specs especially for the occasion. This was something that my real aunt, who'd been a professor at Oxford, would never have been seen dead wearing in real life. Not that Lucy would let a small detail like that ever get in the way of her wardrobe choice for dramatic effect.

Alice, the president of the Sky Dreamer Corp, put down the tablet that she'd been studying since Jodie had handed it to her. 'Lucy, would you like to brief us all on what you've discovered?' she said.

Lucy nodded, making her specs slide down her nose so she had to poke them back up into place with her finger.

'To kick this briefing off, we're going to look at the area where this latest lead is located,' she said.

All the screens around us were filled with a map centred on an ocean just off the northern coast of Cuba. Near the centre of the map was an island labelled the *Isla de la Juventud*.

'This is the area of the ocean where a deep-sea diver called Raúl Fernández and his sister Maricela went missing three months ago onboard their boat *Hercules*,' Lucy continued. 'Debris from it was washed up on the shores of Juventud nearby, an archipelago lying 50 miles south of Cuba. There were no storms reported in the area at the time that their boat went missing, so local news sites have suggested that a whale strike may have sunk it, especially as there has been a significant increase in whale activity across that whole region in recent months.'

Mike tapped his stylus against the side of his tablet. 'As tragic as that is, I still don't see how a whale strike can be linked to a possible waking micro mind, Lucy?'

'We'll get to that part in a minute,' Lucy replied. 'But to start with, I took the liberty of checking the video surveillance footage from one of the military satellites that I've previously hacked into. And what I found is very interesting indeed. Here's an image recorded less than five minutes ago, ten miles away from the area where Fernández and his sister disappeared.'

A zoomed-in image of the ocean appeared on the main screen.

'Looks quiet enough now,' Jack said.

'You think? Look again...' Lucy replied.

The image zoomed in again and it looked just as empty as the previous view. Then I spotted a tiny faint trail on the surface.

'What's causing that wake, Lucy?' I asked. 'The dorsal fin of a whale, something like that?'

'Not in this instance, my little sunflower,' Lucy replied, deliberately using my Aunt's old term of endearment for me when I'd been all of eight. 'I've run some imaging processing to increase contrast and it will reveal what's actually going on.'

The image switched to a false colour view. What suddenly appeared in what had been an empty area of ocean was the unmistakable outline of a very large submarine just beneath the surface.

'The wake that you spotted, Lauren, was caused by that sub's raised scope,' Lucy said.

Tom sat up straighter in his seat. 'Based on that silhouette, that looks like a Russian Graney class nuclear sub to me.'

Lucy's avatar nodded. 'You've hit the nail on the head, Tom.'

'Okay, this is very interesting, especially if the Russians are prepared to send a nuclear sub so close to US territorial waters,' Alice said.

'Then I think you'll be really interested when you see the next image,' Lucy replied.

The view pulled out and started to scroll west until a white ship came into view. It appeared to have a couple of yellow crane arms towards the rear and some sort of garage leading out onto a rear pad.

'What sort of boat is that?' Mike asked, peering at it.

'That's a Russian research ship called the *Retvizan*,' Lucy said. 'But in reality it's actually a spy ship that's rumoured to be equipped with submersible drones that can dive to a depth of twenty thousand feet. They're primarily designed to target undersea data cables between the US and the rest of the world. However, they are more than capable of getting to the bottom of the ocean at that location; it's just a thousand feet down to the seabed.'

Ruby sat forward, elbows on the table, the annoyance that had been on her face about being dragged into this meeting, now history. 'So you're trying to say the Russkies had something to do with the death of those divers?'

'It's certainly one hell of a coincidence if it isn't,' Lucy replied.

'Okay, I grant you that this is certainly suspicious,' I said. 'But I don't see how this supports the theory that this has anything to do with a waking micro mind, especially as there's been no accompanying neutrino burst.'

'That's where the next piece of evidence comes in about a possible cover-up around the divers and their boat,' Lucy replied. 'Examining Delphi's searches, a report surfaced on one of the national Cuban newspaper websites a week before the divers' disappearance. But a few days later that same news article was taken down, no doubt under heavy influence from the Kremlin, going by the presence of the Russian ships in the area. Anyway, thanks to the fact that Delphi stores every single web page on the server centre here at Eden, we can still read it...'

A website news article appeared on the main screen with the headline: *Local Divers Claim to Have Heard Unexplained Sound Coming from the Depths of the Ocean.*

'What sort of,' – Mike scratched air quotes – '*strange sounds* are we talking here?'

'The diver said it sounded like echoey whale song that rose and fell in modulated tones.'

'That certainly sounds like it could have been generated by a micro mind,' I said.

'Certainly based on the Russian activity alone, something significant is obviously happening at that location,' Lucy replied. 'Whether it's anything to do with a micro mind is still up for debate.'

Mike pinched his lips between his fingers. 'There is a way to rule it out either way and that's to place seismic sensors across the area to pick up any monowave quakes. That way if a micro mind is responsible for these sounds, we can triangulate them and detect the precise location, even if it's under the ocean.'

Alice nodded. 'Okay, that certainly sounds like a line of enquiry worth pursuing.'

Tom steepled his fingers together. 'I agree, but aren't we in danger of jumping to conclusions that this is anything to do with a micro mind? After all, with all the Russian military activity and the high level secrecy that's obviously in place, this has all the classic ingredients of a cover-up. Maybe the Russians have a sunken nuclear sub they are trying to recover, hence all the secrecy?'

I understood where Tom was coming from. 'It's just such a shame we can't talk to those missing divers to find out exactly what they heard.'

'Actually there may still be a way to find that out,' Lucy replied. 'You see, both siblings were part of a diving dynasty. Their father, Carlos Fernández, who heads up the diving school they all ran together is still very much alive. From the brother and sister's posts on social media and on their diving school website, it's obvious that the three of them were very close. If anyone might know anything more about what they heard, I'm sure they would have shared it with their dad.'

'So you're saying we should go and track this Carlos guy down in Cuba?' Ruby asked.

'It certainly sounds worth pursuing to me,' Alice said.

'Great! I've always wanted to visit there,' Mike said.

Tom held up his palms. 'Maybe you have, but do I really need to point out that this isn't going to be any sort of holiday in any way or form?'

'Exactly,' Jodie said, frowning at her boyfriend.

'But guys, we're talking Havana here, not to mention the home of the Cubano,' Mike replied.

'The what?' I asked.

But now Ruby was nodding with approval. 'Only one of the best sandwiches in the whole world, Lauren. And I'm so up for that.' She reached across and fist-bumped Mike.

Jack shook his head at the two of them. 'I do wonder about your priorities sometimes.'

They both grinned at him by way of a response.

'The one thing I don't get is if this is linked to a micro mind, why isn't the Russian navy trying to track it down rather than an Overseers' force?' Ruby asked.

'Don't forget that the Overseers' reach extends into all governments around the world, including their military,' Tom said. 'If this has anything at all to do with a micro mind, I can guarantee you that the Overseers will already be pulling the strings of this operation. The Russian military probably have no idea of what their real mission is.'

'It sounds to me like we have no choice but to assume that's exactly what's going on,' I said. 'But if we're going to do this maybe we should also visit the area where the divers disappeared?'

Jack nodded . 'If ever there was a need for a stealth mission, this is it. The problem as I see it is that if the micro mind is on the ocean floor or even buried beneath it, then that's going to present a significant logistical problem as to how we're going to retrieve it.'

An idea immediately sprung into my head and I turned to Jodie. 'You talked before about adapting *Ariel* to be able to travel underwater when we first thought the Atlantis site was actually at the bottom of the ocean. Could that be a viable option here?'

Jodie eyes unfocused for a few seconds as she gazed off into empty space. 'This sounds like a perfect project for my new Forge team.'

'Your what?' I asked.

'Yes, sorry, it's a group of some of our best scientists and engineers,' Alice said. 'Think of it as Eden's very own version of America's Skunk Works, where top secret, cutting edge tech is put together, like the Pangolins that we've been developing.'

'Yes, and for some unknown reason, Alice has put me in charge of this new dream team,' Jodie said.

Alice smiled at her. 'Oh, you're more than qualified to be in charge of them all.'

'If you say so,' Jodie replied, frowning slightly. 'Anyway, converting an X103 craft will be a perfect first project for the Forge team to get their teeth into. We would need to add some sort of thruster system, as obviously the existing multi-mode manoeuvring rockets wouldn't work underwater. But the main problem is that we're talking about a serious amount of pressure at those depths; we need to make sure the craft doesn't get crushed like a tin can.'

'Actually, that's something that I can help you with,' Lucy said. 'I can adjust the REV drive field to create a gravity bubble around an X103. That will protect the hull in much the same way as we currently use it as a forcefield against enemy fire.'

'Okay, this sounds very promising, but aren't we overlooking the very real danger here?' I said. 'The Russians, or at least the Overseers — who are really running the operation, may be able to retrieve the micro mind if there is one there and they'll be long gone by the time we arrive.'

'Not based on the evidence that I've seen from the military satellite feeds,' Lucy replied. 'If anything, activity is ratcheting up; more Russian supply ships are heading towards the northern coast of Cuba, which suggests this is very much an ongoing mission situation.'

'But for how much longer?' Ruby asked.

'Taking into account the depth that they are having to work at, even with the right equipment, it's going to be a serious challenge,' Jodie said. 'It could take them weeks, months even to locate, let alone retrieve anything down there. So if there is a micro mind down there, I think we'll still be in with a strong chance to beat them to it.'

Jodie made a good point and everyone was now nodding.

'In that case it sounds like this is becoming a serious mission proposal that we need to act immediately on. We need to send out a reconnaissance team to get moving whilst Jodie begins the alterations to the craft for underwater use,' Alice said.

Tom sat forward, resting his elbows on the table. 'Then there is something else I'd like to raise. If we are going to do this, especially after the events at the Richat Structure, I'm no longer prepared to send a single ship in. From now on it should be three ships as a minimum. So if we are serious about pursuing this lead I would suggest that maybe we send in *Ariel* and a converted X103, along with another converted Pangolin for heavy weapons backup. Jodie, would it be possible to convert an X104 for underwater use?'

'That would be a bigger engineering challenge and I'm afraid will take longer. If speed is of the essence, I'd say just concentrate on the X103 craft and have one of the existing Pangolin fleet available for backup above the surface.'

'That certainly makes sense to me,' I said. 'And having been caught with the shit hitting the fan during the last mission and being outgunned by a TR-3B fleet, I'd be more than happy to have some serious firepower available to us if it's needed.'

'Then you'll have it,' Alice replied.

I turned to Jodie. 'I hate to try and pin you down on this, but how long do you think all this might take?'

'In a sensible and realistic time frame, probably a year,' Jodie said.

I couldn't hold back the grimace that instantly appeared on my face.

But Jodie was already holding up a hand. 'Relax, Lauren. In the crazy accelerated universe we all seem to exist in within the walls of Eden these days, it might be possible to get it all done in a few weeks, maybe less.'

'Then you'll have all the resources you need to make that goal become a reality,' Alice said.

'I also have a suggestion,' Jack said. 'Whilst we are waiting for the modifications and as it sounds like we're heading to Cuba anyway, why don't we hire someone with a submersible to explore the ocean bed where the divers went missing? At least it's currently well away from all that Russian activity.'

Tom nodded. 'I'll look into it and see if we can charter a suitable vessel with a team to operate it. Ideally, something that won't raise any eyebrows.'

Ruby sat forward. 'Um, Jodie, I hate to add to your workload, but would it be possible to add some underwater weapons systems to *Ariel* too? Maybe even some WASP drones modified for underwater use?'

'Hey, add to my workload why don't you, but yes that shouldn't be a problem,' Jodie replied.

'Now *that* I'm liking the sound of, especially if it means I don't have to get my feet wet,' Ruby said. 'Absolutely loathe the water. All those things with eyes and sharp teeth lurking beneath the surface waiting to bite you.'

'Not a big fan of *Jaws* then?' Mike asked.

Ruby just shuddered in response.

Alice glanced across at Tom. 'Can I leave it to you to get everything organised for an initial reconnaissance mission with Lauren and her team?'

'Absolutely! As time is of the essence, I suggest we aim to head out tomorrow to track down this Carlos Fernández to see what he knows. The sooner we gather some intelligence on the ground about what's going on out there, the happier I'll be.'

'I think you're speaking for all of us, Tom,' I said.

'It will also mean that I can start placing those seismic sensors across Cuba sooner rather than later.'

Ruby clutched her hands together. 'But we'll still be here to see the Osprey Squadron off, right?'

Of course, Ruby wanted to be here to see Jane off on her critical mission to 16 Psyche. And who could blame her? It might be months, longer even, until she saw Jane again.

'I should think so; it will take me a while to get everything organised,' Tom said.

'Oh thank God for that,' Ruby said, slumping back into her chair.

As the meeting broke up and people began to head off, Jack caught my eye. 'Sounds like this is going to be an interesting mission, Lauren.'

'Aren't they always? Anyway, I don't know about you but I'm sure I've got room for some more of Jerry's barbeque.'

Jack stood up and offered me his hand. 'Then let's get to it.'

'Lauren, could I have a word alone with you before you go?' Lucy's voice said from the screen

I raised my eyebrows at Jack. 'Of course. I'll see you there, Jack.'

He nodded but gave me a look as he disappeared out of the door.

'Is everything okay, Lucy?' I asked as soon as the door had closed behind him.

'Not completely. Look, I know Tom isn't keen on me heading out on missions after I managed to get myself shot down, not to mention what happened here in Eden with Red. But the theory is one thing and not being by your side on a mission is completely another. You do know I'm going to be worried sick about you all?'

'I sort of guessed that. But we both know that this is the right call, Lucy. You're just too valuable to throw into the frontline anymore.'

'And you're not?'

'To be absolutely blunt, not as much as you are. Look, I understand how you must be feeling about being asked to stay behind, but I'll rest easier knowing that you're safe here. And if we do discover a micro mind down there on the seabed, then I'm sure that not even Tom will object to you making a field trip to merge with it. So for now, let's park this conversation and revisit it later on.'

'Right...'

Lucy's tone made it evident to me that she was less than happy about the situation. But whether she understood it or not, I knew deep down it really was for the best.

'Okay, how about this for a great idea?' I said, making a very deliberate attempt to lighten the mood. 'Let me go and grab you some of that barbecue and then I'll pop over to E8 so you can try for yourself. I promise you it's going to blow your silicon mind.'

'My mind isn't actually made from silicon like your computer chips, but it would take too long to explain the physics of E8, where my main matrix resides. Anyway, some of Jerry's barbeque sounds wonderful right now.'

'Then I'm all over it and I'll see you in person soon,' I said, heading towards the door. But as I stepped out into the corridor, I also had a sinking feeling inside.

The subject of Lucy remaining behind was something that I'd already discussed at length with Tom. The real truth was that Lucy wasn't the only one who wasn't entirely happy about her not coming along with us. Despite it making sense on so many levels, without the extra edge that Lucy's abilities had frequently brought us – not least being able to simply hop across to the twilight zone when a mission got tricky – if we *did* run into trouble we really would be on our own this time. And that made me more uncomfortable than anything else. But at least on this occasion we were just talking about a recon mission here.

If I'd had any idea about just how wrong that particular thought was going to turn out to be, I would have turned straight round and headed back into the briefing room to plead with Lucy to come with us after all and to hell with the consequences. But as they say, that's bloody hindsight for you.

CHAPTER THREE

As THE SUNRISE crested the jungle, shadows stretched like long fingers across the clearing on the small hilltop that we were sitting on. Jack, Mike, Ruby, me and Jodie, who'd dragged herself along after an all-nighter on the *Ariel's* modifications, had all gathered together for the big moment. Any minute now we should hopefully be about to witness the Osprey squadron's launch to their mission to 16 Psyche. And we weren't alone. Scattered across the hillside were a number of groups who'd all gotten up early to witness the big event.

The Pangolin fleet had been fully loaded with enough building materials to get the second automated factory up and running, as well as building the 3D-printed accommodation domes to allow Serenity Base to begin to expand rather than just sleep in their ships.

I'd seen a few of Troy's reports to Alice and it was obvious from the practically frothing tone that he and his team were in their element. They might have trained for establishing a Mars colony but it seemed they had all taken the change of venue in their stride with the construction of Serenity Base.

I sipped my coffee, the caffeine helping to drive away the cobwebs of sleep that were still mushing my brain up a bit.

Mike refilled his own mug, the last of the dregs from the thermos jug we'd brought with us from the cafeteria.

'You do realise we should all still be tucked up in bed catching as much shut-eye as we can before we head off on our mission in a few hours' time?' he said.

Ruby stifled a yawn. 'No way I wasn't going to be here for Jane's big moment.'

'Just how much sleep did you guys get last night?' I asked, giving her a pointed look.

She grinned at me. 'Enough to get by on. I mean it was my duty to give Jane the send-off she deserves.'

'And that's a duty I know you would have taken very seriously,' Jack said.

Ruby's grin widened. 'Oh I most certainly did.'

Alice appeared from the edge of the jungle to the left of us. She appeared to be using an all-terrain version of her wheelchair, with big chunky tyres and a third smaller wheel at the back. Tom was walking alongside her, rather than even attempting to try to push her, something that I knew Alice would have no time for. The president of the Sky Dreamer Corp was independent to the core of her being when it came to her own mobility.

Mike watched her approach with a thoughtful gaze and reached down to scratch his prosthetic leg, before grimacing and then catching my eye.

He shrugged. 'Old habits die hard. I still get phantom sensations from my missing limb.'

Jack glanced at him and nodded. 'It's a well-known phenomenon, Mike. But it should fall away gradually. As long as you're not suffering from any phantom pains, because there is a cognitive therapy that you can try. Certain exercises can help to rewire your brain and desensitise you.'

'No, I'm good, but the effect of getting an itch in something that isn't there is still the weirdest feeling.'

I nodded as I gave him a straight look. 'And you're absolutely sure you're up to coming on this mission, Mike? No one will think any the less of you if you want to duck out.'

He smiled at me. 'You couldn't keep me away if you tried, Lauren.'

'That's all I needed to know and that's great to hear,' he replied.

I couldn't help it but my eyes glanced towards Jodie. Even though I hadn't said anything, she nodded.

'Before you ask, yes I'm cool with it too,' she said. 'Mike and I have talked it all through. Besides, he'd only sulk if I tried to keep him here and sulking is such a bad look for this pretty boy's face.' She reached up and squeezed his chin, grinning elfishly.

Mike snorted. 'Isn't that the truth? Anyway, you need me and my special brand of expertise on this mission, Lauren.'

'True. If you're both happy, then so am I,' I replied.

'We are,' Mike said, squeezing Jodie's hand. She looked a lot less certain than her partner.

The sound of wheels crunching over the loose soil heralded Alice and Tom reaching us.

'I see you've managed to get yourself a ringside seat,' Alice said as she set the parking brake on her wheelchair.

Jack waved his hand at the panoramic view of the jungle stretching away around us. 'This is so much better than seeing it on a screen down in Eden.'

'I couldn't agree more,' Tom replied, unhitching the small rucksack he'd been carrying, then producing, much to everyone's delight, a fresh jug of coffee.

'So how have you been getting on with hiring us a mini-sub for the Cuba mission?' I asked Tom as he refilled my mug.

'Actually, very well. I managed to track down a French

explorer called Leon Dupont. He's a former hedge fund investor who became a billionaire by the time he'd reached thirty and retired from the rat race. However, rather than just go down the usual super yacht route of most playboys with too much money and time on their hands, Leon dedicated his life to oceanic exploration. Apparently he was following in the footsteps of his great grandfather, who he'd always admired and was one of the pioneers in helping to develop the aqualung. So now, not only has Leon got a state-of-the-art ship by the name of *Venus*, with a thickened hull that cuts through ice for polar exploration, he also has on-board a very impressive Triton deep diving mini-sub too. It's capable of diving down to at least thirty-five thousand feet, so should easily be able to explore the seabed around Cuba.'

'And he's agreed to work with us?' Jack asked.

'Yes, although for now he believes it's a wreck search mission. We've left the fine print out of the negotiations. The best news is that he and his ship are just off the Mexican island of Cozumel in the Caribbean, where he's studying a migrating pod of whales. He's promised that he can be with us within two days.'

'That's great news,' I said.

'I'm not so sure. I'm still deeply uncomfortable about getting a civilian involved in what could rapidly descend into a tricky mission if the Overseers are involved in any way,' Alice said.

'That didn't stop you working with us,' Jack said.

'That may be true, but Tom had run a thorough background check on the three of you. Additionally, you all more than proved yourselves with the Overseers on Orkney.'

'I'm also confident that Leon is a man that we can trust,' Tom said. 'Besides, even if we bought our own submersible, not to mention a ship to use it with, that would take a considerable amount of time that we simply don't have. And that isn't factoring in the amount of training that would be required to use that equipment. Leon and his team's expertise is what's needed and as time is of the essence, we really haven't any other choice.'

'Even so, can we rely on his discretion afterwards?' I asked.

'I wouldn't be too worried on that count. I've promised to make a sizeable contribution to one of his ecological charities. So that should be more than enough to guarantee the silence of him and his crew. And when it comes down to it, we only need this to be kept secret for the duration of the mission and after that it becomes a moot point as we will all have moved onto finding the next micro mind.'

'Then it sounds to me like we have no other choice,' Jack said.

Alice sighed. 'You're right of course, but these days I see the shadows in every situation.'

Jack shrugged. 'I think we all do, Alice.'

Just then my smart watch beeped and Lucy's avatar appeared on the face. 'I thought you'd like to know that the Osprey squadron is about to launch. Hope you brought the popcorn!'

'No popcorn but plenty of coffee,' I said. 'Anyway, thanks for the heads up.'

'Anytime, my little sunflower.'

I caught Ruby smirking as we all turned our attention towards the jungle-covered plateau beneath us. I was *definitely* going to have words with Lucy about her still calling me that.

Word had obviously spread about the imminent launch, as the conversations of the groups around us fell silent.

The sun had now crept high above the horizon to bruise the sky with pinks and purples. The planet Venus shone above us, the planet that I always associated with Spring in my head. Maybe that was because it had been the first planet that my real Aunt Lucy had shown to me shortly after buying me a telescope for my birthday one March. Although it had been hard for my ten-year-old self not to be seduced by those first views of Jupiter and Saturn through it, for some reason it had been Venus's burning point of light that had always meant the most to me. Maybe that had everything to do with my early love of Greek mythology and although I would never admit it out loud, I always saw that planet as the personification of a goddess.

The only movements around us in the stillness of the early morning were a few flocks of scarlet macaws heading towards the salt lick by the river that they loved so much. That aside, it was almost eerily quiet, as though even nature herself knew what was at stake here and was holding her breath.

People began pointing around us towards the jungle below and then I saw it too. Light glistening on the hulls of the three massive Pangolin saucer ships at least a hundred metres across, which had just begun to rise above the canopy of the jungle.

They moved in absolute silence thanks to their newly improved Element 115-filled plasma drive rings. Finding enough of that element had been something of a challenge, but Jodie and her team had set up banks of particle accelerators firing calcium atoms into clouds of americium to produce the rare substance in industrial quantities.

My heart soared with them as they began to rise, every launch from here on out to 16 Psyche carrying so many dreams and hopes with them.

Powered by the improved REV drives, the three ships slowly ascended, the sun glistening off their thickly armoured hulls, which had been built with extra shielding to cope with any solar radiation spikes during their thirty-day journey to 16 Psyche.

'Wow, aren't those quite the sight?' Jack said.

'Aren't they just,' I replied, smiling at him.

The three saucer craft came to a low-hovering stop and then began to rotate on their axis through every orientation, all part of their last minute flight test.

Just like *Ariel*, these craft had been designed with gyroscopically stabilised flight decks that even now would be level whilst the ships rotated around them.

Mike took Jodie's hand in his. 'I'm so flipping proud of what you've been able to achieve in such a short amount of time.'

'Most of this is down to the incredible hard work and dedication of the Forge team that I'm lucky enough to work with,' she replied. 'They have been nothing short of miracle workers.'

'Says the woman who can't take even a small amount of the credit for something that couldn't have happened without her guidance and leadership,' Alice said.

Jodie gave her a small embarrassed smile.

'Maybe you should change your name to Scotty,' I said.

For a moment everyone gave me a blank look, but it was Jack who got there first.

'Oh you mean Scotty as in *Star Trek*, the engineer guy who could work miracles on the *Enterprise*.'

'Hey, good man,' I said, beaming at him.

'Scotty... yes that could work as a nickname for you, Jodie,' Ruby said.

'Oh great, Lauren, thanks for putting the idea in her head,' Jodie said, but her smile indicated that she actually rather liked the association.

'Anytime,' I replied, instantly starting to wonder what nickname I could give Jack, although he was and always would be my very own *blond Viking*.

The three saucers stopped rotating almost in unison and returned to a level position. Even though we'd had plenty of experience flying *Ariel*, watching a craft like this from a spectator's point of view brought home just how strange they were, just hanging there in mid-air without any obvious means of propulsion.

'So, any moment now they'll initiate their thrusters,' Jodie said.

The words had barely left her mouth when twelve discs of blue light appeared in each of the ship's bellies. Then just like that they were the briefest blur as they zipped fast up into the sky without so much as a sonic boom, thanks to the effect of the gravity bubbles surrounding each ship. Left behind each one was just empty air, like they'd never been.

Ruby let out the softest sigh and blinked. It was only then that I noticed the tears in her eyes. She caught my gaze – I was the only person who'd noticed – and quickly smeared the tears away. Ruby might be as hard as nails in the field, but it was nice to see a softer side of this woman who was obviously very emotionally invested in her blossoming relationship with Jane.

'Wow, that was a fast ascent, but I will always miss the thunder and fire of an old-fashioned rocket launch,' Jack said, staring at the spot in the sky where the craft had vanished just to the western side of Venus.

'You think that's fast but they were probably only travelling around Mach 7,' Jodie said. 'But once they are out of the atmosphere and power up their helical particle drives, they'll accelerate up to four hundred million miles per hour.'

'Nosebleed fast,' Mike said, grimacing.

'Yes, I still can't get my head around the fact that it's reduced the journey time to the 16 Psyche to just thirty days,' I said. 'It took the *Voyager* probes around four years to achieve that sort of distance and they weren't exactly dawdling either, thanks to some nifty gravity slingshot work around the planets.'

'Well it's a crucial part of how we're going to defend the world when the time comes,' Alice said, her face becoming drawn.

Any sense of lightness evaporated from the group. Going by everyone's solemn expressions, all of us were once again starkly reminded of what was at stake here.

Tom downed the last of his coffee. 'Well as we're talking of saving the world, we should all head back and get ready for our own mission. I'll see you all in the hangar to sort out equipment. Oh – and a suitable disguise, as we'll be mixing with the Cuban locals.'

'Oh just great, my favourite, we get to dress up again,' Jack said, scowling.

As we stood I nudged him in the arm with my shoulder. 'You love it really.'

Jack narrowed his eyes. 'Yeah, right.'

As we sat in the hangar inside the X103 that we were going to use for the mission whilst *Ariel* was being upgraded, I did my best to suppress a smirk. That wasn't helped by the pissed off expression on Jack's face. He was sitting opposite me on the flight deck in a dazzling Hawaiian shirt, cargo pants and a dark, shoulder-length wig.

Mike had on a faded green canvas shirt and blue jeans, with a patterned cotton snood around his neck. With the trainers and the fluid way that he was now able to move, I would challenge anyone to be able to tell that he was using a prosthetic leg.

Ruby and I had faired a lot better than the guys in our transformations at the hands of Tom. She was rocking the whole exposed midriff look and had a blonde wig on. Me, well I had a loose fitting white cotton blouse and jeans on, but the biggest transformation was my jet black hair that almost reached my bum. I'd always wondered how I'd look with longer hair and now that I knew, I rather liked it.

But it was Tom that had almost made me spit my tea out when he appeared. The master of disguise had gone for what I could only describe as a Dumbledore look, complete with long white wispy beard and straggling white hair.

The key thing was that *I* barely recognised us, let alone anyone else and that was the whole point of Tom's insistence that we all wore disguises. The Overseers had contacts everywhere and we were all very much on the most wanted list, probably more so since Alvarez, a colonel in that secretive organisation, had been killed during our last encounter with him. He'd been buried alive when the glass pyramid we'd discovered back at the Richat Structure had disappeared and the corridor Alvarez had been walking through had reverted to sand. I for one wasn't going to shed any tears over that particular cold-hearted killer's death.

Tom slid the tablet he'd been using into the custom recess built into his chair. 'Okay, that's all of our preflight checks completed,' he said. 'Let's see how Delphi's new flight algorithms by Troy work out.'

'You think the system is ready to take full control like in the old X101s, then?' I asked.

Before he could answer, Lucy's avatar appeared in a window that had popped up on the virtual cockpit.

'If you're worried, don't be. I've been over Delphi's code several times and it all looks good to me,' Lucy said. 'You have plenty of backup safety systems, not to mention the escape pods. And besides, Tom can take over from Delphi if her flying causes any reason for concern...' A tightness filled her voice and her words trailed away.

But before I could ask her if she was okay, Jack jumped in, immediately scoring highly on my empathy radar for other people.

'You do know that staying behind is for the best, right, Lucy?' he said.

'Yes...' This time her voice did catch and she did the very human thing of dropping her gaze in her video window.

It was then that I wished I'd taken the time to have a heart-to-heart with her. 'Lucy, I'd love you to be coming with us, but like we've already discussed...' I lifted my shoulders.

Lucy raised her head and nodded. 'Yes...' She flapped a hand in front of her face. 'Sorry, I need to dial down some of the emotional subroutines. But if you need me – as an actress once famously said to Bogart in a movie that I'm paraphrasing here... *You know how to whistle, don't you? You just put your lips together and blow.* Do that and I'll be straight by your side the moment you recover a micro mind... if you do end up finding one.'

I nodded, but a sense of apprehension had taken hold of me. Without Lucy by our side, our safety net that I'd grown so used to on missions was about to be removed. But that was a cost worth paying to keep her as safe as possible.

'Okay, let's get this mission underway,' Tom said. 'Delphi, you have control.'

'I have control,' Delphi repeated in her silkiest, calmest tone.

'Then please set a course for the preloaded coordinates and launch when you're ready.'

'Understood, initiating launch procedure,' Delphi replied.

Lucy's video window vanished as the virtual cockpit walls glowed into life around us. Now we had a view of the hangar that *Ariel* was parked in. Jodie and Alice were watching us from one side of it and Lucy's merged micro mind star-shaped craft hovered just to our right. Mike's gaze immediately travelled to his girlfriend, who was chewing her nails. He'd been unusually quiet since we'd entered the cockpit. Although he was clearly totally committed to going on missions again, I knew that if I'd been standing in his shoes I would have allowed myself a certain amount of apprehension too.

A very soft hum came from the floor as the Element 115 mark two REV drive was brought online. Slowly, the launch silo door above slid open to reveal a disc of blue sky above us.

An array of indicators glowed green in Tom's pilot seat panel and then our X103 began to rise in almost total silence.

Alice and Jodie waved to us and even though they couldn't see him, Mike returned their gesture.

I glanced at the team around me, people who I'd trust my life with and had done so on so many occasions. At some point along the journey together we'd become a tight-knit team, something that Mike was very much a key part of.

Almost as though he'd been reading my mind, Jack nodded across to Mike. 'It's great getting the band back together, hey?'

'This is like old times,' Mike replied, as we began to accelerate up the shaft towards the expanding disc of blue sky.

Jack caught my eye and winked. Yes, I'd chosen well picking him as my partner.

As our X-craft cleared the silo we burst out into sunlight, the lush green jungle canopy stretching away around us.

Tom sat back and let Delphi execute a perfect, fully automated ascent, climbing away rapidly from the jungle until it was thousands of feet below us and all without even the faintest vibration.

'Peanut butter-smooth flying,' Ruby said, looking at her CIC screen that partly encircled her flight seat. 'Looking forward to seeing this baby hit Mach ten.'

'Yes, thanks to the upgraded REV drive we should be able to reach Cuba in just under twenty minutes,' Tom said.

Jack whistled.' Holy crap, that's a seriously short flight time.'

'Yes, not even time for an in-flight drink,' Mike said.

I shot him an amused look as the ship began to rotate back to the vertical. This was so it could use the REV drive's gravity field enveloped around the ship to create the equivalent of lateral thrust - and a lot of it!

Delphi adjusted our flight path until we were almost flying

directly towards the sun. At that moment, Lucy's face appeared back on an overlaid video window on the virtual cockpit.

'Okay, kids. I'll be waiting for you to whistle so I can get my arse over to wherever you're ready for me to merge with the micro mind, if you find one there. In the meantime, safe journey onwards and good hunting.'

'Amen to that,' Jack replied.

Lucy smiled, caught my eye, then blinked several times.

I felt a tug of sympathy for her as she cut her video feed. I so knew how I would be feeling right now if I'd been watching everyone else set off without me.

'Okay, let's see what this upgraded drive can *really* do,' Tom said. 'Delphi, blank virtual cockpit screens.'

'Blanking screens,' our ship's AI replied.

The screens went dark around us, all part of the secrecy surrounding Eden's location so we couldn't reveal it if we were captured.

Now the only things projected onto the virtual cockpit were the flight stats, including our airspeed, which had already climbed to just over a thousand knots, well beyond the speed of sound. Then, with the barest increase in hum from the REV drive, our speed began to climb. Two thousand knots became six thousand and all with only the softest tug of gravity to indicate the absolutely insane acceleration. A quick mental calculation told me we were moving at the equivalent of six hundred miles per hour.

'Bloody hell, I knew the new drive system was good, but that's incredible,' Mike said.

'Yes, with the improved efficiency of the drive, the sort of G-forces we would have experienced in conventional craft – if it could even go that fast – would basically have killed us by now,' Tom said, looking at his readouts.

'Well if we did have that in-flight drink, I doubt it would even have spilled a drop,' I said.

Jack snorted as we returned our attention to the somewhat mesmerising display of data that was telling us that we were now travelling over six times faster than a speeding bullet. And that was breathtaking, whichever way you wanted to look at it.

CHAPTER FOUR

ON THE RESTORED virtual cockpit view, now that we were a suitable distance from Eden, we had a view of the island of Cuba laid out before us, sitting in the middle of the aqua blue sea. Small fishing boats were visible everywhere around its coast and a commercial jet was making its final approach to the island's main airport.

'So this is the place that nearly ended the world back in the sixties with the Cuban missile crisis,' Jack said, gazing down at the island.

'Yes and it seems that once again what happens around Cuba is going to play a key role in whether our planet survives for much longer,' Tom replied.

'Hey, let's try and keep a positive outlook on this and assume we're going to have a positive mission, guys,' Mike said, shaking his head.

It was good to hear someone who still had a fragment of optimism left inside them, but the truth was that I was feeling more than a little bit unsettled about the presence of the Russian military in the waters. At best, that was going to complicate things and at worst, who knew? I looked down at the tapestry of fields and towns. So many people lived down there and right now, they had no idea that the fate of the world was playing out around them.

Our X103 came to a hovering stop. 'Destination reached. Pilot please stand by to resume control,' Delphi announced.

Tom reached forward and placed his hand on the three axis control joystick and flicked a button. 'I have control, Delphi.'

'You have control,' she echoed.

'So where exactly are we going to land? I think the main airport might raise a few eyebrows, Tom.' I said.

'We have a local asset on the ground. An American ex-pat called Glenn Nelson, who has made Cuba his home and now runs a sugarcane farm there. I've already contacted him and he's set aside a field for us to land in where our X103 won't be noticed or disturbed.' He glanced at his watch. 'We're five minutes early, so we'll hold position here before going in. Everyone should grab the opportunity to check their mission equipment because we're going to head out almost immediately that we touch down.'

'Okay, you heard the man. Let's get to it everyone,' I said, unbuckling my harness.

Soon we all had our heads buried in our lockers examining our packs. As always, my Empyrean Key – a carved stone ball that allowed me to communicate with a micro mind using my visual synaesthesia – lay safely tucked in the bottom of my small rucksack. I also had the tuning fork that I used to activate the Key stowed in there as a backup to the carrier tone that my earbud could generate, in case that failed. In a holster already strapped beneath my shirt was my trusty Mossad .22 LRS. As usual, I had plenty of spare magazines and ammunition for my weapon of choice that over the years had grown into an extension of my arm.

Jack had his Glock 19 safely stowed in a low profile holster beneath his shirt, along with the usual array of grenades. But it was the weapon that Mike was bringing on the mission that caught me completely off guard. As opposed to the usual dart gun that I'd already seen Tom place into his own shoulder holster, I saw Mike slide a magazine into a small pistol.

'What the hell have you got there?' I asked, staring at him.

Mike gave me a small shrug. 'A Walther PPK as favoured by James Bond.'

Jack looked at him. 'Since when are you packing a firearm on a mission, buddy? What happened to our conscientious objector to anything that fired bullets?'

'This...' Mike gestured to his prosthetic leg. 'It sort of changed my perspective when those beliefs didn't stop an Overseer soldier trying to take my life.'

'But we all understood your reason for using a dart gun,' I said. 'Are you sure you're really ready to cross that line and use that pistol in anger?'

'No, but I will if I have to.'

I was taken aback by his determined tone and looked to Tom for support. 'Did you know about this decision?'

'Yes, because I'm the one who has been giving Mike extensive training on the target ranges. This is his decision to take and we should all respect that, even if I think he's making a huge mistake.' Tom gave Mike a pointed look.

I spread my hands wide as I turned back to Mike. 'You really don't have to take this step; I know it's against everything you stand for.'

'I'm afraid that's the more innocent version of the guy I used to be, Lauren. Unfortunately, that man was lost the day he took a bullet that cost him his leg.'

Not able to ignore the hardness that had crept into his tone, I stared at my friend for the longest moment. There was so much that I wanted to say about why he shouldn't do this, but the problem was that Tom was right. At the end of the day, however big a mistake I thought Mike might be making, this was his decision. The problem was that choosing a pistol favoured by a fictional spy made me more than a little suspicious that he had romanticised the reality of being able to put a round into someone. And crossing that line for the first time was unfortunately something I knew way too much about from personal experience.

'Time for the rendezvous,' Ruby announced, gazing at her CIC screen.

Exchanging a scowl with Jack who, based on his deeply furrowed forehead was just as worried about Mike's decision as I was, I headed back to my flight seat and strapped in.

'Okay, let's get going and find out what Cuba is like,' Tom said. He took hold of the joystick, adjusted the throttle and began to descend us towards the island.

A lazy sea lapped around the shoreline, white gulls spiralling out over it as the island began to reveal its details. A mosaic of fields stretched out towards a mountain range that cast a large shadow in the early morning and ran along the spine of the island. The virtual cockpit view was helpfully labelled with tags to identify what we were looking at, the most significant of which was the large and sprawling metropolitan mass of Havana.

I'd always had a strong yearning to visit this island, specifically because of its capital. In my imagination it was filled with people dancing in the streets to salsa as brightly coloured vintage American cars wove their way through them. Whether the reality matched up to that, I was about to find out.

Tom appeared to be flying us towards a remote corner of the island set back from the coast. A few loan farms became visible as we dropped to three thousand feet. I spotted a battered blue van parked alongside a metallic green, old style Cadillac parked in the corner of the field that we were heading towards. It was just like the sort of car I pictured the islanders using.

A faded brown crop filled the view in the bottom half of the virtual cockpit. As we dropped to less than a hundred feet and began to slow, I could see little orange dust devils spinning up dirt in the powder-dry ground around the plants.

'That looks in pretty bad condition for a crop,' Ruby said.

'Yes, Glenn would be the first to tell you that farming isn't exactly his forte, but more of a hobby he dabbles in,' Tom replied. 'It also gives him the perfect cover for his family – he's actually on Sky Dreamer Corp's payroll as a part-time spy.'

Tom slowed our descent down to a crawl as he flipped a switch to extend the landing legs.

Ruby peered at her CIC screen. 'Apart from the two human heat signatures that I'm reading in those vehicles, there's absolutely no one else around,' she said.

'That will be Glenn and his son Antonio,' Tom said. 'However, based on the fact they haven't even got out of their vehicle yet, it would suggest that our chameleon cloak camouflage system is doing an excellent job.'

With a quiet rustle from outside as we descended into the crop, our X103 pushed the stalks apart and flattened them as we gently touched down on the ground with a slight shudder.

'You do realise we have just created our very own crop circle?' Mike said.

'Maybe this Glenn guy will be able to sell tickets to it as an attraction,' Ruby said with a grin 'And talking of whom...' She flicked her hand and the camera feed she'd been watching on her CIC screen was displayed on our virtual cockpit.

A man wearing a white short-sleeved shirt and a slightly fraying fedora hat was peering out of the windscreen of the Cadillac towards our X103 as the stub of a cigar glowed in his mouth. His brow furrowed and then he climbed out of his car. A lad in his late teens, who had to be Antonio, also climbed out of the van and together the duo began to head towards our landing site.

'Ah, the great man himself,' Tom said as he shut down the engine. 'I should maybe warn you now that Glenn is quite a colourful character.'

'In a good or bad way?' I asked.

'Maybe a little bit of both,' Tom said, unbuckling his harness.

We gathered up our kit and by the time we opened the ramp, a grinning Glenn was standing outside with his son, both staring at the magical door hanging in mid-air that we were about to step out of. As we followed Tom outside, Glenn swept his fedora off with a flourish and bowed to us.

'Welcome to Cuba, my friends,' he said in a strong southern accent. Arms outstretched he headed towards Tom, drew him into a hug and kissed him on both cheeks. By contrast, Antonio managed a feeble handshake and couldn't quite manage to look me in the eye when it was my turn, seeming to prefer to concentrate his gaze on my trainers instead.

Jack leant into me as the teenager stepped back, hands stuck into his jeans pockets. 'I think you may have snagged yourself your first Cuban admirer,' he whispered into my ear. 'It's probably your long dark Latino hair.'

'Stop that right now, you,' I whispered back, immediately feeling ridiculously self- conscious in my wig.

Jack grinned at me as Glenn and Tom finished slapping each other's backs.

Tom pulled away, holding the other man by the shoulders. 'Good to see you, you old pirate.'

'Hey, less of the old,' Glenn said, revealing a gleaming gold front tooth.

He then shook hands with Jack and Mike, but kissed Ruby and I on both cheeks as Tom introduced us all.

'My, what beautiful women you both are,' Glenn said with a toothy smile that couldn't have been more roguish if he'd tried.

Ruby, much to my surprise, instead of punching his lights out simply smiled. 'Hey *jamonero*, good to meet you.'

Glenn burst out laughing. 'Just so.'

'Sorry, what did you just say? I haven't powered up my earbud.' Mike said.

'That was Spanish for a creepy, touchy-feely guy,' Ruby replied. 'I did a stint in Venezuela fighting the drug cartels so I picked up the lingo.'

Glenn grinned. 'Oh now this one I like! With the spirit of a Cuban too.'

'Well if you want to give me one of your cigars we can be best buddies,' Ruby replied.

'Now we're talking.' Glenn took one out of his front pocket, offered it to Ruby and gave her a light.

A moment later she was blowing smoke rings with a blissed out expression on her face. 'Oh now that is so damned smooth.'

Glenn looked past us to the X103, the cockpit the only part still visible through the open doorway. 'It looks like you've got yourself a fancy new set of wheels there, Tom. I guess Sky Dreamer Corp has been busy again?'

'Isn't it always?' Tom replied. 'We'll have time later for me to fill you in, but right now we need to get a move on. Mike here needs to head to the western tip of the island to place some seismic probes. Whilst he's doing that we need to interview this Carlos Fernández about his missing children.'

Glenn nodded. 'No problem. Antonio, you can drive our guest out there and look after him.'

'Of course, Papa,' Antonio replied, the blush that he'd been trying to hide finally fading.

'One of us should tag along, just in case the Overseers are already here,' I said, making sure I looked anywhere but at the teenager.

'I'll happily watch his back,' Jack said.

I nodded. 'Okay, Ruby, you're with us trying to track down this Carlos guy.' My gaze travelled to the green classic car with its sloping roofline, built for speed. 'Please tell me we're riding with you in that Cadillac, Glenn?'

He pulled a face. 'You most certainly are, Lauren. But for your information that is something far better than any Caddy. That's a Ford Fairlane Crown Victoria Skyliner, one of the finest four-wheel vehicles ever built on this planet of ours.'

'Apart from the fact it breaks down half the time it's on the road,' Antonio said, the corners of his mouth curling up a fraction.

Glenn waved his hand at his son. 'A mere detail when compared to the romance of riding in such a refined vehicle.'

Antonio shrugged. 'Whatever you say, Papa.'

I had to suppress a laugh. I was already warming to these two.

'Hopefully, it'll be reliable long enough to get us to the diving school that Carlos owns?' Tom asked.

'Hopefully...' Glenn replied, winking at Ruby and I.

Like father, like son.

CHAPTER FIVE

WITH THE X103 fully locked up behind us and its chameleon camo doing a spectacular job to make it basically invisible, no one would realise our craft was there unless they literally walked straight into it.

We'd just finished loading up the vehicles with our kit. Tom and I were in the back of the Ford Skyliner, and I was already in love with the retro white and green patterned leather seats. Ruby rode up front with Glenn.

We drove in a convoy along a dusty track, Antonio's beat-up van carrying Jack and Mike just behind us. The rutted surface was seriously testing the Skyliner's shock absorbers and more or less bouncing our heads into the roof with every rut. Off-roading was so not the intended territory for this car.

We passed a crumbling colonial style building looking out over the beach, with hammocks strung between the trees.

'Your home, Glenn?' I asked.

'Yes, my own little corner of paradise,' he replied with his signature toothy grin.

We headed past the building, continuing on our teeth jarring journey but then, much to the relief of my already aching spine, we reached a junction with a smooth tarmacked main road.

Antonio pulled up alongside us as he got ready to turn onto the main road in the opposite direction to the way we were headed.

Jack leant out of the open window. 'Good hunting, guys.'

'You too. Don't get into any trouble,' I replied.

'We'll do our best,' Mike said, leaning across Jack and holding up his thumb with a big smile.

It wasn't lost on me that Mike certainly looked more lit up than I'd seen him for ages. Yes, maybe coming on a mission had been the right decision after all for him.

With a honk of the horn and a final wave, Glenn turned the car onto the road and we headed away.

As the Skyliner gathered speed I glanced across at Tom who was massaging his neck. 'How are you doing?'

'I have had smoother rides over a rough track,' he replied.

Glenn patted the dash. 'Don't you listen to him, old girl. These gringos don't recognise your charms.'

I snorted and then settled into the seat, looking out at the chain of mountains to our right against the bright blue sky. In the distance ahead, I could already see the city of Havana spread out along the coastline, where lots of small boats were sailing to and fro from its bustling harbour. If the beautiful retro Skyliner we were riding in was anything to go by, the city was in danger of actually living up to my dreams,

Ruby took a long drag of her cigar and blew out a cloud of smoke, pulling me straight out of my reverie as my lungs filled with the fumes. I started coughing.

'Bloody hell, Ruby, seriously?' I cranked down the side window and sucked in a lungful of the clear, ozone-rich sea air.

'Sorry, my bad,' Ruby said, grinding the cigar out on an ashtray already overflowing with butts.

It was a slight improvement, but as much as I loved the style of our ride, my clothes already reeked of smoke. I was certainly going to need a good shower and lots of shampoo to get rid of the stink from my hair.

Ruby took her Sky Wire handset out of her bag.

'What are you doing?' I asked.

'I'm just checking that we have a solid link back to the X103,' she said. 'I have a squadron of WASP drones loaded, which I can activate if we need back-up in a hurry. If it's really serious I can even remotely bring the X103 in to extract us.' She peered at her phone's screen. 'And yes, we're all good; we have a rock solid signal via a satellite.'

'Remember, everyone, that this is just an intelligence-gathering mission,' Tom said.

'Have you ever been on a mission with Lauren where a mission didn't go south?' Ruby asked.

I grimaced and got in my reply before Tom could. 'Fair point, but let's hope this one is the exception.' I gazed at our driver's face reflected in the rear-view mirror. 'So, how long have you lived on Cuba, Glenn?'

'About thirty years, give or take,' he replied. 'I met my wife Benita here on a trip from the States and so I set down roots with her.'

'What led you to working as a spy for Sky Dreamer Corp?' Ruby asked.

Glenn snorted. 'Maybe a spy with a very small s.'

'I wouldn't be so sure about that with your background,' Tom replied.

'What sort of background?' I asked, immediately intrigued.

'In my former life I used to work for the CIA, that's how I got to know Tom,' Glenn replied.

'That sounds a lot like you were working for the secret services too, Tom?' I said.

He nodded. 'Yes, although it was MI6 in my case. Once a spy, always a spy.'

It wasn't the first time that I realised just how little I knew about Tom, the man who'd been responsible for recruiting me and the guys into Alice's organisation, back on Orkney.

As the road opened up and we drew nearer to the coast, I could see windsurfers carving through the waves, bright splashes of red, green and yellow against the sparkling blue sea. In another life maybe I'd come back as a tourist to fully sample exactly what this island had to offer. I had a similar thought about Machu Picchu too. But for now, the possibility that Jack and I could lead some semblance of a normal life including taking holidays, seemed like an impossible dream.

After another twenty minutes of driving we were nearing the outskirts of Havana. As the city drew closer we'd started to see more examples of the immaculate cars from the fifties and even earlier.

At last Glenn turned the Skyliner onto a side road and we began to head down it into a rock-filled ravine covered with moss. We rounded a bend and suddenly the view opened out to reveal an Instagram-perfect, white sandy bay stretching in a horseshoe around a crystal clear ocean.

At the end of the road ahead stood a two-storey white stucco building with pendant banners fluttering from its roof. *The Fernández Diving School* was written in a large flowing script on a sign hanging over the entrance. Beyond it, a couple of boats were moored up to a small jetty but there was no one in sight.

In mission mode as ever, I'd already started scanning for anything out of the ordinary. The next thing I noticed was the distinct lack of vehicles in the car park, that was apart from a small silver Jeep and a truck beside it with the diving school's logo on its door. As to why it was so quiet, that became more obvious as we passed the open gate with a handwritten sign taped to it: *Closed Until Further Notice.*

'Ah, yes, I heard from a local contact that Carlos was broken-hearted about the loss of his son and daughter,' Glenn said, stubbing his cigar out in the car's ashtray. 'Apparently he closed the diving school because he couldn't face running it without them,'

'And who can blame him for that,' I said. 'But hopefully he'll still be open to answering a few questions.'

'I think if we approach it along the lines of trying to find out exactly what happened to his son and daughter, he'll be more than cooperative,' Tom said as we pulled up to the front of the building.

As we all climbed out, I took in the white truck with the scuba tanks in the back of it. Next to it, the silver Jeep looked distinctly less grimy than the truck.

A slight squealing was coming from the PADI diving sign as it rocked back and forth above the door in the gentle breeze. I felt like I was heading for a saloon in a spaghetti western before a big shoot-out. I could already feel something was off here and that impression was compounded by our next discovery.

'Hey, that doesn't look good,' Ruby said, gesturing towards the entrance.

I turned to see that the door, which also had a closed sign on it, was partly hanging off its hinges. The window was damaged and broken glass from it was scattered all over the floor.

I didn't need to say anything as I drew my weapons, because the others already had pistols in their hands.

Tom headed over to the truck and placed his hand on the bonnet. Then he checked the Jeep.

'Okay, the truck's engine is cold, but that Jeep is still warm,' he said. 'I'd say someone just arrived.' He took out his Sky Wire and snapped a photo of the vehicle's license plate. 'We'll run a trace on it later. If someone has broken in, odds are that that Jeep belongs to them.'

'So what's our next move?' Ruby asked, looking at Tom and me. 'And I hate to ask, but who exactly is in charge of this mission because we should sort out the chain of command between you two before we go any further?'

Tom pointed towards me. 'This is your squad, Lauren, so I'll defer to your decisions in all of this.'

I gave him a slightly startled look. 'You trust me that much?'

'Do you really have to ask after you've proved yourself on so many occasions?' he replied.

I gave him a small smile. 'Thanks for the vote of confidence, it means a lot coming from you.' I turned to the others. 'Okay, I think it's best to be paranoid until we know differently. Glenn, you're with Ruby, so go and cover the back whilst Tom and I head in through the front.

Ruby nodded and a moment later she had disappeared around the side of the building with Glenn.

I slipped my earbud in and activated it with a press of my finger as Tom did the same. Then with a nod to him, I took up a position to one side of the door as he did the same on the opposite side.

With a centring breath, I pressed my finger tip to my electronic earbud. 'Are you in position yet, Ruby?' I whispered.

'Roger that, Captain,' she replied, kicking into formal military speak like she always did when things started to get serious.

Despite the evidence of the broken door, I was still hoping that maybe there was an innocent explanation for all of this.

My ears strained to hear any sound out of the ordinary. But apart from the distant sigh of the surf and the squeal of the sign above us, it seemed to be completely quiet inside the building. Maybe too quiet.

'We should call out and flush out any intruder who might be inside,' Tom said.

I glanced across at him. 'Good idea.' I returned my attention to the doorway. 'Hello, Carlos, are you in there?'

No reply came, or – more reassuringly – no sudden shadow of someone diving for cover inside the shop.

I pressed my finger to my ear again. 'Okay, we're going in. Get ready, Ruby.'

'Don't worry, we're already locked and loaded,' she replied.

Without any form of body armour on, I felt distinctly vulnerable as I stepped forward. My shoes crunched on the broken glass as I entered the shop. Holding my pistol in both hands, I swung it in a swift arc to cover the room as Tom slipped through the door behind me.

My eyes took in the usual paraphernalia of diving equipment I'd expect to see somewhere like this. I had some experience of diving schools after earning my own PADI license in the seas of Bali on one very memorable holiday in another life years ago.

Wetsuits of assorted designs and sizes hung from a rail at the back along with a wide selection of flippers and masks. Accessories of every kind, from spearguns to knives, were displayed in glass cases. I headed for the counter, already bracing myself for the sight of a dead body on the floor on the other side. But when I peered over it, there wasn't so much as even a few droplets of blood there. So far so good.

I pressed my finger to my earbud. 'We're in and nothing obvious so far,' I said. 'Enter when you're ready. If the intruder is in here, we can pincer them.'

'Okay, we're about to enter through the back door into what looks like a workshop area,' Ruby said. 'I'll report back if we find anything.'

'Ditto,' I replied.

I pointed towards a doorway at the back of the shop. 'Let's try through there, Tom.'

He nodded and we stepped through the open door, pistols raised, and cautiously crept into what turned out to be a galley kitchen. To one side of the room was a staircase that looked like it led to the upper floor. Through another glass door at the end I could see a workshop that Ruby and Glen were already searching and clearing.

I pointed up towards the ceiling and Tom nodded.

Once again, taking the lead and creeping catlike on the balls of my feet, I made my way to the stairs and peered up, my LRS aimed and ready.

There was a landing at the top with three closed doors leading off it.

With Tom right behind me, my finger on the trigger, I began to creep up the stairs. I'd almost reached the top when on the penultimate step, a board creaked under my foot.

Adrenaline and instinct kicked in as I immediately heard the muffled cracks of suppressed rounds being fired. I threw myself flat just as three bullets ripped through the closed door ahead and whistled over my head.

No time to even think, countless hours of combat training kicking in, Tom and I returned a barrage of semi-automatic fire, punching more bullet holes through the wooden door and splintering it apart. A split-second later we heard running footsteps and the crash of glass.

'Are you hit?' Tom said as he raced up and crouched beside me.

'No, I'm good. Let's get that bastard,' I said, ejecting the spent magazine from the LRS and slipping a fresh one in.

I jumped back to my feet and in one fluid movement, kicked the door open. Keeping low, I ducked into what turned out to be an office. The contents of desk drawers had been emptied onto

the floor and papers were strewn everywhere. Of more immediate significance was the smashed window, the curtains flapping
in the breeze. I rushed over and peered out to see the Jeep racing
away. I emptied my fresh magazine towards it, one of my bullets
smashing the rear window and another sparking off the vehicle's
bumper as it swerved through the gate.

Tom reached my side just as the vehicle gunned its engine
and hurtled away up the lane.

'Whoever that was, we can be pretty bloody certain it wasn't
Carlos,' he said.

A moment later, Ruby and Glenn burst into the room.

'I heard shots! Are you both okay?' Ruby asked.

'Yes, but the intruder managed to bloody get away,' I said,
scowling and pointing towards the Jeep as it disappeared into the
rocky ravine.

'Damn it, I knew I should have brought my Accuracy
International sniper rifle with me,' Ruby said.

'Don't forget that this was meant to be just a reconnaissance
mission,' Tom said.

'Yeah, that part about our missions always going south...'

'Tell me about it,' I replied.

'But on the plus side...' Tom said. He pulled up the images on
his Sky Wire that he'd taken of the Jeep and zoomed in on the
number plate to reveal *F021 016*. 'Delphi has complete databases
of all vehicle registrations around the world. But given that
whoever it was was using a suppressor on a pistol, then you can
pretty much guarantee that we're dealing with a professional
here. If so, we can almost be certain that they fitted false plates.'

'So we've no way to trace whoever it is?' Glenn asked.

'That may be true, but I think our key priority has to be
finding Carlos,' I said. 'Whoever it was that just broke in here,
you can bet they have to be looking for him too. There are some
pretty glaring signs here that his life is in danger.'

'But Cuba is a big place; where the hell are we going to find him?' Ruby asked.

Glenn smiled and pointed to the white board behind us that listed the days of the weeks across several months.

Most of the entries on it were booked lessons with red pen strikes through them. The only appointment I could see that hadn't been crossed out was one for today, Wednesday, where a single entry had been written beneath it: *Chess tournament at La Tropicana.*

'So Carlos is a chess player then?' I said.

'A very good one, according to what I've heard about him,' Glenn said, flashing his golden smile. 'And in Cuba, chess isn't so much a sport as a religion. The man may be grieving about his children, but as the tournament is the only thing not crossed out, I will wager you that's where we'll probably find him.'

'It sounds like a promising lead, but the bad news is that our intruder likely also saw that board and came to the same conclusion,' Tom said. 'They probably waited until Carlos was out to search his office.'

'Kicking the front door in isn't exactly a subtle way to gain entry to a building,' Ruby said.

'Which is probably exactly why the intruder did it, to try and make it look like a regular break-in,' Glenn said. 'Problem is that now we've disturbed them, they also now know someone else is keen to talk to Carlos. We may have forced their hands into making a move on Carlos to find out directly from him about whatever it is that they're after.'

'Shit, you're saying we've put his life in danger?' I asked.

'Maybe not intentionally, but basically yes.'

I felt a surge of guilt and responsibility for the life of a man that I'd never met.

'Okay, then let's get moving and just pray we reach Carlos before that intruder does,' I said, heading for the door.

CHAPTER SIX

AFTER GLENN HAD DRIVEN the Skyliner as fast as he dared without drawing too much attention through the outskirts of Havana, we were finally nearing the heart of the city that was assaulting all my senses and totally living up to expectations. As I'd hoped, the famous 1950s cars that Cuba had imported before America imposed their embargo following the communist revolution, were absolutely everywhere. It turned out that a lot of the taxis were old Chevrolets, the very peak of retro cool. But Glenn had also identified some even more stunning examples of the classic car, like a metallic red soft top Cadillac complete with bat wing tail lights. I would never have described myself as a car woman, but I could have been swayed by the vehicles we saw in that city. The way the cars had been maintained and obviously very carefully looked after, certainly suggested a lot of love from their owners.

The vehicles I'd expected, but the horse-drawn carts I hadn't. They were everywhere as well, many carrying goods of every kind and in one particular memorable example, a well used grand piano jammed in at an angle into the cart, forcing it hard down onto its wheels.

We drove down a broad street with colourful colonial style buildings on either side, offset against the background of an intense blue sky.

The hat of choice for a lot of the older men seemed to be panamas like Glenn's or pork pie hats that I'd seen many a musician wear at gigs over the years. The clothing of choice for the younger generations seemed to be the obligatory shorts and T-shirts. But the other look that stood out, worn by people of all ages, was dressing from head to toe in white. We passed the latest example of this, a woman in her fifties in a long white dress, carrying a basket of bread on her arm.

I looked at the back of Glenn's head. 'Why are so many people wearing white?' I asked.

Glenn took a puff of his cigar. 'They belong to the Santería religion. Priests who are in training wear white and it sort of caught on for everyone else as a uniform to show their devotion.'

'Their laundry bill must be pretty hefty keeping their look that pristine,' Ruby said.

Glenn chuckled. 'Isn't that the truth?'

We reached the end of the road and swept around an enormous plaza with an unmistakable mural of Fidel Castro, the revolutionary leader, on one of the buildings.

'Hey, this place is epic,' Ruby said, taking in the expansive view.

'That's because this is the Plaza de la Revolución , one of the largest plazas in the world and where the biggest rallies in our country's history have been held.'

'*Our* country's history?' I replied. 'I thought you were American born and bred, Glenn?'

'Maybe I am, but Cuba is my adopted home now and also my soul's home; it dances to the music here.'

Tom glanced across at me. 'I don't think you could get Glenn to leave if you offered him his weight in gold.'

'That's right, my old friend,' Glenn replied, beaming his gold tooth smile.

We turned off from the square and headed down a busy smaller road.

I glanced at my smartwatch and felt my anxiety spike as I saw that it had been nearly thirty minutes since we'd left the diving school. The car began to slow because of the sheer amount of traffic and I began to drum my foot on the floor.

'How much longer till we get to this damned chess tournament? I won't be able to relax until we know that Carlos is safe,' I said.

'We're almost there, can't you tell?' Glen said, gesturing to the street that we were driving along.

I looked out to see small tables nearly everywhere along the street, even up on the balconies. People were sitting at each and every one, from the young to the old, and they were all playing chess.

'As I said, chess is basically the third religion of our country,' Glenn said.

'I'm starting to get that impression,' I replied.

With several honks of his horn and a bit of negotiation, Glenn persuaded an old man with a horse and cart filled with mangoes to move along enough that we could squeeze into the parking space behind him.

When we got out I saw that we'd pulled up outside a relatively modern, glass-panelled hotel, a contrast to the far older architecture around it. Over its entrance hung the sign, *Habana Libre*, but of more immediate interest was the blue *Capablanca Memorial Elite Chess Tournament* banner written in English, slung beneath it.

An assault of food smells from the street vendors hit my nose.

There was everything from pizza to churros, complete with some hot chocolate pots on the side to dip the sweet treats into. There were also some fried flat patties that a line of people were queuing for.

'What are those, Glenn?' I asked as we passed by the line, heading for the main entrance.

'Those are one of Cuba's most famous street foods - plantains fried until they're crispy and eaten like potato chips with a dip. And they taste...' he kissed the tips of his fingers.

'And what about the famous Cubano sandwich that Mike's been raving about?' Ruby asked.

Glenn laughed. 'I'm afraid you'll only find that sold in the tourist areas, because people kept asking for them.' He shrugged. 'They are more famous in America now, and the locals here don't even really eat them.'

'Oh God, Mike's going to be so bummed when he hears that,' Ruby said.

Tom raised his eyebrows. 'You do know we're on a mission here and not a food tour?'

Ruby grinned at him. 'Sorry, just getting a bit pulled in by the local sights and smells.'

'Yes, be careful or Cuba will snag a piece of your heart forever,' Glenn said. 'That's what brought me back here...well, that and a beautiful Latino woman who I'm lucky enough to have called my wife for the last twenty years.' He gave us a crooked grin.

I was liking Glenn more and more by the minute. A rough diamond definitely, but one with a soft heart.

We squeezed through the crowds and reached the entrance of the hotel. As we entered the lobby the welcome chill of air conditioning wafted over us.

After the noise of the crowds outside, it was like we'd stepped into the hushed atmosphere of a library. A large bright atrium with green palms scattered throughout opened out into an area where chess tables had been set up in regimented rows. From the balconied area around it, an audience looked down intently, watching the games in progress. At the far end was a large chess board hanging from the wall, where a guy with a long stick had just moved a white knight.

Tom's gaze was already scanning the people. 'On the plus side, if whoever broke into the diving school is already here, at least there are far too many people for them to try anything. On the minus side of that equation is that we still have no idea what they look like. Also we may not be dealing with a lone wolf operation. There's every chance that they could be working with an accomplice.'

'Then we'll just have to keep extra sharp and hope we can get to Carlos first then,' I said. 'And talking of Carlos, any idea where we might find him, Glenn?' I asked.

He gestured towards an easel near the front desk where a list of names were displayed in two columns. 'We can find out if Carlos is currently in a match and if so, who he's playing.'

We all headed over to the board. In a glance I saw that there were a number of blanks on it where names had been removed, presumably players who'd lost their matches. I quickly scanned through the remaining names, but it was Ruby that spotted our man's name first.

She tapped Carlos's name on the board about halfway down. 'According to this he's playing some guy called Yadier Alfonso.'

'That's going to be a tough match for Carlos; Yadier is a Grandmaster and ranked number three in Cuba,' Glenn said. 'But going by the fact that Carlos's name is still on the board, he's still playing, which means he's still here rather than drowning his sorrows in a bar, where he would be a much easier target for whoever is after him.'

'So then, where is our man?' I asked, looking at the rows of chess matches in progress.

Glenn sucked his lip. 'According to the board he's on table twelve so...' He narrowed his eyes as he scanned the players. 'Aha, there's the great man himself.' He gestured towards a match at the far end of the room, just below the display chess board on the wall.

Two men sat across from each other at the table. One had a mane of dark hair and was probably in his forties. The older, grey-haired man sitting opposite him I instinctively knew was Carlos. He had the well-tanned face of a diver and the lean physique of someone who was used to a lot of exercise.

'The guy on the right?' I asked.

'Yes, that's him,' Glenn confirmed.

The old man reached out and moved his rook forward to take one of his opponent's pawns.

At the same time the man moved the rook on the big display board at the back that was presumably reserved for the star match. On the balcony above, people nodded and bent their heads together in whispered conversation, their gazes fixed intently on the two players.

'Well that's a bold move. Carlos has exposed his queen to being taken,' Tom said.

'You play then?' I asked.

Tom held out his hand and waggled it. 'Just a little bit.'

But knowing Tom's general leaning towards understatements, that probably meant he was a Grandmaster too.

I glanced at the board. I'd played a bit of chess myself and the rook move looked like Carlos was just about to throw away his queen. The old man was obviously getting desperate.

Then my gaze swept over all the people watching. 'So the intruder is probably already here?' I said.

'Oh you can count on it,' Tom replied, also scanning the crowd.

'What I really want to know is exactly who they are working for,' Ruby said.

'Based on the fact we have certain vessels just off the coast, I'd say the most likely candidate is the Russian Foreign Intelligence Service,' Tom said.

I furrowed my eyebrows. 'Not the Overseers?'

'Well maybe not directly but even though the agent probably doesn't realise it, the Overseers are almost certainly pulling the strings of this particular operation.'

So we could be dealing with a Russian agent. I'd seen enough movies to know that they would be very highly trained.

I increased my scrutiny of the spectators. But without any clue about who we were looking for, suddenly everybody looked like they could be a Russian spy, even an old grandma sitting at a nearby table, sipping a small espresso.

'So how are we going to spot them?' Ruby said, casting a hawk-like gaze over the crowd.

'Unfortunately, we're going to have to wait for them to show their hand,' Tom said.

I nodded, but I really wasn't happy. We were going to be on the back foot here, waiting for our mystery man or woman to make their move.

I tried to put myself in their headspace. What they did next would depend on their mission objective. The fact that they'd been ready to shoot three rounds through the door suggested they weren't going to play nicely when it came to extracting whatever information that Carlos knew.

A murmur passed through the spectators and I returned my attention to the match in progress. It was then that I realised the Grandmaster hadn't taken Carlos's queen as expected but had instead moved his knight forward to take one of his pawns.

I stared at the board as I realised that Carlos had just been put into check. Then Carlos tipped his king over onto the board and extended his hand to shake his opponent's.

'Why is he resigning?' I asked.

'Because the Grandmaster has him on the ropes; it's checkmate in three moves from here,' Tom said with an approving look.

The two players stood up and nodded to each other with wide smiles.

'Okay, we need to keep sharp everyone, because the agent could literally be anyone here,' Tom said.

I nodded. 'Glenn and Ruby, you keep an eye on the crowd in case anyone tries to make a move. Tom, I think it's time for you and I to introduce ourselves to Mr Fernández, don't you?'

'I couldn't agree more,' Tom replied.

Together we set off towards Carlos, who'd already been surrounded by well-wishers, all trying to shake his hand. Even though the old man had lost, he seemed as popular as though he'd just won.

I scrutinised the people around him intensely, but as far as I could tell, none were acting suspiciously, at least not yet.

We reached the edge of the perimeter of people that had formed around Carlos just as an old woman hugged him. 'I thought you had Yadier,' she said, squeezing his cheek.

'No, he was too slippery for me. The rook was a gamble on my part, but he didn't fall for it. And that's why he's a Grandmaster and I'm a lowly player.'

'You will never be a lowly player, my dear Carlos. You have the spirit of a marlin.'

He smiled at her and kissed her on both cheeks. 'Once, maybe, but that man was gone after I lost my beautiful children.'

She rested her hand on his shoulder. 'Never give up, Carlos, never give up. That's what my sister would have said if she was still here.'

'I know, I know, but now I'm all alone in the world, Mariah.'

'You will always have the rest of your family. We'll always be here for you.'

Carlos held her hands in his and nodded.

I immediately felt a tug of sadness for this old man. Losing his son and daughter had to be the toughest thing to come to terms with. Also, if I was reading what we'd just overheard correctly, he'd also lost his wife. But the fact he'd managed to drag himself out here at all showed to me that the old man had the courage to carry on, even if he did have a broken heart.

And for no reason I could really fathom it was then that I was reminded of Aunt Lucy. She'd always been courageous, whatever life had thrown at her, including a scare with cancer. And despite all of that, Colonel Alvarez had casually snuffed her life out on a road in Exmoor. Immediately, I felt a strong affinity for Carlos and became determined to protect him at any cost.

A waiter reached Carlos just before we did and offered him a glass containing a golden liquid.

He said something in Spanish to the waiter that my earbud instantly translated into – *But I didn't order a drink.'*

'It's from a fan who insisted on buying you Ron Edmundo Dantes, a 25-year-old Santiago rum,' the waiter replied. Once again it was translated by my earbud.

Carlos shrugged. *'Then I will toast my well-wisher his health.'*

The glass was halfway to his lips when Tom darted forward and deliberately knocked into him, sending it flying to the ground, where it smashed.

Tom gave the old man an ashen look. 'I am so sorry, my friend, I didn't look where I was going.'

Carlos glowered first at him and then the spilt drink pooling into the carpet.

Tom held up his palms. 'Please, let me buy you a replace-

ment.' He waved to Glenn and Ruby, who came over immediately.

Tom leant into me. 'We need to find out who brought that
drink and fast.'

I stared at him. 'Got to have been spiked, right?'

'Yes. Maybe even drugged with something to make it look like
Carlos had suffered a fatal heart attack. All in the playbook for a
Russian agent if they wanted to make sure he couldn't talk to us.'

'Bloody hell, we'd better find out who ordered that drink, and
fast!'

Leaving Glenn and Ruby to babysit Carlos, we headed
towards the waiter, who was now installed back behind the bar.

'Who ordered the Ron Edmundo Dantes that you just served
to that chess player over there?' I asked him.

He shook his head. 'Sorry, he said I wasn't to tell anyone.' But
then his gaze flicked to a thin man heading towards a door at the
back of the atrium. The guy was wearing black jeans and a shirt
and had his baseball cap pulled down to obscure his face.

Tom had spotted the barman's subconscious gesture too. He
dug out a handful of American hundred dollar bills and showed
them to barman, then nodded towards the thin man. 'Was it that
man by any chance?'

The barman shrugged. 'You didn't hear it from me, señor.'
Then with a grin he took the cash from Tom's outstretched hand.

We stepped away from the bar as the thin man disappeared
out through the doorway.

'Okay, let's tail him and see where he leads us,' I said.

Tom nodded. 'Exactly what I was about to suggest.'

I pressed my finger tip into my earbud. 'Ruby, we're pursuing
the possible agent. You and Glenn escort Carlos back to the car in
case the agent came here with an accomplice.'

'Understood and will do, Captain,' she replied.

As nonchalantly as I could, I walked with Tom towards the door that the guy had just exited through.

A few seconds later we entered a bright white corridor lined with the usual anonymous framed prints that hotels always seemed to favour. The slap of the man's shoes on the tiled floor came from around the corner of the corridor ahead, but his step wasn't hurried, just another hotel guest in no particular rush to get anywhere so he wouldn't draw any attention. Cool, calm and detached. This guy really was a professional, somebody who knew exactly what they were doing, and that made him extremely dangerous. We needed to step carefully here.

As Tom and I rounded the corner, we saw the man disappearing through a door into the busy street outside.

'It's going to be tricky to keep track of him if he gets into a car,' Tom said.

'I've already had an idea about that,' I replied. I pressed my finger to my earbud. 'Ruby, we are in pursuit of the target. Are we within range of one of your WASPs? We could use an extra pair of eyes in the sky.'

'Yes. I can get one here in less than ten minutes,' Ruby replied.

'Good, then please do it.'

'Understood, Captain. Launching WASP unit now. I'll lock onto the signal from your Sky Wires and have it track you,' Ruby said.

'Roger that and keep us posted,' I said.

We stepped through the door out into the street. The thin man was now about fifty metres away, heading along the pavement in front of a line of small shops.

The musical notes of a guitar being played drifted down from a balcony and the smell of good coffee wafted out of a cafe as we passed. The people out on the street looked relaxed, a stark contrast to how I was feeling on the inside - wired and ready for anything. The thin man squeezed through a crowd of tourists who were following a guide on the pavement, and then crossed the street to the opposite side, still with a casual stride to his step.

'Probably best to stay on this side so we don't draw any attention to ourselves,' Tom said.

'Good idea,' I said, making a mental note that Tom really needed to train me in the art of surveillance techniques.

As we carried on, I started to wonder about why the agent might want to kill Carlos. Was this confirmation that the old man had critical information that the Overseers wanted burying? And if so, was it about what Carlos's son and daughter had heard during their dive?

The thin man paused to looked into a tobacconist's window. We dropped our pace, but as we drew level his eyes met mine in the reflection. Instantly, he ducked sideways and disappeared into a dark alley.

Tom and I set off after him, darting in front of a bus that blared its horn, braking hard. We ignored the shouted protests of the driver and the expletives that my earbud was doing far too good a job of translating. We shot into the alley to see the agent sprinting away from us. Tom took his dart gun out from beneath his shirt as I reached for the LRS in my holster, screwing the suppressor onto it as we took off after the man.

But the guy was fast and although Tom was fit he was starting to fall behind me, probably thanks to all the time I'd spent on treadmills and doing runs through the jungle, upping my stamina.

The agent sped around the corner, but I was gaining on him.

As I hurtled around the corner after him, I had just a split second to register the guy, standing with his feet spaced slightly apart, his body angled to present as small a target as possible, the pistol in his hand aimed straight at my chest. I dived sideways as his bullet whizzed over my head, close enough for me to feel the draught of its flight as I dived flat.

Before I could return fire, or even call out a warning, Tom rounded the corner and the guy fired again. Brick splinters flew from the wall, but Tom's instincts were well honed and he rolled sideways in a fluid move as a second shot missed him.

Adrenaline hummed through my system as I aimed my LRS at the guy and returned fire. But he was already moving and diving behind a dumpster. In semi-automatic mode I emptied my magazine, firing at his hiding place, my shots ricocheting off the dumpster and sending sparks flying.

I was just grabbing a fresh magazine to reload when something came arcing out from behind the dumpster. My brain barely had a moment to register the grenade tumbling towards us.

Instantly I realised that both Tom and I were exposed and worse still, without cover to get behind in time. But as that grenade with our names on it started to fall back down towards us, it exploded in mid-air with a loud bang and a cloud of black smoke.

'Allow me,' Ruby's voice said through my earbud. 'Turns out my WASPs are even faster than I realised if you run them hot enough to almost burn out their motors.'

A drone unit dropped down between the alley walls and sped towards the dumpster, its stubby barrel already pointing towards it.

The man's head appeared and he shot once, twice, both bullets going wide, but his third shot struck the craft, which spiralled into the alley and exploded in a bright blue flash as its lithium battery exploded.

But that moment of frenzied activity had been all the time I needed to slip the fresh magazine into my LRS, aim it at the agent's exposed head and fire. A crack came from the muzzle of my pistol and a cloud of blood erupted from the man's temple as he crumpled backwards.

I jumped to my feet and raced forward, aiming my pistol towards where he'd disappeared. Tom was only a couple of metres behind me as I reached the dumpster to find the man twitching on the floor, an expanding pool of blood spreading from his head. A phone was in his hand, his thumb edging towards a send button.

I kicked it from him and the phone went skittering across the alley. The man's eyes locked onto mine as a shudder went through him. Then his pupils rolled up into his skull.

I stood slowly, my blood humming, and took a deep breath.

Tom checked the agent's neck for a pulse and shook his head. 'So much for interrogating him about who he was working for.'

'Sorry, I didn't have any choice but to take the shot.'

Tom sighed. 'I know.' He checked the man's pockets and then sat back on his haunches. 'No ID, just as I expected.'

'Are you guys okay?' Ruby asked through my earbud.

'Yes, we're all good thanks to you taking that grenade out,' I replied. 'But I'm afraid your WASP has seen better days.'

'Yep, but that was one hell of a shot taking out a grenade in mid-air like that, even for me.'

'Well it's certainly appreciated and we both owe you a drink,' Tom replied.

I crossed the alley and scooped up the agent's phone. I looked at the screen and my eyes widened. On it was a photo of me. It looked like the guy must have taken it back in the lobby of the hotel. Of even more significance were all the biometric markers over my face. Despite my long-haired disguise, the message, *Subject identified, Lauren Stelleck,* was displayed below the photo.

'Tom, that agent clocked me. Look.' I swivelled the screen up towards him.

He frowned. 'Let me see that.' He took the phone and then his brow relaxed. 'Thank God, he didn't get a chance to hit send. We're in the clear for now, although he's highly likely to have already reported in to whoever he is working for, to let them know he encountered us back at Carlos's diving school.'

'So what are we going to do now?'

Tom looked up and down the empty alleyway and then gestured first to the dumpster and then to the spy's body. 'First a bit of spring cleaning, then we'll all need to put our heads together about what our next move should be.'

CHAPTER SEVEN

WITH THE SPY'S body buried beneath a pile of bin bags in the dumpster and the remains of the WASP in another, we headed back to a rendezvous point that Tom had arranged with Glenn in one of the nearby streets.

'That was a bit of a close call,' Tom said, patting down the dust from his trousers.

'Yes, if it hadn't of been for Ruby I doubt either of us would have made it,' I replied.

'I very much agree. However, a spy using a grenade in the field was unheard of in my day.'

'Well if the Overseers are behind this operation, I think the rulebook that all sides played by is probably long gone.'

A horn sounded and we both looked up the street to see Glenn waving to us through the windscreen of the Skyliner. Sitting next to him was Carlos. The Cuban gave us a questioning look as we climbed into the back seat alongside Ruby.

'Everything okay, guys?' Glenn asked, looking at us in the rear-view mirror.

'Yes, our dirty laundry is all sorted,' Tom replied, tugging his own ear.

'Good to hear,' Glenn said, with that signature gold tooth grin of his. He gestured towards Carlos. 'Let me make some introductions. These are some very good buddies of mine, my friend. They are very keen to talk to you and offer assistance to find out what happened to Raúl and Maricela.'

Carlos's eyes widened. 'Everyone else has refused to help. Why are you so willing to help a stranger?'

'Because we believe your children may have made a significant discovery, if what was reported in the news before it was taken down is correct,' I said.

'You mean the strange whale song that Raúl recorded when they were searching for the wreck?'

'Yes. Actually, what wreck is that?' Tom asked quickly.

But immediately Carlos's face became guarded. 'Oh nothing of interest, just an old cargo boat that went down at the location they were diving at.'

I didn't know exactly what my subconscious was picking up on, but I had the distinct impression the old man was now lying through his teeth. But if so why?

'So about this recording, do you still have it?' Tom asked, either oblivious to the lie or just playing along for now, which was more likely.

'Yes, back at my diving school. Why, would you like to listen to it?'

I traded looks with the others. Could this be what the agent had been after? But based on Carlos's offer he had no idea that his shop had just been broken into.

Glenn beat me to it, breaking the news to him. 'That would be most kind of you, my friend, but I have to let you know we were just there looking for you. Unfortunately we managed to disturb an intruder who'd broken into your shop.'

'Hijo de la chingada!' Carlos said, which my earbud translated into *Son of a bitch.*

'I thought I saw someone suspicious hanging around when I got a lift with my sister's wife Mariah into town for the tournament,' Carlos continued in English. 'There was a silver Jeep parked up on the road near my diving school. I spotted a thin-faced guy in it watching me as we drove past him. There was something about him that – how do you say? –, *creeped me out.*'

'That sounds like the same man we just met; his vehicle was parked out the front of your place when we got there,' I said. 'And I'm afraid he's made a huge mess of your office.'

Glenn gazed at the old man. 'We suspect he was looking for information linked to Raúl and Maricela's disappearance.'

Carlos's eyes narrowed. 'In other words, just like you all are. And who's to say it wasn't you who really did this and have now turned up pretending to be my friends and trying to make me trust you?'

'Look, I'd probably feel the same in your situation,' I said. 'But for what it's worth I can promise you that we weren't involved in any of that. We actually tried to stop him.'

'Yes, if anything, we're very much on your side and want to help,' Tom added.

The old man looked out of the windscreen. 'And what about the bodies of my children that have never been found? I tried to persuade the authorities to organise a search mission to examine the seabed, but they wanted nothing to do with it. Will my new friends really help me do that or are you just telling me what I want to hear?' Tears suddenly beaded his eyes. 'All I want to do is lay my children to rest and give them a proper burial.'

I felt a surge of compassion for the guy. He was obviously still grieving for his son and daughter. I thought of Aunt Lucy's old friend Sally, a fellow lecturer who'd lost her son in a motorcycle accident. Her life had fallen apart afterwards and she'd ended up separating from her husband. As Lucy had told me at the time, no parent should ever have to cope with the soul- destroying grief of outliving their child.

Tom reached out and patted the old man's shoulder. 'We'll do whatever it takes to recover Maricela and Raúl's bodies and that's a promise.'

I realised immediately that that promise was something that we couldn't necessarily keep even if the intent was there. But right now this was all about gaining Carlos's trust.

The old man gave Tom a long look. 'Sweet words that a father wants to hear, but if I don't agree to share this recording with you, what then?'

'I can't lie, that will be a big setback to us, Carlos,' I said. 'But at the end of the day that's your decision and we'd have to respect that.'

'Really?' he asked.

I sighed, resisting the urge to cross my heart. 'Really.'

Carlos gave me the longest look and then nodded. 'You remind me of my daughter, you know that? Sorry, I didn't catch your name?'

I paused for a moment. I could give him the alias that Tom had supplied me with along with the fake passports, but maybe the truth started here. 'It's Lauren.'

'Then, Lauren, I think I can tell when someone is being sincere, so please don't end up disappointing an old man and leave him feeling gullible after falling for a promise from a pretty lady. Do we have an understanding?'

I held out my hand. 'We do.'

Carlos reached out and shook my hand with a smile. 'That is good to hear.'

I gave him my best *you can trust me* smile. 'Now we've got that all sorted, I can't tell you how anxious I am to hear that recording.'

'Even though it's just whale song?' Carlos asked.

I gave him a small smile. 'Even if it's just whale song.'

Ruby had taken the precaution of calling up another WASP to escort us back in the Skyliner to the diving school in case we were being followed. But thankfully the drive had proved to be totally uneventful. Ruby had also taken the precaution of posting another drone on guard duty over the diving school itself in case another agent turned up.

We parked up outside the diving school and when we got out, Carlos growled like a very pissed off bear when he saw his kicked-in shop door.

'I hope the bastard who did this gets run over by a truck and then it reverses over him just to make sure,' he said as he examined the splintered frame.

'Oh don't you worry, Carlos, people of his type always pay the price eventually,' Tom said, his perfectly neutral expression not giving anything away.

I tried to make sure my own expression was also suitably poker-faced. 'Sorry, I don't want to rush you and I realise you probably want to check things over after the break-in, but about that recording, Carlos?' I said.

'Yes, yes...please follow me.'

But rather than walk into the diving shop, Carlos headed around the side to the jetty, where a white boat was moored up. It was about ten metres long and had diving tanks in the back. He jumped onto its deck and headed to the cabin, then a moment later emerged with an ignition key in his hand. He unclipped a rubber-coated USB stick from the keyring.

'You're telling us it was here all this time?' Tom asked.

'Yes, we always have a memory stick on dives and Maricela

made a point of copying the files off the underwater camera onto this as back-up,' Carlos replied. 'The whale song Raúl captured is on there; I hope it's useful to you.' He handed it to me.

'Thank you so much, Carlos,' I said, taking it from him.

I opened the rubber panel that covered the ports of my Sky Wire and with a sense of anticipation, I slipped the memory stick into the device. At once a folder opened up on the screen filled with hundreds of video and photo folders.

Carlos's face became drawn. 'I'm sorry, the last photos of Maricela and Raúl are on there and it still breaks my heart to see them. You will need to look at them by yourselves.'

Glenn met his gaze. 'I'm so deeply sorry for your loss.'

The old man nodded. He squeezed his eyes shut for a moment, then turned and headed towards the end of the quay to stare out at the tranquil sea.

'God, that poor guy,' I said.

'I know and I hope you meant it when you said you'll do whatever it takes to find their bodies, Tom,' Glenn said. 'The death ritual is an important part of the grieving process on Cuba.'

'We certainly will try to do our best,' Tom replied.

'Good, because if we can help him achieve closure in any small way, it certainly gets my vote,' I said.

Glenn gave me an appraising look. 'You, Lauren, have got a good heart.'

'I try to,' I said.

Ruby gestured to the memory stick. 'Guys, I hate to drag us back to the mission, but we need to see what's on that thing and get out of here sooner rather than later.'

'Yes, sorry, you're right, Ruby,' I replied.

'Don't sweat it and I didn't mean to bust your balls, Lauren. But we may be about to discover something crucial here.'

'You're right. Let's see what we have.'

I began to examine the folders, pulling up the video folder

to start with. In it were lots of files that seemed to span a two-year period. I selected the very last one and opened it. Immediately, a video of a guy in an old-fashioned diving suit made from faded brown fabric with a brass collar plate, appeared. The young man was sitting on the bow of the boat and was well tanned. He also had similar, distinct facial features to Carlos.

'That has to be Raúl, because he's the spitting image of his dad,' Ruby whispered so Carlos wouldn't hear.

I nodded as a beautiful Latino woman with dark eyes and long hair appeared and picked up another camera that had been filming the scene. She had to be Maricela. We watched her carry the camera towards a copper diving helmet and mount it inside of it before closing the faceplate. Then she picked the helmet up, with the camera inside now filming out of the faceplate, towards her brother.

'Wow, talk about being your double with her long flowing locks, Lauren,' Ruby blurted out. 'No wonder you reminded Carlos of her.'

I noticed the old man's back stiffen. 'Oh great, let's just twist the emotional knife, why don't we?' I said in a hushed voice as we all returned our attention to the video.

Maricela was now lowering the helmet over Raúl's head. Then she began to lock it into place with metal clips.

'I've done a bit of diving, but that suit looks seriously heavy to me,' I said.

'Eighty-six kilograms, you have to have the strength of a bull to move it even a fraction on land,' Carlos said, without looking round at us. 'I should know because that's my old diving suit. Raúl always loved the sea and begged me to let him use it. His mother and I always joked that our children were born half-fish...' His words trailed away as he blinked hard, fighting back the tears.

In that moment I became determined to make good on our

promise to Carlos about recovering their bodies, impossible promise or not.

On the video, Maricela was pivoting a boom with two ropes towards Raúl. She hooked the carabiners at the end of the rope onto two eyelets on top of the metal collar of the suit. That was followed by an air hose, which spooled out from a long reel on the deck and connected to the top of Raúl's helmet.

Now, with Maricela in frame and Raúl suspended like a marionette from his harness, he was swung out over the water. His sister pressed a button and the winch began to lower him into the waves. The clear blue sky and gentle lapping disappeared and then suddenly, we had an underwater view through his faceplate of the sea stretching away around us.

A gurgling sound came from a valve in the helmet as Raúl breathed in and out. He glanced down into the murky gloom and then he began to descend towards it.

Whatever Raúl had heard on the day of that dive, hopefully any moment now we'd hear it for ourselves. The question was, would it give us the answer we were looking for?

Raúl glanced back up towards the surface where the old trawler sat, the winch cable to the suit taut, the air hose snaking down alongside it.

As he was slowly descending into the depths, the ocean grew steadily more gloomy around him. Raúl's arm came up into view and on his diving watch it showed a depth of four hundred feet.

'Bloody hell, the deepest I've ever managed on a scuba dive is thirty metres,' I said.

'Yes, my son was pushing the suit to its maximum depth of six hundred feet at that site,' Carlos said, again not looking round. 'I suppose I should tell you the truth about the wreck that my children were searching for.'

My gaze tightened on his back. 'The cargo boat you mentioned?'

He sighed. 'That was just a cover story that we all came up with to hide what they were really looking for, something that both myself and my father before me had also searched for. I had to be sure that you weren't just rival treasure hunters trying to discover information that could lead you to the wreck.'

'Treasure?' Ruby asked, her eyes widening.

Carlos turned round to face us, tears streaming down. 'Yes, but none of that matters to me now that I've lost my children. So, I may as well tell you the truth. You see, they had unearthed a clue that led them to the location that they were diving at. My children became convinced that the site was the location of the sunken ship of Bartolomeu, a famous Portuguese buccaneer. The rumours were that Bartolomeu had managed to capture a treasure galleon bound from Cartagena to Havana, but the ship foundered in a hurricane on the rocks of the Jardines de la Reina. Raúl and Maricela, following the family obsession, tried to find that wreck, an obsession that ultimately cost them their lives.'

Glenn raised his eyebrows at us and then joined the old man at the end of quay, draping a companionable arm around his shoulders as Carlos hung his head.

My thoughts were whirling with the revelation that we'd just heard. We were actually talking about a real life search for pirate treasure here.

The video was still playing as I returned my attention to it, even more intrigued about what we might be about to see. On it the gloom was pressing in on every side as we listened to Raúl's breathing deepen.

It was at that moment that I was struck by the strong analogy between Raúl and his air line, and an astronaut doing a space-walk back in the sixties in the Mercury programme. Rather than the self-contained modern spacesuits used by astronauts now, back then they'd had an air line that connected to their capsule, supplying oxygen to keep them alive. In so many ways, Raúl and those brave astronauts who put their lives on the line were cut from the same cloth.

Fine particles were drifting past the faceplate of the helmet as the darkness started to deepen even more around Raúl. Then his gloved hands were fumbling with something; a beam of light lanced out from the torch that he was holding. He angled it downwards, illuminating the ocean beneath him, where there were small boulders and little else. A moment later, like someone on a very slow motion parachute jump, Raúl touched down on the seabed.

I noted how regular his breathing still was. I knew in his situation I would have been hyperventilating by that point. A dive to thirty metres was scary enough with the water pressing in on you, but at this depth I couldn't even begin to imagine what it was like.

With a gurgle of bubbles from the helmet's valve, Raúl set forward, each slow footstep in the dirt sending up a billow of mud.

'Vamos, belleza mía, dónde estás?' we heard Raúl whisper.

Come on, my beauty, where are you? my earbud translated.

Then Raúl then let out a sharp breath. 'Shit!' he said in English.

Something was glowing in the distance and growing bigger fast. Too quick to make out, the thing rushed past him at high speed, the wake behind it powerful enough to knock Raúl off his feet. He sprawled backwards and then suddenly we were looking up at the surface.

'What's the hell was that thing?' Ruby asked, staring at the screen.

But before I could answer, the mic picked up a distant echoey cry like haunting whale song. It made the hairs on my neck stand up.

On the video, Raúl, who'd now slowly pushed himself back to his feet, was also looking everywhere for the source of the sound.

From his rapid breath it was obvious the guy was rattled – who wouldn't be by whatever it was that he'd just witnessed?

His hand rose up and tugged hard on his tether. A moment later Raúl was rising from the seabed, his breath thundering inside the confines of the helmet. The point of light was already becoming a fading ember as it sped away into the ocean, the whale song growing quieter with it.

None of us said a thing as we continued watching until Raúl at last broke the surface. Maricela was staring down at her brother from the railing of the boat as he frantically gestured to her to get him back aboard. A few seconds later the video ended.

'Was that thing a micro mind zooming around the ocean like it owned the place?' Ruby asked.

'I didn't get a good enough look at it, but it certainly could have been,' I replied. 'But I think we should upload this footage for Lucy to analyse and tell us what she thinks.'

Tom nodded and then turned towards Carlos. 'I don't remember seeing any report of a glowing underwater object in that news article?'

'That's because we didn't tell them anything about it,' Carlos said. 'Apart from anything else, Raúl didn't want to tip anyone off about why he and Maricela were in that particular location.'

'But he obviously still told them about the strange whale song,' I said.

'He did, but only to see if anyone knew what it might be. But nobody did. So, they went back time and again to the same spot but they never saw the glowing light again. Sadly they didn't find Captain **Bartolomeu's** ship either. And then one day, on a blue sky day just like today, my son and daughter didn't come back home. Despite numerous searches their boat was never found. A few items that had been on the deck of the boat were washed up on Juventud, but that was all.

'I'm guessing you don't believe the story that their boat may have been hit by a whale then?' I asked.

Carlos shook his head. 'Far more likely that rival treasure hunters got wind of what they were up to and murdered my children trying to discover the whereabouts of **Bartolomeu's** sunken ship. They probably thought they were onto something because, well - do you know what the original name for Isla de la Juventud was?'

'No idea – please enlighten us,' Tom said.

'It was called *Treasure Island.*'

We all gawped at him.

'You've got to be shitting me?' Ruby said.

'Not at all. It's rumoured that the famous book was actually inspired by that very island. Which isn't surprising, because this whole region was once a haven for pirates.'

'*Pirates of the Caribbean?*' I said, grinning.

'The very same,' Carlos replied.

'Well then,' Tom said. 'Sounds like our next step is to investigate that area for ourselves.'

I nodded. 'Apart from anything else, we may be able to turn up some evidence of what happened to your children, Carlos, and if the worst case is true and they *are* dead, recover their bodies if the wreck of their boat is at the bottom of the ocean.'

His eyes met mine. 'You would do this for me, Lauren?'

'Of course I would,' I replied. And I meant it. The old man's plight had really got to me and had been made even realer by seeing his children alive and full of life on the video.

Tom nodded. 'We have someone arriving tomorrow on an exploration ship with a submersible. We will make locating Raúl and Maricela's boat an absolute priority. However, to help our search, could you provide us with the coordinates of their last known position?'

'Yes, Raúl wrote down all their dive site locations in a journal

that he kept under the counter in the shop. I can supply you with
the GPS coordinates from that.' He gave Tom a wistful look. 'A
submersible you say?'

'Yes, a state-of-the-art one that can get down to extraordinary
depths,' Tom replied.

'Oh how I would love to experience a ride down into the
ocean on it,' Carlos said.

I glanced at Tom. 'Is there any reason that Carlos shouldn't
join us on this voyage, even if he just tags along as a spectator?
After all, we are talking about the fate of his children here.'

Tom made a sucking sound between his teeth. 'If I was being
hard-headed, I'd say no...'

I opened my mouth to object, but Tom had already held up
his hand to stop me.

'Before you launch into a blistering tirade about what we
should do in this particular instant, I didn't say I was hard-
hearted. Besides, from a practical point of view it would be useful
to have local knowledge about the currents in that area when we
go diving. And as we agreed already, this is your mission and
you're calling the shots, Lauren.'

I smiled. 'Thank you. In that case, we're doing this.' I turned
to Carlos. 'So what do you say? Would you like to accompany us
on the voyage of a lifetime and try to achieve some closure about
what happened to Maricela and Raúl?'

The old man stepped forward, reached out, and clasped both
of my hands in his. 'Of course I would. Thank you so much,
Lauren. Even though what we may discover may break my
heart.'

'You'll be our honoured guest.' I glanced up at the sky, where
I knew high above us Ruby's WASP drone was hovering out of
sight somewhere. I was increasingly, painfully aware that if we
stayed here longer than we had to, it might make it more likely
that another agent would follow through to find out what had

happened to their comrade. But for Carlos's benefit I put a slightly different spin on it.

'I think in light of the break-in and especially if a rival treasure hunter group is trying to muscle in on what your children were searching for, maybe it would be a good idea if you stayed somewhere else tonight.'

Glenn nodded. 'I absolutely agree with Lauren; in fact you should all stay with me. I have more than enough rooms for everyone and they have incredible views of the ocean.'

'That's very kind of you, but then I must insist on paying for my keep by supplying the rum,' Carlos said. 'I have a few rather special bottles put aside and I would like to toast our new friendship and our success in this endeavour.'

'If that includes a good mojito, then I'm all in,' I said.

Glenn thumped his chest. 'I make the best mojitos.'

'Then I'd better contact Jack and Mike, because apart from getting up to speed with how they've been getting on, we need to tell them to get ready for some real Cuban hospitality.'

'You better believe it,' Glenn said with a beaming smile.

CHAPTER EIGHT

THE SURF ROLLED IN GENTLY on the beach in a rhythmic beating of white lines over the coral sands. Now joined by Jack, Mike, and Glenn's son Antonio, we all sat on a large deck area built to face out to the sea, lit by flaming lanterns that framed the view on either side. Behind us, across a wide lawn edged with palm trees, stood Glenn's crumbling stone mansion, complete with arched windows.

We were all grabbing a chance to mellow out, as the next day promised to be a hectic one. But for now I allowed myself to kick back and soak in some of the magical Cuban atmosphere.

Whilst Carlos and Glenn had been in the house sorting the first round of drinks, Tom, Ruby and I had briefed Jack and Mike on our fun-filled day. But unfortunately our host had returned with Carlos before we'd had a chance to hear how the others had got on, and although I was keen to be as open as possible with Carlos, there were still some things that it was probably better not to discuss in front of him.

I took a sip of my very excellent mojito, which almost tasted of the sunset we were all being treated to. Everyone else was sipping Carlos's special rum and making appreciative noises.

'Of all the places I visualised you living before we arrived in Cuba, Glenn, I have to say it was nowhere like this,' Tom said.

'Ah, the decaying luxury of the past,' Glenn replied. 'But there are mansions like this dotted all over the island. They were built by the Americans who came over in the fifties and made Cuba their decadent playground before they were thrown out - or fled – during the revolution. Of course, I barely have enough money to maintain it, but I think all the cracked plasterwork and rampant vegetation running all over it sort of add to the place's character.'

'Shabby chic, hey?' I said.

Glenn smiled. 'Pretty much, Lauren.' He held up his glass towards Carlos. 'Anyway, I'd like to propose a toast to Carlos for supplying us with this fantastic rum.'

We all raised our glasses to the old man.

He smiled. 'You're very welcome, my friends.'

Ruby took a long drag of her cigar and blew out a perfectly formed smoke ring. 'And here's to you Glenn for sharing with me some of the best damned cigars I've ever tried in my life.'

He winked at her. 'Then I'll have to make sure you're supplied with a box before you leave Cuba.'

'Oh now that I can drink to,' she said, clinking her glass against his before draining it.

Glenn peered at the empty bottle. 'Ah, looks like we need another refill. Carlos, would you like to accompany me to my cellar and choose an appropriate rum? I've quite a collection.'

'That sounds like an excellent idea,' Carlos said, smiling as he stood up.

As the two men headed away, I put my mojito down and looked expectantly at Jack and Mike. 'Okay guys, I'm dying to know what your day was like?'

'It was a lot less exciting than yours, but we managed to get all the probes planted right around the island and the network patched into Delphi on the X103,' Mike replied. 'The moment any monowave seismic activity hits we should be able to get a pretty accurate fix on the epicentre and hopefully from that, the location of the micro mind.'

'That's great news,' I replied, noticing once again just how animated Mike looked. I just hoped that he would still feel that way by the end of this mission.

Jack's gaze tightened on me. 'But getting back to what happened to you guys. So not happy that you and Tom nearly got taken out by a damned grenade.'

'Not as much as I. And neither of us would be sitting here now if it hadn't of been for Ruby.'

'Hey, right person, right time, and thankfully right place as I managed to get my WASP to you in time,' she said. 'And talking of which, just for peace of mind after what happened, I've got three WASPs patrolling the grounds here in case we get any unwelcome visitors.'

'I think that's a wise decision,' Tom said. 'We still have no way of knowing if that agent was acting alone.'

'You still think he may have an accomplice?' Jack asked.

'It's certainly possible, so we all need to be on guard,' I said. 'At least we got lucky this time and they weren't able to report in, especially as the agent was able to identify me.'

'So much for wearing a disguise,' Jack said, scratching under the neckline of his wig.

'The Overseers have obviously got some very sophisticated biometric software running that they are supplying directly to their operatives,' Tom said. 'Short of everyone wearing a latex mask, I think our days of wearing disguises in the field are probably over.'

'Oh thank God for small mercies,' Jack replied with a thin smile.

'Not a fan of dressing up then, big guy?' Ruby said, grinning.

He shook his head. 'That's the understatement of the century.'

My Sky Wire warbled and I glanced at the screen to see that I had an incoming call from Lucy.

'Aha, hopefully this is news from Lucy about Raúl's underwater video footage,' I said. 'I sent it through to her to analyse and maybe give some idea of what that glowing, dart-shaped crystal was.'

'If definitely looked like some of Angelus tech to me,' Mike said.

'We should hopefully know for sure in a moment,' I replied, putting my Sky Wire into speaker phone mode. 'Lucy, are you there?'

'Yes, but getting bored out of my mind mooching around the lab whilst you crazy kids are off having a great time on Cuba.'

'I'm not sure I'd call it all a great time. But that aside, did you manage to analyse the video I uploaded?' I asked.

'Yes, and the good news is that I've been able to identify that glowing light. Based on the footage I'd say we are looking at a Guardian patrolling those waters.'

'And what's a Guardian when it's at home?' Ruby asked.

'A level three AI semi-autonomous drone, that like it says on the tin, was designed to guard something. Of course, micro minds like me are level one AIs and if you'll excuse me blowing my own trumpet, we are far smarter. But more basic level AIs like Guardians are often used to protect significant installations.'

I sat up. 'What sort of significant installation?'

'There I have no idea because of the massive holes in my substrata memory matrix, thanks to that damned Kimprak virus. But the sound picked up by the camera's microphone during

Raúl's dive was definitely coming from that Guardian drone. It would also suggest that there was a micro mind awake somewhere in the vicinity controlling it.'

My eyes widened. 'If that means that this is confirmation of an active micro mind then it sounds like our mission has already struck gold.'

Jack set his drink down. 'So then, how about cutting to the chase and just sending it a message, Lucy? Maybe just tell it to come and merge with you and save us a whole lot of time trying to track it down?'

'I would if I could,' Lucy replied. 'The strange thing is that even though the micro mind is evidently awake, I'm not picking anything up from the quantum communication system that active micro minds normally use to stay in touch with each other. The last time I encountered anything similar was with Red.'

'Please tell me we're not dealing with another rogue AI?' Mike said.

'No, not necessarily. In Red's case he chose to disconnect himself from our network, as he treated everything external to him as a threat. But there is a strong possibility that this micro mind suffered some sort of partial technical failure, meaning that even though it's operational it can't access the network. And if that's true, it may also mean that it was never infected by the Kimprak virus.'

My eyes widened. 'Are you saying that for the first time we may be about to discover a micro mind with a fully intact memory?'

'If you could see me now, you would be able to see me grinning from ear to ear because that's exactly what I'm thinking, Lauren,' Lucy replied. 'An uninfected micro mind would change everything.'

But Tom was holding his hands up. 'I appreciate your enthusiasm, everyone, but please slow down for a moment. There are a lot of maybes in play here rather than any definites. The one thing that has become an even bigger priority after hearing this is that we need to locate this micro mind as fast as possible, wherever it is.'

'Absolutely, and because of that, I say we call it a night now and get as much sleep as possible,' I replied. 'We need to be as sharp as possible, because apart from the micro mind, the presence of a Guardian suggests a very important structure as well, which could make this our most important mission yet.'

Tom nodded. 'Absolutely. I agree we should draw things to close here.'

'Well in my opinion you two are both total buzzkills,' Ruby said.

'I think that's part of my job description,' I replied.

'Apparently so,' Jack said, smiling at me.

And of course it was at exactly that moment that Glenn and Carlos returned with a fresh bottle of rum.

'Oh you're going to like this bottle, it's very special,' Carlos said as they reached us.

I made a T-shape with my hands. 'Sorry guys, you're going to need to put that on ice for now but maybe bring it with us to the ship tomorrow, because I'm hoping we'll have something to really celebrate if everything goes according to plan.'

Glenn raised his eyebrows. 'Oh really?'

'Really. We'll brief you tomorrow,' Jack said, discreetly gesturing his chin towards Carlos, before draining the rest of his glass.

The sun still hadn't risen as we stood on the shore, watching the approaching helicopter's spinning blades getting steadily louder as it swept over the ocean towards us. When it had still been a

speck in the distance, Tom had somehow already correctly identified it as an Airbus H155, which according to him was capable of
carrying up to eight passengers.

We stood there free of our disguises, with our bags of kit at
the ready. Of course I'd had to explain our sudden transformation
to Carlos, saying that we'd been working undercover investigating
the organisation that had sent the agent to break into his house.
He'd immediately fired a dozen questions back at us, that so far
I'd been able to sidestep by telling him that he just needed to
trust us. I knew that explanation was going to get old rapidly, but
for now it was better for his own sake that he didn't know the
whole truth.

Carlos stood with Glenn, shielding his eyes from the coral
sand being kicked up by the helicopter's rotor blades as it came in
to land. Ruby, who was a little further away, was keeping her eyes
on a live feed from one of the WASPs overhead.

'No other aircraft in the area,' she said through my earbud
over the roar of the slowing rotors.

'Good and you're all set here when we take off?' I whispered,
so Carlos wouldn't hear next to me.

'Yes, Glenn is going to give me a lift back. I'll be sticking to
you like glue and no one will know I'm there.'

Jack, who'd also been listening in, gave her a thumbs up. 'I for
one will be much happier knowing you've got our backs covered.'

'Always, if I have anything to do with it,' Ruby replied.

As the rotors slowed to a stop, a guy with a full beard and a
long ponytail to rival Jack's old wig emerged from the helicopter.

The man was wearing a blue shirt and shorts, and had a red
snood around his neck. He had something of the look of a roadie,
based on his muscular build and wide shoulders. The guy also
had arctic blue eyes, which immediately latched onto mine like
some sort of heat-seeking missile and gave me an immediate
uncomfortable vibe.

'Leon, good to meet you at last,' Tom said, sticking out a hand.

So this was Leon, the wealthy French explorer – not that you would have realised it to look at the guy. The only major give-away of how much money he was worth was the helicopter he arrived in, complete with *Leon Dupont Oceanic Exploration Group* on the side.

'Tom, I presume?' he said, shaking Tom's hand.

'The very same. Good to meet you. I'd also like to intro-duce my associates, Lauren, Jack and Mike.' He gestured towards Carlos. 'This is Mr Fernández, the father of the two people whose boat that we'll be looking for on the seabed.' He gestured towards the others and finished making the intro-ductions.

Leon shook everyone's hands, but when he was introduced to me, he took my hand in his and then kissed it. 'I'm charmed to make your acquaintance, Lauren Stelleck.'

I felt a blush creep across my cheeks. To be honest, the guy was rather good-looking, at least if you're into chiselled features and a sexy French accent.

'You too, Leon,' I replied, trying to ignore the barely supressed scowl Jack was giving him.

'Well my dear Lauren, we will need to get a move on if we want to begin the search for this boat today. A storm front is moving in and I am keen to get my submersible launched as soon as possible before we lose our window.'

Glenn turned to us. 'Then this is where we say goodbye for now.' He stepped forward and shook Carlos's hand. 'Good hunt-ing, my friend. I hope this expedition brings you the answers that you deserve. But do make sure you look me up when you get back, because I have a lot of fine rum to be sampled and I think I may have discovered a new best friend.'

'You can count on it,' Carlos said with a broad smile.

With pats on the back and hugs from Carlos, we bid our own

farewells before leaving him behind with Ruby as we headed off towards the helicopter.

'I have a feeling that Leon is quite the ladies' man,' Jack said, giving me a pointed look.

'Hey, I've done absolutely nothing to encourage him.' I said.

'Ah yes, about that,' Tom said. 'Leon does have something of a reputation with romancing women, if you catch my drift.'

'Way too clearly,' I replied.

'Don't worry, he's mostly harmless,' Tom said, as a smiling Leon held the door open for us and we boarded the helicopter.

As the H155 roared into life, Leon handed us all headsets. The moment I put mine on, the active noise cancellation kicked in and the bellow of the rotors was muted to a whisper. We'd barely strapped into our seats as the craft began to rise into the air.

Compared to the magic carpet flight of the X103, this craft felt prehistoric by comparison. The whole helicopter shook and rattled as though it was starting to tear itself apart. But thankfully, that bone shaking vibration began to subside when the pilot levelled off at about five hundred feet above the sea. We began to swing back towards the shore.

We flew over the others on the beach, waving up at us, and then started to climb over the island until the opposite shore and the shimmering sea of the Caribbean beyond became visible.

Carlos was craning his head to get a view of the island speeding past beneath us, his eyes drinking in every detail.

Leon smiled across at the old man. 'Something tells me you haven't seen your home from the air before, is that right?'

The old man nodded. 'This is actually my first time flying ever. Cuba looks even more beautiful from up here.'

'Oh I think it's pretty special from ground level too,' I said.

Carlos beamed at me. 'That we can certainly agree on, Lauren.'

Within ten minutes we'd already crossed the island and were speeding out over the ocean towards a large island to the south. Beyond it, in the far distance, lay the thin neck of South America.

Carlos gestured towards the sea below us. 'We're flying over an area now that was once the playground of pirates back in the sixteenth century. The seabed is littered with wrecks of the Spanish treasure ships that they plundered.'

'Who in turn plundered the Aztecs and relieved them of their gold and silver,' Jack said.

'That is also true, my friend,' Carlos replied with a smile.

Just to the left of the nose of the helicopter I could see a white foam carving the way through the crystal sea.

I pointed it out, my stomach already knotting, because it might be another Russian sub. 'What's that?'

But Leon turned to me with a wide smile. 'That, my dear, Lauren, is a Bryde's whale. On the way here we detected considerable activity around many different whale species.'

'Is that not normal for this region?' Jack asked.

'Not for this time of year it isn't and certainly not in the numbers that we've been seeing,' Leon replied. 'It's almost like they are being drawn to this area for some reason.'

I made sure I didn't catch Jack or Tom's eye. It was hard to imagine that this wasn't something to do with the Guardian's song that Raúl had recorded beneath the waves.

As the others gazed down to watch the whale, I scanned the sky around us but couldn't see any distortions in the air to give away the presence of Ruby's X103 tailing us.

I discreetly powered up my Sky Wire and sent a text. *'Ruby, are you there?'*

Her response came straight back. *'Hell yeah, a mile out from your port side and tracking you.'*

I glanced out through the left window, where I now knew the X103 was but still couldn't see a thing. The chameleon camo system was obviously doing a great job as usual. It was certainly reassuring to know that back-up was close to hand if we did run into any of the Russian vessels and things began to get *interesting*.

The large island ahead of us grew steadily closer over the next twenty minutes until a jagged rocky outline became visible. A quick check of the Sky Wire's map confirmed it as the Isla de la Juventud. Since Carlos had told us that it had once been called Treasure Island, it was easy to envisage pirate ships moored around its many bays.

Because I'd become so transfixed by the spectacle of the island, I hadn't noticed the growing white dot in the sea ahead of us until Mike pointed it out.

'Is that your ship, Leon?' he asked.

I looked down to see a large, white, funnelled ship at least a hundred metres long. It had a long rear deck with a helipad next to a hangar.

'Yes, that's *Venus*, the second love of my life. She has a crew of fifty and facilities of every sort, including a wet lab to analyse the new species that we've discovered.'

'Impressive – and your first love is?' Tom asked.

Leon gestured towards the rear of the deck, where a bright red mini sub was being connected to a hoist by a team of people dressed in white coveralls. 'That's my first love, *Neptune*, and she's being prepped for immediate launch. She has a solid titanium hull a metre thick and is capable of diving to the deepest depths of any ocean.'

I nodded as I gazed down at the ocean. It was a much darker blue than the aqua green of the shallow sea around the island. What secrets lay at its bottom? I was certainly keeping everything crossed that we'd find the sunken wreck of Raúl's and Maricela's boat – and hopefully also their bodies – but also that we might have our own encounter with the Guardian drone.

I glanced across at Carlos, whose eyes were also studying the ocean, his face drawn.

I reached out and squeezed his hand. His eyes met mine and he slowly nodded, before his gaze returned to the ocean beneath us once more.

Yes, this man needed closure – and with any luck, we were about to give it to him.

CHAPTER NINE

WE SETTLED onto *Venus's* helipad with a gentle shudder. As the rotor blades began to slow, one of the crew, wearing ear defenders, ran forward and opened the passenger door for us.

'Welcome to my kingdom,' Leon said, ushering us out of the helicopter towards the rear of the pad where *Neptune* was waiting.

The bright red sub had two large propellers at the back and three blister viewing canopies built into the nose of the craft. It sat on two large metal skids and two insect-like arms with pincer hands were built into the nose. Thruster units were built into several places around its hull. The way into the craft appeared to be through a hatch set into its roof, fastened with huge bolts that looked like they might have come straight off of the *Titanic*.

We approached the team surrounding the sub. 'Get ready for immediate launch,' Leon said.

In a flurry of choreographed activity the air and power lines were disconnected from the bulbous vehicle.

'No safety briefing first?' Tom asked.

Leon shook his head. 'No time. Look at that.' He gestured

towards the northern horizon, where a thin band of darkness was just visible. 'We have a category three hurricane rolling in within the next couple of hours and we want to be back onboard *Venus* long before that beast reaches us. As far as a safety briefing goes, basically assume the brace position to kiss your arse goodbye if anything goes wrong. We'll be killed almost instantly at the depth we're going down to if the hull fails.'

'Now there's a cheery thought,' Mike said, chewing his lip as he gave the craft a suspicious look.

Leon noticed it. 'I only have space for two passengers anyway; it's very cramped onboard *Neptune*. So who's it going to be?'

Tom gestured towards me. 'This is your call, Lauren.'

If we were about to discover the clues about a micro mind, or even come across a Guardian, then my synaesthesia – which allowed my brain to interpret the audio to visual language of the Angelus – would be essential on this dive.

'Okay, I should go, for obvious reasons,' I said.

Jack crossed his arms. 'Hang on, why should it be you? Let someone else take the risk for once.'

Of course, he already knew the answer to that because with my synaesthesia, not to mention the Empyrean Key stowed away in my rucksack, I was the only one who would be able to communicate with the Guardian if we ran into it.

But before I could take Jack aside for a serious chat, Leon was already waving his hands at him. 'Please relax. Diving to this depth will barely tax *Neptune* and although I can't stand here and promise you it's a hundred percent safe, it's pretty damned close.'

Jack's forehead furrowed as he gazed into my eyes. 'Are you sure about this?'

'I'm afraid I am, Jack.'

Mike and Tom were looking between us like this was a tennis match.

'Sounds to me like you have lost the argument, mate,' Mike said.

Jack dragged his hand through his hair and sighed. 'It does, doesn't it? But I should go with you. If this does end up involving an ancient wreck, that falls under the realm of archaeology, albeit with an underwater spin.'

I started to nod, but Carlos stepped forward, his hands clutched together. 'Please let me go on this dive, Lauren. If you discover *Hercules* down on the seabed and my children are onboard it...' He placed his hands to his heart, beseeching me.

I held his gaze, thinking. What if we did discover them? Even worse, what condition would their bodies be in after three months down there? Despite his words, how would he really react to that? I knew if I was in his shoes I would probably suffer a breakdown there and then, not exactly ideal within the confines of the submersible. Surely if there *was* a grim discovery, it would be better to come back to the surface and break it to Carlos gently rather than expose him to what could be a brutal experience?

'I don't think that's a good idea, Carlos, for all sorts of reasons,' I said.

He placed his hand over his heart and gave me a pure big-eyed Bambi look. 'Please, Lauren, I need to do this. Imagine I was your father standing here and it was you who had died down there. Would you deny him that request?'

That statement pierced my emotional armour like nothing else could. Carlos had no way of knowing that I'd lost both of my parents in a house fire when I was younger. Of course, no one had let me anywhere near the bodies to identify them. That had fallen on the shoulders of a close family friend. I knew everyone had been trying to protect me, but it had left a deep scar. One moment my dad had been reading me a bedtime story and the next I was being dragged out into the street as our house raged with fire and smoke. Even though I knew it would have been the most awful sight to see their burned bodies, if I had been an adult I would have insisted on it. Just like Carlos was now. This was all about closure, something that I'd never ever achieved over the loss of my parents. It had left a gaping hole in me ever since.

All these thoughts flashed through my mind in a matter of seconds.

Then before I knew it, I found myself slowly nodding. 'I understand, of course I do, and if you're absolutely sure of this, the third seat is yours,' I said.

Jack took my arm in his. 'Are you really sure about this?'

'No, but how can I stand here and deny Carlos this request? Seriously?'

He glanced across at Carlos, then slowly nodded. 'Yes, I think you may have a good point there, but what if...'

His words trailed away but I knew exactly what he was talking about. What if we ran into a micro mind down there?

'We'll just have to cross that bridge if we get to it, but leave it to me.'

Jack nodded. 'Okay.'

A look of utter relief filled the old man's face. He stepped forward and kissed me on both cheeks. 'Thank you, thank you so much.'

Mike was nodding with approval, but Tom's expression was unreadable. He almost certainly didn't approve that I'd let my heart overrule my head. But as Tom himself had said, I was the one in charge and this was my call.

Leon clapped his hands together. 'Good, then as that's all decided, let's get this dive underway. Just one thing that you should know – during the dive there won't be any way for us to communicate with the surface, and vice versa.'

'So in other words, we won't know the outcome of your mission until you surface again?' Tom said.

'Pretty much,' Leon replied.

'Then once again, please remember that this is just a reconnaissance mission, Lauren,' Tom said. 'If it turns out to be anything more, you should surface straight away and then we can discuss our next steps.'

'Okay, but have the coffee ready for when we get back,' I said.

'You can count on it,' Mike said with a smile.

Leon was already clambering up a ladder, heading for the open hatch leading into the submersible.

Carlos walked up to *Neptune* and stroked its hull. 'Beautiful,' he said to himself, before – with some assistance from the crew – he climbed the ladder and disappeared into the sub.

I turned to Jack. 'Thank you for understanding that I should be the one to go.'

'I didn't have a lot of choice, did I?'

'No, but thank you anyway.'

I drew him in for a kiss and a smile flickered across his face as I pulled away.

'Just be careful of any mermen you meet down there,' he said.

'Hmmm, I think the only merman I need to be a little wary of is our new friend Leon.'

'Yep, he really is a ladies' man if ever I saw one,' Mike said.

'Trust me, only in his own head, although there will always be a few who fall for that sort of guy,' I replied quickly, as Jack was now frowning again.

I hugged Mike and then even Tom, who looked slightly taken aback by my show of affection. Considering the guy was only in his forties he was seriously stiff upper lip and *don't show your emotions*, old-school British.

A moment later I was climbing down the ladder into *Neptune* to join the others.

As I set foot on the deck of the cramped cockpit, I saw Leon and Carlos, already laid out on their fronts on two couches, their heads peering out through viewing blisters in the sub's nose. A constellation of lights lit up around Leon's couch as he powered up the sub's systems.

I headed to the remaining couch, on Leon's right, and slid myself along it until my head was within my own blister window, which I could see was reassuringly thick. Through it I could see Jack, Mike and Tom watching me. I gave them a thumbs up, which Jack half-heartedly returned. He was *so* not happy that he wasn't accompanying me, even if he got my reasons for letting Carlos take his place.

I glanced to the left of my blister window to see that Leon had taken hold of two complex controls fixed to pivoting rods. As he moved his hand through the air, the mandible claws outside replicated his movements. Then, when he squeezed his hands, the pincers clamped shut.

Beyond him, in the far blister window, I could see Carlos's head, his eyes wide with wonder. And who could blame him? This thing must have felt like a spaceship compared to the ancient diving suits that he'd was used to exploring the sea in.

Leon spoke into the headset that he'd just pulled on. '*Venus* control, main tanks fully pressurised, power is at one hundred percent charge and *Neptune* is running under her own power. Ready to launch.'

'Roger that, *Neptune*, hoist lift commencing,' a woman with an Italian accent replied.

A whine came from outside as several winches kicked into life. With a slight lurch the mini-sub began to rise from the deck by a crane, then was pivoted out over the sea.

Through the blister on the deck I could see Jack, Mike and Tom all waving, which Carlos and I returned. A moment later I lost sight of them as *Neptune* was lowered towards the water.

The immaculately painted hull of *Venus* slid past, gleaming white, with not a dot of rust to be seen anywhere.

I took a last glance at the horizon. Even though the storm was still a long way off, the crests on the water were already starting to build.

'Okay, brace yourselves for a gentle impact,' Leon said as the waves rose to meet us.

With a slap of surf that jolted us on our couches and sent a spray of foaming water over our windows, *Neptune* settled onto the surface. I clung to my seat's arms as the waves began to rock the sub to the right, before it settled back into an upright position.

For all my bravado about insisting it should be me on this mission, it was only as we began to bob around on the surface that I remembered I didn't have a great stomach for sailing. That was something I'd discovered in truly spectacular fashion during a girls only sailing trip around the Greek islands. I'd spent most of my time with my head over the railing, puking into the sea. This was much to the delight of the fish, who'd risen to eat it all up like some sort of gourmet chum that people use to attract sharks.

'Hey, Leon, I don't suppose you have any sea sickness pills on board?' I asked.

He cast me an amused look. 'Actually, I do, Lauren. But please relax. I promise you that once we get beneath the waves it will be a silky smooth ride from there on out.'

'I just hope you're right,' I replied.

'Trust me,' Leon said. He pressed a button on his console and spoke into his mic. '*Venus*, release harness on my mark.'

'Roger that, *Neptune*, waiting for your order,' the Italian woman replied.

Leon scanned his readouts. 'Three, two, one...release.'

With a lurch the harness shot away and the submersible immediately settled deeper into the water.

'Flooding main ballast tanks,' Leon said, flicking a switch above him.

A gurgling sound came from the belly of the craft beneath us. Then my stomach lurched as we began to descend into the water. Within moments the waves were lapping up over our blister windows.

My eyes drank in the last view of the blue sky then it was gone as we submerged. The large hull of *Venus* sat to our starboard with its anchor line stretching away into the depths below.

It was then I noticed two sharks swimming further out, the caustic light patterns across their backs refracting the sunlight coming through the surface of the sea above.

I gripped the sides of my couch harder. 'Damn it, there are bloody sharks out there, guys.'

Carlos peered out and then a smile filled his face. 'So beautiful. Those are Blacktip Reef ones.'

Leon shot me an amused look. 'And before you panic, they are pretty harmless, Lauren, although they might give you a nip if you get too close.' He made a show of biting down and flashing his bright white teeth at me.

Yep, this guy was a regular predator in every sense and I'd come across his species plenty of times in bars and clubs over the years. I knew how to handle them.

'Okay, let's see what awaits us down below,' Leon said, totally unaware that I had mentally categorised him into *that* box. 'Starting up motors and increasing angle to diving planes,' he continued, pushing a control yoke in front of him forward.

A whine came from behind us and with a velvety smooth bit of acceleration the nose of the *Neptune* dropped and we began to move forward while quickly descending.

The Blacktip sharks swam briefly over to us to inspect our strange red craft trailing ribbons of bubbles behind it.

Despite being told that they were relatively harmless, I found it distinctly unnerving as the bigger of the two sharks, almost a couple of metres long, swam past. My window slightly magnified the shark and made it appear even bigger, which really didn't help. Its white-rimmed iris eyeballed me as though it could almost smell my unease through the window.

'I'm starting to feel like a human exhibit in a reverse aquarium,' I said.

'We are the exhibits to the Blacktips out there,' Carlos replied with a laugh, pressing his hand to the window as if he wanted to tickle the shark's nose.

We began to spiral down, following the anchor line from the ship above, the sub tilting slightly in the turn as Leon applied the rudder by twisting the joystick.

Leon glanced across at Carlos. 'So what do you think so far?'

'It's spectacular, but I just wish my children were here to share this moment.'

Leon expression fell. 'Of course you do...'

After that, not surprisingly, we all fell silent, each of us lost in our own thoughts.

I'd once watched a *Falcon* rocket launch on YouTube and had heard one of the astronauts describe the ship as a living breathing dragon as it left the Earth's atmosphere. That was exactly what I was experiencing here, as the soft whir of the electric motors propelling us were increasingly overwhelmed by the slightly alarming creaks and groans coming from the submersible titanium hull around us. Also, there were gurgling noises that sounded very much like my own stomach after taco night at the Rock Garden. But what really wasn't helping was the odd pop and hiss that had my imagination working overtime, imagining rivets exploding from *Neptune's* metal body. However, when no cracks appeared in my blister window and there wasn't a sudden jet of water to drown us all, I started to relax a fraction. I just needed to keep reminding myself that statistically, this dive was *almost* totally safe...

With a considerable act of willpower, I concentrated on the view through the window rather than the paranoid churn of my own thoughts.

Leon flicked on *Neptune's* headlights, which lanced down into the gloomier waters beneath us.

As we descended, small particles swirled past the window, caught in the sub's headlights like tiny stars. Talking of which, our own sun, still visible through the sea's surface overhead, had grown considerably dimmer as we dived deeper.

There were also more of the silhouetted Blacktip sharks swimming around *Venus* on the surface, but they seemed just curious rather than waiting for an unlucky crew member to stumble overboard and become a quick snack. Yes, maybe *Jaws* had a lot to answer for regarding my attitude towards those beautiful creatures.

The ocean beyond our windows was gradually turning from light green to a deeper ultramarine as the odd fish flickered past. At one point, a whole shoal of shrimp, catching the light like a field of diamonds, swam by.

As we continued our descent, the seabed was gradually becoming visible. On first glance, it appeared to be littered boulders sticking out of a silt that surrounded them like a thick grey icing that softened every sharp edge. An abundance of plant life, including coral, rose from the seabed despite the depth. Then to my surprise, I saw a turtle pass us with lazy strokes.

'Wow, I had no idea turtles could dive this deep,' I said.

Leon glanced at a display. 'We're only at eighty-three fathoms, otherwise known as five hundred feet; that's nothing for a turtle. They can dive down to nearly a thousand feet if they put their minds to it. At this depth we're still in the sunlight zone and there is still plenty of luminescence to support photosynthesis.

Because of that, life thrives down here as there's plenty to eat for everyone. Isn't that right, Carlos?'

The old man seemed to stir himself out of a reverie. 'Yes, and that's despite the pressure at these sorts of depths.'

I did a quick mental calculation. 'So, at roughly forty-five psi per one hundred feet, that's a pressure equivalent of around two hundred and twenty-five pounds. Talk about uncomfortable.'

'Exactly and you have to be extremely fit and strong to be able to dive to these depths to cope with it, just as my children were...' His voice trailed away and he returned his attention to his window.

Leon caught my eye and grimaced.

I looked down through my own window. Would we find their bodies partly buried in that grey mud, like everything else that had ended up down here?

We continued our descent until the seabed was at last only a car's length beneath us, and Leon finally levelled *Neptune* out. A boulder field stretched away from us and in the distance lay a coral field of hills and valleys. Little flickers of bright colours caught in our headlights gave away the presence of hundreds of fish swimming among the rich feeding ground of canyons and coral mountains.

'This is a scuba diver's paradise,' I said.

'Not at these depths it isn't,' Leon said. 'This is strictly the realm of subs and deep sea divers, although one record-breaker managed a thousand feet in scuba gear. However, the bends are a serious danger and it took the diver over fifteen hours to return to the surface in a series of staged ascents.'

I nodded, imagining what four hundred pounds of pressure must have felt like on a human's body.

I gently patted the inside of the padded hull. 'Well *Neptune* is definitely designed to easily withstand it.'

'Ah, she may be, but a diving suit is still a magical experience,'

Carlos said. 'I miss being down here, exploring, seeing what so many eyes have never seen. And that's a passion that I passed onto my children.'

Leon smiled and nodded. 'Yes, I know all about that. You see, my father was a marine biologist who fuelled my own love for the sea and that's something that never left me.'

The two men exchanged a knowing look.

When I saw the wistful expression on Leon's face as he returned his attention to the controls, my mind was already starting to recategorise him. Yes, he might be a player, but it was obvious the guy also had a good heart too.

I glanced at my smartwatch to see twenty minutes had already passed. 'We really should get this search underway before that weather window closes in on us.'

Carlos let out a long sigh and his shoulders dropped. 'Okay, let's discover what happened to Raúl and Maricela.'

Part of me wished that Carlos had stayed on the surface and that it was Jack down here with me right now. In future, maybe I was going to have to listen my head rather than my heart.

Leon pressed a button on his display and an underwater chart of the seabed appeared, complete with contours.

'Tom sent me the last known location of *Hercules*. I have loaded it into the VMS.' He pointed towards a marker on the screen that, according to the scale I could see printed next to it, was about a hundred metres out from our current position.

'VMS?' I asked.

'That stands for Voyage Management System. It uses digital charts in combination with *Neptune's* other sensors to work out where we are. Obviously GPS signals don't work down here.'

'Of course, but if Raúl and Maricela's boat did sink, surely it would have drifted some distance?' I said.

Leon nodded and pressed a button on his screen. A blue circle appeared around the marker.

'Allowing for typical oceanic currents around this region, this is our search area for the wreck. It's about a thousand metres wide.'

'I understand, but I do wish you would stop switching between feet and metres; I find it confusing,' I said.

'Just the vagaries of history. Traditionally altitude for aircraft is measured in feet and the same goes for underwater, although strictly speaking that's measured in fathoms, which is the equivalent of six feet.'

'That's even more confusing; you'd think they'd try to standardise everything to metric by now.'

In the far blister window, Carlos shook his head. 'That's never going to happen, Lauren, because you'll never be able to get everyone to agree.'

I sighed. 'Yes, the same old.'

Leon nodded. 'Anyway politics aside, let's get this search underway.'

He pushed the accelerator lever forward and the motors hummed louder. *Neptune* surged towards the marker on the VMS, gaining a bit of altitude, so we had more of an aerial view of the coral landscape mountains and valleys below.

Once again, everyone fell silent, all of us painfully aware of what we might encounter at any moment. A bigger issue for me, that was growing realer by the moment, was how Carlos would react and how we could deal with it. Talk about my decision making life difficult for us.

As we closed on the marker, the old man's expression became one of utter concentration as his gaze flicked over the seabed, looking for any clue as to the fate of his children's boat.

The distance counter on Leon's VMS map ticked down past ten metres and a moment later a soft chime came from the console.

'These are the exact last known coordinates for the *Hercules*,' Leon said in an almost reverential tone.

I looked down at the coral landscape. Apart from dozens of sea anemones, their fronds waving gently in the underwater current, there certainly wasn't any sign of a wreck down here.

'Now the hard part starts,' Leon said. 'I'm going to take us through a spiralling out search pattern from these coordinates. If *Hercules* did go down at this location, a thousand-metre radius should hopefully be enough to locate it.'

'I pray to God that it is,' Carlos said quietly as he crossed himself.

We all settled in for the long haul as Leon began to take *Neptune* out in growing circuits. I was uncomfortably aware that I hadn't had a loo break before starting this voyage, and I was pretty sure that the sub didn't come with a loo. I wasn't about to ask what the alternative arrangement might be.

Silence settled over the cabin, with Carlos the epicentre of that mood. Leon and I both picked up on it. I could hazard a guess at what was going through the old man's mind right now – dread, numbness, possibly even relief that this might soon all be resolved one way or the other.

My body was growing increasingly cramped inside the claustrophobic cockpit of the submersible and that was starting to take its toll on my body and mind. I couldn't wait to get back to the surface, feel the wind on my face and have a damned good stretch.

Ten minutes dissolved into twenty and then became forty. The area that we had already covered was now shaded red, and we were nearing the edge of the search zone without seeing a thing. Then Carlos suddenly tensed and pointed through his window.

Just ahead of us, in a canyon running between two tall outcrops of rock, was a trawler-sized vessel lying on its side.

'That's *Hercules*...' Carlos whispered. Then he let out a stifled sob, tears filling his eyes.

In the cramped conditions there was no way that I could reach the old man to comfort him. Instead I was forced to watch as he silently wept, his eyes locked onto the wreck partly buried in silt, with lichen already beginning to grow over it.

But what exactly would we find when we examined the sunken boat? I couldn't suppress the shudder that passed through me as I imagined the states of Raúl and Maricela's bodies.

'Okay, I'm taking us in for a closer look,' Leon said, his face grim.

He pushed the control yoke forward and we began to head towards the broken hull of *Hercules*.

CHAPTER TEN

CARLOS, his eyes bright red, had been unable to bring himself to watch as Leon steered us to within ten metres of the sunken ship that had belonged to his children.

My heart clenched as I took in the holes peppering the boat's hull, many below the waterline.

'Tell me that's not bullet fire,' I said.

Carlo's head snapped up and he stared at the damage. 'Oh God...'

Frown lines radiated around Leon's eyes. 'I'm afraid that's exactly what it looks like, Lauren. But who would do something so barbaric?'

'Other treasure hunters, it has to be,' Carlos said, his voice bitter.

'Treasure hunters?' Leon asked, staring at the old man.

'It's a long story for later,' I said, heading off any more conversation on the topic. It was the last thing Carlos needed right now. As it was, I was having a huge surge of guilt about bringing him down here at all. Yes, I definitely wasn't going to let my heart overrule my head in future.

I looked across at Carlos, completely understanding his anger at this awful discovery. But of course, there could be a far more ominous explanation than ruthless rival treasure hunters. Unfortunately, any information about the Overseers' likely involvement was one nugget of information that I couldn't share with the other two, at least not if I didn't want to put their lives in danger after this was all over.

'So much for it being a whale strike,' Leon said. 'Anyway, we'd better see what else we can discover.' He gave me pointed look which I knew was code for *search for Raúl and Maricela's bodies.*

I took in the tight crevasse that the boat was wedged into. 'That looks like a difficult space to manoeuvre *Neptune* into, Leon?'

'It is and that's why we're going to send in *Bad Dog,*' he replied.

'*Bad Dog?*'

'Sorry, that's our nickname for the underwater drone that *Neptune* carries with her. It's so named because of the number of times that drone has managed to get itself wedged into a space that we end up having to haul it out of using the tether. I always think of it as a lead.'

'Got you. So where is he - presumably it's a he?'

He gave me a wolfish smile. 'Of course *Bad Dog* is a he. The drone is stowed in a hatch, under the nose. Give me a few seconds and I'll launch him.'

Leon reached up and pivoted down a secondary display with another joystick control attached to it. He flicked a number of buttons, and with a gurgle a swarm of small bubbles erupted from the *Neptune's* nose. At the same moment the screens above mine and Carlos's dive couches also flicked into life to show a wide angle camera view of the seabed ahead. Leon spun a thumbwheel on the back of the joystick and with a distant whir, a small, fluorescent red craft emerged, trailing a tether behind it. It had a bulbous camera eye behind a dome and was equipped with two pincer claws, just like *Neptune*, but on a far smaller scale.

The screens in front of us relayed *Bad Dog's* view, as Leon dipped its nose and began to dive it towards the sunken boat. A needle of light shot out from a lamp mounted in the drone's belly, playing over the side of the hull and settling on the name, *Hercules*.

'Well that settles that, not that there was any real doubt,' Leon said.

Carlos nodded, wiping a tear from his eye. 'I would recognise that boat anywhere.'

'Look there's no need for you to watch this. It could be extremely difficult for you,' I said.

He shook his head. 'No, I have to know, Lauren.'

I nodded. Of course he did, just like I would have wanted to know if I'd been in his position. I returned my attention to watch *Bad Dog's* progress.

The diminutive craft was already being investigated by a couple of curious fish who quickly gave up on it before returning to their pursuit of food among the coral.

Leon deftly steered the underwater drone around until it was facing the back of *Hercules'* stern and then slowly manoeuvred it towards the boat's cabin.

A brief image of bloated corpses filled my imagination and I wished I could reach across to hold Carlos's hand in preparation for whatever we were about to discover.

I held my breath as Leon edged *Bad Dog* forward towards the open door of the cabin.

The tension ratcheted up across my shoulders as the craft's spotlight stabbed into the gloom. I almost jumped out of my skin when a shape flashed out of the darkness. I just had a chance to register the large eel as it shot past *Bad Dog* and snaked away through the water.

'Just a whiptail conger,' Leon said. 'They love to take up residence in wrecks.'

'Right,' I replied, hoping my heartbeat might drop back to a normal level anytime soon. So much for me being a battle-hardened soldier.

Leon propelled the drone forward again with little blasts of its thrusters, fine-tuning its manoeuvre through the doorway. Then he brought it to a dead stop.

'Okay, let's see what we have in here,' he said.

He slowly revolved *Bad Dog*, its spotlight swinging round the cabin to reveal nothing other than the chaotic detritus of a boat thrown around after tipping onto its side. But the important thing was, there was no sign of any bodies in there.

I exhaled a long, deep breath. 'Oh thank God for that,' I said, before I could stop myself.

Carlos's face had tensed and I immediately felt a huge surge of guilt. Finding nothing in here was in many ways the worst possible outcome for him.

Leon breathed through his nose. 'Okay, so let's look around the wreck site now.'

I knew immediately that it was a *hail Mary*, because if Raúl and Maricela hadn't been in the boat when it hit the seabed, surely the current could have carried them a considerable distance? Or worse, they could have been eaten by a whole host of marine life over the three months since the boat had been lost.

If Leon knew that too, he didn't let on because he spent a good twenty minutes meticulously looking over the surrounding area, but not spotting a single thing.

Throughout, Carlos stared out like a statue from his blister window, closed in on himself and lost in his thoughts.

Leon spun *Bad Dog* around for yet another sweep of the area.

The wreck was now in the foreground with *Neptune* hanging like a spacecraft in the water behind it.

'I'm sorry. I don't think their bodies are here, Carlos,' Leon finally said.

The old man's face crumpled. 'Thank you for trying so hard, but at least I know now that I'll never find them. The sea has obviously claimed them for its own.'

'I'm so sorry,' Leon said. His lips thinned as he started to rise the drone over *Hercules* to bring it back home to us.

And it was then that I saw it on my video monitor - a hose, dropped over the side of *Hercules'* hull, disappearing into the silt. It was just visible, snaking away from the sunken ship along the crevasse.

'Stop *Bad Dog*!' I shouted, my brain briefly appreciating the irony of that particular statement.

Leon immediately killed the thrusters. 'What is it, Lauren?'

I pointed at the screen to show them what I had just seen. 'That's an air hose isn't it?'

Carlos was staring at it too. 'My God, you're right.'

Then Leon's eyes widened. 'You think that Raúl or Maricela may have been diving when the boat went down?'

'There is only one way to find that out,' Carlos replied. 'And if we do find Raúl or Maricela, at least then I'll be able to lay one of my family to rest.'

'Then let's see where this air hose leads us,' Leon said.

He spun *Bad Dog* back round and sent it off along the ravine, the tether extending out behind it. With his other hand he started up *Neptune* again and we started to edge forward, trailing the drone that to all intents was the perfect metaphor of someone walking an actual dog.

The hose was barely visible in places, as so much silt had been piled up over it by the ocean currents. But there was still enough of a ridge running along the floor to indicate where it lay hidden underneath the mud. Following that telltale clue, Carlos and I watched as Leon manoeuvred the drone between the coral canyon walls that had begun closing in on either side of it. Then, dead ahead on my screen, I saw the hose disappearing into a dark cave entrance about twenty metres across, hidden beneath a large, overhanging rock.

'Oh, now this looks very promising,' Leon said, edging *Bad Dog* towards the entrance.

Inside, protected from the currents, the hose sat on the surface of the seabed, trailing away into the gloom.

Carlos had become absolutely still, his gaze locked onto whatever we were about to find at the end of it.

Leon brought *Neptune* to a stop as *Bad Dog* disappeared deeper into the tunnel, trailing its tether behind it, its spotlight delivering a cone of illumination that picked out stone walls on either side.

My heart rate was already accelerating in anticipation of what we were about to find. The air had grown so tense inside the cockpit that I could almost feel the static of our combined expectation washing over my skin.

Then we saw a glint of light reflecting back at *Bad Dog's* camera.

'What do we have here?' Leon said.

I clenched my jaw as *Bad Dog* rotated towards the object.

Carlos let out a gasp as we all took in what the drone could see.

Raúl's diving helmet, the hose still attached, lay on the cavern floor. More significantly, there wasn't a body next to it.

'What the hell?' Leon said. He spun *Bad Dog* around but there was no sign of a corpse anywhere.

I didn't want to voice my thought in front of Carlos because it was so upsetting, but Leon did it for me.

'Maybe the sharks have already been here,' he said quietly.

'But if so, it should be easy to confirm. We'll look through the faceplate; their teeth would have got through that helmet.'

'Jesus, you're saying they decapitated him?' I said, before I could stop myself.

'Unfortunately, yes,' Leon replied.

As all my *Jaws* nightmares came home to roost and I cast a guilty look towards Carlos who was now ashen-faced.

'You may want to look away for this,' I said gently.

The old man shook his head. 'No, I must see what happened to my son with my own eyes.'

'I understand...' But if I'd had the power to teleport Carlos back to the surface at that moment, I would have so hit the button. Instead I nodded to Leon, who began to manoeuvre the drone into position.

As the helmet's faceplate came into view I braced myself for a grisly sight. But then I let out a long breath of relief, because there was absolutely nothing inside. Nothing, that was, apart from Raúl's camera still on its mounting plate, pointing out through the faceplate.

'But I don't understand,' Carlos said, staring at it.

'Maybe his helmet got ripped off his suit when *Hercules* was sunk?' I said.

'No, not possible. Just look at the clips, they've been unfastened manually. If Raúl's helmet had been pulled off, it would have sheered the bolts connecting it to the collar.'

Leon peered at him. 'Are you saying that you think he deliberately took it off?'

'That's what those helmet catches say,' Carlos said. 'Maybe he decided that rather than suffocate when the pump failed as the boat sank, he wanted to end things quickly...' His voice trailed away as he closed his eyes.

I shimmied back on my couch and reached over Leon to

squeeze Carlos's arm. 'I'm just so bloody sorry that you had to see this.'

He patted my hand. 'Don't be, because this is exactly what I needed to know. There's a good chance that Raúl's body could be somewhere in this cavern. Please look for him, my friends.'

'Don't worry, I intend to,' Leon replied.

I slid back into position on my couch, as with a quick blast of the thrusters, Leon rotated *Bad Dog* until it was pointing towards the rear of the cavern again and started it forward.

The darkness felt like it was closing in on the drone, no longer visible through my window as it travelled deeper and deeper into the cavern.

Then Leon gasped. 'Holy shit!'

We all gawped at *Bad Dog's* video feed. On it was the unmistakable shine of a gold bar.

'Please head further into the cavern, Leon,' Carlos whispered.

The Frenchman nodded, and then pushed the accelerator forward.

Bad Dog's spotlight played across the ground...then my heart leapt as we saw another gold bar, then another. But Leon was ignoring all of them, accelerating the craft forward, and then I saw why.

They say that there are some moments that are going to be carved into your memory for as long as you live, and this was definitely one of those.

Jammed into the far end of the cavern was a large wooden galleon, its three masts ripped off and part of its hull smashed to pieces. Lichen-covered crates lay everywhere, some broken, gold bars spilling out of them across the cave floor.

'Oh my God! My children discovered Bartolomeu's shipwreck after all,' Carlos said, his eyes wide with wonder.

My thoughts began to whirl as I already knew exactly what this meant. Leon voiced it before I could stop him.

'Hang on – if your children were killed for this treasure, considering there must be an absolute fortune down here, how come this site isn't swarming with divers to recover it?' he said.

Carlos nodded. 'You're right, it doesn't make sense. So...I wonder what really happened here?'

I looked across at the two men. Of course, I'd already realised that only one organisation would be prepared to overlook that sort of treasure haul – one that was desperate to keep its secrets clutched to its chest. I might not want to tell either of them about the Overseers, but I also needed to find out for definite what had happened here. And thankfully, I already had an idea about how to do exactly that.

'Leon, just how much can *Bad Dog* lift?' I asked.

'It's not powerful enough to lift a solid gold bar, if that's what you mean?'

'No, not that, but how about a diving helmet?'

'Yes I think so...' Then he stared at me. 'The camera inside it! You're thinking it may be able to show us what happened to Raúl?'

'It's certainly a chance worth checking out.'

'Okay, then let's do it.'

He began to swing *Bad Dog* round towards the diving helmet, just visible in the distance, picked out by the spotlight.

One thing was certain - I couldn't wait to see what was on that camera. Every instinct I had told me we would find some significant answers on there.

CHAPTER ELEVEN

A GURGLING SOUND came from the other side of the hatch built into the floor as we waited for the water to be expelled by the pumps in the airlock and equalise the pressure in the cockpit.

On his couch, Leon watched the red light cycle to green, like someone hungrily eyeballing the microwave as it counted down to ready.

I was just as impatient, drumming my fingers on my knees over and over. We might be able to find out some real answers about what had caused the disaster that had unfolded here. The only one of us that seemed disinterested was Carlos, who'd remained on his couch, lying down and staring out of his window towards the cave month. He'd been like that since *Bad Dog* had returned with Raúl's helmet and entered *Neptune*'s airlock.

I'd resisted the desire to strike up a conversation with Carlos to ask him how he was doing. I didn't need to be a psychologist to tell that he needed a bit of space, something that was a slightly tricky proposition in a cockpit less than two metres wide. How much easier it would have been to break all of this to him gently, back onboard *Venus*.

When the light at last turned green, Leon practically tore the door off its hinges in his haste to get into the airlock.

The fluorescent red underwater drone sat in the middle of the metal floor, water dripping off it, Raúl's helmet clamped in its pincers like a dog that had retrieved a stick for its master. All they needed to do was add a tail to *Bad Dog* and he'd be all set.

Leon stuck his hand in through the neck of the helmet and took hold of the camera, then found the clip and released it. A moment later, he closed the hatch, the camera safely retrieved. He looked at Carlos and I. 'So, who else wants to see what's on this baby?' he said.

'Do we have time? What about the storm?' I said. I knew the camera might throw up something that would prove difficult to explain away. And with the storm coming in, our need to *see* that something might just have to wait a little longer...

'I need to see it. Please.' Carlos said quietly, his eyes desperate. 'My son...'

I sighed, knowing that not letting him see it would potentially convince him that not only were we hiding something, we might even have been involved in the attack on his children's boat. Nope, if the video did raise any tricky questions, I would just have to deal with it.

With no real choice, I picked the lesser of the two evils and reluctantly nodded to Leon.

'She's a way off yet,' he said, 'We do have time.' He cracked open the camera's waterproof housing to reveal a USB port, and then connected a cable, which he plugged into the monitor.

I mentally held my breath as an icon spun on the screen, and then a series of folders appeared. Leon clicked on the video folder, opened it and scanned the list.

'The twenty-eighth of May is when they went missing isn't it, Carlos?'

The old man nodded.

'There's a video file here with that date stamp on it.' He double clicked on the folder and a familiar view appeared. I'd last seen it on Raúl's video, the one taken on the deck of *Hercules*.

In the footage, Maricela was looking in through the faceplate at Raúl. She fired off some Spanish that my earbud translated to, *So let's see if today is our lucky day, brother, because I have a good feeling about this.*

I noticed Carlos stiffen at the sound of her voice.

'*Yo también,*' we heard Raúl say, which was translated into, *me too.*

Then, just as I'd seen on the first video, Raúl was swung out by the harness and lowered into the water.

'I think we should fast-forward to where he found the boat and take it from there,' I said.

Leon nodded. He started to scrub through the video until the entrance of the cave came into shot. 'Okay, here we go...' He hit the play button.

Raúl took slow steps into the cavern, his torch penetrating the darkness ahead of him. His breathing was slow and steady, as was the sound of bubbles escaping from the valve on the helmet; a regular background beat. Then just as *Bad Dog's* spotlight had done, his torchlight fell upon a glitter of gold on the cave floor. In an instant, his breathing rate shot up as he peered down at a gold bar. It only accelerated further as he stepped deeper into the cavern and spotted more gold scattered across the floor. But Raúl ignored them all, just as Leon had done, and pressed on until he was confronted with the wreck of the galleon.

He whooped, the sound amplified inside the confines of his helmet. He raised his arm, hand clenched into a fist, and punched the water.

A sheer moment of joy before whatever was about to happen to him. If only the guy had known what was coming next.

We watched Raúl as he walked up and down the wreck,

punctuating the silence with whistles and whoops. But that only increased my sense of foreboding; that after all the joy of one of the biggest moments of that young man's life, all this was about to go so catastrophically wrong.

At last, Raúl seemed satisfied that he'd seen enough for this first dive. He turned round and headed back towards the cave entrance, the pool of light growing larger with every step.

It was then that the exact moment that I'd been dreading actually happened. The tether, which had been lying on the ground like a sleeping python, suddenly flew up through the water and caught on the top of the cave mouth, going taut. It yanked Raúl off his feet and dragged him head first towards the entrance as it was reeled in.

As the cavern walls rushed past, the footage kept shaking as Raúl's helmet clanged and bumped over the uneven floor, his arm thrashing around for purchase but finding nothing to grab onto. Then he had a sudden reprieve – the line that had been rubbing on a lip of rock snapped, sending the man skidding to a stop. Over his panicked and laboured breathing, I could hear the hiss that proved that at least his airline was still intact. But for how much longer? What had just happened surely had to be linked to *Hercules* being attacked?

Slowly, and with some difficulty, Raúl got back to his feet. As fast as his diving suit would allow, he began to move towards the cave entrance.

'Maricela!' he cried out, his voice echoing inside his helmet.

He reached the entrance, and the camera view tipped as he looked up. The air caught in my throat. There on the surface, like huge, predatory sharks, two black speedboats were circling around *Hercules*, flashes of muzzle fire illuminating the gentle waves. The old trawler was already listing heavily in the water.

Leon hissed. 'So someone did fucking attack them?'

Carlos visibly flinched, his face now pale.

'I'm afraid it looks that way.' I said.

But there was now no question in my mind that this brutal assault on the unarmed boat had all the hallmarks of an Overseers' operation.

Hercules was now heavily listing, its hull shredded with bullets. Then almost in slow motion it began to slide beneath the surface, helm first. A splash came from just in front of the prow as a distant figure leapt into the sea, bullet trails zipping past them.

'Maricela!' Raúl cried out again, his voice filled with sheer panic.

As the boat sunk beneath the waves, the hiss of air that had been keeping Raúl alive stopped dead. The air compressor on the deck of *Hercules* must have flooded with water. Raúl was forced to watch helplessly as some of the hundreds of rounds being fired into the water struck his sister, and she twitched violently. A plume of blood began to stain the water as her limbs stretched out, and then she stilled, her dark hair gently waving in the water like jet black seaweed.

Tears filled my eyes as I listened to Raúl gasping and sobbing for his dead sister even as he suffocated. And still Carlos hadn't turned round to witness his children's death, although I could see his shoulders shaking with silent sobs.

'We can stop the video, Carlos,' Leon said gently, hitting pause.

'No. You keep watching, for their sakes, so we know exactly what really happened here,' the old man replied.

Leon shot me a grim look, then pressed play.

As we watched *Hercules* begin its long and slow descent towards the seabed along with Maricela's body, it was like watching a heartbreaking, slow-motion dance of death.

Raúl's breath began to rattle in his helmet.

A lump rose in my throat and unexpectedly, Leon's hand

sought mine out as we both bore witness to the young diver's death.

The man's breathing finally rattled to silence as he collapsed backwards into the cave, the gurgle of the helmet's valve forever silenced.

Tears filled my eyes. Those bastard Overseers had done it again – needlessly thrown away innocent lives that had got in their way. But *why* on this occasion? They obviously had no interest in the wreck.

Leon was just about to stop the video, when there was a flash of light. He paused, his finger hovering in mid-air over the controls.

His hand fell away as the light grew stronger, illuminating the cave ceiling for the camera that was still filming. Was it another diver, coming to rescue Raúl too late?

But then I blinked in astonishment as a glowing blue crystal came to a stop directly over the dead diver. The Guardian. Its brilliance bathed the cavern in intense blue light, before the image broke up and the video went black.

Leon gave me a shocked look. He dragged the play bar back ten seconds and began stepping through the frames one by one. And there it was again, exactly as I'd suspected, a tetrahedron-shaped crystal of a Guardian. This image was much clearer than the last footage I'd seen. The Angelus device was slimmer and far more elongated than a micro mind; a dart shape if anything.

Leon gawped at it. 'Is that some sort of underwater military drone...maybe launched by the same bastards who attacked *Hercules*?'

Although I was certain about what we were looking at, Leon's explanation was the perfect cover story.

'Maybe it was some sort of top secret military test that Maricela and Raúl stumbled across, and they were killed to keep their silence?' I said.

For the first time, Carlos turned his tear-streaked face round to look at us. 'You're saying somebody's military murdered my children?'

'It's only a guess, but possibly,' I replied. It felt awful not just coming out and telling him the truth, but I couldn't go there right now, for both their sakes.

'Then *somebody* needs to be held to account over this,' Leon said.

'One day, I'm sure they will,' I said.

Leon gave me the sort of look that told me he realised I knew more then I was letting on. That I was being economical with the truth. His expression hardened. He pivoted the monitor back upwards into the submersible's ceiling and took hold of the control yoke. Maybe he was waiting for us to be out of earshot from Carlos onboard *Venus* before he laid into me and asked me what the hell was really going on.

'We should head back to the surface and show the world what we have just found out,' Leon said, his tone flat.

'Of course,' I replied, grateful that I wasn't having to look him in the face.

He pushed the throttle forward and in a turning circle, we climbed away. We began to head up towards *Venus* on the surface, where the waves were visibly starting to build around its hull.

Carlos had returned to his seat, his gaze locked onto the cave where his son had died, until it was lost from view.

Despite the awful atmosphere in the cockpit, I laid back on the couch, lost in my own thoughts. Why had the Guardian turned up like that? Could it have been aiming to rescue Raúl, but had arrived too late? And if so, could the micro mind be close by too? That would certainly explain why the Overseers had been in the area.

'What is that thing?' Carlos said, pulling me back out of my reverie.

I turned my head to see him pointing down towards the seabed.

Then I saw it too. Elation surged through me at the sight of the glowing point of blue light, a few hundred metres out on the seabed.

'Is that the thing that we just saw in the video?' Leon asked, also staring down at it.

If it was a micro mind, I needed to confirm it, if only so I could come back later to retrieve it with the others. I could always pass it off as military technology, continuing the lie I'd already started spinning. In for a penny, in for a pound.

I looked him square in the eye. 'There is only one way we're going to discover that.'

Leon nodded. 'Then let's go and find out for sure.'

With a blast of full throttle, a fresh sense of hope filled me despite my grief for Carlos's loss. *We could be close to making a breakthrough.* I crossed my fingers as *Neptune* surged down towards the distant beacon of light glowing in the gloom.

CHAPTER TWELVE

THROUGH THE SURFACE of the sea, far above us the sky had begun to turn from blue to steely greys. Our window of opportunity was starting to close and having already checked with Leon, at most we only had an hour until the hurricane hit. But technically this was still a reconnaissance mission, as I'd be pointing out to Tom when we got back.

The ocean bed stretched away below us, the canyons of coral smoothing out into a bed of silt and sand, across which crabs scuttled. A dense shoal of tiny fish swam through the water ahead, parting in complex patterns as *Neptune* passed through their midst, thousands of tiny eyes taking in our progress. There was a distinct lack of seaweed at this depth apart from the odd hardy specimen determined to make a go of it. In my imagination I pictured the submersible manoeuvring through vast kelp forests, but that was never going to be a thing. I knew from my own scuba diving experience that they only grew in depths of about thirty metres. But that aside, what we were about to discover would be infinitely more interesting than any seaweed we might encounter. We closed in on that glowing point of *come and get me* light.

If it really was the Guardian, had it somehow been shot down by the same Overseers that had sunk *Hercules* and murdered Raúl and Maricela? But if so, why hadn't they attempted to recover the Angelus's AI? The one thing I was pretty sure of, based on the fact there was still light coming from whatever it was, suggested that its systems were still active. That might mean there was a way for me to communicate with it, and that excited me more than anything.

I checked my bag, putting my hand on the Empyrean Key. The next problem was how I was going to come up with a remotely plausible explanation for getting the stone ball out and striking it with a tuning fork.

Yes, Carlos and Leon, this is all part of my daily mindfulness mediation practice, which I just have to do as regularly as clockwork at this time every day, or my mind falls apart...

I sighed inwardly.

The light was growing steadily stronger as we neared it. I strained my eyes trying to make it out and then its shape suddenly became sharper. But rather than being a dart-shaped object as I'd hoped, what we actually saw was a slab pushing up through the silt.

'Okay, so maybe not our mystery military drone, but it looks as though it's something just as intriguing,' Leon said.

'It looks like a giant glowing gem,' Carlos said, peering through his blister window at it.

But my heart was already racing. I'd first encountered something very similar one stormy night near the ancient Skara Brae site on Orkney. This was just like one of the Angelus runes that had formed a large spiral pattern, with Lucy at the centre. And the fact that this one was glowing had to be significant.

Leon throttled back the thrusters and slowed our approach to crawl as we closed in on the object. Our headlights picked up its highly reflective surface in the silt covering it. Like the roots of a tree, its crystal tendrils buried themselves in the silt. This rune was easily twice the size of any I'd seen before – at least two metres across. But frustratingly, we still couldn't see any inscription on the top surface because it was partly buried in silt.

'Is there any way you can clear away the dirt on the top of that structure, Leon?' I asked.

'Yes, there's an air hose built into the hydraulic claws designed to do exactly that,' he replied. 'I just need to be very careful not to damage whatever that thing is, although it certainly looks strong enough.'

Once again, I had to bite my tongue because I knew the structure was built from solid crystal. Leon was in more danger of damaging the claw rather than the other way round.

'Go for it,' I said.

Leon brought *Neptune* into a hover right in front of the object, the light from it illuminating our cockpit through the windows.

Our captain took hold of the grips and the arms outside swivelled towards the buried rune. With the precision of a surgeon at work, he began to gently scrape away the dirt with the hydraulic claw, not hurrying, just taking his time.

My expectations grew by the minute as Leon cleared the surface. Jack would have got such a huge kick out of this. It was, in every sense, underwater archaeology in action.

I let out a loud breath as a petal geometric symbol began to appear. Yes – absolutely no question – it was an Angelus rune.

'It looks incredible, but what is it?' Carlos asked.

I resisted the urge to whoop and then give him a gushing explanation.

'That certainly doesn't look like military to me,' Leon said.

Carlos nodded. 'If it's some sort of Aztec artefact that the Spanish plundered and lost, it's like nothing I've ever seen before.'

I had to bite my tongue again, as Leon turned his head towards me.

'Any thoughts, Lauren?' he said, giving me a very probing look.

I held his gaze for a moment. I knew then there was no way I could continue to get away with my charade. But rather than tell him and Carlos everything, I needed to share just enough of the truth that I dared to.

'Okay, there *are* some things I should have told you before now. My friend Jack, back onboard the *Neptune*? Well, he's actually an archaeologist, and this symbol matches others that we've found at other ancient sites around the world.'

Leon stared at me. 'And you're only telling us this now, Lauren?'

'Sorry, but we do have our reasons for keeping this secret,' I said.

Carlos was narrowing his eyes at me now too and shaking his head. 'I asked you not to make an old man look foolish by lying to him. Look at what you've done!'

I felt my heart break a fraction. Carlos was right. I had lied to his face, even if my reason for doing so had been noble and had been all about protecting others.

The old man clicked his tongue against his teeth. 'Just promise me that you and your associates had nothing to do with the murder of my children?'

So there it was. The next logical step for his mistrust to leap to.

I stared at him, feeling the colour drain from my face. 'Oh God, one hundred percent, Carlos.'

He stared harder at me. 'This is the absolute truth?'

'I swear to you with all my heart.'

Carlos looked at me for the longest time. 'Then don't make me regret giving you a second chance, Lauren.'

'Thank you and you won't...' I turned my gaze towards Leon. 'And how about you?'

A smile filled his face. 'If Carlos is prepared to trust you, then who am I to argue? Plus when a beautiful woman tells me something, I tend to believe them. One of my many weaknesses.'

I let out a long breath. 'Good to know. But I have to ask you both to keep what you're about to see to yourselves; *absolutely* to yourselves. I can't stress how important it is that you don't tell anyone you know – your family, your friends... and that includes your crew, Leon.'

'Okay, but what exactly have you dragged us into here, Lauren?' he asked.

So here I went, crossing that line. 'Something where we're about to make a real difference.'

'Then show us,' Carlos said.

'In that case, get ready to have your minds well and truly blown. But first, I'm going to try something that will hopefully enable me to communicate with that glowing device out there.'

I took the Empyrean Key and tuning fork out of my bag, then sat up on the couch with the orb between my elbows. The two men gave me questioning looks as I struck the tuning fork against the stone.

The single clear note was very loud inside that tiny cockpit and for a moment nothing happened. Then relief rushed through me as a single shimmering icon materialised, hovering over the stone orb. The icon itself appeared as two adjacent green triangles, pointing in towards each other like geometric butterfly wings.

'Thank God...it's worked,' I said.

'What's worked?' Leon asked, staring at the empty air over the Empyrean Key. Of course only I could see what was going on, thanks to my synaesthesia.

'Hopefully you're about to see,' I replied. With the shimmering icon selected, I flicked my wrist forward.

If I'd had any idea of what was about to happen next I would have thought twice about that particular action.

Both men gasped as a pulse of light came from the geometric petals carved into the quartz crystal, which now shone with the intensity of white hot metal.

'What in the name of dear God is that thing?' Leon asked. Out of the corner of my eye, I saw Carlos make the sign of the cross on his chest.

But before I could even attempt any sort of watered-down explanation, something even more extraordinary happened, something that I'd never seen before.

It was like little blue flickering signal fires were being lit one by one on the sea bed, stretching away into the distance across the ocean.

Carlos gasped. 'Are more of those things lighting up?'

I slowly nodded. 'I think so.'

My heart was soaring because I could already see that they curved away to the left in the distance. And if this was a spiral in a similar pattern to the one found around Skara Brae, then at the end of this metaphorical yellow brick road would be a micro mind, just waiting for us to make contact with it.

But then a rumbling sound began to grow, becoming louder. We all exchanged questioning looks.

Through my blister window I saw bubbles tracing glowing points of light together, racing towards us like a dot to dot puzzle. My mouth went dry as the seabed began to undulate beneath the submersible. Then almost too late, my brain caught up with what was actually happening.

'Leon, get us out of here! I think that's an underwater quake!' I shouted.

'Shit! Hang on to whatever you can!' he called back.

As Carlos and I locked our hands onto the side of our couches, Leon grabbed hold of the control yoke and pulled it back hard, pushing the throttle to maximum.

We began to turn away from the rune, which was now burning with blinding brilliance as *Neptune* started to gain height.

But then with a roar, the ocean seemed to erupt with frothing water, shoving *Neptune* sideways as the shockwave slammed into us. The submersible began to roll, the floor becoming the ceiling and flinging the three of us around the cockpit. Multiple alarms screamed out as *Neptune's* hull let out groans and the world gyrated around us.

Leon fought an impossible battle as the sub tumbled sideways towards the seabed. With a bone-jarring crash, we slammed into it, scouring a great groove through the silt and throwing up a cloud of debris.

Every bone in my body shook as *Neptune* skidded to a stop with a long, groaning shudder, the cabin floor at a forty-five degree angle beneath us. Every light in the sub went dark. The roaring bellow of shifting earth and rock continued outside, the seabed bucking beneath us and rattling us like pebbles in a can.

My brain was numb as I watched the shockwave of bubbles speeding away. Then at last the quake began to subside, and my eyes were already scanning for any sign of cracks in the thick Perspex windows. If it breached at this depth, I knew it would implode, killing us all in a split second. I was already kicking myself. My own impetuous stupidity, charging in and activating that rune, might not only cost me my own life, but also the lives of the two men I'd dragged along on this mission.

Darkness lapped around us, the only illumination coming from the rune, which was beginning to fade again. Then I noticed the flashes of light from the surface. I glanced up to see lightning flicker in the stormy black sky above the waves.

My stomach knotted as creaks and groans came from *Neptune's* hull around us.

'Is everyone okay?' Leon asked, his tone ridiculously calm.

'Yes, although I do have a few bruises that I didn't start this dive with,' Carlos said, rubbing the back of his neck.

I sucked in a breath, but after a quick physical inventory I realised that apart from some serious knocks, I'd made it through without any broken bones.

'I'm shaken but otherwise okay. More importantly, how badly damaged is *Neptune*?' I asked.

'Well, the power failing isn't exactly a good sign,' Leon replied. 'Unless I can get it back online we are going to die down here.' He flicked on a small battery lantern that pushed back the gloom.

'Bloody hell, you don't pull any punches do you?' I said,

Carlos shrugged. 'It's the best way to be in a situation like this, Lauren. Sweet stories are for children at bedtime; they don't help in a life or death situation.'

'Wow, you two are cut from the same cloth,' I replied. But I took a mental note to learn something from both of these men about what real heroism in the face of adversity looked like.

Leon smiled at Carlos. 'Let's see what we can do about not dying down here. Meanwhile, I suggest that everyone remains quiet to try and save what little oxygen we have left.'

I nodded, clamping down my next question about what our odds of survival were. Instead I watched as Leon began to unscrew the butterfly nuts on a panel. As he pulled it off, the smell of burnt wiring filled the cockpit. Despite the dim light, I saw the scowl fill his face as he pulled out a charred circuit board. That did little to help the nausea that was already having a party in my stomach.

I turned back to my window and stared out. I could almost feel the ocean pressing in on the hull, trying to get to us. Without doubt it was beautiful and serene down here, but undeniably, if anything went wrong we'd very likely all end up very dead, very quickly.

As I waited, trying to stop myself imagining how it all might play out, I began to mentally pick over what had just happened. Waking up the rune had obviously created some sort of cascade effect through the other runes connected to it. It must somehow have been that which was responsible for the underwater quake. The one comforting thought, if you could call it that, was that if we did end up dying down here, at least the quake would definitely be picked up by Mike's seismic sensor network across Cuba. Armed with that data he should be able to locate the epicentre of the earthquake, and hopefully through that the exact location of the micro mind.

The minutes stretched on as Leon worked frantically away, swapping out circuit boards and quietly cursing to himself in French. Carlos, despite everything that he'd just gone through, looked relaxed and lost in his element down here. An old diver coming home maybe? Whatever the reason, it was obvious he had made some sort of peace with himself, despite finding out what had happened to his son and daughter. Maybe he was ready to die down here too and join them wherever he believed they were now. As for me, well, the only reason I wasn't kicking and screaming to stay alive was because that would have used up more oxygen.

Another ten minutes passed, and what I could see of the sky through the surface was looking distinctly choppy. It couldn't be long until the storm hit with full force.

The air in the cockpit was starting to taste noticeably stale and was also tinged with the hint of sweat. I was just wondering if I should start searching for a piece of paper to leave Jack a note declaring my undying love for him, when without ceremony, Leon pushed a circuit board back and flicked a switch.

With a whir of pumps starting up somewhere in the submersible, deliciously fresh oxygen started to pump back into the cockpit.

'Oh you absolute miracle worker, you,' I said.

'We're not out of the woods yet,' Leon replied. 'At least two of the thrusters on the port side, which we need to right us, are still buried in the silt.'

'Shit, so you're saying we're stuck down here?'

'Oh, I wouldn't give up hope just yet.' Leon said. 'I'm going to purge the ballast tanks and hopefully that will be enough to lift us out of this mess we've got ourselves into.'

'Have faith, Lauren,' Carlos said.

'I'm certainly trying to,' I replied.

Leon flicked several more switches on a console over his head. 'Okay, hang on everyone, purging tanks now,' he said.

I grabbed onto the side of my couch, throwing out a silent prayer in case any deity who happened to be in the vicinity might give a damn about any of us.

Leon pressed a button and a loud gurgling, hissing sound came from outside. A flurry of bubbles erupted beneath *Neptune*, kicking up silt and blocking out the view. Then, with a long groan, the floor began to tilt back to the horizontal position.

Immediately, Leon was on the case, spinning the thrusters up to full power. With a whine of electric motors, we began to rise.

I whooped and clapped, then reached across and slapped Leon on the back. 'Well done that man.'

He grinned at me, but Carlos's gaze was focused on something on the seabed.

'What is that white thing down there?' he asked.

I glanced at where he was indicating to see a white cylinder mounted on a pole, sunk into a large concrete block.

'That, if I'm not mistaken, is an underwater listening post,' Leon said. 'I've come across similar devices around the Baltic coast during a dive and they almost certainly belonged to the Russian navy. It's the sort of the thing they use to detect enemy subs trying to sneak into their waters. You can guarantee that whoever dropped this one now knows that we're here.'

My blood instantly turned to ice. 'Leon, we need to get back to the surface and get *Venus* away from here as fast as we bloody can.'

'Why?' Leon said, staring at me.

'Because I think we may have just stirred up a hornets' nest. The same nest that Raúl and Maricela ran into.'

Leon scowled at me and without another word, gunned the motors and spun us round hard. Then we were heading rapidly back towards the surface, the growing storm churning the surface of the sea far above us.

CHAPTER THIRTEEN

WE GLIDED through the water in *Neptune,* heading for where we'd left the marker for *Venus.*

'Okay, now we're no longer in imminent danger of death, we need to talk about that quake, and what caused it, Lauren,' Leon said.

I knew the question was coming. Leon and Carlos were bound to quiz me about what had just happened. 'I really had no idea that was going to happen when I activated that rune.'

'Activated the *rune?* That in itself begs a hundred other questions about how you woke it up with what looked like a fork and a stone ball.'

'I'm more than a little curious about that myself,' Carlos said.

I sighed. 'Look, guys, I really can't get into it for your sakes. There are people out there who are determined to keep this sort of thing a secret. So as much as I would love to tell you, I really can't, so let's please just leave it there.'

Carlos drew in a long breath. 'I see...' Then he nodded. 'But I also understand that the authorities can sometimes bury the truth and will do anything to keep it hidden.'

'Exactly,' I replied.

'Okay, then just tell me one thing, Lauren. Are you fighting against these people?'

'Oh God yes, with every fibre of my being.'

'In that case, I wish you every luck,' Carlos said.

Leon blew the air between his teeth. 'You do realise you nearly killed us by not being straight with us? If you had at least told us about the risks involved, I may have thought twice about assisting you on this mission of yours.'

My guilt trip did a few honorary laps around my head as I nodded back.

'Look, you have every reason to be pissed off with me, but I honestly had no idea about what would happen down there. I'm so sorry about everything that's happened. I had no right to drag you into this.'

Leon shook his head. 'I doubt anyone could have anticipated triggering an underwater quake.' Then he chuckled. 'In so many ways this whole trip has appealed to my explorer's soul. I've seen a lot down of amazing sights at the bottom of the ocean, but none as incredible as that spectacle. So just between us, I wouldn't have missed it for the world.'

Carlos was smiling now too. 'Yes, I agree completely, my friend. It was a vision of wonder. It will leave me with even more awe at what is beneath the sea around Cuba.'

I felt some of the tension that I'd been carrying drain away. 'Thank you, guys, for understanding. Just know that I would tell you more if I could. But talking of what's at the bottom of the sea...what about that incredible wreck your children found, Carlos?'

'Yes, the discovery of a lifetime! But I've no interest in it now, not after...' He paused, swallowing hard. 'No. Leave it for others to discover. After all, what good is money to an old man?'

'Then maybe you should be thinking of your legacy,' Leon

said. 'I run a number of charitable trusts for disadvantaged children around the world and you could look to set something
similar up. If you want to honour the memory of Maricela and
Raúl, I can think of no better way to put in place something that
can make a real difference to so many lives.'

So Leon was a philanthropist too. I was going to seriously
have to rethink my first impression of this man.

Carlos's face lit up briefly before his expression fell again.

'That's a wonderful idea, but sadly we lost our dive boat. And
I am too old to dive anyway,' he replied.

Before I could suggest anything, Leon absolutely excelled
himself with his next offer.

'I've already thought of that,' our captain replied. 'I'd be
delighted to offer you the services of *Venus* and my crew to help
you recover the treasure.'

I beamed at him. 'You really are one of the good guys, aren't
you?'

'Oh, I try to be,' he said.

Carlos stared at Leon with wide eyes. 'That would be incredible. Obviously I would share any treasure with you that we
recover.'

Leon chuckled. 'As generous an offer as that is, do I look like I
need any more wealth? No, I will happily do it for free. All I ask
is that you make a real difference with the money you make
from it.'

'I will, my friend. Thank you so much.'

I was pretty sure that if we hadn't been in the confined space
of the *Neptune*, the old man would have given Leon a very big
hug, something that even I felt like doing despite my initial reser-
vation towards the Frenchman.

'For a billionaire, you've got a very good heart, Leon,' I said.

'Hey, not all of us are just in it for ourselves,' he replied, smiling. 'Maybe there's still a chance for me to be admitted through the pearly gates after all.'

I snorted at him. Flickers of light from the surface lit up the ocean around us and I peered through the window to see countless expanding ripples, hinting at heavy rain pouring down from the now present storm. We could hear the muffled booms of thunderclaps through the water.

Leon glanced at his chart. 'Okay, we're a couple of kilometres out from *Venus*, but this is going to be a tricky manoeuvre getting *Neptune* back aboard. However, if anyone can pull it off, my crew can. The alternative is that we wait out the storm on the surface, which won't be pleasant, but at least it will be safer.'

'No, that's not an option. Whoever planted that listening device is bound to send somebody out to check out what it picked up,' I replied. 'Trust me, the further we are away from this location, the better it will be for all of us.'

'In that case, we'll go for it,' Leon said. 'We need to surface briefly so we can make radio contact with my ship.'

He pulled the yoke back and *Neptune* rose rapidly through the last ten metres of the sea. Then with a torrent of water over our blister windows, we broke the surface, straight into the full-blown fury of the storm.

The large swell of towering mountains and valleys of water immediately began to lift and drop *Neptune,* as the wind howled around us.

In the distance we caught glimpses of *Venus* between the rolling landscape of waves, lit up like a Christmas tree.

'Okay, let's make contact with them,' Leon said, unclipping a radio set.

Suddenly my earbud burst into life with a crackle.

'Lauren, are you reading me? This is urgent, over,' Ruby's voice said.

'Yes, loud and clear! We're about to radio *Venus* to come and recover us.'

'Don't! They've been boarded,' she responded.

'What?' I said, a sense of dread building inside me.

'You heard me. Whatever you do, you must maintain radio silence with them and don't give away your presence.'

Leon was pulling on his headset, his hand reaching for the button to activate the radio.

'Hey, stop!' I shouted. 'Don't try contacting *Venus*.'

His hand froze. 'Why not?'

'Because your ship has been boarded by those people that I mentioned...'

I pulled my Sky Wire from my pack and turned on its speaker mode.

'First of all, how the hell did you allow *Venus* to be boarded without doing anything about it, Ruby?' I said, unable to suppress my panic as I imagined the worst case scenario of dead bodies littering the ship.

'Because,' she said, just as briskly, 'a damned attack helicopter came in low over the water at high speed from the opposite side of the ship. That shielded it from my radar, so I only saw them when they popped up over the rear deck. Then six soldiers in full combat gear rappelled down and started taking hostages before I could do anything about it. If I try to intervene now, a lot of innocent people are going to get caught in the crossfire. The only good news I can give you is that so far no one seems to have been hurt. The bad news is that I've lost contact with our guys because the assault team deployed some sort of comms jamming system when they boarded.'

'Oh my God, we have to save my crew,' Leon said. He stared at me. 'This is because of what we found down there isn't it?'

I gave him a helpless look. 'I'm so bloody sorry.'

'Sorry isn't going to fucking save my people, is it?' Leon snapped, almost spitting the words at me.

Carlos raised his hands. 'My friends, please calm down. If they have hijacked your ship, these soldiers must be after something if they haven't just started executing people.'

My stomach churned as I thought of the others. 'I'm afraid it's probably only a matter of time,' I said. 'Someone out there is desperate to suppress the truth and will interrogate anyone onboard *Venus* who can tell them what we're up to down here. Then they will almost certainly kill all remaining witnesses to silence them.'

Leon hissed, 'Merde!' – which I didn't need my earbud to translate to *shit*. 'We have to save them!' he continued in English.

'And we will, Leon, but we need to come up with a plan and fast,' I replied. 'Ruby, have you got a live feed of what's happening onboard *Venus* that you can relay to my Sky Wire?'

'Sure, hang on...sending you the video from my infrared camera now.'

Immediately a false colour video of *Venus* pitching up and down in the storm appeared on my screen. On the rear deck were the heat signatures of a large group people lying face down, their hands tied behind their backs. Two people stood over them, with stick shapes in their hands that I was sure were machine guns.

I angled the Sky Wire's screen so the others could see it.

Leon hissed. 'The bastards!'

'I promise you that we're going to do everything we can to save your crew,' I said.

He glared at me. 'You're damn right you are. It was your people who dragged us into this shit show.'

Carlos shook his head. 'No, if you want to be angry at anyone, be angry at me for wanting to know what happened to my children, Leon. Don't forget that was a big part of the reason that we were down there.'

Leon blinked. 'I'm sorry, I didn't mean to...' His words trailed away as the fire disappeared from his eyes.

The old man smiled at him. 'I know you didn't, but I'm sure that it was these same people who murdered my Raúl and Maricela. They are the monsters you should be angry with.'

'Yes, yes, you're right. I'm sorry, Lauren, I'm just worried sick about my people.'

'And I would be worried sick in your position too.' I said. I resisted adding *and how do you think I feel about my friends?*

'So what are we going to do?' Leon asked.

'Leave that to us,' I replied. 'Okay, Ruby, let's get this plan put together. Do you know where our team is on that ship?'

'Oh, I've got a pretty good idea,' Ruby said.

The thermal camera view pivoted forward towards the bridge. We could see four soldiers at the base of the stairs on either side of the bridge, the muzzles of their weapons occasionally flashing as they fired up towards it. Then my heart leapt as I saw two rounds of return fire coming from the bridge's windows.

'Looks like they're holding their own for now,' Ruby said.

'But for how much longer? They are severely outnumbered. We need to mount this rescue mission and fast.' I looked out through the window at *Venus* in the distance. 'Leon, could you submerge us again and get me close enough so I can climb aboard?'

He stared at me. 'Are you mad? In this storm you wouldn't stand a chance; you would be swept away in seconds. Besides, if anyone should try something so reckless and stupid, it should be me.'

'Absolutely no way. You're a civilian and I'm a trained soldier.'

Both men stared at me.

'You are?' Carlos said.

'She is and she kicks ass, so get over it already,' Ruby said over the radio link.

Leon blew his cheeks out. 'It sounds like you've got the job then, whoever you really are, Lauren.'

'Maybe one day I can tell you all about that, but this so isn't that moment. Just know that we're the good guys and we're going to sort this out, whatever it takes.'

'Please do. Those people on that ship are my family,' Leon said quietly.

'You've got it,' I replied, my determination hardening. 'Ruby, how about launching your WASPs and swarming those bloody soldiers?'

'I would if I could but that storm is blowing way too strongly now; they'll be as good as useless in this weather. Alternatively, I could try to pick them off with my miniguns, but there is a real danger I could hit some of the hostages if I try that.'

'No, that's not an option. We need feet on the ground, which basically means me,' I said.

'Not liking those odds, Lauren,' Ruby replied.

'It's the only play we have, so we're going to do it my way.'

Leon shook his head. 'If you're still talking about trying to sneak *Neptune* up so you can try to board the ship...like I just said, it will be impossible in this storm unless someone winches you aboard.'

'Winches me aboard...' I repeated as an idea popped into my head. 'Ruby, can we borrow a page out of the hijackers' book? Can you airlift me in on a line?'

'Fuck, you really are batshit crazy. Are you sure you want to do this, Captain?'

'Captain?' Carlos asked. Then he waved a hand. 'Yeah, I know, you'll tell us all about it another day.'

I gave him a grateful nod. 'To answer your question, Ruby, yes I am sure. Can you lower a line with a bag on the end of it, with full combat gear? Oh, and an MP5 with lots of extra magazines? Throw in a bunch of flashbangs for good measure too. Then I'll clip myself to that same line and you can lower me onto the forward deck, well away from where those soldiers are trying to storm the bridge.'

'Sounds like a plan, but it needs a bit of tweaking,' Ruby replied. The guys were looking at me as though I'd turned into Bruce Willis in *Die Hard*. 'Looking at the firefight down there, even if our ship is fully stealthed, they will spot you if I try to drop you straight down onto the deck. If you're determined to do this, I'm going to need to bring you in low over the water. Then at the last moment I can jink up and drop you onto the prow. But you do realise there's still a massive risk that someone might spot you? If that happens, you'll lose any element of surprise.'

'Then maybe you need to come up with a way to have everyone look the other way when you try this mad plan of yours,' Leon said.

'A distraction...' Ruby said. Then we heard her snap her fingers together. 'Damn, I know just the thing. Their attack helicopter is holding off about a mile to *Venus's* port side. If I bring that chopper down it will be the perfect distraction to make everyone look the other way.'

'Good grief, have you got your own military helicopter up there too?' Carlos asked.

'Something much, much better,' Ruby said, chuckling over the radio. 'Anyway, get ready. I'll be with you in a few minutes, Captain.'

'Understood. We'll be ready,' I said. I absolutely knew that it could all go so badly wrong in a dozen ways, but that wasn't going to stop me from trying, even if it cost me my life.

CHAPTER FOURTEEN

I STOOD on top of *Neptune's* hatch, kitted out in a black combat uniform with Kevlar body armour and a helmet with a flip-down HUD. I was going to need every edge I could get heading into this fight.

The submersible rocked violently under my feet in the huge swell, knocking my balance all over the place, but I managed to clip myself onto the line.

Leon stood on top of the sub next to me, staring wildly up at the sky directly over our heads, where the invisible X103 was leaving a circular-shaped hole in the hammering rain.

'What the hell is that thing?' Leon shouted over the roar of the storm.

'Just add it to that growing list of things I can't tell you about,' I replied, as Carlos's head emerged from the open hatch. He handed me the MP5 with the suppressor already screwed onto its barrel.

'Why am I not surprised to hear you say that?' Leon said, shaking his head.

'Yes, same old, I'm afraid,' I shrugged.

A wave crashed over the sub, sending some of the water washing down through the open hatch over Carlos.

'Get that hatch shut before *Neptune* gets flooded,' I called out. 'Hopefully I'll live to see you on the other side of this.'

'I'll look forward to that, but how will we know how you got on?' Carlos asked.

'I suspect it will be pretty obvious, but I've left my Sky Wire in the cockpit just in case. Wait for our signal when it's all over.'

'We will,' Leon said.

Carlos reached up from the hatch and squeezed my hand. 'Good luck, Lauren. Make those bastards pay for what they have done.'

'I will. And Leon? Just know I'm going to do whatever it takes to save everyone.'

Much to my surprise, Leon leant forward and hugged me. 'I know you will.' He pulled away. 'Good hunting, Captain.'

I nodded to him and a moment later he had disappeared back into *Neptune* with Carlos, closing the hatch behind them.

'Okay, Ruby, let's do this,' I said into my helmet's mic.

'Roger that. Get ready to be lifted, Captain,' Ruby replied. There was none of the slight mockery she had once used when she called me that. At some point during our journey together, our mutual respect had grown into a real thing.

The steel cable that had been flapping in the gusting wind suddenly grew taut. I shot up into the sky and came to a stop less than ten metres above the waves. For some reason my mind served up the totally appropriate soundtrack, *Ride of the Valkyries*. And with that now playing in my imagination, the X103 surged forward, towing the line with me on it. We sped over the sea towards the hijacked ship, its lights twinkling in the squalling rain.

The swelled peaks reached up towards me as *Venus* rapidly grew larger. The X103 shone with the faintest blue aura, just visible in the pitch black. But thanks to the whisper-quiet REV drive, all I could hear was the crash of the waves below and the distant boom of thunder.

Flying through the air in a wild sea storm was a deeply surreal experience, especially as it really did make me feel exactly like a Valkyrie straight out of Norse mythology, getting ready to *smite* their enemy.

'Okay, we need to create that distraction about now,' Ruby said through my helmet's speakers. 'I'm boosting the signal feed to your helmet to get past their jamming field. I'm also relaying an image of the helicopter I'm tracking on the far side of the ship.'

A small video window popped up on the top left of my HUD. It showed a helicopter battling to stay in a level hover as the storm raged around it.

'Permission to open fire on it, Captain.'

I didn't even hesitate. 'Permission granted,' I said.

I spotted a port open briefly in the invisible ship above and one of the X103's JASSM-ER missiles burst from it. A second later its rocket ignited and streaked towards its target.

The video in my HUD switched to a missile nose camera view as it sped over the *Venus,* straight towards the helicopter. The pilot's instincts were sharp - they'd obviously already spotted it, as they were trying to bank away, firing off clouds of chaff.

But it was too little, too late.

The missile sped towards the body of the helicopter, its cockpit windows filling the view in the last hundredths of a second. I tensed instinctively as the missile struck, then I exhaled as the video blinked out at exactly the same moment that a distant fireball lit up the far side of *Venus.*

I briefly registered the helicopter plummeting down towards

the sea, as the ship's hull came racing towards us. My heart clenched; I was convinced that Ruby was about to smear me into a bloody pulp on the side of *Venus*.

But at the very last moment, when I could literally count the individual rivets in the hull's panels, we started to slow. My line began to swing forward just as Ruby raised the X103 the last few metres necessary for me to clear the railing. As the X103 came to a dead stop and I reached the end of my pendulum swing, I hit my harness release and dropped onto the deck.

I resisted the urge to whoop that we'd managed to pull off so crazy a manoeuvre. Instead, breathing hard, adrenaline making my blood sing, I whipped my MP5 out, ready to take down any soldier who might have seen me land.

But exactly as we'd hoped, the two that I could see from my vantage point – behind a pile of crates on the pitching deck – had their attention locked onto the helicopter slowly sinking beneath the waves.

'Are you okay, Captain?' Ruby said.

'Yes, I've made it down in one piece thanks to some extraordinary flying on your part.'

'No problemo. I'll be holding position next to the ship, so just call if everything goes south and I'll rip with the X103's weapons.'

'Let's hope it doesn't come to that,' I said.

I found a useful bit of cover behind a crate on a pallet lashed to the front deck and began to study the thermal video of the boat that Ruby was already piping into my helmet's HUD.

The two soldiers at the rear of the boat, where the crew were being held, had already moved away from the railing back towards their hostages.

'One bad guy helicopter dusted and I'm playing them at their own game and blocking all communications so they can't radio for backup,' Ruby said over the link. 'Go and do your stuff, Captain.'

'Oh, don't you worry, I intend to,' I replied.

With the rain lashing down on the deck, I started to make my way forward, but cautiously.

I'd only taken two steps when the cracking sound of machine gun fire came from some stairs ahead. I froze, bringing the MP5's sight up to my visor, ready to return fire. But the rounds hadn't been intended for me. Instead, bullets sparked off the metalwork of the darkened bridge above.

My gut tightened. Jack, Tom and Mike had to be up there, but the question was – were they still alive?

Trying to ignore the sudden sense of panic threatening to take hold of me, I turned on the image intensifier system built into my helmet.

Suddenly, a soldier that had been invisible in the darkness became clearly visible in my HUD. Not that I would have needed any help seeing him a moment later, because he let rip with his machine gun, lighting him up as he fired towards the doorway leading into the bridge.

There was a momentary lull and then I saw Mike lean out and let loose with a PPK, firing straight down at the assailant. Bullets pinged off the metalwork around the enemy soldier, who threw himself flat. Then a larger calibre round smashed into the doorframe just above Mike's head, forcing him to duck back inside.

I looked for the source of what had to be a sniper shot and then spotted the guy behind a lifeboat, resting the barrel stand of a high-powered sniper rifle on it.

Luckily for me, with his eye to his weapon's scope, all of his attention was on the bridge. But to be sure of a kill shot I was going to have to close the distance.

I kept low and to the shadows as the storm roared around us. Spray peppered my visor, which was now running with water. Despite the helmet's sophisticated vision electronics, I was as good as useless with these storm conditions obscuring the target behind sheets of rain. I pivoted up the HUD panel to give me the view that I needed.

I crept forward and got ready to take a shot. But then the ship rolled beneath me as a large wave hit, and the man's head, which I'd just centred within the MP5's sight, swung out of view.

I cursed silently and cut the distance down to twenty metres. Suddenly, the clatter of the other soldier's machine gun roared again from the stairs directly above. In that same instant the sniper glanced up from his sight. It was at that moment our eyes locked.

Before I could even think, I aimed, fired, and a perfect hole appeared just beneath the lip of the sniper's helmet. He slumped onto his rifle.

Now for the second soldier.

I was moving, running on the balls of my feet, when the clatter of the machine gun suddenly stopped. I rounded the base of the stairs to the bridge to see the soldier crouched on the steps in a firing position, already loading a fresh magazine. But some sort of sixth sense must have kicked in, because his back stiffened and he spun round, a pistol already in his hand.

I dropped to my knees as his bullet whizzed over my head, then I fired a short burst from my MP5, which slammed into his body armour.

Knocked back onto the steps, the guy raised his pistol to fire again. But then a shadow loomed from behind him...Mike fired his PPK straight into the man's skull, killing the soldier instantly.

I stared at the man I thought I knew, who'd once insisted he'd have nothing to do with guns. The same man now staring down at his victim with eyes of flint. Then those same hard eyes were raised back to me and they instantly softened.

'Lauren! Thank God you're okay,' he said.

'You too, Mike. What's the situation on the ground here?'

'We have two other soldiers on the far side of the bridge; Jack is doing his best to hold them off. But the bad news is that Tom's been hit.'

My mouth went dry, but Mike must have spotted my expression because he held up his hands. 'Don't panic, just a flesh wound to the chest. Jack says he'll be fine.'

I nodded, relief surging through me as I unclipped a flashbang from my webbing belt and handed it over the corpse to Mike. 'Give this to Jack. I'm going to make my way to the other side of the deck. Then we'll really bring the fight to those bastards.'

'Got it,' Mike said. He turned and disappeared up the steps.

I headed back down the stairs towards a door that stood swinging open in the storm. Beyond it appeared to be an empty corridor. I entered it, senses electric as I crept along, my MP5 aimed towards a closed door at the far end. And with every step the sound of gunfire grew louder as I closed in.

I reached the door and opened it a fraction to see a soldier silhouetted by the muzzle flashes of his machine gun, which was aimed up towards the bridge. But this guy seemed a lot more disciplined than the guy Mike had just taken out. He actually seemed to be aiming, rather than randomly spraying bullets.

The door on the bridge opened and a grenade came arcing out of it. It bounced down the stairs towards the soldier.

I ducked back into the corridor as the sound bomb detonated with a satisfying bang and a flash of light that cast bright shadows through the portholes. I yanked the door just as Jack leant round the corner, firing his Glock twice into the soldier now groaning on the floor.

I stepped out onto the deck, relief surging through me at seeing him unhurt.

'Lauren, look out!' Ruby shouted through my helmet's speakers.

Shit! The other soldier that Mike had warned me about... Too slowly I spun round with my MP5, but the soldier already had his machine gun trained on me and was squeezing the trigger.

But in that same split-second, a shape came barrelling towards the ship from out over the ocean and slammed straight into the soldier, sending him and his weapon flying. Before I'd even registered what had hit him, I fired into the guy's head. He twitched and then stilled as his blood dripped down the white cabin wall behind him. Buried into his chest was the broken WASP that had crashed into him.

'You're welcome,' Ruby said over my helmet's speakers.

I drew in a long gasp, not quite believing I was still alive. 'I thought you said it was too windy to fly?'

'Not for an accurate shot maybe, but for a kamikaze run like that I just about had enough control. Besides, I couldn't just sit on my hands and watch you get taken out. Anyway, using that same trick...'

I saw two other WASPs come blurring in at high speed on the waves, then they disappeared from view towards the rear deck. That was followed a moment later by a loud scream and a clatter of a gunfire, which abruptly died.

'And then there were none,' Ruby said. 'The two remaining soldiers literally didn't know what had hit them. They're shark snacks now.'

'Bloody hell, Ruby! I owe you big time.'

'So what's new?' she replied. I could absolutely hear the grin in her tone.

I turned to Jack as he stepped over the dead soldier on the stairs and headed for me.

'You certainly know how to make an entrance,' he said, shaking his head.

'Well you did dial up the *cavalry riding to the rescue* emergency service, didn't you?' I said, smiling at him.

He laughed and grabbed hold of me, swinging me around as we hugged each other hard.

CHAPTER FIFTEEN

WITH LEON and Carlos safely back on board after *Neptune* had been retrieved from the sea, *Venus* was now sailing towards Havana at maximum possible speed, with Ruby escorting us in the X103. Tom had advised Leon that it would be the safest place to go to avoid any reprisal from the group responsible for the hijack. Naturally, he didn't mention the Overseers by name.

The sea had grown considerably calmer now that the hurricane had thankfully blown through. We sat in Leon's quarters, which we had borrowed for our debriefing with Ruby and Lucy via Sky Wire, whilst the captain checked on his crew following their ordeal.

'Thank Christ you turned up when you did, Lauren,' Jack said as he applied a bandage over Tom's stitched wound. 'You definitely helped to tip the battle in our favour.'

'You guys looked like you were pretty much holding your own,' I replied.

'I'm not sure we could have held out for much longer before your timely intervention,' Tom said, wincing as he pulled his shirt back on.

'My only regret is the way I was forced to take those three soldiers down,' Ruby said via Tom's Sky Wire. 'For somebody who prides themselves on their sniping skills it was a bit of an embarrassing way to end a hijack.'

'It got the job done, which is the thing that mattered,' I said.

'I just wish I'd been there to help,' Lucy said. 'Tom, I couldn't by any chance get you to reconsider letting me join in with the mission, after all this?'

'It's still no. You know why,' he replied.

She sighed. 'Yes I do.'

'You know I have more than a little sympathy for your situation,' Tom said. 'But this is the right call. You're just too valuable to expose to any danger more than we absolutely have to.'

'Okay, okay. God, you humans are just so damned stubborn.'

Everyone smiled at her mild tirade with the exception of Mike, who'd been uncharacteristically subdued throughout our debriefing and was currently peering out of the porthole. I could hazard a guess as to why he was so being so quiet.

'Was that really you that I saw going all Rambo in that shoot-out, Mike?' I asked.

He looked at me. 'I just did what needed to be done,' he said, his voice strained.

Tom gave me the briefest head shake and I immediately knew not to pursue the matter. For Mike – someone who'd previously relied on dart guns during combat missions – killing someone had to have been a difficult line for him to cross... just as it had been for me. When we had time after this mission was all over, I'd have a proper heart-to-heart with him to see how he was really doing, because I could already hazard a guess that it was very badly.

Tom propped his elbows on the table as he leant in towards the Sky Wire. 'Ruby, have you any ideas about where that helicopter came from?'

'Because it was flying so close to the ocean and was blocked from the X103's sensor by *Venus* until the last moment, all I can tell you is that it flew in from a westerly direction,' Ruby replied.

'Could it have come from that Russian spy boat?' Jack asked.

Lucy's voice piped up. 'Actually, no. I've checked over the military satellite footage and was able to backtrack its flightpath. It first appeared from an area of the ocean off the western tip of Cuba, and that Russian spy boat was nowhere near there at the time.'

'You're saying you don't have satellite footage from before that point?' I asked.

'No, I'm saying that it literally appeared out of nowhere,' said Lucy.

'But that's not possible. Helicopters don't simply materialise out of thin air,' Jack said.

'They might if they were covered in some sort of adaptive electronic skin like our Chameleon cloaking system,' Tom suggested.

'That was my first thought,' Lucy replied. 'That was until I looked more carefully. I'm loading the original satellite video of the area down to your Sky Wire now so you can look at it for yourselves.'

A video of an empty area of ocean appeared on the satellite phone. We all watched as the helicopter's nose appeared first and then, as though an invisible tarpaulin was being pulled back, the rest of its body was revealed.

'Is that the cloaking device being turned off?' Jack asked, peering at the screen.

'That's certainly what it looked like until I ran some frame by frame analysis, looking for the slightest differences between them,' Lucy replied. 'I'm downloading the processed video to you now so you can see what's really going on.'

Presented in false colours, a thermal image had been overlaid. I stared at the screen and saw that a large angular boat with sloping sides was now dwarfing the helicopter. It soon became clear that the helicopter was emerging from some sort of rear hangar onto a landing pad.

'You're telling me the Overseers are using bloody invisible ships now?' Mike asked, shaking his head in disbelief.

'Absolutely and looking at its shape I'd say that it's an adapted USS Zumwalt class destroyer,' Lucy said. 'Those ships aren't normally fitted with stealth systems, so it's probably been adapted with some top secret tech.'

Tom nodded. 'I believe the Zumwalt programme itself was cancelled, apparently because of significant budget overruns.'

'Well, somebody has deep pockets,' Ruby said.

'Exactly,' Tom replied. 'This sounds suspiciously like a US black budget project and we all know who really controls that.'

I blew my cheeks out. 'Okay, if we're saying the Overseers are prepared to commit a top secret ship like that to a mission, you can pretty much guarantee that there is something very significant in the area.'

'A Guardian drone, plus you setting off a significant underwater quake when you activated that rune, is already more than confirmation that there has to be a micro mind in that area,' Lucy said.

'In that case it's just become even more urgent that we track both the micro mind and the Angelus facility down.' I turned to Mike. 'About that quake...please tell me your seismic sensors picked it up?'

He managed a faint smile and nodded. 'They did. I've looked at the data they managed to record as the monowave hit Cuba. The epicentre appears to be at a location that's a couple of thousand feet down, on the seabed to the west of Cuba.'

'The same area where that stealth battleship is situated?' Tom asked.

'Based on my own analysis, almost exactly the same to within a couple of miles, to be precise,' Lucy interjected. 'And Jack, you need to tell Lauren the punchline that I ran past you before this meeting started, when I told you the position of those coordinates.'

My gaze swivelled towards Jack, who was looking distinctly guilty. 'Look, I want to say straight off that I didn't really consider it to be a viable option, as some have even called it an outright hoax. And here I am now kicking myself for writing it off too quickly.'

'Come on, put me out of my misery and just tell us already,' Mike said.

'Okay, but first a bit of back story for you all. In 2001, a Canadian company was on an oceanic survey mission, working with the Cuban government. They were using an underwater drone with sonar to map out the seabed at a considerable depth when they saw something incredible in the images that they captured. Their initial analysis revealed what appeared to be various pyramid and circular structures made from large stone blocks that could have been constructed from hewn granite.'

'Seriously, you're trying to tell us there are pyramids on the seabed off the coast of Cuba, and you're only just mentioning this now?' I said. 'Shouldn't we have started the search there, Jack?'

If possible he looked even more uncomfortable. 'Look, it was one of those stories that briefly appeared in the news then vanished again. And for a while they even called it the *lost sunken city of Cuba*, some putting it forward as a candidate site for Atlantis, but as we now know, that's nowhere near the real site. Also, when it became clear that the site was over two thousand feet down – even allowing for the possible collapse of a geological land bridge to the American continent over five thousand years ago that it *might* have been built on – the site was still way too deep to have been accessed by people at any point in history. Because of that, and in my defence, along with nearly every other archaeologist I know, I'd just written it off as a misinterpretation of data. I felt certain that it had to be some sort of natural rock formation on the seabed because there was no way that a human structure could have naturally gotten down to that sort of depth.'

I leant forward. 'Maybe not a human one, but how about an alien one?'

'Exactly. That's why I could kick myself now for not challenging my own assumptions.'

'Please stop being so hard on yourself, Jack,' Lucy said. 'The rune, and Raúl and Maricela's disappearance, happened in a completely different location. Besides, even I didn't think it was relevant because the distance was so great. There was certainly no way it could have been linked to the two until I saw the data from Mike's seismic probes.'

Mike nodded. 'Yes, based on that data, it appears the scale is at least ten times that of the rune formation we discovered around Lucy back at Skara Brae.'

'The main thing that matters is that we know about it now,' I said, giving Jack a gentle look. He slowly nodded back at me. Then I returned my attention to the others. 'So taking into account its highly inaccessible location, it again supports the idea of a very significant installation, one that the Angelus didn't want our species inadvertently discovering.'

'But what could be that important?' Ruby asked.

'Unfortunately, thanks to that damned Kimprak virus there are no intact records of anything at that location,' Lucy said.

'The one thing I know for certain is that we need to find that location and fast,' I said. 'But there is certainly no way I'm going to ask Leon to sail us there after what happened.'

'I agree. Also, as impressive as *Venus* is, she will be no match for the state-of-the-art Zumwalt destroyer, especially when it's invisible,' Tom said.

'Aha, I have good news there,' Lucy said. 'You know what a miracle worker Jodie is. Well, she has only managed to get the underwater retrofit on *Ariel* completed several days ahead of schedule. The Forge has even managed to fit out that second underwater-capable X103, which will be escorting her out to hand *Ariel* over to you.'

I stared at the phone. 'So what are waiting for, Lucy? Get her to send it here ASAP. Then we can find out exactly what's at the centre of that quake site without putting anyone else in danger.'

'I agree,' Tom said. 'However, I think we are far past the point of this just being a reconnaissance mission. We need to go in ready for combat. We should definitely deploy a Pangolin, maybe with Niki onboard to form a squadron with us.'

Jack nodded. 'If it made sense before, it's even more necessary now to head in with the big guns. It won't take the Overseers long to realise that one of their helicopters is missing; they'll be on high alert by the time we get there.'

I gave a low whistle. 'It sounds like we may be heading into something that will rapidly become a combat zone.' I glanced at Tom. 'Rather than trust our lives to Delphi's flying skills – even if they *are* based on Troy's incredible abilities – I'd like you to fly *Ariel*. Something tells me that we're going to need your experience. You might not have planned to become a mission pilot, but as you more than proved back at Area 51, you can certainly handle yourself in the air.'

'There are more experienced pilots back at Eden we could bring in,' he replied.

Jack shook his head. 'Maybe, but none I'd trust my life with quite as much as you, Tom.'

A smile filled Tom's face. 'Then I'd be delighted. However, there is one other matter that we should clarify up front for this next phase of our mission. A squadron needs a commander and my vote goes to Lauren to take on that role.'

'But surely you're more experienced in something like this?' I said.

'No, you really are the ideal candidate, even if you don't realise it yet. You've already proved yourself in the role of captain and shown that you're ready to step up to the role of squadron commander.'

'Are you sure?'

Tom folded his arms. 'I am, but maybe you want to run this past the rest of your team?'

I looked at Jack and Mike. 'Are the rest of you happy with this?'

'Do you really need to ask?' Jack said, smiling at me as Mike nodded.

'Yep, that goes for me too and I'm certain the rest of the squadron would agree,' Ruby said over the Sky Wire. 'Whether you realise it or not, Lauren, you've developed quite the reputation in Eden. Just as you trust Tom to pilot us, a lot of people would trust you with their lives too.'

I immediately felt the weight of responsibility pressing down on my shoulders as well as feeling incredibly humbled. When had people started believing in me like this when often I barely did?

I lifted my chin up and met the expectant gazes of the others. 'Okay. If you all insist, I'll do it. So with my new hat on we'd better start putting a mission plan together. To start with, Lucy, how long until Jodie can get *Ariel* to us along with the rest of the squadron?'

'First thing tomorrow, after the final bits of equipment are fitted.'

'That could work out well. We should be back in dock by then,' Tom said.

'In that case I suggest we all grab what rest whilst we can, because I for one am bloody knackered,' I said, and I meant it.

We stood on the quayside next to *Venus* under the burnished sky of a new dawn, no hint of the previous night's storm in sight. It was time to say our goodbyes to Leon and Carlos.

I hugged Carlos. 'Now you take good care of yourself, do you hear me?'

'I'll do my best, although it seems I'm going to be pretty busy between that wreck and setting up a charity.'

'Don't you worry, I'll be helping you every step of the way,' Leon said.

'And you'll both do a great job. Carlos, I think if Raúl and Maricela could see you now, they'd be very proud of their dad.'

'I hope so,' he smiled.

'I know so,' I said, smiling back and giving him another hug.

Tom stepped forward. 'The only thing I ask of you both is that you please wait for the all-clear from us that it's okay to go back to the wreck site. We have to deal with the people behind the hijack, but once we've done that it should be safe for you to return to recover the wreck. I've also made steps to ensure that you're protected from any further hostile action.'

'What sort of protection are we talking about here?' Leon asked.

Tom tapped the side of his nose. 'Once again, much better for you not to know.'

'Are you absolutely sure there is nothing more you can tell us about what's really going on?' Carlos asked. 'Don't you think we have a right to know?'

I took his hands in mine and gazed at him. 'Yes you do, and as much as I would love to tell you everything, as Tom said, it's honestly better that you don't know.'

The old man sighed. 'Maybe we'll find out one day.'

'The moment that day comes, I promise that you'll be the first to know.'

Leon cleared his throat. 'And you really will deal with the bastards who attempted to hijack *Venus*?'

'Oh, you can count on it,' Jack said.

'Be sure to send them my love.' Leon said grimly.

I laughed. 'I'll make sure I do that with extra kisses.' I held out my hand to shake his. But Leon ignored that and drew me into a hug as Jack raised his eyebrows at me over the other man's shoulders.

I gave him a guilty smile. 'What can I say? We all got very close on that voyage onboard *Neptune*.'

'So it would seem,' Jack replied, unable to suppress a smile.

Leon glanced at him as he pulled away from me. 'Lauren is one in a million.'

'Yeah, she certainly is,' Jack said.

With a beep of a horn, Glenn swept into the dock in his Skyliner and pulled up next to us.

'Hey, my friends, what have I missed?' he said with a wide smile.

'Okay, time to go,' Tom said.

With a final wave to Carlos and Glenn we climbed into the car.

Jack cast a wistful glance back towards *Venus*. 'What I'd give to be part of the exploration team heading down to that wreck.'

'True, but think about where we're heading now, Jack,' Mike said, patting him on the back. 'This Cuban underwater formation sounds right up your alley.'

'It does, apart from the fact that it also sounds as though its likely to be crawling with damned Overseers by now.'

I shrugged. 'Then I pity them when we show up to spoil their party.'

'You make it sound so easy,' Jack said.

If only, I thought to myself. With the Overseers already on high alert, I strongly suspected we were about to head into the trickiest battle of our lives. The fact that that was going to turn out to be something of a considerable understatement was truly saying something.

CHAPTER SIXTEEN

THE FOLLOWING MORNING, we grabbed a lift with Glenn in his Ford Skyliner under the light of a golden dawn and headed out towards the sugar cane field where we'd first landed. I cranked the car window down, breathing in the moist air, thick with the scent of rich earth, thanks to the heavy rainfall from the night before.

Glenn was leaning over his steering wheel, looking up into the sky. 'Any idea when your ride will get here?' he asked.

I glanced at my Sky Wire and the GPS marker on the large scale map. Three blips were heading towards our location at incredible speed. There was already a static one just ahead of us – Ruby, already touched down in the X103.

'They are about fifty miles out, but it looks like Ruby's already here and waiting,' I replied.

Glenn looked straight ahead at the field that we were heading towards, where absolutely nothing was visible except for the crops. 'I'll have to take your word for it, Lauren.'

We pulled up in the corner of the field and began to unload our kit from the vehicle.

As Mike grabbed his bag he glanced along the coast. 'Glenn, you'll need to ask Antonio to recover all those probes that we buried across the island. If someone stumbles across them it will raise too many questions.'

'No problem. I'll wake him when I get back to the house and send him out to round them up,' Glenn said.

I heard a rustling sound approaching and turned to see Ruby emerging from the sugar cane crop.

'Good, you're all here at last. Niki just radioed in to say he's coming in to land,' she said.

'Wow, they're here already?' Jack asked.

'Yes, those mark two REV engines can really shift some butt when they need to,' Ruby grinned.

'That's good news because the sooner we get to the structure site, the happier I'll be,' I said.

I looked up, trying to spot the telltale sign of the shifting Chameleon camouflage that would give any hint of the two X-craft presence as they arrived. But it was impossible to spot them in the early morning light. Also, the fact that the new drive was basically silent meant that the first we knew of their landing was when the sound of sugarcane crops being squashed flat reached our ears from the middle of the field.

'That will never get old,' Jack said, shaking his head as we began to walk between the stalks towards the sound.

Within moments we were standing by the edge of four large circles. The three smaller ones had the distinct shapes and dimensions of X103s. I figured they were Ruby's X103, *Ariel* – fresh from her underwater refit, and *Ariel's* escorting craft, which was apparently called *Artemis*. According to Tom, the *Artemis's* pilot had taken over *Ariel's* systems to fly her to us like a new car delivery service. The fourth compressed circular imprint was easily four times the size of the others and had to be Niki's Pangolin.

'When we're gone you'll be able to charge the tourists to see your crop circle collection, Glenn,' Jack said, smiling.

Glenn chuckled. 'Now there's a great idea.'

A shimmer passed through the air and then the three new arrivals suddenly appeared before us as they uncloaked. The Pangolin in particular looked built for war, with its thick slabs of armour and weapons pod bulges on the top and underside of the craft. But it was *Ariel* that I was most interested in. I was keen to see Jodie's modifications to her for underwater flight.

Glenn stared slack-jawed at the craft. 'Seeing these with my own eyes I can tell Sky Dreamer Corp has been seriously busy.'

'You can say that again', Ruby said. She was already examining the new circular intakes around *Ariel's* hull, which were currently covered with closed hatches. 'This must be the new impeller system that Jodie fitted.'

'Apparently she has programmed Delphi with a briefing package about how to use them,' Tom said. 'It also covers the new underwater weapon systems that we're both going to have to familiarise ourselves with, Ruby.'

'Never been one for instruction booklets, so hopefully there's a quick start guide,' Ruby replied with a grin. She disappeared up the ramp into *Ariel* with a definite spring in her step, obviously itching to get her hands on the updated craft and its controls.

With a slight hiss, the ramp in the Pangolin lowered and Niki appeared. He walked down it towards us.

'I hear you've been having an interesting time out here,' Niki said as he reached us.

'Yeah, the same old rollercoaster ride,' Mike shrugged.

From the other X103, Erin and Daryl, the recently qualified flight crew that we'd been introduced to back at the 16 Psyche landing party, emerged together.

They made straight for me, came to a halt, and then both snapped me a salute.

'Reporting for duty, Commander,' Daryl said. Erin stood to attention with a ramrod straight stance.

I caught the smile on Jack's face before he quickly hid it.

'So it will be you two joining us on this mission then?' I replied.

'Absolutely. We both volunteered for the chance to work with you and your team,' Erin said with far too much enthusiasm.

'And I just wanted to say what an honour it is to join you. I promise that we won't let you down,' Daryl added.

'I'm sure you won't,' I replied with a smile. I gestured towards the Pangolin. 'Your new craft certainly looks the business, Niki.'

'You mean *Thor,* as we've christened him. We're looking forward to putting our new ship through its paces in a combat mission.'

'Talking of which, we need to discuss tactics,' I said. 'To start with, seeing how Erin remotely piloted *Ariel* from her craft gives me an idea. Could we do the same with the X103 we arrived in? That way you take control of it from *Thor,* effectively using it in the battle as one massive drone?'

Niki nodded. 'I like it. That way we can have a second craft at our disposal above the surface if things get interesting whilst you guys head underwater.'

'Talking of getting ready for combat, I wouldn't be surprised if the Overseers had some TR-3Bs patrolling the area just to make life difficult,' Jack said.

Niki grinned. 'And won't they get a surprise when then run into *Thor,* armed to the teeth with missiles, a railgun and six mini-guns? And even if they do get a lucky shot in that manages to breach the gravity shielding, Jodie promises that the ablative armour-plating fitted to the X104 can soak up a lot of damage.'

'Ablative armour?' Mike asked.

'It's designed to dissipate any weapon damage, including the Overseer's new laser turret that you ran into at Atlantis.'

'It certainly looks the business,' Jack said, giving the craft an admiring glance.

At that moment, a sliding metal sound came from behind us and we turned to see the weapons pods on *Ariel* opening to reveal the silver noses of two missiles. At the same time, a *whoop* came from the interior of *Ariel's* cockpit.

'That will be Ruby discovering her new toys then,' Niki said, shaking his head. '*Ariel* and *Artemis* have been equipped with an arsenal of Spearfish heavy torpedoes.'

'Permission to speak to explain about our new weapon systems, Commander,' Daryl said.

For a moment I didn't realise that he was talking to me, but then I got it. 'Oh yes, sorry, please go ahead. But in future, you don't need my permission to speak up.'

'Understood, Commander, and noted,' Daryl replied. 'So, starting with the Spearfish missiles. They can be guided by wire or use their own autonomous sonar to take out other enemy subs or ships up to fifty-four klicks out. Additionally, the flechette munitions loaded in the modified miniguns are effective up to about three hundred metres, but really are for close range combat only. There are also twenty brand new WASP drones loaded onto *Ariel* that your tactical officer requested. They have been adapted for underwater use and are also equipped with flechette dart rounds.'

Jack chuckled. 'So in other words, Ruby's birthday and Christmas presents have all been rolled into one.'

'It certainly sounds like it to me,' I said.

Tom tapped his watch. 'Time to get into the air I think.'

I nodded. I turned to Glenn, who'd been standing at the edge of our group, quietly listening to our exchange with ever widening eyes.

'It looks like it's time to say our goodbyes,' I said. 'I just want to thank you for everything and to ask you to maybe keep an eye on Carlos for us? He could probably do with a friend right now after what he discovered happened to his children.'

'I was already planning to do exactly that and regularly pop over to see how he's doing,' Glenn replied. 'Anyway, it's been a real pleasure to meet you and the others.' He drew me in and kissed me on the cheeks. Then he proceeded to shake everyone else's hands, before taking a wooden box from a bag he'd retrieved from the boot of his car. He handed it to Tom. 'Please give this to Ruby for me, my old friend. Tell her these are some of my finest cigars and I hope she likes them.'

'If I know Ruby, she'll adore them,' Tom said.

Glenn nodded and looked up into the clear sky. 'Whatever you're heading into, at least you're going to have better weather for it than you did last night. But please take care, especially if your undersea encounter was a taste of what you'll be up against.'

I tapped *Ariel's* hull. 'Oh, I think we can look after ourselves pretty well this time round.'

'I hope so, my friends, I hope so...'

On the virtual cockpit, the contrast to the stormy weather of the previous night couldn't have been more stark. The ocean shone as soft twinkling sunlight danced across its surface. In any other situation it would have been an uplifting view, but not today, in light of the potential confrontation that we were heading straight towards.

Displayed either side of us, even though the other X-craft were in stealth mode, were their rendered 3D representations on the virtual cockpit that encircled the flight deck. *Thor,* under Niki's command, and the X103 that we'd flown out on, were flying off to our port side. Meanwhile, Erin and Daryl onboard *Artemis* were off to our starboard. It wasn't lost on me that the combined firepower of our four craft was substantial. Despite it all, the one thing I knew for certain was that I would have felt far more relaxed if Lucy had been flying with us as part of our squadron.

'We're about ten miles out,' Tom said, looking at his nav screen.

'Any hint of that Zumwalt destroyer yet?' I asked.

'No, but we've got at least one of those Russian spy fishing boats,' Ruby replied. She pressed an icon on her CIC screen and in a pop-up window on the virtual display, the squat outline of a ship was shown in the ocean. The people on the deck were barely visible, just specks moving around the deck, but more noticeable was a white blob dangling from a crane at the rear of the vessel.

'That looks like another submersible to me,' Mike said.

'And bang over the mystery site at the bottom of the ocean by the looks of it,' Ruby replied.

'I think that more than confirms that they are actively investigating that site,' I said. 'Is there any chance you could get a clearer image so we could get a better idea of what's going on, Ruby?'

'Sorry, *Ariel's* imaging system is already at maximum magnification as it is.'

'Then allow me,' Lucy said as her face appeared in another pop-up window, making me jump in the process and causing Jack to spill the water he'd been drinking.

'Damn it, can you at least warn us when you make a house call?' he said, wiping the water from his combat uniform.

'Sorry, my bad,' Lucy said, grinning at him. 'Anyway, welcome to another mod that I managed to get Jodie to fit before the squadron left Eden. Your craft have been fitted with the new QEC – quantum entangled communication – radios. Thanks to that, not only will you be able to keep in contact with Niki when you're submerged, but I also fitted a dedicated channel so I can tag along in virtual form using my avatar. If I can't be there in person, at least I can be there in spirit.'

'So you mean there is basically no way that we can get away from you now?' Jack said, grinning.

'As if you'd want to. Anyway, you were asking about a clearer look at that image. You know that bit in the movies where someone asks the expert to enhance the image and they press a few buttons and hey presto, the thing that was a vague blob suddenly becomes a pin sharp image?'

'You can do that?' I said, impressed.

She snorted. 'As if. Beyond a bit of sharpening, that's all Hollywood make believe. However, what I can do is supply you with a satellite feed playback of that boat. It's fitted with a two hundred megapixel camera that passed overhead about an hour ago and you're so going to want to see what it captured.'

A new video window appeared and on it was a very clear close-up of the Russian spy ship. The submersible's hatch was open and a man's head was visible, talking to a woman standing on the deck. They were too small to make out any real detail other than that.

'I don't see the significance, Lucy?' Jack said.

'Oh you will. Just give it a moment as the satellite tracked closer and then you'll get a better view,' Lucy replied.

Sure enough the image continued to draw nearer to the ship and then suddenly we could clearly see who the two people were.

'Oh bloody hell! I thought you got rid of him on your last mission,' Mike said.

My stomach had dropped into my feet. The man who I saw climb out of the submersible and stand next to the woman was instantly recognisable as Alvarez, the Overseers' colonel who had made our life a living hell on so many missions.

Ruby hissed. 'How the hell did that bastard survive being buried alive in the sand under that pyramid?'

'That's what I'd like to know,' I said.

Ever since our last encounter with the Overseer colonel at Atlantis, otherwise known as the Richat Structure, I'd felt a certain weight come off my shoulders knowing the man was dead. Now that anxiety came rushing back with a vengeance and I could feel it crushing me down into my flight seat.

Jack leant forward, staring harder at the video footage. 'And tell me that woman with him isn't that bitch, Professor Evelyn Fischer?'

'The archaeologist working for the Overseers that you ran into at Machu Picchu?' Tom asked.

'The very same,' Mike said, answering the question for him.

Jack sighed. 'Fischer's presence has to be significant. It suggests that the Overseers already found something major on the ocean bed at that location. Lucy, any chance I could have a quick word with Poseidon? I want to pick his brains about the underwater structure.'

'Your wish is my command,' Lucy said with a grin.

A moment later, her image was replaced with Poseidon, the micro mind AI that we'd first encountered at the Richat Structure.

The first thing that was hard to miss was his rather significant change in wardrobe. Gone was the toga suitable for the god of Atlantis and in its place were white jeans and a cotton shirt. But somehow Poseidon still managed to look godly with his beard and penetrating eyes – just an omnipotent being who'd moved with the times.

Jack didn't even batter an eyelid at the change of appearance as he addressed the AI. 'Poseidon, I need to ask you about the Cuban underwater formation. I don't suppose you have any record in your database about anything that might at least give us a faint clue as to what's down there?'

Poseidon shook his head. 'I'm afraid as Lucy has already told you, nothing directly, Jack. That's not necessarily surprising as there are so many gaps in the substrata database thanks to the Kimprak virus destroying much of it. However, there is one severely truncated record about a facility that drew a vast amount of energy from the E8 dimension to power its systems. Although I have no record of it being at this particular location, what I can tell you is that it was a significant facility, even if I can't tell you what its purpose is.'

'So, based on the fact it's at the bottom of such a deep part of the ocean, along with the presence of a Guardian, there's a good chance that this could be this mysterious Angelus megastructure?' I asked.

'I think that's certainly a possibility,' Poseidon replied.

'Then what are we waiting for?' Ruby said. 'To kick this show off, I say we take down that spy ship with an ASSAM missile right now, killing Alvarez and Fischer in the process. Then we head straight down there to retrieve the micro mind. That sounds like a great day's work to me.'

'No, you absolutely can't do that, at least not yet. Let me show you why,' Lucy said.

The video windows disappeared to reveal the virtual cockpit again. Now the spy boat was barely a spec on the horizon. But about five klicks to the right of it was a rendered 3D image of the cloaked Zumwalt class destroyer superimposed into the scene.

'Are you trying to tell us that that stealthed-up warship is guarding that bloody spy boat?' Mike asked.

'I most certainly am. Actually, the only reason that you're able to see it at all is that I'm analysing all the visual data coming from your squadron's cameras and I'm looking for even the slightest discrepancy between frames. By analysing this and constructing a 3D model, I can then feed through this information to the squadron's CICs and, even more importantly, to your targeting system.'

I felt the tension ratchet up across my shoulders. Thanks to the warship's presence and even with the new hardware at our disposal, instinct was already screaming at me that this mission wasn't going to be anything like a walk in the park.

'I'm pretty sure I could sink even that destroyer with a well-aimed railgun round,' Niki said over the open channel.

'You probably could, but you can guarantee we would quickly be dealing with a squadron of TR-3Bs pretty soon after,' Jack replied.

'Then as tempting a target as that spy boat is, we all need to remember what our real priority is here and that's to recover the micro mind,' Tom said. 'Based on all this activity on the surface, the one thing you can almost certainly guarantee is that they haven't yet recovered it.'

I marshalled my thoughts as I nodded. 'Yes, we should only tip our hand about our presence here if we absolutely have to. But if we have to – and if that means taking that bastard Alvarez out in the process – none of us is going to shed a tear about that.' As I was speaking I could feel my thoughts starting to crystallise. 'So let's go with our initial plan. Niki, you and your crew will command the slaved X103 and keep guard up here, ready to step in the moment things start to look dodgy. Meanwhile, *Artemis* and *Ariel* will land on the surface and then we'll make our way below towards the site.'

Everyone nodded around me.

'Sounds like a good strategy to me, Commander,' Erin's voice said over the link.

'To me too,' Niki added.

'One small complication, guys,' Lucy said. 'That submersible has just launched with Alvarez and Fischer onboard, so you're likely to run into them down there.'

'Now wouldn't that be a pity? I might just have to try out those dart rounds in our adapted miniguns for a bit of target practice,' Ruby said, a broad grin on her face.

'We'll have to see about that,' I replied. 'Erin, get ready to land on the surface.'

'Roger that,' the young pilot said.

I returned my attention to the virtual cockpit. 'Tom, please take us down and prep our underwater drive system.'

He nodded. A moment later, in utter silence, *Ariel* with *Artemis* next to us, began to descend towards the surface of that cobalt blue ocean.

CHAPTER SEVENTEEN

THE WATER LAPPED GENTLY around *Ariel's* hull and the sound bubbled all around us.

'Flooding ballast tanks now,' Tom announced, his gaze half on an electronic tablet that he seemed to be following the instructions from, which wasn't exactly filling me with confidence. But to his credit, Tom had already been at pains to point out that if he wasn't sure about anything he would simply ask Delphi to take over control during the dive.

Above us, thanks to the enhanced virtual cockpit, semi-transparent rendered versions of *Thor* and our X103 slaved to it hung in a stationary hover. The sight was incredibly reassuring. Whatever happened beneath the ocean, at least someone would be covering our backs above the surface, specifically when it came to that bloody Zumwalt destroyer.

At last Tom seemed happy with his pre-dive checks. Taking hold of the controls he began to slip *Ariel* beneath the surface. To our port side, the *Artemis* was barely visible beneath the rendered version superimposed over it, but its presence was still given away by a faintly transparent bubble trail around the edge of the craft.

I pressed the comms button. '*Artemis*, is there some sort of problem with your Chameleon cloak? You still appear to be partly visible.'

'So are you, Commander,' Erin's voice replied. 'But Jodie explained that this might happen. Because of the gravity field from our REV drives, it creates a slight distortion due to the refraction effect of the water, which is impossible to completely compensate for.'

'So in other words, we are not entirely invisible down here?' I asked.

'Not a hundred percent, but pretty close unless you are within a hundred metres or so of either craft.'

'Now she tells us,' Ruby said, shaking her head.

'Sorry, there was just so much to brief you on before, but I should have mentioned it,' Erin said. 'I'll try to do better in future, Commander.'

'The priority was getting the mission underway. It's ok. But now we know about it, we can allow for it,' I said.

'Yes, Commander,' Erin replied flatly.

Tom gave me a nod, obviously approving that I hadn't balled the young pilot out. I knew that she would learn from the mistake and so I could leave it there. But inwardly I was less than thrilled at the news. Even though it was unlikely that anyone would get close enough to spot us, it was still a faint possibility and I needed every edge that our technology could give us when heading into the unknown.

We began to dive diagonally towards the ocean depths, our descent far faster than Leon had managed to achieve in *Neptune*. Part of me wished the French explorer was with us now just so I could see the look on his face.

Ruby pressed a button on her CIC screen and a depth gauge

appeared over the virtual cockpit. We'd already passed the two hundred fathoms mark, way deeper that we'd managed at the rune site, yet we were still nowhere near the bottom. Above us a shoal of what might have been barracuda swam past, their changes in direction mesmerising us and catching the sunlight like hundreds of mirrors. But far below, the water was growing darker as we dropped.

Jack took in the view, shaking his head. 'Wow, isn't this something?'

'Isn't it just?' I said, enjoying the fact that I was getting to share this experience with him in the moment of calm before we encountered whatever was waiting for us.

'It looks seriously dark down there,' Ruby said, peering down at the depths on the virtual cockpit.

'That's actually called the bathypelagic region of the ocean, also known as the twilight zone – just like our nickname for the waveform dimension,' Mike said. 'It runs down to over two thousand fathoms. Beneath that is the abyssopelagic zone, which is pitch black at those depths and is better known as the abyss for that reason.'

Ruby's face lit up. 'Just like the movie.'

'Oh great, thanks for that. Now I'm going to be thinking of a bloody great big alien sea monster waiting to capture us,' Mike replied.

'Anytime,' Ruby smirked, but she edged her hand a fraction closer towards the weapons control panel.

The gloom started to press in around *Ariel*. Everyone had fallen into an uneasy silence, our default setting when we were heading into extreme danger.

There was a flicker of white ahead of us, then every one of us in that cockpit jumped as a ridiculously large squid, at least two metres long, shot between both craft.

Ruby gasped, gripping the minigun's joystick control so tightly that her knuckles went white.

'Careful there or you'll turn into calamari before you know it, Ruby,' Mike said.

Our weapons officer merely *humphed* loudly, then relaxed her grip on the joystick.

The darkness was growing deeper. But despite that, very much unlike *Neptune*, there wasn't so much as a groan coming from the hull. And that was just as it should be as the gravity bubble did its thing to keep the pressure around us at surface levels on our hull.

I opened up a comms channel. 'Niki, are you still able to read us over this new QEC radio?'

'Loud and clear as though you were in the next room. This quantum entangled radio system is certainly delivering what Lucy promised it would.'

Lucy's avatar immediately appeared in an overlaid window on the cockpit. 'Did you expect anything else from yours truly?'

'I should certainly know better by now,' Niki replied.

'So your link to us is obviously working well too, Lucy?' I asked.

'Like a dream.'

'Good to know that we'll at least be able to pick your brains if we need to,' Mike said.

'Oh, you can pick my brains anytime, handsome,' Lucy said, grinning at him.

'Anyway, back to the mission,' I said, rolling my eyes. 'How are things looking on the surface for you guys, Niki?'

'All quiet here since Alvarez's submersible launched from that spy boat. The Zumwalt destroyer is just slowly patrolling around the area, so it looks like so far, no one knows we're here.'

'Good, let's hope it stays that way,' I replied.

The depth gauge had ticked past two hundred and fifty fathoms now. In another eighty or so we'd reach the bottom.

'External pressure is now six hundred pounds per square inch or twenty atmospheres,' Ruby said, peering at the display on the CIC screen that encircled her.

'Any sign of any leaks yet?' Lucy asked, with a totally unnecessary amused tone.

'I'll give you bloody leaks,' Jack muttered under his breath.

It had grown so dark now that it was getting hard to see beyond twenty metres outside.

'Any chance you can enhance the view, Ruby?' I asked.

'Our thermal cameras won't work well down here because of the cooling effect of all this water. But I can overlay the passive sonar information if it detects anything interesting alongside the existing map data. The problem is that we can't use active sonar; it would give our position away to that damn destroyer.'

'Okay, then let's give the overlaid sonar data a whirl please.'

She nodded and toggled a few buttons on her screen. Immediately the gloomy view on the walls was superimposed with pixel points for the seabed stretching away below us. In the distance, radiating circular lines were pulsing around an object above, which was descending far more slowly than *Ariel*.

'Is that Alvarez and Fischer's submersible by any chance?' I asked.

'Damned right it is,' Ruby said. 'Just one little flechette round and we could open that thing up like a can of sardines.'

'No doubt, but then we'd have to deal with all the fun it would bring down on our heads,' Tom said.

'You can't tell me you're not tempted,' Ruby sniffed.

He held a forefinger and thumb out with the slightest gap between them. 'Maybe a *tiny* bit.'

'So where is this underwater formation anyway?' Jack interjected, peering at the enhanced view.

'I'm overlaying its position for you now,' Lucy said.

A pulsing blue marker appeared dead ahead of us in the distance with a four-kilometre marker next to it. It was also exactly where Alvarez's submersible appeared to be heading.

'Not long till the big reveal then,' Mike said, glancing across at Jack.

'If it really is a city of underwater pyramids, I'm all ready to have my mind blown,' Jack smiled.

The sense of anticipation was growing inside me. Whatever this was, I knew it was going to be significant, but the question that kept looping through my head was *how so*?

Tom dropped us to less than twenty metres above the ocean floor and Erin matched his manoeuvre precisely in *Artemis*. If she was trying to impress me with her piloting skills, she was certainly doing a good job of it so far.

Ridges rose and fell away in front of us like a series of gentle rolling hills. Far above, the rendered hull of the Zumwalt was growing steadily closer as we neared the site. Holding further back in the sky were the familiar shapes of our X-craft squadron on the surface.

Beneath the enhanced view of the dots, following the contours, the ocean bed was just visible in the twilight. At these depths, it was barely illuminated by the faint light, creating a palette of muted greys and dappled greens.

Once, while visiting the London aquarium, I'd almost dropped into a trance while watching the fish swimming around their alternate universe. It was the same here; caustic light patterns rippled across the ocean floor and strange fish darted away as we approached them. Then I became instantly alert as I spotted hundreds of tiny blue points of light ahead of us.

'What the hell are those things?' Ruby said, peering forward.

The question was soon answered for us as we drew closer to

one of the floating blue lights. It was a jellyfish, its delicate undulating structure lit up with blue and green beads of light, tenta-
cles wavering in the water behind it.

'Wow, they almost look like space ships straight out of that
film, *Close Encounters of the Third Kind*,' Jack said.

I shot him a look. 'You do realise that you're impressing me
again with sci-fi knowledge?'

'Maybe that's because I have something of a relentless
teacher.'

'Hey, you love it really,' I said, smiling at him.

'Yes, maybe I do,' he replied, giving me an equally wide smile.

'They may look innocent enough, but have you ever been
stung by a jellyfish? They sting like a bitch,' Mike said. 'Happened to me once when I was surfing and I had to get a mate to
pee on me.'

'Ewww, gross!' Ruby said.

'No, you don't understand. Apparently it's meant to take the
pain away, but it made absolutely no bloody difference.'

'I'm afraid that's just one of those urban legends, although the
idea is sound enough,' Jack said. 'What you really need to do is
use a strong salt water solution to bathe the area, which
neutralises the venom.'

'The things one learns on your missions,' Tom said, raising his
eyebrows.

We heard Niki snort over the comm link. 'Isn't that the
truth?'

I snorted and switched my attention back to the countdown
marker, which had now ticked passed three klicks. It was then,
without any warning, that an eerie sound passed through the
cockpit, rising and falling in a haunting note.

Mike sat up straight. 'Is that a micro mind calling out?'

'No, gorgeous, that's actually whale song,' Lucy chimed in.

'Looking at the passive sonar data, I'd say it's a blue whale and we're not picking just one up either. There seems to be a large pod of them down here with us.'

'Seriously, at this depth?' Mike said.

'Actually they are just above you at around three hundred metres, which is still very impressive,' Lucy replied. 'However, according to a Wikipedia entry I just checked, the record for a deep dive goes to a Cuvier's beaked whale. It had a satellite tag on it, which showed that the whale managed to dive to a depth of two-thousand metres at one point.'

Jack whistled. 'Now that's seriously impressive.'

Everyone fell silent again as Tom manoeuvred us beneath the whales swimming leisurely above. The creatures were vast, absolutely dwarfing our not exactly small X-craft.

The whales began calling again to each other, the sound bringing tears to my eyes. It was so intensely beautiful. There were younger whales in the pod too, keeping close to their mothers. How anyone could hunt these wonderful creatures was beyond me. Some things were very wrong in our world and that was definitely one of them.

The pod moved past us and swam away with gentle and powerful flicks of their huge tails. No wonder people like Leon and Carlos had dedicated so much of their lives to being down here, when you got see astonishing sights like that.

'On my goodness, I've never seen anything quite so incredible,' Tom said quietly.

When I glanced at him I caught him wiping away a tear. That deeply touched me more than anything. The guy was normally all business and laser sharp focus on getting the job done, I'd never seen a softer side to him. He was always something of a loner, even at Eden.

I made a mental note that I really needed to put some effort into getting to know Tom better. There was obviously a lot more to him than a man who was just married to his job.

A large shallow valley, where the marker for the underwater site was located, was slowly coming into view. Unfortunately, it was too dark for us to physically see it yet. We wouldn't even have known about it if it weren't for the vague shapes representing the pyramid and circular structures on Lucy's overlaid data.

We had closed in to less than two klicks when suddenly a cone of light appeared from somewhere inside the valley and shot upwards into the sea. The beam locked onto Alvarez's submersible, which was descending towards the middle of the valley.

'Okay, the fact that they have a spotlight down here suggests some sort of Overseer facility,' Tom said.

I nodded. 'I agree. We should creep in as quietly as possible—'

But before I could finish my sentence, a loud, warbling alarm cut off my words.

A pulsating red marker appeared straight ahead of us at the edge of the valley.

Ruby stared at her screens. 'Crap, we seem to have just triggered some sort of acoustic listening device.'

'Damn it, this has to be similar to what we ran into back at the rune site,' I replied.

Erin's voice cut in over the link. 'I don't understand. How can they detect our ships when we are fully stealthed?'

'As effective as your ship's systems are, the new impeller drive system isn't completely silent,' Lucy replied.

'Then kill all our motors right now, Tom and Erin,' I said.

'Affirmative, Commander,' Erin responded.

Tom drew the throttle back to a neutral position. We slid to a dead stop as *Artemis* did the same alongside us.

Jack stared into the distance. 'Do you think they're going to send someone to check out the contact?'

'I certainly would if I was responsible for guarding a site and I picked up an unexpected hello,' Ruby said.

'The Overseers hijacking an unarmed ship is one thing, but seriously, what can they even do to us down here? We're talking about two underwater flying saucers that pack a serious military punch.' Jack said.

The phrase *him and his big mouth* had just leapt into my mind when at that moment the HUD went crazy. A massive, pulsing, red triangular symbol was dead ahead, glaring *enemy contact detected* for us all to see.

My blood froze. 'What are we looking at here, Ruby?'

'Not sure. Our systems are barely getting a lock on whatever it is.'

'Damn it! Lucy, can you help us?'

'Hang on, processing all available incoming data and...oh no, that's really not good.'

My blood grew even colder. 'Care to elaborate?'

In answer, a small rectangular box appeared and grew larger to fill half of the virtual cockpit. Within it we could just see a slight distortion in the water. Then lots of data points began to appear all over the vague shape, growing denser by the moment until a large submarine became visible.

'That's not that Yasen-class, hunter-killer Russian sub?' Tom said, his face tense.

'Afraid so, and with the same active camouflage system that the Zumwalt destroyer has been fitted with,' Lucy said.

'It looks like another of the Overseers' special book projects,' Tom said, peering at the enhanced image.

'Should I open fire, Commander?' Ruby said, her hand already on the weapons control panel.

Shit, I don't know, I wanted to say. But instead I forced my mind to come up with an answer. 'They can't actually detect us with their sonar equipment can they, Lucy?'

'No, because our gravity field is masking our signature. However, that underwater mic will pick up on any noise you make inside this cockpit that radiates out through the hull. So, like in all those old sub movies you humans love, where they are being hunted down by a minesweeper, you need to be absolutely quiet for the next few minutes unless you want them to detect your presence.'

That made perfect tactical sense to me, but the other urgent question was whether or not we engaged the threat. Do that and we would blow any element of stealth that we had. And all eyes, even Tom's, were looking at me for the answer to that particular riddle.

'What are your orders, Commander?' Erin said, her voice strained.

My eyes started scanning the ocean bed. Just to our right was a dark ravine under a towering pinnacle of rock. Maybe there was a way we could still escape detection...

'Tom, can you drift us down into there?' I said, pointing towards the ravine.

'If I adjust our REV drive's lift to act like the equivalent of a ballast tank, then it shouldn't be a problem.'

I nodded. 'Okay, then do it. I need everyone to keep completely quiet until we're out of danger. If we're lucky, that sub will pass right over us and write it off as a false contact. Erin, follow Tom's lead.'

'Understood,' she replied.

With gentle adjustments using the REV drive, Tom began to angle us down towards the shadowed cover of the ravine, with *Artemis* tucked in behind.

The fine stream of bubbles trailed from both craft as we

watched the distance indicator to the enemy sub tick down to a thousand metres.

'Torpedo ports are already open on that damned Yasen sub. They're not taking any chances,' Ruby whispered, as we dropped lower and began to enter the ravine.

'Hopefully, that's just standard combat procedure until they've checked out the contact,' Tom replied.

'Okay, but just in case, *Artemis* and *Ariel* be ready to open fire on my orders,' I whispered.

'Roger that,' Daryl replied from onboard our sister craft.

Ruby toggled several icons that lit up red, before taking hold of the targeting joystick.

The darkness of the ravine began to envelop us as we dropped into it. *Artemis* was only twenty metres or so above us and was also about to enter. The distant beating of the enemy's propeller grew steadily louder as we descended into cover.

Tom was calmly focused on his flight screens as he made small, delicate movements to the REV drive control. He began to slow our descent as the rocky walls slid past *Ariel*.

I was just starting to think we were going to be okay when a grinding sound came from above. My gaze shot up to see that *Artemis* had caught the lip of the ravine, sending boulders dropping through the water around us.

And that was all it took to give us away.

'That Yasen has just launched a torpedo! Five seconds to impact, Commander!' Ruby said, her knuckles pure white as she clenched the joystick.

'Then get us out of here and engage!' I shouted.

Tom was already reacting, speeding up the thrusters to maximum as he increased the lift. We shot out of the ravine like a startled rabbit bolting from its burrow.

I looked back to see the *Artemis* still emerging from the

ravine... just as the sub's torpedo streamed out of the gloom and slammed into the towering finger of rock above the X103.

My stomach clenched as with a huge shockwave, an explosion boiled out from the impact, ripping through the rock edifice. In slow motion it began to crumple in on itself, collapsing downward into the path of the rising X103. Then I lost sight of the ship as the missile's shockwave slammed into us and spun *Ariel* around.

Tom quickly compensated, bringing us to a total stop as the flight deck gyros protested, fighting to keep it level.

On the virtual cockpit, there was another burst of bubbles from the nose of the enemy sub as it turned directly towards us.

'Second torpedo away!' Ruby said, her voice suddenly way too calm.

'Take it out!' I shouted.

'Already on it.'

Thudding sounds came from above and below us as a trail of flechette rounds raced out from our miniguns, straight into the path of the torpedo speeding towards us. The steel darts scythed through the torpedo and it exploded with a bright flash, the roar of its destruction echoing through *Ariel* as another shockwave slammed into us.

'Permission to fire Spearfish torpedoes, Commander,' Ruby said, her eyes steel.

'Do it!' I said, any sense of detachment gone. Despite the crew I knew had to be on that sub, this had fast become a kill or be killed scenario.

Tom looped us back around. Jack and Mike tightened their seat harnesses as *Ariel's* hull spun around us, although our stabilised deck remained level during the extreme manoeuvre.

'Spearfish locked and away,' Ruby said.

The missile leapt from our weapons port and tore straight

towards the Russian sub, which had begun to turn, its rudder at maximum, propellers churning hard through the water leaving a vortex in their wake. But the sub was far too close to avoid being hit and it was certainly way too slow in this underwater dance of death. The Spearfish effortlessly adjusted its own path to compensate and slammed straight into the side of the enemy craft.

With a deafening roar, audible even through the hull of our craft, a vast hole opened up in the side of the Yasen sub as air exploded from it in a torrent of bubbles. Then it seemed to crumple in on itself as the incredible pressure of the water tore it apart. The stern broke away first, small flashes of fire spitting from it as the two sections began to sink towards their watery grave at the bottom of the ocean.

I barely had to time to register the truly shocking loss of life before my attention snapped back to *Artemis*. The X103 still hadn't emerged from the ravine, into which huge boulders continued to fall.

My heart clenched into a ball. 'Erin, please tell me you guys are okay.'

'No...' Erin replied, her voice flat. 'We have a partial hull breach and Daryl has been crushed to death by a beam.'

I exchanged a shocked look with the others, almost too numb to fully comprehend what she'd just told me. 'What about you? Are you okay, Erin?'

'Trapped under the same beam. Also, although the REV drive is still online, *Artemis* is taking on water fast and the escape hatches are jammed shut under the rock fall. I'm afraid my mission is over, Commander.'

I clenched my hands into fists. 'No it's not, do you hear me? I need you on my next mission. You hang in there and that's a bloody order.'

We all heard Erin take a shuddering breath. 'Roger that,' she replied.

I turned to the others. 'What the hell are we going to do?'

Tom muted the comms, his face drawn. 'I don't know, but whatever it is we need to do it fast before she drowns.'

I stared at the column of bubbles rising from the ravine as nausea swirled through me. What on earth could we do at these kinds of depths? If I didn't come up with an answer to that right now, another one of our own would lose their lives.

CHAPTER EIGHTEEN

A LARGE STREAM of frothing water was now rising from the hull of *Artemis* as we looked down at it from our virtual cockpit. Its Chameleon system was clearly offline too as it had become visible beneath the mound of boulders that had partly trapped it in the ravine.

My mind was whirling, desperately trying to come up with a plan to save Erin before it was too late.

Niki's voice cut in over the comm. 'That Zumwalt destroyer has just opened its missile hatches.'

Tom shot me a worried look. 'Those ships have vertical launch torpedoes and you can guarantee they will know we're down here by now.'

'Permission to open fire on that ship, Lauren?' Niki asked.

My stomach knotted. 'But that will give away your presence,' I said.

'I think we're long past that point. This has become a battle for survival,' Jack said, his expression drawn.

'Yep, a damned torpedo has just launched and is arcing over, ready to enter the water,' Niki shouted. 'Permission to fire on it, Commander?'

It seemed the decision had been made for me. 'Take it out, Niki!' I replied.

'Roger that.'

Over the speakers we heard the rattle of the Pangolin's miniguns opening up.

An explosion appeared above the surface of the ocean, the intense bright light briefly illuminating the gloom around us, casting sharp shadows across the ravine before fading again.

'Okay, that certainly got their attention,' Niki said. 'But now we're coming under heavy anti-aircraft fire from that damned destroyer.'

'Has your Chameleon system failed?' I said.

'No, they're just concentrating their fire on where we were when our miniguns started getting busy. Thankfully, thanks to swift thinking on the part of my pilot, that's two miles away from our current position.'

I felt a surge of relief. 'In that case keep moving around the sky like your arse is on fire and take out any more of those bloody torpedoes as they launch them.'

'On it. I'm throwing the $X103$'s miniguns into the mix too. Between the two ships we should be more than able to deal with any threat from that Zumwalt.'

'Okay, but we just need cover until we can rescue Erin,' I said. 'After that, fall back.'

'Understood.'

I returned my attention to the others in the cockpit and killed the comms channel so Erin couldn't hear the next bit of our conversation. 'Okay, we need a plan to save Erin and fast. Does anyone have any ideas? I've got nothing.'

'The first problem is that we haven't got the kind of advanced pressure suits we need to operate at these depths and even if we did, I'm not sure how we could get into the ship with those boulders on top of its hatch,' Jack said.

'What about the new WASPs, would they be powerful enough to clear the debris away so *Artemis* can get out of there?' Mike asked.

'Nothing like, I'm afraid,' Ruby replied. 'Looking at the specs, their new propulsion system is designed for manoeuvring and has nowhere near the power to clear those boulders. Also, I hate to point it out but our X103s aren't fitted with an airlock, which is going to make a rescue almost impossible.'

I tried to fight the panic rising in me. 'Shit. There must be *something* we can do to save her?'

'Actually there is,' Lucy's voice said, as her avatar popped up. 'I've been running the numbers and if you can get *Ariel* close enough then I can extend part of her gravity field in a bulge. Utilising that, together with Ariel's auxiliary pumps to increase cabin pressure, I can effectively create an underwater passageway clear of water from your ramp to *Artemis's* top hatch.'

'You mean we could literally drop down on *Artemis* and clear the rubble by hand?' I asked.

'I can't see why not,' Lucy said.

Fresh hope burned through me. 'I could seriously hug you right now, Lucy, if you were here in person.'

She beamed at me. 'Hold that thought for later. Meanwhile, I'll run the necessary alterations to your REV drive's gravity field. It will take me a few minutes to code a patch in though.'

'As fast as you can, Lucy.' I pressed the comms button. 'Erin, we have a plan and we're coming for you.'

'What are you going to do?' Erin called out over the radio link, the noise of rushing water audible in the background.

'Something batshit crazy, as you'd expect from our team,' Mike said.

'Right...' Erin replied.

I nodded towards Tom. 'Okay, take us in as close as possible. Everyone else get ready to form a rescue party.'

'On it, Lauren,' Tom replied.

With a gentle nudge of our thrusters, Tom began to manoeuvre us closer. As *Ariel* descended back towards the ravine, bursts of light kept illuminating the ocean – the continuing cover fire that *Thor* was dishing out against the Zumwalt's torpedoes.

Jack looked towards the silent firework display happening on the surface. 'It looks like Niki and his crew are doing one hell of a job up there.'

'And thankfully keeping us all alive in the process,' I said, as Tom settled *Ariel* into a hover directly over the top of *Artemis* with only a couple of metres between our craft.

From this close we could see that multiple panels on *Artemis* had buckled under the rockfall that the craft had been caught in. Sparks of electricity were also coming from an exposed section of the torus accelerator of the REV drive. Of more immediate concern was a single large boulder sitting on top of the main hatch.

'That looks like it's going to be really heavy to lift,' Ruby said, eyeballing it.

Jack unclipped his harness and headed towards a tool locker at the edge of the deck. 'We can use the winch on the ramp exit with a harness to drag that boulder clear once Lucy opens up that gravity air tunnel of hers.'

I nodded. 'Talking of which, how's it coming along, Lucy?'

'Just another minute and it will be ready.'

'Okay, everyone get ready because every second is really going to count here. Ruby, you stay onboard and operate *Ariel's* weapons in case any of those torpedoes get past Niki.'

'Understood, Commander,' she replied.

I was just unclipping my harness when a line of green light

shot out from the Zumwalt battleship above us. The beam swung around the sky in sweeping arcs like a searchlight until it seemed to lock onto something.

'Shit, they've just fired some sort of laser that has taken out our Chameleon cloak,' Niki said. 'I need permission to take offensive action directly against that destroyer.'

'What's that meant to mean?' I asked.

Tom stood up and turned towards me. 'He means he needs to take out that Zumwalt.'

I stared at him. 'But there are people on that ship!'

Mike and Jack were looking between us, appalled.

But Tom's eyes held mine, his gaze unflinching. 'This is now a fully fledged battle. You have to choose between our people's lives or the lives of the people who are trying to kill us. Your choice, Lauren.'

His words were hard, but I knew they had to be in a situation like this when the truth, however brutal, was a matter of life or death. And in that moment I had absolutely no choice other than to issue the order.

'Okay, Niki. Ruby, too. You both do whatever you have to do to sink that bloody warship.'

'Spooling up power to the railgun now,' Niki said calmly.

'Arming a Spearfish torpedo,' Ruby confirmed. 'Target solution locked on and firing now.'

With a loud gurgle of water a Spearfish leapt from one of our ports and streaked up towards the destroyer's hull.

'Railgun round fired and... oh fucking hell!' Niki exclaimed.

A flash of light came from the Zumwalt, followed by a distance boom as a white cloud of water erupted around the enemy ship. Then, even though there was a vast expanse of water between us, a loud boom still reached us through *Ariel's* walls. The Spearfish torpedo reached the turbulent boiling water and then suddenly veered away at a right angle.

'What the hell?' Ruby said, looking at her weapon targeting display.

Then we all saw for ourselves what had happened. The boiling water began to settle, revealing the destroyer still sitting on the surface of the sea, looking totally unscathed.

'How the hell is that thing still floating? Why was our torpedo just deflected?' Ruby asked.

'Probably the same reason *Thor's* railgun round didn't do any damage,' Lucy replied as her avatar appeared. 'The really bad news is that the Zumwalt seems to be using some sort of gravity shield to envelop it. It seems that the Overseers have been taking notes from their previous encounters with our latest X-craft.'

'You mean we can't even hit that damn thing?' I asked.

'If even a hypersonic round can't scratch it than I'm afraid it looks that way, Lauren,' Lucy said. 'Meanwhile, with the destroyer's gravity shield still up they can fire that laser weapon of theirs straight at a target with impunity, unlike us, who have to drop our gravity shields to fire.'

'Okay, as bad as this all is, there is at least one bit of good news,' Niki's voice cut in. 'Thankfully our ablative armour did its job and absorbed the blast, but we won't be able to take that sort of punishment indefinitely. So we'll do our best to keep them busy, but you'd better get on with your rescue, Lauren.'

'Understood, but you still need to fall back as soon as we've finished down here. Lucy, please tell me you're ready with that gravity field tunnel to link us to *Artemis*?'

'I just finished coding the patch for the REV drive. Activating now,' she replied.

A gurgling sound came from outside *Ariel* and then something that resembled a – to be perfectly, revoltingly honest – giant snot bubble appeared in our craft's belly. It began to grow downwards into a tentacle that was reached out towards *Artemis's* partly buried hatch. Then with a popping sound, it latched onto the other craft.

'Gravity umbilical connected. You need to get a move on, guys,' Lucy said. 'If they launch a torpedo whilst our gravity is stretched thin like this, we'll take a significant amount of damage.'

'Okay, let's move it, people,' I said.

Jack activated the ramp controls and began to unwind the winch.

Even though I knew what to expect, the air still caught in my lungs as what was outside waiting for us came into view.

An undulating tunnel of water led down from the bottom of *Ariel*, directly onto *Artemis's* hull. The walls shimmered with the light from our cockpit as the gloom of the deep ocean pressed in round it. It resembled one of those transparent underwater tunnels you sometimes get in the really big aquariums, where you can see the fish swimming all round you. The big difference between them was that down here, there were no acrylic walls to stop the water rushing in if the gravity field failed for any reason.

'This is completely safe, Lucy, right?' Mike asked, peering down at it.

'As much as I can make it,' she replied.

'Then that's good enough for me,' Jack said as he headed towards the end of the ramp with the winch cable hook in his hand.

The rest of us slipped earbuds in to maintain comms contact with Erin and Ruby, then joined Jack on the ramp. He was using a remote to slacken some more line from the winch.

I could see *Artemis's* hull just a few feet below, its hull still glistening with sea water and silt from the landslide. The large boulder was still sitting on top of the hatch. Even though it was a small leap down, I found myself casting a sideways glance at Mike's prosthetic leg, which he caught me doing.

'Don't sweat it, Lauren, I can manage this.'

'Sorry, I didn't mean to—'

He waved my apology away. 'Don't worry. I'd be wondering the same in your position. But I promise you I'm match fit. And all that exercise in the gym to prepare me for active missions again has to count for something, right?'

I smiled at him. 'Right.'

I got ready to drop down, aiming for a spot towards the summit of *Artemis's* hull, and leapt. I landed with a *thunk* on the metal surface as the seawater splashed off my boots. I was followed a moment later by Tom.

In this, the strangest of impossible corridors linking our two ships, I could immediately feel the chill of the ocean around me. The intense smell of brine was already flooding my nostrils.

I glanced up to see the destroyer's green laser beam firing at its assailants. Without the virtual cockpit to render the enemy ship, the only other clue to its presence was the smooth bulge in the water that its hull was making.

With another *thunk*, Mike landed next to us with not so much as a slip as he crouched to absorb the landing. He gave me a wink.

Jack was the next to land, trailing the harness down with him. He immediately began to tow it towards the large boulder.

I pressed my finger to my earbud. 'Erin, we're standing on top of *Artemis* and should be with you any moment now.'

'You're what? But how?' she replied.

'Long story and too little time to explain. Right now all you need to know is we're starting to clear the rocks from your top hatch and we will be entering shortly.'

'Understood and thank you, however you're pulling this off.'

Jack finished trailing the wire around the boulder and looping it back through its hook. Then, grabbing the remote box from his belt, he pressed a green button on it. At once the winch on the ramp began to wind in the slack. The wire went taut and with a squeal, the rock began to grind its way backwards off the hatch. As it began to tip over the edge of the sloping hull, Jack released the cable.

The boulder tumbled away down *Artemis's* hull towards the water lapping around the base of the gravity tunnel. It crashed through the invisible barrier with a splash, sending ripples radiating out through the walls as the rock dropped away into the ravine.

'Ah, I was wondering what would happen if one of us slipped,' Tom said as we watched the huge boulder disappear.

'Yes, I should probably have mentioned that part,' Lucy said through our earbuds.

I raised my eyebrows at Tom as we all set to work moving the rest of the smaller rocks by hand, sending them on their way to join their larger cousin at the bottom of the ravine. It was hard work, but in less than another minute we'd cleared it enough to open the hatch.

'Shit! Heads up people, we have incoming,' Ruby said over our earbuds.

With clattering booms, *Ariel's* minigun let loose, and the projectiles lanced straight up towards a torpedo that was hurtling down towards us. The stream of flechettes scythed through the missile and it detonated with a flash of light and a cloud of expanding foaming water. The shockwave reached us a second later and both ships shook. More alarmingly, cracking sounds came from what was left of the stone pillar before it stilled again.

'Take that, you son of a bitch,' Ruby snapped.

Niki's voice broke in over the comm. 'Sorry about that. Those sneaky bastards launched that last torpedo when we were making a high speed manoeuvre.'

'Thankfully Ruby was on the case. Are you doing okay?' I asked.

'As well as can be expected, but our armour-plating has

soaked up a fair number of direct strikes. We're going to have to fall back sooner rather than later.'

'Hopefully, we won't be much longer, Niki. We should be able to get Erin and get clear from *Artemis* any minute. Then we can work out together what we're going to do about that bloody destroyer,' I said.

'Roger that,' Niki replied as Jack and Tom grabbed hold of the lip of the hatch and heaved it open.

Erin stared up at us from her flight seat, her foot trapped in place by a beam that had collapsed from the roof. My gaze travelled the length of that same beam that had crushed Daryl's skull into a bloody pulp. Grief for the young weapons officer pulsed through me as bile filled my throat. The guy was too young to die like this.

Tom and Jack traded grim looks and began to clamber down the ladder into the cockpit.

Mike glanced down into the cockpit and grimaced. 'Oh God, that poor guy.'

'I know...' I shut my eyes momentarily. I needed to focus on the living, not the dead.

I drew in a deep breath and started to descend the ladder into the darkened cockpit, lit only by a low red light from the emergency battery backup system.

The bottom third of the cockpit had already been flooded by the water cascading down from several cracks in the hull's metal panels.

Tom had thankfully found a flight jacket from somewhere and draped it over Daryl's head for dignity. Meanwhile, Jack tried to pull the beam off of Erin's foot, which was twisted at such a shocking angle that it could only be broken. The poor girl stifled a yelp of pain as Jack tried to lift the beam clear and only succeeded in making it shift a fraction.

My own nausea forgotten, I crossed to Erin and took her hand in mine. 'How are you doing there?'

'Oh, I've had better days, Commander.'

'Look, enough with this *commander* nonsense already. You call me Lauren. Understand?'

She gave me a small smile. 'Okay, Lauren,' but as Jack tried to shift the beam again, this time with Tom, she practically crushed my hand as she whimpered.

I glanced at the ceiling, far too aware that a torpedo was probably going to land on our heads at any moment, and caught Mike's gaze. He looked thoughtful.

He disappeared and a moment later reappeared with the winch harness in his hand. 'You guys should probably try this.'

'Good thinking,' I said.

But Jack frowned. 'Sorry for the straight talking, Erin, but I'm not sure that a winch is going to be powerful enough to shift that beam.'

She gave him a slow nod. 'Got it. Then just leave me with a pistol to end it and get yourselves to safety.'

I stared at this young woman, not sure I could be quite so brave if I was in her place. I certainly wasn't going to listen to that sort of talk.

'Absolutely not on my watch,' I said. 'Tom, Jack, we'll all try pushing together as the winch starts to take the slack. Hopefully, that will be enough to shift this damned thing.'

'Got to be worth a try, because I'm with Lauren on this,' Jack said. 'There's no way I'm going to leave you to die in here, Erin.'

'That goes for me too,' Tom said as he patted her gently on the shoulder.

Erin breathed in through her nose and nodded, a single tear running down her cheek. It made me even more determined to save her, especially after the awful loss of Daryl.

With Jack's help, I was looping the winch wire around the beam when Ruby's voice rang out over our earbuds.

'Hey, I don't want to worry you, guys, but that last torpedo shockwave seems to have loosened a few more rocks on that pillar and it has begun to shift again. The headline is that you need to move it.'

'Understood,' I replied. 'Guys, we need to hurry this up.'

Jack grabbed the remote box and pressed the green button. Mike joined us as the wire began to take up the slack, then we all got our hands under the beam. Bracing ourselves as best we could, we began to heave and push. A shudder passed through the beam as Erin squealed in pain.

Gritting my teeth, I pulled with everything I had.

'Will you bloody move, you son of a bitch!' Jack said as the muscles on his neck started to cable.

Despite the chilled air flooding the cabin from the open hatch, beads of sweat began to pop out all over my forehead.

The collapsed beam trembled again, but it still wasn't shifting. Despair was starting to creep in, an emotion I could see mirrored in everyone else's expressions too.

'Dear God, just leave me here. This isn't going to work,' Erin said, her face pale.

'Not with that attitude it's not, Erin,' Tom said, his tone sharp. 'So rather than just sit there will you bloody well give us a hand?' Then a rare smile cracked his face.

And just like that the mood shifted. I pulled harder than I ever had in my life, my muscles singing with the strain almost as loudly as the winch wire that hummed like an out of tune harp.

Jack braced his back against the beam, his feet shoving against another pillar that had burst through the floor. Then with all of us pushing with everything we had, the beam suddenly groaned and bent sideways. Erin's foot was suddenly, thankfully free.

'You see, I told you it would be okay,' Tom said, panting hard.

'Yes, and now I believe you,' Erin said with a smile, gasping for breath.

None of us was going to hang around for a victory lap though. Jack had already helped Erin up from her chair and was moving her to the ladder as she gritted her teeth with every jarring step. Then Jack pulled her over his shoulder and with a fireman's lift, carried her up the ladder and out onto the hull with some assistance from Mike.

I climbed out next with Tom right behind. But then any sense of relief that had briefly filled me was swept away as a violent vibration suddenly ran through *Artemis's* hull.

'That pillar of rock is fucking giving way,' Ruby shouted through my earbud.

I glanced up to see the massive stone formation starting to tip straight down towards us.

Erin screamed in pain as Jack threw her onto *Ariel's* ramp and we followed her up onto the hull. At that same moment, a massive boulder about three metres across broke loose and began to plummet towards *Artemis*. Jack and Mike dragged Erin, whimpering, up into *Ariel's* cockpit as Tom's head began to emerge from the hatch.

In that frozen moment, I had a second to register it as he glanced up towards the plummeting rocks, and then his eyes found mine.

Time stopped. And that moment was something that was going to haunt me for the rest of my life.

A look of utter calm and acceptance filled Tom's face.

Then time sped up again as the boulder crashed straight through the gravity tunnel and down onto *Artemis*. The hatch slammed shut, trapping Tom inside the other craft. With an explosion of water, the gravity tunnel shattered as *Artemis* was shoved downwards by the massive boulder's impact, bubbles bursting from its hull as it started to buckle.

'Tom!' I screamed as the saucer plummeted away into the darkness and a wall of seawater surged towards me.

Then strong hands were dragging me upwards onto the ramp, but I fought them even as freezing water crashed over me. I was yanked backwards past Mike, who'd slammed his hand on the emergency close button. Multiple warning alarms filled the cockpit as the view of the ravine disappeared. But still I struggled, trying to get back to Tom. Then the geysers of water that had been erupting around the edge of the ramp finally slowed to gentle dribble.

'You have to get *Ariel* clear,' Tom's voice said over my earbud.

'No, we're coming back for you,' I sobbed as Jack finally released me.

'No time, the cockpit will be flooded by then.'

'But you have to let us try to save you,' I pleaded, even thought I could hear the certainty in his voice.

'No, I'm going to activate *Artemis's* self-destruct sequence. Hopefully, that will be enough to convince that bloody Zumwalt destroyer that any threat down here has been neutralised.'

'But you can't throw your life away like this,' I whispered.

'I'm dead anyway, Lauren, and I'm sorry. Goodbye my friends. Delphi, initiate *Ariel's* emergency escape procedure to one klick. Override order, authorisation Overlord.'

'Authorisation Overlord, command accepted,' Delphi calmly announced from the cockpit.

I felt *Ariel* surge away, its thrusters humming with full power. I turned and ran back up into the cockpit to see that Erin had dropped into the pilot's seat.

'Stop *Ariel*, we have to go back for Tom, Erin,' I said.

She held up her hands. I could see the joystick and throttle moving by itself. 'I can't,' she replied, tears in her eyes. 'Tom has temporarily locked me out with that override command.'

'But there has to be a way! Lucy, is there anything you can do?'

Her avatar appeared in a video window, her face tense. 'I'm so sorry, Lauren. All those safety protocols that were built in after Red's shenanigans mean I can't override Delphi when an executive order has been issued.'

'You mean there's absolutely nothing we can do to save Tom?'

Lucy simply shook her head, her expression ashen.

Ariel was gaining speed as Delphi manoeuvred us away. The rocky pillar crumbled downwards into the ravine, burying *Artemis* under tons of rock.

Then a huge pulse briefly rocked *Ariel* as an explosion boiled up from the canyon with a flash of light. A second pulse of light, stronger than the first, lit up the ocean bed. Then just for a split second our virtual cockpit went dark and our lights flickered. A moment later, with a high- pitched whine, the view was rebooted and we could see outside again.

'Some sort of magnetic pulse, probably *Artemis's* fusion reactor letting go,' Ruby said, staring at her CIC screen.

'I'm afraid *Artemis* has been destroyed,' Lucy said, her voice catching on the last syllable. 'It might be little comfort right now, but the destroyer does seem to have bought Tom's bluff and has stopped launching missiles.'

So even at the end, Tom had succeeded in trying to save the rest of us.

I clenched my hands into fists, driving my fingernails into my palms hard enough to draw blood. As I slumped into my seat, my heart shattered into a million pieces.

CHAPTER NINETEEN

TOM IS DEAD... The thought kept looping through my head. Nothing made sense anymore.

I was only dimly aware of what was happening around me. The retreating view of the pillar of rock as it crumbled down into the ravine, while Erin, even with her broken ankle, manoeuvred us away from the site at high speed. The bellow of *Ariel's* pumps evacuating the water that had managed to get into the cockpit before the ramp had closed. Jack, giving our new pilot a shot of adrenaline. Ruby, frantically scanning her screens for any sign of a further attack.

Tom is dead...

Then Mike was kneeling before me and looking into my eyes. 'Lauren, what are your orders?'

What were my orders? To turn *Ariel* round and get away from here as fast as possible. To stand on the shore of Cuba and scream at the sea for taking my friend's life in such a callous manner? To curl up in bed with Jack's arms wrapped around me and sob my heart out?

Mike gently took my hands in his and peered into my eyes. 'Lauren, look we're all in shock but we need to do something.'

Do something?

My mind felt locked up, the shock of the suddenness of Tom's death so overwhelming that my mind had frozen like a crashed computer.

I looked across at Erin, her foot twisted at an awful angle to her leg and tears streaming down her face, but who was still flying the rivets off *Ariel* now she'd regained control from Delphi. As she headed us away from the pillar of rocks that had become Tom's tombstone, I hated myself. I couldn't regret giving the order to save Erin's life but the price we paid for it would haunt me forever.

But Tom's life hadn't been the only casualty. Daryl's life had been snuffed out just like that and one look at Erin's face told me she was grappling with the death of a close friend, just like I was.

I needed to be better than this.

'Lauren, tell us what to do?' Mike repeated.

I gazed back at him numbly.

'Oh for fuck's sake, Lauren, will you bloody pull yourself together? We need our commander right now,' Ruby snapped.

Her words cut through the log jam of thoughts in my head.

Everyone around me was doing their jobs and I needed to do mine. It was exactly what Tom would have said if he'd still been here. A kick up the bum when I needed it most.

I wiped the back of my hand across my cheeks, leaving them streaked with the tears that I hadn't even known I'd been crying. Time to reboot myself. I would have to grieve later. Just like Erin and the rest of the team.

I sucked in a deep, shaky breath. 'Okay...'

Jack shot me such a look of compassion that it nearly set me off again. Every person in the cockpit, even Ruby, was watching me with genuine concern.

I exhaled and met my team's gazes in full. 'Okay, our mission objective remains the same. We still need to get to the underwater formation. So, let's go and kick arse, because that's exactly what Tom would want us to do.'

'And she's back,' Mike said.

The lives of everyone onboard this craft depended on what I decided to do next and also those of Niki and his crew, still slugging it out with the destroyer back on the surface.

I turned on my comm channel to talk to *Thor*. 'Niki, please report in. What's your situation?'

We heard the background clatter of minigun fire as his voice came on. 'Shielding down to thirty percent, but the good news is that that destroyer has stopped launching those damned torpedoes, as you probably noticed.'

I knew then that Tom would have been pleased that his sacrifice hadn't been in vain. Now I needed to play my part to honour what he'd done.

I breathed out slowly. 'Niki, you need to disengage from combat with that destroyer and pull back to a safe distance for now, whilst we head over to investigate the site,' I said. 'But it might be an idea to call for more backup.'

'Already done. We have a squadron of six Pangolins on the way,' Niki replied. 'They should be with us within sixty minutes.'

'Good, now get yourself safe because...' My voice trailed away. There was so much I wanted to tell Niki about how Tom's sacrifice had bought us valuable time. But even thinking about Tom brought a stabbing pain to my chest.

'We will. Good luck, Lauren,' Niki said, filling in the pause for me.

I turned my attention to Ruby. 'Right, rather than just go storming in there, because God knows what other surprises they have waiting for us, I suggest it's time to try out your new underwater WASPs and scout out the area first.'

'Good plan, Commander,' Ruby replied, all brisk and businesslike again. 'Delphi, launch WASP swarm.'

'Launching WASP swarm now,' Delphi repeated.

Ruby flicked a few buttons and twelve small video windows appeared on the virtual cockpit. They showed the live camera feeds of the WASP drones mounted in their racks in the loading bay. Water gurgled up around them as Delphi flooded the compartment.

Then a hatch opened beneath them and one by one, trailing a data cable that spooled out from a dozen reels, the drones dropped out through the hatch and into the sea. They rapidly split apart like dandelion seeds caught in the breeze, each heading for the lip of the valley about a klick away from us.

I turned to the rest of the crew and had to avoid Jack's soft gaze, which threatened to unlock the grief that I was doing my best to keep at bay.

'Okay, whilst we're waiting to see what the swarm discovers, I suggest we land on the seabed,' I said. 'That way there'll be no chance of one of those bloody underwater mics picking up our thrusters and realising there's still a craft down here.'

'Now that sounds like a good plan to me,' Jack said.

I nodded, still avoiding his gaze. 'Erin, please take us down to land on the seabed.'

With a deft nudge of the controls she sent us down into a gentle dive, landing with the barest shake onto the bottom.

The laser fire from the destroyer had ceased above us, indicating that Niki had now pulled back to a safe distance. At least that was one thing I could relax about.

As the rest of us watched the live feeds from the WASPs heading towards the target, Jack had a moment to check on Erin.

'Okay, let me have a look at that busted ankle of yours,' he said.

But Erin shook her head. 'No, even looking at it will make me pass out. As good as Delphi's flight routines are, a human pilot is better in this sort of situation. So for now just some more painkillers will do nicely. Afterwards, I'll happily hand everything back over to Delphi and you can do whatever you want to my ankle. Deal?'

'Are you sure?' I asked, properly meeting her eyes.

She nodded. 'It will help take my mind off Daryl. But I just want you to know that if I could, I'd swap positions with Tom in a heartbeat so he'd still be here with you now.'

That had me fighting down a stone in my throat. I nodded, hoping tears wouldn't betray me. 'Okay. Deal,' I eventually said.

'You should know that once I get an idea into my head I'm pretty stubborn,' Erin continued.

'That reminds me of a certain someone I know,' Mike said, giving me a smile.

Even though my heart was broken, his words brought a smile to my own lips. 'You better believe it.'

It took every ounce of self-discipline to force myself to concentrate on the video feeds as we all waited to see what the WASPS had discovered. In any other circumstances I would seriously have considered asking Jack for a sedative, but just like Erin, I needed to stay sharp.

Jack pointed up towards the surface. 'Wow will you look at how many there are now?'

I looked at the feed he was gesturing towards to see hundreds, maybe a thousand even, of whales of every species, circling slowly around the circumference of the valley ahead.

'There's no way that's normal behaviour. Whales don't gather in those numbers,' Mike said.

I watched, mesmerised, and nodded. 'Leon mentioned something about running into a lot of whale activity in the area and I think we may have just found the reason why. They're obviously drawn to this area for some reason. But any idea why exactly, anyone?'

Lucy's avatar popped up on the screen. She gave me a quick look, then cleared her throat. 'My money would be on it having everything to do with the active micro mind sending out a broadcast carrier signal on the same frequency that the whales use to communicate.'

'So going on the fact that the whales have gathered here at all, that suggests the micro mind is still here?' Jack asked.

'I think it's increasingly likely,' Lucy said.

'Well, we're about to get our first proper look at the site,' Ruby said. 'One of my WASPs has almost reached the edge of the valley, so maybe we'll see for ourselves any moment now.'

She transferred the feed from her CIC to the virtual cockpit for us all to watch.

The drone had reached the edge of the rocky ridge, which suddenly fell away to reveal a large valley. There was a combination of gasps and whistles as we all took in the view.

Laid out at the bottom of the valley were a least a dozen stone pyramids and dotted between them were large cylindrical stone buildings. There were also tall columns that finished in a point. But as incredible as that sight was, what took it completely over the edge into something truly mind-bending was that the structures had pulses of light dotted all over them.

Jack shook his head. 'Jesus, that place is lit up like a Christmas tree. This is like a far bigger version of what we found at the Richat Structure.'

Lucy's gaze lingered on mine for a moment. I could tell there was so much she wanted to say to me about what had happened to Tom. But instead of addressing that particular elephant in the cockpit, she directed her energy to answering Jack's point.

'Even though neither myself nor Poseidon recognises this site yet, we're both certain that this is Angelus technology. Frustratingly, I feel I know the answer to exactly what this is and it's on the tip of my tongue. It's moments like this I feel like I suffer from the AI equivalent of amnesia. But what I can tell you is that there is definitely an active micro mind down there powering all those systems.'

'In that case, Ruby, can you direct all the WASPs towards the source of that quake?' I said. 'But take it slow because I don't want to give away their presence to any more of those underwater mics.'

'All over it, Commander,' Ruby replied.

The views from the drones now showed different aspects of the structure as they started to descend towards it.

As the drone dropped towards the valley floor it soon became obvious that the pyramids were massive, easily at least six hundred metres high. But unlike the last Angelus pyramid that we'd encountered back at the Richat Structure, these were covered by a thick carpet of lichen and were made from stone rather than crystal.

Several of the WASPs reached the edge of the site and began heading down what looked very much like streets. But the structures that towered over them looked distinctly strange, more like lightning conductors than anything.

As the drone proceeded along the street, it began to open out and then at last we caught our first view of what sat at the heart of this Angelus megastructure.

Immediately Ruby killed the forward momentum on the drones. 'What the holy fuck is that?' she said, voicing the thought for all of us.

On several of the video feeds we now had a view of a wide plaza that was at least two kilometres wide and sizewise, put Cuba's Revolution Square to shame. But it was what was going on within it that really snagged our attention.

Human made structures were everywhere, from banks of

what looked like missile launchers, to some sort of large white underwater habitation on tall hydraulic legs, its portholes blazing with light.

'Whatever that thing is, the area looks heavily defended with what I'm guessing are torpedo launcher emplacements,' Ruby said.

'So can you neutralise them with your drones if we head in to take that base out?' I asked.

'I'm not sure I can, even if I station all of my WASPs around each one. My concern is that *Ariel's* defences might be quickly overwhelmed.'

Mike gave me a hesitant look and then I understood why when he spoke.

'Look, I know this is a painful subject to bring up, but I have a pretty good idea what Tom would say if he was still with us.'

'Go on,' I said in a small voice.

'That we should gather as much intelligence as we can and then put together a plan, rather than go in all guns blazing.'

I felt that pain in my chest stick its claws into me again. But grieving for my lost friend would have to wait until the right time to look it in the face.

'You're right, Mike, and thank you for the reminder.'

He smiled at me.

'Ruby, can you send just a single WASP unit in for a closer look at that underwater base?'

'Absolutely, Commander.' She selected an icon and a single video feed from the WASP unit nearest the plaza filled the virtual cockpit. 'Okay, Delphi, give me control of WASP unit nine.'

'You have control,' Delphi announced.

Ruby took hold of the joystick. With a small amount of throttle she began to propel the small drone forward, keeping it so low to the seabed that it almost scraped through the silt.

The structures either side of the craft fell away and then it was out in the plaza with a distinct lack of cover.

'Come on little fella, you can make it,' Mike whispered to himself, but loud enough for us to hear.

Our drone flying at little more than walking speed meant the underwater base seemed permanently stuck in the distance. But slowly, metre by metre, the WASP closed in on what had to be an Overseer facility.

I noticed as a pile of shattered crystal appeared in the silt ahead of the drone. For one awful moment I thought the Overseers had destroyed the micro mind. But then I saw that the profile was far too slim.

'That's a Guardian that's been shot down isn't it, Lucy?' I said.

She frowned. 'I'm afraid so, Lauren. And it's not just one of them either.' Highlight boxes were appearing all across the square now, each marking a pile of crystal remains. 'It seems the Overseers have been doing their best to destroy the AIs that were defending this facility. That would also explain why it's taken them so much time to recover this particular micro mind.'

Mike scowled. 'Those absolute bastards. We're talking sentient entities here.'

'Exactly,' Lucy replied, grim-faced.

The WASP slid past the remains of the Guardian and headed on towards one of the large supporting legs of a torpedo launcher. As it neared we all got a clearer view of the weapon system. It seemed to be on a rotating mount, but it was only as we passed that I noticed something more significant.

'Hang on, is anyone else picking up on the fact that the torpedo battery is pointing inwards towards that underwater base?'

Lucy nodded. 'You have a point there, Lauren. After

analysing the feeds from the rest of the swarm it seems that all the torpedoes are doing the same.'

'You don't think they're targeting their own base after taking out all those Guardians?' Mike said.

'Maybe they have already recovered the micro mind and it's in that base, so it's some sort of security measure in case it tries to escape?' Jack said.

My heart sped up at the idea. 'Hopefully we'll learn the answer to that riddle before long, and if the micro mind is in there, that's another reason not to go storming in.'

'Absolutely, Commander,' Ruby said.

The WASP was now drawing closer to the base and from its low angle, thanks to Ruby hugging the floor with it, we had a view of the belly of the raised structure. At one end was a rectangular opening, through which we could see water lapping on the surface of a pool. On that sat Alvarez's white sub. A walled metal room with curved beams was visible above it.

'So that explains where Alvarez and Fischer are hiding,' I said.

'Yes, it looks like they entered the base through the dock on the underside of the facility,' Lucy said. 'The air pressure inside that room obviously keeps the water at bay.'

'Safer than relying on an airlock connection, I guess,' Erin said.

'Exactly,' Lucy replied.

As the WASP closed in we began to get a clearer look at the rear of the base. Three corridors led out towards what appeared to be a ragged hole in the middle of the plaza, about three metres across. Over it was a large gantry and slung beneath it were three winches with large cables, two of which disappeared straight down through the hole. The third cable was connected to a round white metal craft with portholes all over it. The craft was connected to one of the corridors by an airlock built into the side.

Jack gestured towards it. 'That looks like some sort of bathysphere.'

'Like the old-fashioned diving bells that divers originally used to explore the deep?' I said.

'Pretty much the same thing,' Lucy replied before Jack could. 'Looking at the design and the thickness of the hull around those portholes, I'd say it was designed to dive to a considerable depth.'

I glanced at the submersible. 'Deeper than their sub can get to?'

'Definitely. The round design of a bathysphere is all about surviving extreme pressure. So it looks like wherever that hole leads, it's somewhere very, very deep indeed.'

A tingle of excitement ran down my spine. 'Okay, somehow we need to get down there too, but the obvious problem is that that hole is way too small for *Ariel* to fit through. Besides, the moment we try to get closer we'll have all those mics picking up the noise from our thrusters, not to mention those torpedo batteries. So we need to brainstorm our next move.'

Jack sucked the air between his teeth. 'We really need a sound to mask the audio signature of *Ariel's* thrusters, something that sounds natural in this environment.'

My gaze snapped up to the whales still circling the crater. 'Like whale song?'

Lucy nodded. 'The WASPs are fitted with electronic oscillators, which vibrate the hull, turning the drone into one big speaker when needed. So we could certainly program them to broadcast something pretty convincing.'

Ruby gave a sharp nod. 'Hell yeah. Then I could manoeuvre them past those mics, sounding just like a passing whale pod, and *Ariel* can sneak on by.'

A plan was starting to form in my mind. 'Okay, how about this for a plan? So we neutralise those mics and sneak past them. Then... Lucy, can we use a gravity bubble to connect us to their dock? If we can, then we can enter the base, neutralise anyone who's in there and recover the micro mind.'

'And if it isn't there?' Mike asked.

I gestured towards the bathysphere. 'Then we take that thing down the shaft. The Overseers wouldn't have gone to all that effort for no reason. I strongly suspect the micro mind will be down there.'

Erin gawped at me. 'Seriously, there are so many things that could go wrong with that plan.'

Jack grinned. 'Welcome to the world of *seat of her pants planning* that is Lauren's speciality.'

'Isn't that the truth?' Ruby muttered as she turned the WASP round and headed it back towards the buildings at the edge of the plaza.

CHAPTER TWENTY

Ruby had finished manoeuvring her WASP swarm into position around the underwater mics that she'd managed to locate running along the lip of the valley.

'Lucy, how's that whale song coming along?' I called out. 'Are we ready for a performance?'

'Downloading them into the WASPs now,' she replied as her avatar popped up on the cockpit's virtual screen. 'I've put some minke song in there along with a backing track of blue whales. It's quite the mixtape if I say so myself.'

'All I'm worried about is that it will be enough to convince whoever is monitoring the feeds from those mics,' I said.

'Oh don't you worry yourself about that. If I were a whale I'd be convinced,' she said loftily. 'Okay, the last few lines of code and...done! A new icon should be appearing in your CIC screen any time now, Ruby. Just hit that and your swarm will start singing.'

'Then let's give this a whirl,' Ruby said, pressing the green pulsing icon that had just appeared in front of her.

At once, the incredibly haunting sounds of whales calling to each other came from all around us beyond *Ariel's* hull.

'Wow, you weren't kidding, Lucy. That sounds like the real thing,' Jack said.

Ruby nodded. 'So let's manoeuvre the WASPs around to make our floor show even more convincing for our audience.'

The video feeds from the dozen drones began to slowly swoop and dive, keeping to our side of the valley's rim to make sure that no one in the underwater base could actually eyeball them and realise they weren't actual whales.

And then something truly extraordinary happened.

In the distance, far above us, replying calls came from the whales circling the facility.

'Bloody hell, you've even convinced the locals,' Mike said.

'Maybe, but time to put it to the real test,' I said. 'Erin, please take us in, nice and slow.'

'On it, Lauren,' she replied.

Erin began to move *Ariel* forward, stealthily creeping along, the thrusters barely ticking over as we rose from our resting place on the seabed. Three of Ruby's drones came into view beneath us, positioning themselves in a leisurely line that matched the curvature of the valley rim.

The anticipation built inside me as we crested the top of that same ridge. Ruby synchronised the pod of whale decoys to our path as we headed over the lip to mask our movements from one of the mics, less than a hundred metres to our starboard. I held my breath, praying that a barrage of missiles wouldn't be the last thing I ever saw...

Then, just like that, the ancient underwater structure came into view. It was so breathtaking that I forgot to be scared. Instead, the tension dribbled away as I took in the sight before me.

I glanced at Jack, whose expression matched my own. 'Wow,' he mouthed at me.

Lights were everywhere over the structures, many at the summits of the buildings like the blinking warning beacons found on the top of skyscrapers.

We began to track down the slope, following the contour towards the structures laid out tantalisingly before us.

'So far, so good,' Ruby said, looking at her CIC screen readouts. 'I left two WASP units down there specifically to monitor those damned torpedo batteries, and they haven't picked up any activity.'

'Then it seems like the first part of this plan has actually worked,' Erin said.

'Yes, Lauren's plans have a way of surprising everyone like that,' Jack grinned.

'Thanks for the vote of confidence,' I said, managing a smile.

He shrugged, the corners of his mouth curling again. 'Anytime.'

I watched Erin for a moment. She seemed to be doing an amazing job of piloting *Ariel*, especially considering her foot was sticking out sideways at totally the wrong angle. It made my stomach turn every time I looked at it. Her handling of *Ariel's* controls was far subtler and more precise than Tom had ever managed. And it was testament to her character that despite losing Daryl, she was holding it together. A shining example for me to draw inspiration from after the loss of Tom.

We finally reached the bottom of the slope and just as Ruby had done earlier with the drones, rather than fly us over the top of the structures – which could have made us easier to spot – Erin flew between them along the broad streets. The pyramids towered over us, massive and mysterious. We were far too deep for any coral formations down here, but the gold and green lichen covered the structures in almost abstract patterns.

'How long do you think these things have been down here, Jack?' I asked, gesturing towards them.

'Based on the thickness of the lichen cover, a very long time indeed. But the thing I'm surprised at is that there's no sign of any erosion. It's like these things have lasted forever.'

'That suggests to me that there is some sort of self-repairing going on,' Lucy said as she appeared in her window. 'And that could be very significant as it also suggests that this facility has never been dormant.'

'So you're saying that's confirmation that the micro mind was never taken out by that Kimprak virus?' Mike asked as we reached the edge of the plaza.

'It's increasingly starting to look that way. And you all know what that means. We really may be about to discover a micro mind with its memories intact.'

'Bloody hell, the priority for recovering this micro mind just went through the roof,' Mike said.

'Then I say we make sure that that happens to honour the memories of Tom and Daryl,' Jack said.

I felt a physical surge of love for the man because that was exactly the positive focus I needed to focus away from my grief, which was bubbling just beneath the surface, threatening to escape.

Erin was already nodding. 'Heck yes.'

'Then let's take that underwater base for both of them,' I said.

'Booyah, let's do this thing!' Ruby said, fist punching the air.

As we passed one of the torpedo batteries, I held my breath, waiting for the death and destruction to rain down on our heads at any moment, but still none came. Okay, maybe I could really start to believe that we might actually pull this off.

Ahead of us the base was steadily growing closer. The structure, with its thick metal walls, was mounted on six tall hydraulic legs. There was enough clearance beneath it for a submersible to reach the built-in dock and thankfully, it was just high enough for *Ariel* to squeeze in beneath the other sub.

In the murk of the ocean, the bright porthole lights seemed slightly out of place. This was such an alien environment that it was hard to imagine anyone living and working down here. The Overseers might be on the wrong side of this fight, but I had to admire their ingenuity.

'Okay, we need to get ready for a boarding mission,' I said.

'We'd better use hollow-nosed bullets so we don't accidentally punch a hole through the walls and cause a breach,' Ruby replied. 'It's the same ammo air marshals use on flights.'

'Jesus. Have you seen what those rounds do to internal organs?' Jack said. 'I should know, because I fought to save the lives of soldiers hit by them.'

Ruby shrugged. 'Yes, I do, but we can't take any chances, Jack.'

He sighed. 'Yeah, I get it.'

I noticed the grimace that flashed across Mike's face. It seemed our newly converted Rambo still had some reservations about killing people and that was a good thing in my book. Yes, like the rest of us he had proved he could take a life. The problem was living with yourself afterwards.

Jack headed to the weapons locker and started handing out the hollow-nosed rounds for our pistols. Ruby loaded her favoured pistol, a Colt M1911A1 and I did the same with my LRS. But when Mike approached, rather than take the Glock, he helped himself to Tom's dart gun instead.

'An interesting choice of weapon there, Mike,' Jack said, raising his eyebrows.

'Yeah, who was I trying to kid? Shooting that soldier in the head is something that I never want to have to go through again.'

Jack patted him on the shoulder. 'And in my humble opinion that's a very good call.'

I could already tell, based on the sense of relief flooding through me, that Mike had absolutely made the right decision.

We might never get the old Mike back, but I could certainly do with his perspective of only using force when it was absolutely necessary – which had been exactly Tom's philosophy too.

Everybody started strapping on body armour and we shared out some smoke grenades, but this time no flashbangs. Ruby pointed out that their effect would be severely amplified in the confines of the base and could have just as devastating effect on us as the people we were about to attack. So instead she equipped us with tear gas canisters, also issuing us with breathing masks to use beneath our combat helmets.

As *Ariel* neared the base, crawling at the rate of a sea slug, everyone had fallen quiet and tension was visible on everyone's faces. We were effectively going in blind and everyone knew it. But one positive was that the base itself wasn't that big and could at most probably hold less than ten people. However, I knew we could really do with more of an edge.

'Lucy, can you begin to hack into the base's systems and kill any comms systems they may have, along with the lights?' I asked.

'Actually, yes, they seem to have some sort of wi-fi system on that base. As soon as we get close enough, I'll begin.'

'Good. Be careful to make it look like it's some sort of malfunction rather than their base coming under a cyber attack,' I replied.

'Leave it with me and I'll see what I can do,' Lucy said, smiling.

Erin closed the distance in *Ariel* until she had finally moved us into position, almost directly beneath the base's dock and Alvarez's submersible.

'On the plus side, if they do spot us now we're way too close to their base for them to risk using a torpedo on us,' Ruby said.

'Good point, but we need to be ready with *Ariel's* weapons if they do try anything,' I replied.

'Already covered. I've slaved the systems to Delphi, but I'll be able to take over control via my Sky Wire if necessary.'

'Then it sounds like we have the bases all covered with a full-blown assault party,' Jack said. 'Now all we need to do is actually pull this off.'

I nodded. 'How's hacking into their systems going, Lucy?'

'I'm almost through and...tut, tut, tut. Their security protocols are really lax and have been way too easy for me to bypass.'

'I don't suppose they thought hackers would be much of an issue when they were two thousand feet beneath the surface of the ocean,' Mike said.

Lucy chuckled. 'Yes, fair point. Anyway, I now have access to their internal security cameras including one in the docking bay, which I've already disabled. The good news is there are only six people onboard, although they are all military. The bad news is that there's no sign of Alvarez and Fischer.'

My gaze turned towards the cables disappearing into the hole, visible through the rippling tunnel of the gravity field expanded passageway.

'If they're nowhere on there, they have to have taken one of those bathyspheres down to whatever is through that hole,' I said.

'So we follow them, right?' Ruby asked.

I nodded. 'If it turns out that the micro mind isn't in the base – and we suspect by the fact Alvarez and Fischer aren't there that it isn't – then absolutely. At least, once we have dealt with the soldiers in this base, we will. Lucy, are you in a position to kill the lights yet?'

'I am. One power cut coming up,' Lucy announced. 'Oh and I made it look like it's a fault in their battery room. But the only comms I could find was a laser system that it uses to signal ships on the surface, which I've already disabled.'

'Great work like always, Lucy,' Mike said.

She beamed at him, then with a flicker the base above us plunged into darkness.

'Okay, that's our cue,' I said. 'Lucy, can you extend our gravity field up into the dock?'

'In progress. There's a ladder built into the side of the dock that protrudes down into the water. I'll extend the gravity passageway around it. That'll allow you to gain access without getting an icy cold water dunk that would also crush your bodies at the same time.'

'We'd certainly appreciate not doing that,' Jack said, pulling a face at the rest of us.

A shimmer appeared around *Ariel* and then, like a thin elephant's trunk, a tiny trail of bubbles started to extend from the top of our hatch towards the bottom of the ladder just above our ship.

'Increasing the gravity field now and pumping air into it,' Lucy said.

The trunk grew larger and then with a faint pop of air just audible through the hull, it became a passageway.

'Okay, you're safe to open the top hatch now,' Lucy said.

A moment later, Jack was lowering the ladder and climbing up to the hatch. But he paused before pressing the release button. 'I know we've done this routine before, but you're absolutely certain that this is safe, Lucy?'

'Oh you are such a worry wart,' she replied. 'There is a ninety-five percent chance that it will be fine.'

Mike pulled a face. 'So this is where you tell us about the five percent chance where it won't be?'

Lucy made an embarrassed chuckling sound. 'Hey, those are still pretty good odds you know.'

'Then that will have to do,' I said, slipping my earbud in. 'Go for it, Jack.'

He nodded, but I tensed, ready for a sudden deluge of icy

death as he pressed the green button. With a hiss and nothing more, the hatch swung open accompanied by a popping in my ears as the pressure equalised to the air corridor above us. Thankfully, apart from a few dribbles of water splashing down onto Jack's face there was nothing further.

Mike let out a long breath. 'So your ninety-five percent rule was golden after all, Lucy.'

'You see, ye all of little faith,' she replied.

Shaking his head, Jack already had his Glock out and was aiming it up through the hatch. I was next onto the ladder, LRS in hand, with Ruby and Mike bringing up the rear. Mike's dart gun was primed and ready for action and I noticed the look on his face was a lot less haunted. Yes, that had definitely been a good call on his part.

'Okay, kill the lights in the cockpit, then everyone turn on their thermal vision systems. It's going to be pitch black up there without any power,' I said.

Everyone nodded.

Erin flicked a switch and the virtual cockpit display dulled to a faint red, night vision glow.

Lucy's avatar gazed out at us from her window. 'I've killed the rest of the security cameras that have a separate backup power source. That way, hopefully, they won't be tipped-off about this being a raid until it's too late.'

'Good thinking,' I said, slipping my breathing mask on.

The strong smell of rubber filled my nostrils. The others were just silhouettes now in the darkness, so I flicked down the HUD built into my helmet and turned the vision system on. Immediately, the team became visible as ghostly glowing shapes.

Jack climbed out onto the hull with me right behind him. I went to step onto the ladder up into the dock first, but Jack shook his head.

'Lauren, just this once you shouldn't be in the frontline,' he said.

Ruby nodded. 'Yeah, you and your Empyrean key are way too critical to pulling this mission off.'

I was about to argue that I should always go first, but Jack just looked at me with that challenging look of his that he seemed to specialise in when he needed to pull me into line. Maybe this time he had a point.

'Okay, okay. I'll cover you then rather than waste time getting into an argument about it.'

A brief smile flickered across his lips. 'Good that you're seeing sense for once, *Commander*.'

I scowled at him, but the effect was totally lost when he could only see me in thermal vision mode.

We peered up through the underwater passageway into the dock above. It appeared to be empty with no guards in sight. It made sense though, after all who would expect any uninvited guests to enter the dock at this sort of depth?

I watched as first Ruby, then Jack ascended the ladder, with me ready to shoot anything that might even vaguely look like a threat. But they reached the top of the ladder without incident and disappeared for a moment. Then, much to my relief, Ruby reappeared and gestured to Mike and I.

'We're all good, guys. Erin, keep the engine running,' she said over the comms channel, her voice slightly muffled by her mask.

'Got it. Don't be too long, I don't want to get a ticket,' Erin replied.

Snorting, Ruby turned away and disappeared into the dock.

I nodded to Mike, who was already taking deep breaths.

'Ready?' I whispered.

'As I'll ever be, Lauren,' he said, cocking his dart gun.

Then with my LRS in my hand and a sense of the calm before the storm settling over me, I began to ascend the ladder into whatever was waiting for us.

CHAPTER TWENTY-ONE

WE SPREAD out round the small indoor area of the dock with Alvarez's submersible floating in it and *Ariel* submerged beneath the other craft.

'Lucy, to play things on the same side in case Erin needs to make a fast getaway by herself, kill the gravity field corridor to *Ariel*,' I said into my mic.

Erin immediately cut in. 'Hey, hold up. I'm not going anywhere without you guys.'

'You may have to if this mission goes wrong,' I replied. 'Better to have at least one of us report back and return for a rescue mission.'

A long sigh followed. 'Okay, I want it noted that I'm not happy about it, but if you order me to, I'll pull back if that moment comes,' Erin replied. 'So let's just hope it doesn't come to that.'

'Now there's something we can all agree on,' Ruby replied.

I nodded at her. 'Lucy, please retract the gravity corridor.'

'You got it,' Lucy said.

With a gurgle, the passageway back to our ship collapsed and water flooded into it. That was it – we were cut off and on our own until the other side of this thing.

Beyond the door leading out of the dock, I could hear the distant murmur of voices and cursing in what sounded like Serbian, which was being translated into a string of expletives by my earbud.

'Lucy, can you give me a fix on the current location of the crew?' I asked.

'Looking at the schematics, if you exit the dock through the door at the end, you'll enter a short corridor. The main power supply room is the room off it on your left. There are two soldiers in there right now trying to work out what the hell is going on. The other four soldiers are in a control room at the end of the corridor off to the right. So far no one's realised that they've lost comms with the bathyspheres because I'm feeding false data to their screens, which they are running on emergency power.'

'You may not be here in your micro mind, but you're already making a hell of a difference to this mission, Lucy,' Jack said.

'Hey, you crazy kids just can't do without me,' she replied, clearly amused.

Ruby glanced towards the door. 'So how do we want to play this, Commander?'

'We need to try and take out the two soldiers in the power room as stealthily as possible,' I said. 'Then hopefully, with the element of surprise on our side, we can storm the main control room.'

'An alternative strategy is that we split into two assault groups,' Ruby replied. 'Jack and I can head for the control room whilst you guys deal with the power room. With a simultaneous assault, there'll be less chance of anyone raising the alarm.'

'Okay, I like your plan better,' I said. 'Mike, you're with me to storm the power room. Jack, when you're in position with Ruby, let me know and we'll coordinate.'

'Will do,' he said, taking hold of the circular handle that would release the bolts from around the edges of the frame. Ruby took up a position to one side of it with her Colt drawn.

Mike and I hung back, weapons ready as Jack spun the pressure door handle as slowly as possible to keep the noise down. But when its hinges let out a teeth-grinding squeal, I tensed, ready for the immediate shout of a challenge. Thankfully, none came.

So far so good.

Ruby stepped out first, followed by Jack. A second later, Mike and I followed them out into the corridor. Jack and Ruby were already disappearing down it, heading to the right.

Less than five metres away was another pressurised door with another round handle. It looked like the base had been designed to be able to seal off any flooded sections, just like in every submarine movie I'd seen. Mike and I crept along the corridor towards it, grateful for our helmets' image intensifiers in the pitch black.

The murmured conversation on the other side of the door grew louder as we closed in. It took one look at the circular handle for me to realise it would screech to hell if we opened it. That alone was going to make it near impossible to sneak up on the soldiers on the other side of it. We needed a different approach.

'We're in position,' Jack whispered through my earbuds.

I looked back along the corridor. Jack and Ruby were either side of the far door and were ready for my order. I held up a hand, palm forward just as Tom had taught me, to tell them to stop. Mike gave me a questioning look.

'Trust me,' I whispered. Then I raised my fist and gave three sharp raps on the door.

On the other side the conversation stopped dead.

'Sta?' a man called out, which my earbud translated into *what?*

I ignored the question and rapped again.

This time I didn't need my earbud to translate the curse. Footsteps approached and I immediately made a hand chopping motion to Jack and Ruby - the signal for attack.

I breathed in as Mike stepped to one side of the door, his dart gun raised.

My LRS safety was off, my body primed and pumped for combat. The door began to open. At the other end of the corridor, Jack began to spin the wheel to unlock the door in front of him.

I'd hoped the soldiers would assume we were their colleagues come to check on them, especially in this darkness. What I hadn't counted on was the guy that opened the door, with a massive torch that would give a searchlight a run for its bloody money. As the burly guy cracked the door open, the blinding beam from his torch overwhelmed my image intensifier system.

My brief hesitation was all that the man needed.

He shoved the door hard into me, knocking the LRS from my hand. At the same moment, shouts came from the end of the corridor, followed by the staccato burst of semi-automatic pistol fire.

But as the burly guy reached for his own holstered weapon, he suddenly gave me a shocked look and crumpled to the ground, a dart poking out of his neck. Then before I could stop Mike, he charged past me into the room. A shout came from inside, followed by the crack of a bullet.

My stomach clenched as I dashed into the room, sweeping my LRS left and right to target the bastard who'd just shot Mike. Then my mind caught up with the scene before me.

Mike stood panting in the corner, looking down at a giant of a guy that made the first soldier look like a wimpy kid. But as huge as the man was, the dart sticking out of his shoulder had obviously done its job. The goliath was still twitching, his eyes shut, a pistol still in his hand. Mike grabbed the weapon from him and stowed it in the back of his own belt.

I gave Mike a sharp nod, partly stunned by the foolhardy bravery that he'd just shown, but mainly stupidly proud of him. But there wasn't any time for praise – weapon fire was still echoing from the corridor. Then, like a switch had been thrown, it all went ominously quiet.

I spun round and headed out into the corridor, holding out my LRS in both hands. At the far end, the door was open and there was no sign of Jack or Ruby.

I was already reaching for a tear gas grenade as I stalked towards the scene, blood pounding in my ears. Ready to pull the pin, I stood to one side of the door and prepared to lob the grenade through the gap and then slam the door shut to let the gas do its worst.

But then Jack appeared, his hands raised. 'Woah there, Lauren, we're all good.'

I pulled off my mask and took several deep breaths as I clipped the grenade back onto my belt. I steeped past Jack into the control room, the only light coming from the numerous displays. The smell of cordite from the discharged weapons assaulted my nose as I took in the scene.

Ruby was holstering her Colt, standing over a woman who lay dead at her feet, still clutching a pistol. A torch on the floor cast a spotlight cone across the walls. My gaze flicked around the room to see three other soldiers in black uniforms, all lying slumped in their seats, ragged wounds peppering their bodies.

I took a deep breath to steady the thumping of my heart. 'Thank God, you're both okay.'

'You too,' Jack said, squeezing my shoulder. 'Looks like you dealt with your guys okay too?'

'It was actually Mike who did the heavy lifting. It was pretty impressive to be honest.'

'That's big praise coming from you,' Mike said behind me.

I turned and found myself hugging him. 'You were bloody spectacular back there, mister.'

'Seems all that extra combat training I did with Niki paid off.'

'Since when?' Jack asked.

'Hey, I don't have to tell you guys everything.'

Despite the life and death situation of a moment ago a laugh bubbled up inside me. I pulled away, resisting the urge to ruffle Mike's hair like a kid brother, although maybe in a way that was exactly what he'd become to me over the years.

'Lauren, would you like me to restore the lights now?' Lucy said through my earbud.

'Please. Also can you make a start of seriously hacking into the computers in here to see if we can learn anything useful?'

'Already almost finished doing exactly that.'

The lights flickered on as the four of us raised the HUD reticules on our helmets.

'I also have control of all the base's torpedo batteries.' Lucy added.

'Nice! That could come in useful if we get any more company,' Ruby said.

'Precisely. You should also know that I have now fully accessed the security camera playback. According to the footage I just analysed it does indeed look like Fischer and Alvarez took one of those bathyspheres to wherever that hole they blasted through the rock leads to.'

'Any reference to what that might be stored in this base's computers?' I asked.

'There's certainly nothing about a micro mind and nothing

has been recorded by any of the security cameras to suggest that it's been here. The only thing I can find is a mention of a lot of heavy excavation equipment on a transport manifest, which was shipped down through that hole.'

Jack's eyes widened. 'That sounds like it could be for one of Fischer's not-give-a-damn archaeological digs.'

'Sounds like the next stop on this ride, then,' I said as I turned back towards the door.

I closed the hatch behind us in the bathysphere. If I'd thought *Neptune's* cockpit was cramped, it was practically palatial compared to the tight space the four of us were now squeezed into. Making it an even tighter squeeze was all the extra ammo and grenades that we'd crammed in, including Ruby's Accuracy International sniper rifle with a Starbright KL303 that she'd absolutely insisted on bringing.

A heater was blowing out a constant stream of hot air but was doing little to counteract the freezing temperature of the walls encircling us. Our breaths were clouding like four steam trains in the confined space.

The walls and floor were lined with six portholes and there was also a depth indicator display by the door, indicating that the bathysphere was currently at just over two thousand feet.

Ruby was looking intently at the screen of her Sky Wire and following the live feed from the WASP unit tethered to *Ariel*, which she'd sent out ahead to scout out the shaft before we were lowered down into it.

'How's it looking?' I asked.

She scowled and swivelled the screen towards me – it was filled with nothing but static. 'It's not. I lost the signal to the WASP about ten seconds ago.'

I sat up straighter. 'Was it taken out?'

'No, I was getting warnings about electrical interference interrupting the signal before I lost it completely.'

'But surely that shouldn't happen? It was using a tethered connection,' Mike said.

Ruby frowned. 'Yeah, that's what's got me confused as well.'

I pressed my finger to my earbud. 'Lucy, presumably you were listening in to that. Any insights?'

'I was actually monitoring the WASP's feed before we lost contact with it. There was a significant power surge as it entered the shaft and that's probably what overwhelmed its systems.'

'So in other words, we have no way of finding out what we're heading into?' Mike asked.

Ruby cracked her knuckles. 'I could always pop back to try and get an answer out of that prisoner we brought round with that shot of adrenaline. I can be very persuasive when I need to be.'

We'd tried everything with the giant of a man to get him to talk, but he'd just glowered at us. In the end Jack had knocked him out with a shot of tranquiliser and we'd left him and his buddy securely tied to one of the bulkheads.

'We're so not stooping to Alvarez's level just yet,' I said. 'Jack, Mike and I have far too much personal experience of his expertise with torture to wish that on anyone else, even one of his soldiers.'

'Damned right,' Jack said, giving me an approving nod.

Ruby held up her hands. 'Hey, it was just a suggestion, guys. Anyway, let's shake our tushes and get down there already.'

'You heard the lady. Lucy, can you start lowering us?' I said.

'Will do. Good luck, folks,' she replied.

'I'll be here keeping that engine warm for you, as always,' Erin said.

'Good to know,' I replied. The thing I didn't voice was that I was uncertain what real help Erin could provide when there would be no way of reaching us once we headed down the shaft.

With a lurch the airlock retracted back into the corridor that we'd entered the bathysphere through. Then our ride began to descend towards the shaft entrance that the two other cables were already leading down into.

Through the portholes in the bottom of the bathysphere I could see there seemed to be a pinprick of light at the end of a long stone tunnel beneath. As we descended into it, I grabbed a last look at the base and at *Ariel*, still fully cloaked, which made her almost impossible to see. Far above us, the stealthed Zumwalt destroyer was still prowling, no doubt ready to drop more instant death down onto our heads if ordered to. Hopefully, that was now extremely unlikely as Alvarez and Fischer were somewhere down here rather than up there.

The depth display ticked passed two thousand five hundred feet and if anything our descent was actually speeding up.

Around us, as the blast walls skimmed past, I started to notice vertical grooves running through them. I pointed them out to the others. 'Any idea what those lines might be?'

'They certainly aren't natural rock formations if that's what you're asking,' Jack said.

'Maybe something to do with the Angelus technology down here?' Mike suggested.

Whatever the explanation, the strange markings slid past the portholes for another few minutes and the depth indicator had already passed three thousand feet when at last the end of the tunnel rushed towards us.

Then we descended into one of the most extraordinary things I'd ever seen in my life.

We had dropped into a vast underwater chasm at least ten kilometres wide and maybe the same again deep. Above us, a smooth, domed stone roof arched away from the shaft, which had been punched straight through the middle of its summit. The grooves that I'd seen in the shaft radiated out down through the roof in tangents, making it clear that it was anything but a natural rock formation. If there were any lingering doubts left in my mind, they were soon swept away by what awaited us below.

Dotted around the vast chamber were vast tree structures at least the height of the tallest of the world's skyscrapers, all made from shining crystal. The columns seemed to be made from strands woven in a spiralling shape. The caps on the top of the structures had filigrees of light lines running through them like the branches of a tree, which pulsed brighter every so often. Small luminous fibres connected the strange towers to the walls like glowing spider webs.

If that wasn't jaw dropping enough, beneath them was a huge, bowl-shaped floor that seemed to be constructed entirely of giant hexagonal glass plates. They reflected the scene like a huge fragmented mirror, making it impossible to see what was beyond the floor.

A faint light radiated around the bathysphere as we descended through the middle of the enormous chamber and a slight electrical humming sound came from the craft's walls.

My mind was left reeling by what was around us, the scale almost beyond comprehension.

'Bloody hell,' Mike said.

'That is a serious understatement, buddy, even for you,' Jack said.

With a sense of absolute awe, I stared out of the portholes, taking in the mind-bending scene, unable to string together a coherent thought. I wasn't alone; everyone had fallen silent, content to just absorb the incredible spectacle.

With a distant crackle, a giant spark of energy suddenly leapt from the crystal trees and earthed itself onto the chamber walls. The walls glowed briefly around the impact points before fading away, as a tingle of static brushed over my skin. No wonder the WASP's systems had been fried when it tried to enter this place.

The bathysphere felt like an ant compared to the vast chamber, as we sped towards the bottom. I noticed the depth indicator on the door had just ticked past ten thousand feet and our ride still wasn't showing any signs of slowing.

It was Ruby who finally found a voice. 'What is this place? I mean, what was it built for? It was obviously built for something, right?'

'Well, this is certainly an Angelus megastructure and whatever it was designed to do was clearly something on a very large scale,' Mike said.

An incredible thought struck me. 'Could this be the device that the Angelus planned to use to defend Earth from an external threat?'

'What, you think it could fire some sort of massive energy weapon into space, Death Star style?' Jack asked.

'I wouldn't rule anything out – will you just look at the size of the bloody thing?' Mike said.

'Whatever it does, it looks like we won't have much longer to wait because we've nearly reached the bottom,' I said, pointing downwards.

The hexagon glass floor was getting closer fast. The cables of the other two bathyspheres were dangling through a shattered hole that had been punched through the floor, presumably with underwater charges. Framed within the broken section was what I could only describe as an inverted swimming pool, the surface of which was facing down into the area below the glass panels. Through the rippling surface we could see the two other bathyspheres already on the ground beneath the glass roof.

'Looks like the end of the line is coming up,' Jack said. His eyes suddenly widened. 'Have you seen how deep we are?'

I turned to the display to see eight thousand feet tick past.

'That noise can't be good,' Mike said.

For the first time I tuned into the sounds around me, hearing creaks and groans coming from the spherical metal walls.

'Based on the fact that we are still breathing, and there are already two other bathyspheres on the seabed in what appears to be an area filled with air, I think we're going to be okay,' I said, trying my best to sound absolutely convinced.

At last we started to slow, as our bathysphere dropped towards the rippling surface.

'Okay, get ready everyone in case there's a reception committee waiting for us,' I said.

Immediately, everyone was pure combat focus, checking over their weapons and ammo. In my case that also meant checking the Empyrean Key was safely stowed in my rucksack. If this all went according to plan, when we found the micro mind – and after seeing all of this I was now absolutely certain that we would – I would need it to communicate with what was obviously a very wide awake Angelus AI.

We broke through the upside down surface of the water, which totally messed with my head, and then we descended through a wide open area beneath the glass floor. As we slowed to a stop next to the other two bathyspheres, much to my relief I couldn't see a single person to greet our unscheduled arrival with a storm of bullets.

With a soft shudder the bathysphere settled onto the ground. A chime came from the door panel and a message, *air pressure stabilised, door unlocked* was displayed on it.

'I think that means it's safe to open,' Ruby quipped.

I slung the MP5 with its thirty bullet magazine over my shoulder and slipped the safety off my LRS as Jack placed his hand on the wheel that opened the door.

'Keep sharp everyone; we have no way of knowing what we'll be up against,' I said.

'If I didn't know that Alvarez, Fischer and probably a whole lot of trouble wasn't already down here, I'd actually be looking forward to this,' Jack replied.

Ruby connected the sight to her sniper rifle. 'Then it's time to go and hunt us some bear.'

CHAPTER TWENTY-TWO

RUBY WAS PEERING OUT of the portholes like an astronaut on a lunar lander. And in many senses that was exactly what this whole experience was like. Impossibly, we seemed to have entered a vast, air-filled chamber nearly thirty-five thousand feet beneath the surface of the ocean. I suspected the rush I was feeling wasn't a thousand miles away from what Neil Armstrong and Buzz Aldrin must have felt as they prepared to step out onto the surface of the moon for the first time.

'I can't see any hint of a welcoming committee out there,' Ruby said.

'We can't assume there isn't one, so we all need to stay on it. Be ready for anything,' I reminded.

Not for the first time I wished that Lucy was with us. I would certainly feel a lot more relaxed if we could shift over into the twilight zone right about now.

Weapons ready, numerous grenades clipped to our belts, I patted the reassuring shape of the Empyrean Key in my bag as Jack turned the handle on the hatch in the floor. It swung open. Moments later, we'd all climbed down the ladder and were standing on the sea explorer equivalent of the lunar surface. On their hydraulic legs the bathyspheres even resembled the lunar modules, albeit with a bit of a Jules Verne steampunk vibe. This was another world in so many ways and apart from Alvarez and his people, we were almost certainly the first people outside the Overseer organisation to visit this site, considering how impossibly far beneath the surface we were.

Around the landing zone there were signs of human activity everywhere and the immediate area resembled a builders' yard. Everything from pneumatic drills and shovels to even small diggers had been lined up in regimented rows. There was a wide, well-furrowed track with numerous tyre marks leading away into the gloom.

Banks of arc lights had been set up around the site, making it hard to see what lay beyond, where the distance was only faintly lit by the luminescence of the tree-like structures towering over the vast glass ceiling above.

One of the twisted crystal shafts of the tall mushroom structures intersected the ceiling about a hundred meters away, its trunk passing through it into the rocky floor. Other trunks were also visible, stretching away into the distance like a supersized crystal forest.

A gentle lapping sound was coming from beyond the glass, as the odd alarming creak and groan echoed throughout this impossible place at the bottom of the ocean. There was also a strong smell of rich earth rising from the thick carpet of lichen that covered most of the floor, and some sort of vine wound around the trunk of one of the mushroom towers, continuing up towards the roof and creeping across it, vines dangling down. How those plants could thrive in this deep underwater location was beyond me. Maybe it was an undiscovered species that could thrive on the little luminosity from the chamber?

Standing in the pool of light I certainly felt very exposed. We were surrounded by the cobwebs of shadows and darkness of whatever this place had been built for. I flicked down my thermal HUD and was quickly reassured when I couldn't see any silhouettes of people waiting in the darkness to ambush us.

'Talk about Alice stepping through the looking glass! I feel like I have just been transported to another planet,' Jack said.

'You're not the only one,' Mike said, peering into the distance at the glowing forest of strange structures. He gestured up towards the blasted-through panel in the roof that was rippling like an upside down swimming pool. 'This all has to be Angelus tech; there's obviously some sort of gravity field holding that water back.'

'Almost certainly, but the question is why keep this area clear of water at all?' I asked.

Ruby gestured to a track marked every fifty metres or so with green beacons. 'Maybe we'll find the answer along the yellow brick road, because I don't think we're in Kansas anymore, Dorothy.'

I agreed. 'Presumably wherever that leads we'll find Alvarez and Fischer and the rest of their people, and hopefully the micro mind too.'

'Oh, I'm so looking forward to getting up front and personal with that guy for some serious payback,' Ruby said.

'You'll have to get in line behind me, but I'd be much happier knowing what was at the end of that track, waiting for us,' Jack replied.

'It's just a shame we didn't bring one of your WASPs. We could so do with it scouting ahead for us, Ruby,' I said.

'Hang on, even if we haven't got a WASP, I can still do this the old-fashioned way and scout ahead on foot,' she said. 'I'm far lighter on my feet that any of you baby elephants.'

I raised my eyebrows. 'I love you too. But scouting ahead does sound like a good plan. Just keep in contact via the radio channel on your Sky Wire. One upside of standing in a giant air bubble is that radio waves should still work down here.'

Ruby nodded and with her image intensifier screen pivoted down over her eyes, set off at a light jog into the darkness.

'So, time to see where this particular yellow brick road leads,' I said.

Following in Ruby's footsteps we moved to the left of the track about a hundred metres out so we wouldn't bump into anyone coming from the opposite direction. We set into a steady rhythm, with me leading the column in order for us to present less of a target in case we did run into Alvarez's soldiers.

It wasn't long before our chosen route took us closer to the base of the nearest mushroom structure. The crystal cables that knotted together to form the trunks appeared to have a root-like system burrowing into the moss and the ground beneath. Faint pulses of light ran through them, up into the structure.

Everything about this place screamed purpose. The problem was that until we made contact with the micro mind we would have no idea what that purpose actually was.

As we headed past the base of the mushroom structure its scale became clearer. It was easily at least a hundred metres wide, making us look like ants at the trunk of a giant redwood.

We had just passed it when Ruby spoke over the comms.

'Guys, you're not going to believe what I've just found,' she said.

'What?' I replied.

'Uh, you really need to see it for yourselves. It's about two klicks out along the track that you're on. I'll push on to check the coast is clear.'

'Roger that, but why won't you tell us more?' I asked.

'Because I simply haven't got the words, Lauren. Also, I'm not sure I trust my own eyes right now.'

I glanced back at Jack and Mike, who both shrugged.

This so wasn't like Ruby on a mission. She was usually the very definition of professional detachment. But right now she sounded way more confused than I had heard her in a long time and that intrigued me as much as anything else down here.

'Okay, understood. We should be there in another eight minutes,' I replied.

'You'll know it when you get there,' Ruby replied.

Without me needing to say anything, all three of us picked up our pace, keen to discover whatever the big mystery was that Ruby had just discovered, especially as she was being so cryptic.

Thanks to the gloom, even with my helmet's thermal vision system, it was barely possible to see much of anything ahead of us. We'd been walking for around seven minutes when Jack's voice came through my speakers.

'Are you seeing what I think I'm seeing?' he asked.

I turned to see him staring off into the ten o'clock position. I peered at where he was pointing, then I saw them. My heart skipped several beats as I began to take in faint shapes in the distance...ships.

'Bloody hell, we'd better check this out,' Mike said, his eyes wide.

'Sounds like you've reached those ships,' Ruby said over the link.

'No wonder you weren't sure about your eyesight...neither am I now,' I said.

We veered off as one, heading straight towards the ships, which slowly became clearer as we closed in on them. There was a large fishing trawler, a tanker, and what even looked like an old warship, all covered with a thick blanket of moss.

'Oh my God, that's an Illinois class pre-dreadnought,' Jack said, staring at the warship in awe.

'I damned well knew it,' Ruby said over the link. 'They started building those around the 1900s, am I right, Jack?'

'I believe so,' he said, shaking his head, eyes wide in disbelief.

I made a T-shape with my hands. 'Okay, time out here, people. First things first, what the hell are these three wrecks doing down here?'

'Um, I don't think it's just three wrecks, Lauren,' Mike said. He nodded to the left of the tanker and this time even I couldn't stifle a gasp.

Stretching away beyond it was an elephants' graveyard of ships of every description from every possible era. From small pleasure boats and a shattered three-masted sailing ship to a tug and a wood-panelled pleasure cruiser. There were even planes, including what I was pretty sure was a Corsair Second World War fighter that I'd once seen in an American military aviation museum.

The other startling thing, especially considering how long some of the vessels must have been down here, was that they hadn't dissolved into rust in the oxygen rich atmosphere that we were breathing in, which tasted anything but stale. But many of the ships had evidence of significant damage that had almost certainly directly led to them sinking, from large holes in their hulls to a tanker that had been split completely in two.

'Oh Jesus, I think I know what this might all be connected to,' Jack said.

I turned towards him. 'What?'

'I can't believe I'm actually going to voice this out loud as a serious explanation, but you do realise that we're very close to the edge of the area known as the Bermuda Triangle? So...' He made a sweeping gesture towards all the boats and planes before us.

I looked first at him, then at Mike – who was gawping at his friend – and then back to the graveyard of ships.

'You're seriously suggesting these craft were lost in the Bermuda Triangle?' Ruby said over the link.

'I know I'm in danger of sounding like Fox Mulder here, but

if the damn Greek god Poseidon had its origins in an Angelus AI, then the Bermuda Triangle isn't so far beyond the realms of possibility, right?'

'You're not saying that the micro mind deliberately sunk these craft?' I said.

Jack shrugged. 'I have absolutely no idea. But I guess it's certainly a possibility we should consider. Maybe we are dealing with another rogue micro like Red?'

But it was then I spotted something beyond the Corsair fighter that made everything fall into place.

'I don't think the micro mind was responsible for any of this. Look...' I pointed towards a trawler that had been converted into a deep diving vessel. I'd instantly recognised it from the footage of Raúl's dive video...a ship with barely any moss...

'Bloody hell, it can't be!' Mike said.

' I'm absolutely certain that trawler is *Hercules*.'

'No, not that, *that!*' Mike said, pointing with a trembling finger. 'Tell me that's not *Artemis*?'

'You're shitting me?' Ruby exclaimed over the link. "How did I miss that?"

'He's absolutely isn't shitting us,' I said as my heart leapt at the sight of the lost craft. Then the obvious thought struck me... *what about Tom?*

Artemis was sitting on the rocky floor beyond the last boat. It's upper hull had been partly crushed from the landslide that had landed on top of it, the bottom of the saucer completely blown away by the self-destruct charges that Tom had activated.

I was already running towards the craft before my mind even had a chance to catch up with what my subconscious was desperately hoping for.

My lungs were burning as I skidded to a stop before the X craft. A large gash had torn through the hull and holes were punched through it like a Swiss cheese. *Artemis's* full complement of WASPs were visible in their racks through the launch bay doors that had been twisted partly open by the blast.

A moment later the others caught up with me, both men breathing hard.

Even though I knew no one could have survived the blast, I still called out, 'Tom are you in there?'

The tiny flickering flame of hope that I'd allowed myself to believe for just a moment, spluttered and died when there was no response.

Mike put his hands on his head as he stared at our sister craft. 'Shit, you remember when our systems blinked out for a minute with that magnetic pulse? That must have been when whatever it was transported *Artemis* here.'

Fresh wild hope filled me. 'What if it was in time to save Tom?'

Before the others could answer, I turned towards one of the holes in the X103 to crawl through it. But then I felt a hand on my arm. Jack gazed at me with soft eyes as he gently shook his head.

'There could still be a chance,' I said, answering his unspoken words.

'You and I both already know the answer to that,' Jack said quietly but firmly.

I tried to pull away from his grip. 'But I still need to check.'

'*Somebody* needs to check and I've seen more dead bodies than you have. So please, Lauren, let me do this. It's better that you remember him as he was, rather than what we might find in there.'

I gazed into his eyes and saw nothing but love and concern. Jack didn't want me to be traumatised by what we might be about to discover.

I gave him a slow nod. 'Okay, okay...'

Jack gave me a sweet smile, his hand lingering on my arm for that all important bit of human contact. Then he headed past me and squeezed through the hole into the cockpit.

I listened to his footsteps echoing around the interior of the X-craft, my mind already imagining in vivid gory details the mangled state of Tom's body that Jack was about to find.

But then his head reappeared at the opening. 'Okay, so the really *weird* thing is that there's no sign of Tom's body.'

Mike tucked his chin in. 'Then what the hell happened here?'

'Maybe Tom had a chance to walk away from this?' I said, refusing to let my hope die.

But this time it was Mike who was shaking his head. 'No, I think that whatever transported *Artemis* here, probably also removed his body. Don't forget that Tom had already activated the self-destruct before that electrical pulse happened.'

I felt something inside me crumble, any last hope that somehow he'd miraculously survived was now gone. 'But there might still be a way that Tom survived.'

Jack gently took hold of my shoulders and made me look at him. 'Lauren, you and I both know that's a near impossible hope. The only way we are going to get any real answers is by talking to the micro mind.'

'Yes...' I said, barely able to hold his gaze.

Ruby's voice came over the link. 'About that. I think I've just detected its whereabouts. But you're really not going to like it.'

I traded a worried frown with Jack as we clambered back down from the wreckage of *Artemis* and headed back to Mike.

CHAPTER TWENTY-THREE

THE MOSS-COVERED boulder field that we'd been walking through as we headed towards the pool of light in the distance had started to give way to strange Angelus crystal structures that resembled round gas cylinders. They were connected by a spiderweb of conduits to large, faintly glowing pillars of crystal about six metres high, around which the conduits were wrapped like wiring looms of an electric motor.

As we closed in I could feel the static in the air beginning to tickle over my skin again but this time it was accompanied by the growing smell of ozone. As we walked through this alien sculpture park of towering monoliths, I could hear a low level humming coming from the strange structures.

'I tell you what this place reminds me of – a power station,' I said. 'We had a small sub-station back at Jodrell Bank that sounded a bit like this, albeit this is obviously on a far larger scale.'

'It certainly looks like some sort of energy management system,' Mike replied. 'And if so, going by the hundreds of crystal pillars, whatever it's designed to power needs a heck of a lot of energy.'

'Maybe this really is designed to power some sort of Angelus mega weapon,' Jack said.

I nodded. 'That could certainly be one explanation and I wouldn't rule anything out, taking into account the sheer, jaw-dropping scale of this place.'

The pool of light that we'd been steadily moving towards as we'd followed the track was now close enough for us to see moving dots silhouetted against it. Jack pulled a pair of binoculars out of his pack and aimed them towards the distant specks.

His eyebrows arched as he looked through the binoculars. 'You're going to want to see this for yourself, Lauren,' he said as he handed them to me.

I peered through them to see that the dots were actually teams of workers. The source of the glowing light actually seemed to be coming from a small quarry behind them. A large dug ramp dropped down into it, on which diggers were trundling up and down to deposit their loads of rocks into piles around the edge.

'That looks like the centre of some sort of serious operation,' I said, handing the binoculars back to Jack.

'Odds on that's going to the location of our micro mind,' he replied. 'Going by the look of it, this has all the hallmarks of one of Fischer's not very subtle excavations.'

'Then we'd better get a closer look to make sure,' Mike said.

We set off again between the crystal power stations and as we slowly drew nearer, a thumping soundtrack of pneumatic drills became audible, echoing under the glass roof.

'Yeah, it's never a trowel to do the archaeological work when Fischer's around,' Jack said with a growl.

Something crunched under my boot and I glanced down to see shattered crystal shards beneath it. The fragments stretched away in a line from the debris towards the intact nose cone of a Guardian tetrahedron crystal.

'Looks like it was shot down by something,' Jack said, squatting to examine the remains.

'Not just that one, look...' Mike said. He gestured round us.

The destroyed remains of at least a dozen Guardian crystals littered the ground. 'What the hell shot all those AIs down?' I frowned.

'I'd lay good money on it being something to do with those,' Jack said, pointing towards the excavation site, more specifically two white, dome-shaped objects mounted on the back of a flatbed.

'And *they* are when they're at home?' Mike asked.

'Two C-Ram defence phalanx systems. They're equipped with Gatling guns that can fire twenty millimetre high-explosive incendiary rounds at 4,500 rounds per minute. Basically they're designed to take out a missile or even an incoming mortar round in flight.'

'And also Guardian AIs by the looks of it,' Mike said, pursing his lips. 'They were probably trying to defend the micro mind from the Overseers in that excavation site.'

'But we've never run into anything like these Guardians defending a micro mind before,' I said.

'Once again it all points to this being a high-value target,' Jack replied.

'We really could do with some more intel,' I said. 'Ruby, have you got eyes on whatever is in that quarry yet?'

'Affirmative, Commander. I've just finished climbing one of those crystal pillar things for a sniping position and now have a clear view down into the quarry from here. I'm relaying a live feed – it's quite a doozy.'

A video popped up in the corner of my HUD. Partially buried in the strata of rock was a spherical ball of glowing energy

about thirty metres wide and partly transparent. Workers were
using pneumatic drills to break away the sections of rock that
trapped the shimmering orb. The sphere itself was strobing very
slowly with light that poured into it from a network of conduits
connected to it from the surrounding soil. And then I saw what
was just visible at its heart and my pulse shot up. There, like a
glowing blue seed in an apple, was a crystal tetrahedron – a very
much awake micro mind AI. But just to make life really interesting there were at least fifty soldiers standing guard around the
edge of the quarry.

'Are we looking at some sort of force field around that micro
mind?' Jack asked. He'd been watching the live feed on his HUD,
as had Mike.

'I think so. It would certainly explain why the Overseers
haven't been able to recover it so far,' Mike said.

'Okay, so the next obvious question is how are we going to get
to that micro mind if it's behind a force field?' I asked.

'Actually, I may have an idea about that,' Ruby replied over
the link.

The view in the feed shifted towards a short stone pillar
mounted near the edge of the quarry's rim. The view zoomed in
until we could see a circular shallow depression on the top of the
pillar.

'Tell me that's not just the right shape to fit your Empyrean
Key, Commander,' Ruby said.

'I think you could be right, especially based on its proximity
to the micro mind,' I agreed. 'But to point out the blindingly
obvious here, how are we going to get anywhere near it when
those soldiers are almost on top of it?'

'I've got an idea about that too,' Ruby said. The view started
to move again, this time down towards an area in the middle
distance where some vehicles were parked, including a few
special forces open dune buggies with roll cages and large calibre

machine guns mounted on them. Next to those stood two soldiers, who were smoking cigarettes and looking towards the excavation site.

'How about this for an idea?' Ruby said. 'I take those two guards out and then one of you can use one of those buggies to draw the rest of the soldiers away?'

'That could work,' Jack replied. 'Mike, can you drive whilst I get busy with one of those heavy MGs to get the attention of our little friends?'

'Yep, that works for me.'

Jack turned to me. 'So how about it, Lauren?'

'It works for me too. And whilst you guys are keeping them distracted, I can slip past and try my luck with that control pillar.'

'Sounds like a suitably batshit crazy plan for our team,' Jack said.

'Doesn't it just?' I grinned. 'Ruby, get ready to take those guards out when we're in position.'

'I'll be waiting for your call to get this party started,' she replied.

We set off across the moss, staying clear of the faint pools of light cast from the power crystals just in case either of the guards happened to look our way. Creeping between the shadows slowed us down considerably, so it was a good five minutes before we reached the last of the pillars between us and the two soldiers next to the vehicles, about three hundred metres away from our position.

I thumbed the sector on my MP5 submachine gun to full auto mode just in case this all went wrong. 'Okay, Ruby, we're in position. Take those two soldiers out whenever you're ready.'

'Roger that, Commander,' she replied.

There was a faintly suppressed *crack*, followed by a dim muzzle flash from the top of a pillar about two hundred metres to our right. Then one of the two soldiers slumped backwards clutching his chest. As the second guy started to turn, his head erupted with blood as Ruby fired a second round.

I was just about to commend Ruby on her shooting when her voice cut in over the link.

'Shit, the first guy is still alive and he's got a radio in his hand. Taking another kill shot.'

We heard the whistle of a bullet and the guy with the radio who'd been struggling to sit up collapsed.

They say in the military that even the best plans often don't often survive that critical first contact with the enemy and this was *so* one of those moments.

An alarm warbled out from the quarry as search light beams came on and swivelled out towards the parked buggies.

Jack shook his head. 'Crap, that guard did manage to call it in before he died.'

Another whizz of a bullet and one of the spotlights exploded as Ruby took it out.

A burst of return gunfire immediately crackled out and bullets ricocheted off the crystal pillar she was positioned on. Then at least twenty soldiers started to race towards her hiding place, firing as they went.

'Shit, there's no way we can get to those vehicles in time to draw them off now,' Mike said.

I quickly scanned the terrain between us and the buggies, looking for suitable cover to give us a tactical advantage. Experience told me that the situation was going to descend rapidly into an inevitable firefight.

There were a number of large, squat, rectangular crystal junction boxes with conduits blossoming from their sides like spider legs. The nearest one was between us and the advancing line of soldiers bearing down on Ruby's position. Tactically that looked like it would give us a reasonable amount of cover to take on the enemy, who would be in a much more exposed position out in the open.

'We're going to try and catch the enemy in a crossfire situation, Ruby,' I said over the link.

Another whistle of a bullet and one of the soldiers dropped. 'Good, because it's only a matter of time before they overrun my position,' Ruby replied.

'Understood,' I said. 'Follow me, guys,' I said to Jack and Mike.

The three of us broke into a crouched run, heading towards the junction box. Glints of light kept erupting from Ruby's crystal pillar as more bullets pinged off it.

We reached the junction box and dropped into cover behind it. I peered over the top to see the group of soldiers had now split into two squads. One glance told me everything I needed to know, thanks to Niki constantly drumming military tactics into us during countless training exercises.

'They're trying to outflank Ruby and pincer her from two different directions at once,' I said.

'Damn it. The squad on her right flank will be completely out of range for us,' Jack said.

'Then we'll just have to take down as many of them on this side as we can,' I replied, grim-faced. I was already dreading the odds of us surviving this one. 'I'm afraid, Ruby, the rest will be down to you.'

'Doing my best to trim down their numbers here,' she replied over the crack of a bullet that found a home in one of the soldiers furthest away, dropping him like a bowling pin.

The group nearest us was now less than fifty metres away from our hiding place and were beginning to circle round on Ruby's position.

My mouth was bone dry, in contrast to the eerie sense of calm that always kicked in when I was facing mortal danger.

'Okay, make every round count, guys,' I said.

'Oh don't you worry, I intend to,' Jack replied, his face tense.

Mike nodded as he checked his dart gun's magazine.

If it came to it, I knew we'd all go down fighting to our last breath.

Thankful for the shadows to disguise our presence, I aimed my MP5 over the top of the conduit, directly at the nearest member of the enemy squad.

Once I would have felt conflicted about springing what was effectively an ambush on someone, but not anymore. Too much experience of real world combat had hardened something inside me forever.

'On my mark,' I whispered. 'Three, two, one, open fire!'

With a bark of automatic fire, Jack and I sprayed the advancing soldiers with bullets, both of us dropping two of them instantly. Mike took out a third guy with a tranquilliser dart to the face. The soldier managed to take just three faltering steps before he collapsed.

The rest dived for cover behind another of the crystal junction boxes. Although we'd thinned out their numbers a fraction, my blood chilled when I heard my very own personal nemesis Alvarez barking orders to another group of around twenty soldiers. They ran from the quarry to reinforce the rest, who were already attacking us.

As I knew it would with him now on our case, a hailstorm of incoming fire erupted around our junction box, forcing us to duck down.

'Jesus, we've got to fall back,' Jack hissed as bullets whistled over our heads.

I stared at him, too appalled to even think about retreating. 'But this could be our only opportunity to make contact with the micro mind.'

'Lauren, what if we covered you to make a dash for that rune?' Mike said as he reloaded his dart gun with fresh rounds.

'No way she'd make it through that hornet's nest that we've stirred up now,' Ruby replied before I could. 'If only I had my bloody WASP swarm with me then I'd show them.'

Then, in the middle of my desperation, a possible answer to our impossible situation popped into my head.

'Ruby, when we found *Artemis* the drones were still intact. Could you control them via your Sky Wire?'

'Yeah, that's a distinct possibility, Commander. But with the power offline to that ship, they'll need to be manually rebooted before I can get them into this fight. I would go back and do it myself, but I'm a bit busy being pinned down by gunfire and trying to stay alive right now.'

'Leave it to me,' Mike said.

Before I could stop him, he was on his feet. Keeping his head down, he tore back the way we'd come.

A barrage of bullets whistled past him, fired by the soldiers advancing on our position who had now grown to at least twenty in number.

'Bloody hell, Mike!' I said. 'Next time, we have a conversation about this first. You're too damned brave for your own good.'

'Just making sure I earn my place on the team,' Mike replied.

'We are so having words about this later if we live long enough.' I looked at Jack. 'Time for a bit of covering fire.'

'Damned right,' he agreed.

The two of us popped up again and sprayed rounds into the enemy's ranks, taking out at least three more soldiers before a firestorm of return fire forced us back down into cover. But at least they had stopped firing at Mike long enough for him to escape into the distance.

Then just when I thought we might have a faint chance, things got seriously worse.

Alvarez bellowed more orders and a moment later one of the C-Ram batteries swung its Gatling gun towards us. With the angry buzz of high-speed incendiary rounds, a blazing trail of red erupted from the turret and raced towards us. We ducked, then the crystal junction box shook as the bullets began slamming into the far side of it.

My heart was thumping hard as I glanced over towards Ruby's crystal monolith to see it receiving similar treatment from the other C-Ram. Crystal shards were exploding from the structure.

'Fuckity, fuck!' Ruby said over the comm channel.

The batteries ceased firing for a moment and I sucked in several breaths before popping up again to trade fire with the soldiers. Then, with a roar praising instant death if one of their rounds hit us, the C-Rams opened up once more.

The world felt like it was tearing itself apart as the unrelenting barrage of the large calibre rounds pounded into our cover, gradually destroying it. Despite the active hearing protection of our combat helmets, my ears were ringing to hell. At the rate our cover was disintegrating it would only be a matter of minutes before there was nothing left to shelter behind.

'Okay, I've made it back to *Artemis*,' Mike's voice said over the link. 'But the bloody launch hatch is jammed solid.'

'Do whatever it takes to get it open; we're absolutely relying on you now to live through this,' I said.

'Don't worry, I'll find a way,' Mike replied, his tone strained.

As the C-Rams finished their latest barrage, just to add to our really fun day out, a lobbed grenade bounced onto the ground right next to us.

Jack just had time to grab hold of it and lob it back before it exploded in mid-air.

'Let's return that favour with interest, Jack,' I said.

'I'm so with you on that,' he said, wiping the sweat from his brow.

Jack and I pulled the pins on two fragmentation grenades each and threw them over the top of the junction box. Their explosions were answered with instant shouts and screams.

'Hey guys, they seem to be up to something in that quarry, look at this,' Ruby said.

A video appeared in my HUD. There seemed to be frantic activity around the quarry site; the workers were swarming like a nest of stirred ants. Of most immediate interest, people were setting small boxes around the forcefield sphere.

'Crap, it looks like they're setting boxes of C4 all around that forcefield thing,' Jack said. 'Alvarez is probably going all scorched earth on us, destroying that micro mind rather than let it fall into our hands.'

'Then we'll have to see what we can do about that,' I said, loading a fresh thirty-round magazine into my MP5. Then I caught sight of a flurry of movement out of the corner of my eye. I turned to see a group of three soldiers trying to move past us to our left flank. That would leave us totally exposed and it would be game over for us if they made it.

I gestured towards them. 'Jack!'

'On it!' He threw his last flashbang straight into the middle of the group and I just had time to cover my eyes as it exploded. But even with my eyes squeezed shut, the afterglow still burned through my eyelids. Barely able to see anything, I blinked them open and randomly opened fire in the direction the soldiers had been a split second ago.

But what about the rest of the squad?

I glanced over at what was left of our junction box, my eyes still burning. My blood ran cold as I caught the silhouettes of figures running forward, firing as they came. Gritting my teeth, I desperately returned fire alongside Jack, the stock of my MP5 growing slick in my hand.

Then Jack clicked empty. 'Shit, that's it, I'm out!' he shouted over a fresh barrage from the C-Ram as the rounds exploded around us.

'Shit!' I screamed, dropping flat.

Jack threw himself over the top of me, trying to protect me from the incoming fire by using his body as a shield. And with no Lucy here, there'd be no ducking into the twilight zone this time round.

There was no sense of calm left inside me now, only sheer terror at the thought of being ripped apart in an agonising death by those large calibre rounds.

Jack's hands clawed onto mine as we braced ourselves for the end. And it was at that exact moment, when I'd given up on any hope of living through this, that Mike's welcome voice finally came through the link.

'The hatch is bloody open at bloody last and the bloody drones are bloody powered up,' he said.

'Then launching WASPs now!' Ruby confirmed.

Then the C-Rams opened up for a final barrage and I just prayed the WASPs would arrive in time, because if the batteries didn't kill us first, the squad sweeping in certainly would.

CHAPTER TWENTY-FOUR

CRYSTAL SPLINTERS WERE EXPLODING ALL around us and I felt a hot sting as one slashed through the back of my hand. I swallowed down the bile that filled the back of my mouth.

'Is this a bad time to say how much I love you?' Jack said as he continued to shelter my body with his.

'It's never a bad time,' I replied.

Someone upstairs obviously had a sense of irony because it was at exactly that moment,

with the wail of a banshee, a lone WASP screamed past overhead. One became two, became a dozen in the blink of an eye. Then suddenly the C-Ram fire was swinging away from us and trying to shoot down the crazed drones swarming all over the battlefield, attacking the soldiers.

Jack rolled off me and together we peered out to see the WASPs swooping and diving as they fired at the enemy. They were already carving through the soldiers, their rounds dropping people wherever they stood or crouched.

The survivors were firing wildly upwards, trying to hit the darting drones with little or no success. But then I saw what was happening to the rounds that missed. The bullets were punching holes in the glass roof, cracks spreading wildly as the panels began to give way. The C-Ram batteries even stopped firing when four of the WASP units started to fly directly over the top of them, presumably for that same reason. With no incoming fire to worry about, Ruby rained drone fire down on the weapon systems. With a roar, the ammo boxes for the first exploded, quickly followed by the second, both turrets billowing smoke as their rounds caught ablaze and detonated like fire crackers.

Then Alvarez was running forwards towards his soldiers, waving his arms. 'Stop your fucking fire, you idiots!'

But his soldiers were too panicked to register the order as Ruby's WASPs continued to decimate their numbers. As the last soldier toppled backwards with half of his head missing, his final round hit the already crazed section of glass above and it suddenly gave way with a massive bank. Shards rained down, shattering onto the floor around the man, one large piece about a metre wide slicing straight through his body.

I braced myself for the inevitable deluge of water that should have followed. But instead of a tsunami of death the water rippled on the other side of the glass, held back by the gravity shield that once again created an upside down swimming pool. The difference this time was that this one had already begun to bulge downwards.

'Crap, how much longer can that hold?' Jack said, eyeing it.

'Hopefully, long enough for me to make contact with that micro mind,' I replied.

More soldiers had appeared and were now rushing after Alvarez, who'd already leapt into one of the vehicles. As a soldier leapt onto the back and grabbed hold of the mounted machine gun, the colonel started the engine and began to drive away along the track.

Certain he was coming to finish us off I desperately sought

fresh cover to take shelter behind.

Other buggies were starting up, but Ruby had already directed her WASPs' attention towards the remaining soldiers as they started to follow Alvarez. One of the WASPs sped in low to the ground, heading straight for one of the buggies. With a blaze of tracer fire, it sprayed rounds into the vehicle and the fuel tank exploded in a fireball that sent a dark cloud up towards the bulging roof.

There was almost nothing left of the junction box that we were hiding behind as the convoy raced along the track towards our position.

I rolled over and drew Jack into a tight hug. At least I was going to die in the arms of the man I loved.

But rather than a storm of bullets from Alvarez's vehicle, he didn't so much as slow down as he closed on us. Instead, all of his attention seemed to be fixed in the direction of where we'd left the bathyspheres. The rest of the convoy was following his lead, completely ignoring us.

As they raced past, Alvarez glanced at us. I had a brief moment to register his badly scarred face, no doubt everything to do with the glass pyramid we'd buried him alive under, leaving him for dead. A sneer filled his face as our eyes locked. And then he was gone, his convoy following in his dirt trail as Ruby harried them with drone fire.

Confused as to why Alvarez hadn't grabbed the opportunity to pepper us with bullets, I stood with Jack as workers in coveralls and hardhats rushed past us on foot. They ignored us too, continually looking at the ceiling with terrified expressions. And then we found out why as Mike, who'd been sprinting back to us, skidded to a stop.

'There are too many holes in the roof for the gravity field to be able to plug the gaps anymore,' Mike panted, clutching his sides.

I stared at him. 'You mean this chamber is about to get flooded?'

'Yes. We need to get back to those bathyspheres along with everyone else. They are the only way out of here before the whole place floods.'

Ice rushed through my blood. 'But Alvarez and his thugs will be long gone before we can get anywhere near them.'

'What about all those workers?' Jack said, gesturing towards the men and women running after the retreating vehicles.

'Oh what a surprise, that bastard Alvarez is leaving them to die while he saves his own skin,' Ruby said, joining us. She had a nasty cut across her face, but incredibly, she seemed otherwise unharmed.

She turned to me. 'So, Commander, any suggestions about how we can live through this shit show of a mission?'

Then they were all looking at me, expecting me to have the answer as always. And just like that, I suddenly did. Maybe my brain worked best when I was facing certain death.

'Our mission objective remains the same. I have to get to that control pillar. If we can do that I might be able to activate a link to the micro mind, and then we can cross over to E8 to ride this out. It could be our only chance to survive this.'

Everyone nodded and within seconds we were all racing towards the excavation site. In less than a couple of minutes, our boots digging into the loose soil and rock, we climbed the slope towards the lip of the quarry. We reached the top and as we peered down my eyes began to take in the details.

The pneumatic drills and diggers had been abandoned all around the glowing sphere. The micro mind hung suspended as energy rippled out from it into crystal conduits connecting it to the floor. The C4 charges were clearly visible around the force-field. It was only then that I spotted the one person that had remained behind, a woman standing with her back to us, who appeared to be unarmed. She was watching the forcefield as though it was an art exhibit in a gallery. As we raced around the lip, circling towards the control pillar, Jack tripped, sending a small avalanche of stones tumbling down the slope towards the woman. She turned and stared up at us. It was only then that I recognised her. Professor Evelyn Fischer, who'd I'd last seen this close up when she blew up the solar observatory at Machu Picchu.

Fischer watched us, stony-faced, as we reached the control pillar. 'You're too late to stop this,' she shouted, crossing her arms.

'Oh, we'll see about that,' I replied. I yanked the Empyrean Key out of my rucksack.

'You need to think again,' she replied, holding out a small box with a button on it.

Jack stared at it with narrowed eyes. 'What the hell have you got there, Fischer?'

'Our insurance plan. We need to make sure that you can't capture this micro mind intact. One little push and this trigger will have a chat with the C4 charges planted all over the roof. When they blow, the gravity field trying to protect this chamber will be completely overwhelmed and the place will flood within minutes. However, just before it does that, a second set of C4 charges around the micro mind will detonate. They should be enough to finally breach its forcefield. When that happens anyone still down here will be killed.'

'But you'll be throwing your own life away too,' I called back. 'Why?'

'Because I vowed never to let terrorists like you and your alien allies take over our world,' she said. 'Something for which I am prepared to sacrifice myself, for the greater good of humanity.'

'You're mad if you even think that Alvarez and his kind are anything like that, Fischer,' I said. 'We're the ones fighting for our species' survival. You're the ones throwing away any chance we have of surviving the Kimprak invasion.'

Jack nodded. 'You're so on the wrong side of this fight, Fischer.'

She laughed. 'Oh I don't think so, Professor Harper.'

I spotted her thumb beginning to tense, getting ready to press the button, and I pulled out my LRS. But then a single shot rang out and the control box flew out of Fischer's hand. Mike immediately leapt forward, sliding down the quarry slope to retrieve it as Fischer stared in horror at the bullet hole through her hand.

I turned to see Ruby lowering her Colt. 'We haven't got time for this crap. You need to make contact with the micro mind before it's too late, Commander.'

I gave her a sharp nod and dropped the stone ball into the semi-circular depression in the top of the column. But before I could activate the carrier tone in my speakers, a clear note rang out from the column and lights lit up around the Empyrean Key. With a shimmer in the air, a single icon appeared over the orb. Thanks to my synaesthesia I was the only one who could see it.

A distant boom made us all turn round to see a fireball billowing down from a section of roof between us and the bathyspheres, which were now rising out of the chamber. The charges had just blown.

With the sound of a million wine glasses being broken all at once, the ceiling gave way, falling to the ground in a hailstorm of glass. Immediately a huge blister of water began to bulge downwards as the sea above began to push down in the chamber.

Fischer was clapping despite her ruined hand. 'Bravo Colonel Alvarez. It would seem that he had a fallback plan. I guess he didn't trust me to blow the charges after all.' She gave me a manic smile as Mike clambered up the slope towards us. 'You're too late to stop this, Lauren Stelleck.'

A second explosion detonated, this time much closer, and a

waterfall broke through into the chamber.

I stood, transfixed for a moment by the shocking spectacle as the flood began to grow rapidly into an expanding wave spreading out across the floor. Then someone was shaking me, Jack.

'Lauren, whatever you're going to do, do it now!' he shouted over the tumult.

I nodded and turned back to the column to examine the icon. But then my heart crunched into a ball when I realised it wasn't the control for E8 that might have saved us. Instead it was a segmented, circle-shaped icon, one that I'd never seen before. But maybe there was still a chance that whatever it did could still save us from the nightmare death that was coming. I took a breath and activated it with a flick of my wrist.

Immediately, the column glowed fiercely as a rumbling sound came from the ground beneath our feet. Then the micro mind was blazing with light behind its forcefield as energy strobed from the light down through its crystal root system. Those same pulses of energy sped throughout the length of chamber towards the towering crystal tree trunks, shooting up into them, then the branches, which blazed with light in the sea-filled chamber. A split second later a deafening sound like a gong being hit with a sledgehammer rang out, making every bone in my body vibrate as we all cupped our hands over our ears.

'I think you just found the on switch,' Jack called out as we stared at the spectacle unfolding before us.

I thought my eyes were tricking me when far above, the curved ceiling that we'd first dropped through in the bathysphere began to move. I realised that the lines we'd seen in the ceiling were growing larger as the roof started to pivot upward from the edges, separating into opening petals in the middle of an expanding iris. Flashes of lightning were coming from the structures above on the ocean floor.

In the far distance, the tiny spec of the Overseers' underwater base was now tumbling down in slow motion through the opening chasm into the chamber. Then, as though it was being struck by an invisible hammer crushing its walls, the base began to collapse in on itself as the intense pressure overwhelmed its structure. I thought of the two prisoners that we'd left tied up there and felt a spasm of guilt as the structure was torn apart.

The remnants of the structure spiralled down, straight into the path of the three bathyspheres heading straight up towards it. With no propulsion system to avoid the thing that was heading towards them, they were sitting ducks. Part of the structure crashed into one of the bathyspheres, which exploded as the craft's hull gave way. The other two immediately severed their cables, which were being dragged down by the falling gantry, and began to float up towards the growing hole in the ceiling as its petals pivoted open.

I stared at the unfolding disaster, bitterness filling my mouth as Fischer howled with laughter behind us.

Another massive boom shook the quarry as the last C4 charge detonated directly over our heads. I just had a chance to wrap my arms around Jack as the roof completely shattered. Over his shoulder I saw Fischer looking exultant, raising her arms a split second before a ring of explosions went off around the micro mind's forcefield. The firestorm engulfed her, then the expanding shockwave threw us all flat. The shattered roof exploded into a million tumbling glass pieces, carried by a torrent of water that rushed down in a roaring, frothing mass.

As fire and water boiled towards us, Jack grabbed onto me and hugged me hard. The last thing I registered was a needle of light growing bigger fast through the foaming tumult. And then there was darkness, complete, absolute and suffocating as we all died.

CHAPTER TWENTY-FIVE

It was pitch, can't see your hand in front of your face, black. I couldn't breathe, my lungs clawing for oxygen that wasn't there. And then my mind caught up. If I was still trying to breathe, I couldn't be dead... or could I?

In the far distance a single point of luminance appeared.

Ah, so that was it, my own tunnel of light was about to drag me into the afterlife. Fine, then. As long as they had a bar though, because I so needed a stiff drink right now. Perhaps it might even be happy hour...

Oh for God's sake, Lauren, you're dying and all you can think about is getting a cheap drink? Seriously?

But then the light reached me and was rushing past, growing brighter. Much to my surprise I tasted the sweetest pure mountain air. I gulped it in, greedily filling my lungs with as much of the stuff as I could breathe in.

The light became a uniform white void around me in which I was floating. Then I could feel something solid beneath my feet, a floor on which I was suddenly standing. But when I looked down, it was absolutely featureless. There were no reflections, including my own, not even a sheen, as if the floor only absorbed light and didn't bounce any back. There were also no edges either, the floor merging seamlessly into the walls and the ceiling.

The only thing in this white void of a world was me. I was dressed in the same combat gear that I'd been in a moment ago, during the battle. My LRS was in its holster on my belt, my MP5 still slung over my shoulder. Even the Empyrean Key was in my hand, although I couldn't remember removing it from the stone column as the torrent of water from the collapsing ceiling had struck us.

'Hello?' I called out.

There was nothing for a moment, but then in the far distance I heard a voice.

'Lauren, is that you?' Jack called back.

My heart leapt. 'Yes!'

'Well shit me senseless, what the hell is this new crazy?' Ruby's voice said next.

She was followed by Mike. 'Well if this is someone's version of heaven, it's as bloody boring as hell.'

In this impossible situation I actually found myself laughing.

'Isn't that the truth?' I shouted back. 'Everyone keep talking and let's see if we can find each other.'

'Sounds like a plan,' Mike said. 'So I'm guessing you managed to shift us over to E8 judging by the whole surreal nature of where we are?'

'Actually I didn't do this,' I said. 'There was this flower icon that I activated and it seemed to turn on whatever that facility was. Did you see the ceiling of that huge chamber split open?'

'Yeah, what the hell was that all about?' Jack said, his voice getting louder as a black dot appeared in the distance, then became him as he drew closer.

'Lauren definitely found the on switch for that giant machine by the looks of it,' Ruby said, her voice louder too as she appeared from the opposite direction. 'But how is it we're alive, not that I'm complaining?'

'Was it anything to do with that glowing light that swept down through the water towards us?' Mike asked, so close that he made me jump.

I turned round to see him standing there and hugged him. 'God, it's good to see you,' I said.

'So almost getting killed is what it takes to get a hug out of you these days,' he said, squeezing me back.

I grinned at him. 'Yes, it looks that way. And to answer your question, I did see that light.'

'Yeah, I got a good look at it before everything went black,' Jack said as he reached us and joined what was fast becoming a group hug. 'I'm pretty sure it was a Guardian crystal.'

'Hang on, are you saying it transported us here?' Ruby asked.

As we all broke apart, I turned round to see her standing in front of me. Our reunion was rewarded with a round of fist bumps.

I felt a huge surge of relief wash through me. Somehow, we'd survived. Before I could pursue whether the Guardian had been involved in our rescue, more specks appeared in the distance.

We all traded looks.

'Maybe we're about to find out the answers from whoever or whatever *they* are,' Jack said as we started to head towards them.

But somehow, as I knew they would be, the specks gradually resolved into people. Some were moving towards us, others huddling in small groups, but many were hanging suspended in pearlescent balls of translucent light.

'Okay, this is going to get interesting,' Ruby said, as a man in a bomber jacket with goggles around his neck reached us first.

He put his hands on his hips. 'Are you the people who brought us here? Because I for one would like to know what the hell is going on!' he said with a distinctly mid-western American accent.

Then a fisherman in a yellow waterproof gabbled something in French, but unhelpfully my earbud was offline and wasn't translating. Then came others, some wearing contemporary clothes, but many looking like they'd been plucked straight out of the pages of a history book, including a guy who had what looked like Spanish armour from the sixteenth century. They surrounded us, all talking at once.

I held up my hands, which had no effect whatsoever. Then there was loud whistle.

'Will you all please shut up and listen to the woman?' Ruby said, withdrawing her fingers from her mouth and gesturing at me.

Everyone fell silent, their expectant faces all turned in my direction as though I was the one with all the answers. So nothing new there then.

But before I could attempt to come up with anything sounding vaguely like a coherent response, I spotted a familiar face among the crowd, pushing through them to get to me, tears running down his cheeks.

I stared in disbelief at the man that I instantly recognised as Raúl.

'You're alive!' Jack said, also recognising him.

Raúl gave Jack a confused look as if to say *who the hell are you*, but then his face twisted with grief. 'I should be dead, but an angel spared me. Please help me...' A sob broke from his mouth as he took hold of my hand. He towed me towards one of the nearest spheres of light and then placed his hand on it.

The light intensified where his hands touched the surface. Then I saw who was within it and for a moment I was rooted to the spot as surprise rushed through me.

Within the partly opaque glowing sphere, tucked into a foetal position, was a woman in a bikini with flowing dark hair. Even though I couldn't see her clearly I immediately knew that it was Raúl's sister, Maricela, with several bullet wounds in her back.

Raúl let go of my hand and dropped into a kneeling position before the sphere as fresh tears sprung from his eyes.

The sphere encasing Maricela was just like hundreds of others around us, quite a few with a similar scene playing out as people grieved before them.

I knelt by Raúl and put my arm around his shoulder. Sobbing freely now, he leaned his head into me as the rest of the team joined us.

Then Mike gasped and pointed towards two other spheres close by. When I looked at who was inside them, my heart shattered for the second time that day.

In the nearest one was Tom, while in the one next to it was Erin's co-pilot, Daryl.

I was immediately up on my feet, racing to them. I pressed my hands on Tom's sphere, trying to break through the surface, desperately, impossibly believing for a moment that he might still be alive. But as ethereal as the sphere looked, it was as unyielding as steel no matter how hard I pushed against its surface.

I stared at Tom, looking for even the tiniest breath moving his lungs, but saw none. Then with an awful realisation, I was as certain as I could be that my dear friend was dead.

The crowd had gathered around us, many watching me with compassion and understanding in their faces. But the only one I had eyes for was Tom. He looked at peace, his face smooth and free from worry, just as I'd seen him before that massive boulder had hit *Artemis* and driven it down into the ravine.

A sob rose up through me and broke free from my mouth. Then Jack was by my side as hot tears flowed, not saying anything but just cradling me in his arms.

My sobs began to slow as my tears began to subside. Then my

grief gave way to bewilderment, the same expression I'd seen on Raúl's face a moment ago.

'What happened here?' I asked Jack.

Jack smudged my tears away with his thumbs. 'My guess is that in the same way that a Guardian AI rescued us and Raúl, it also did the same for those it was too late to save.'

'You mean if Tom hadn't set that self-destruct sequence, he might still be alive?'

Jack raised his shoulders a fraction. 'There's no way to know that for sure, Lauren. But what I do know is that Tom's selfless action was enough to convince a Zumwalt destroyer that there was no longer a need to keep launching its missiles. So try to hang on to the fact that he gave his life to save ours. That is every definition of a hero that I can think of.'

I slowly nodded, feeling the grief loosen its claws in my soul a little.

I turned my face back to the sphere to gaze at the serene face of my friend. 'You're right... and Tom almost looks at peace now.'

'His race is done, and what a race it was,' Jack said with a faraway look in his eyes.

'That's a very poetic way to put it,' I said.

Jack leaned in and kissed me on the side of the head. 'I put that particular romantic streak down to my ancient Scottish ancestry. It tends to make an appearance at times like these.'

Then Mike appeared, casting a sideways grimace towards Tom and Daryl's spheres, before returning his gaze to us. 'Guys, you're going to want to hear what Raúl has just told Ruby and me.'

Jack gave my shoulder a last squeeze and offered his hand to me.

I grabbed onto it, wrapping my fingers around his and not letting go. Hand in hand we followed Mike back towards Ruby and Raúl, who were standing next to Maricela's sphere.

'Can you tell them what you just told us about the last thing you remember before you arrived here, Raúl?' Mike said.

Raúl raised a tear-streaked face from where he'd been gazing at Maricela. 'Like I said, an angel came for me.'

Jack peered at him. 'And what exactly did this angel look like?'

'A shining light that rushed towards me. The next thing I knew, I arrived here to see my sister encased in this ball...' A fresh sob cut off his words.

I held his gaze. 'The Guardian saved you, saved all of us, but wasn't in time to save your sister. Just as it was too late for our friends.'

Raúl blinked back tears and nodded.

I glanced round at the spheres. This place, apart from being somewhere that the survivors had been bought to, was a mortuary for those less fortunate.

'But that's not the most significant bit, Lauren,' Ruby said. She turned to Raúl. 'Tell them *when* this happened.'

'Just a few minutes ago,' he replied.

My initial confusion was replaced by sudden comprehension as I looked thoughtfully at the crowd, the people from throughout history. This had to be everything to do with Jack's Bermuda Triangle theory, where the countless people who'd disappeared over the centuries had ended up here, saved by the Guardians patrolling the seas.

I spoke up so that they could all hear. 'Those of you who speak English, can I ask if you arrived just moments ago?'

At least half the people in the crowd nodded.

I turned back to the others. 'I'm sure it hasn't been lost on any of you that some of these people, even if they don't realise it, have been stuck here for hundreds of years.'

'Then you know what this means. Based on the fact that time

is obviously frozen here, that suggests we have made it over to E8 after all,' Mike said.

'Okay, even if that's true, how long in our time have we been here?' Jack asked. 'Could years have already passed and the Kimprak have already arrived and destroyed our world?'

'I wouldn't jump to any conclusions about that,' Mike replied. 'Remember that in E8 time is a very fluid concept and the fact this place is still being generated by a micro mind, suggests that it is still very much intact and our world along with it.'

'But if that's true, where's the micro mind that has to be behind all of this?' I asked.

Jack raked his hand through his hair. 'Maybe to get the answer to that it's time to ask your magic eight ball, Lauren.'

I raised the stone orb still clutched in my hand to see a single triangular icon hovering over it, the same as I'd previously used to summon Lucy. Maybe that was exactly the reason that I'd arrived with it in this place, to allow me to make contact.

'That looks promising,' Jack said. It was another confirmation that this was E8. With or without synaesthesia, they could all see the control icons on the Empyrean Key for themselves whenever we were there.

'Then let's hope the micro mind is in a talkative mood, because I for one could certainly do with some answers,' Ruby said.

'Can't we all?' I replied. I selected the icon and flicked my wrist forward.

In a pulse of light everyone around me disappeared and then I was standing alone in the white endless room... alone that was, apart from the glowing, featureless female made from flowing plasma who was standing before me.

'I see that you have an Empyrean Key and know how to use it,' she said in soft neutral English.

'Yes, but where have my friends gone and all the others?' I

asked.

'Don't worry about them. They are perfectly safe within the stasis field.'

'That's how you've frozen time there?'

'It is,' the figure replied.

I tried to gather my thoughts as my fresh grief about Tom echoed through me.

'So I'm assuming you're the micro mind's avatar, but what should I call you?'

'Yes I am. You may refer to me as Eranos, although in your human tongue that would roughly translate to *operator*.'

'As in the operator of that huge machine beneath the ocean?'

'Yes. That machine is called the Resonancy Generator.'

As I realised I was about to find out its purpose, my anticipation rose. 'And what exactly does that machine do, Eranos?'

'It will awaken every other brother and sister of mine on this planet,' Eranos replied.

I stared at the AI as I processed her words. 'It will activate all the micro minds that we haven't found yet?'

'Yes, that is its core purpose. However, my connections to my kin were severed when they were attacked by a Kimprak virus that was designed in part to disrupt our communication network. When that happened, this facility activated a defence algorithm that cut me off from the rest of the network so that my systems wouldn't be compromised.'

I wasn't sure I dared to believe what she was telling me. 'And this Resonancy Generator has been activated? That's why that light show happened back there and the roof started to open?'

'Yes, that was the initial booting up of the system. When it is fully activated it will send out a low frequency pulse. To use a human analogy, think of the Resonancy Generator as a hammer, which will be used to hit the bell that is your planet and that will change the frequency forever.'

I stared at her. 'You're talking about Earth Song aren't you, the frequency tones that our planet radiates out into space?'

'Yes, although I am not familiar with that exact phrase, we seem to be describing the same thing. Every micro mind that has been shut down has an emergency protocol that will be waiting to hear the carrier tone.'

A sense of excitement was building rapidly inside me; if I had understood Eranos correctly, this could change everything.

I hardly dared to ask my next question because the implications were so huge. 'And when they do hear this new version of the Earth Song, they'll awaken?'

'Precisely,' Eranos replied.

After all the grief of the day, the sudden surge of joy was like a shaft of sunlight on the darkest winter day. 'That's incredible news.' But now to find out whether Eranos also had the answer to my other burning question. 'Do you also know the secret about how the micro minds will help defend us from the Kimprak invasion?'

'Sadly no. The significance of that particular secret is so great that our creators felt it prudent to keep that knowledge hidden, even from me. It is only to be revealed when it is absolutely necessary; a last resort.'

I'd been hoping for answers and what I'd already learned would change everything. Whatever the big reveal was would just have to wait. But for now, this was more than great news. Just like that, our search for the remaining micro minds would be over and that was incredible.

'Okay, that aside, tell me about all the people you brought here, including us?'

The glowing figure nodded. 'Ah yes. I have tried to save those where I could, giving them a reprieve from certain death by transporting them here.'

I thought of Tom, Daryl and Maricela. 'Some, but not all?'

A note of sadness crept into the AI's voice. 'You are correct. My Guardians couldn't reach some of them in time to save them. However, I still retrieved their bodies because one day I hoped to be able to return them to your world when I was given permission to do so.'

I thought of Tom and once again my grief swirled inside me and I had to push it back down.

'Who can give you permission to return all of us?' I asked.

'As you possess an Empyrean Key, you have that authority. However, I must warn you that if I try to return you now to where you were saved from, you would all be drowned. It is almost completely flooded.'

My stomach knotted. 'Please say you're not telling me there's no way to get back?'

'The hell she isn't, my little sunflower,' a familiar voice said from behind me.

I turned to see Lucy standing there. I rushed to her and threw my arms around her neck in a fierce hug.

'Goodness, it's good to see you too, Lauren.'

I pulled away from her. 'But how can you be here?'

'Because the Operator activated the substrata communication network when you used an Empyrean Key to enter this E8 reality bubble she created. That activated communication protocols and through that she can now talk to any awoken micro mind, AKA me and the other merged AIs within me.'

Fresh hope flooded through me. 'So how do we get everyone out of this place and back to the real world?'

'It may be the real world to you, but as I can assure you, E8 is very much our reality,' Eranos replied.

Lucy nodded. 'That philosophical point aside, Lauren, there is a way to return you and your team. But it's going to be very tricky and the timing is going to be awfully tight. Right now the Resonancy Generator is just starting to fully power up and when it does, all hell is going to break loose as it's basically going to cause an earthquake in the immediate vicinity. And that's not forgetting the humongous whirlpool that will be created when it transmits the signal.'

'But why generate a whirlpool?' I asked.

'Because the Resonancy Generator is a large audio chamber and it needs air rather than water to work with as a medium.

Suddenly, what had been staring me in the face the whole time finally made sense. The curved glass floor was shaped that way for a very specific reason and bore a striking similarity to something I had plenty of previous experience of working with.

I tilted my head to one side and looked at her. 'You're saying that entire chamber is a bit like a scaled up version of the Lovell radio telescope back at Jodrell Bank?'

'A perfect analogy,' Lucy replied. 'But in this case the Resonancy Generator has been built to transmit, rather than receive a signal, and to wake the other micro minds up with an alarm call. The bad news is that this whole facility is a one-time use device and will tear itself apart in the process. If that wasn't enough of a problem, because of the Overseers' actions the lives of everyone here and even Eranos herself are in serious danger.'

Eranos was nodding. 'Back in your reality in its current timeframe, milliseconds have passed since I was able to snatch you away from certain death. The shock waves from the charges are still expanding into my energy shield and are about to overwhelm it. I am going to have to launch my micro matrix crystal now to have a chance of surviving. That should just give me time to escape the blast. When I have done that, as intended by the design of the Resonancy Generator, I will move into position to become the focal point for its parabolic bowl to transmit the signal.'

I nodded, grateful that my previous experience as a radio telescope operator meant that I could understand what she'd just said. 'So rather than a receiver box like we had mounted above Lovell's dish, you'll become the transmitter yourself?'

'Correct,' Eranos replied.

Lucy tapped an imaginary watch. 'Look, literally even a few milliseconds is of the essence here if we're going to pull this off. I also need to get you up to speed with what the plan is, Lauren.'

'Go ahead,' I replied.

'Back at Eden, Alice gave me permission to launch and I'm on the way right now to merge with Eranos once the Resonancy Generator has finished sending its broadcast.'

'But what about that Zumwalt destroyer on the surface? I can't see it sitting it out whilst a great big alien megastructure starts to power up on the seabed. '

'Actually, it's even worse than that because the Overseers have sent serious reinforcements and they're heading towards the site in the form of three TR-3B squadrons.'

'Damn it, that's going to make this even more difficult. But what about the reinforcements that Niki called in?'

'They'll be here in five minutes in your time, but by then it may be too late. Eranos's only hope, and the lives of everyone she is protecting, is that *Ariel* gets into the fight and protects her as she launches.'

'In that case we need to get me and my team back onboard *Ariel* and fast.'

'I was hoping you'd say that, but I probably understated it when I said it was going to be extremely tricky, Lauren,' Lucy said. 'It's also going to be extremely dangerous.'

I crossed my arms. 'So when has that ever stopped us? Just tell me how we can make this happen?'

My friend nodded. 'Okay, don't say I didn't warn you...'

If I'd known what she was about to suggest, even I would have had second thoughts. Our day was just about to go from bad to much, much worse.

CHAPTER TWENTY-SIX

THE WHITE WORLD vanished around me and was replaced by one of thundering water roaring so loudly that it made my ears sing. I found myself standing on top of *Artemis's* wrecked hull, floating on the surface of the churning water as it rose rapidly towards the roof as the chamber flooded.

The air shimmered as Jack, Mike and Ruby materialised alongside me. They stared with their mouths open at the horror show around us. But I was already scanning the chamber above, looking for any sign of the next stage of the plan kicking in.

By my own estimate we'd only been away for a few seconds, probably less. The blast of the fireball from the C4 charges around the micro mind were just fading away to the east of us. One of two remaining bathyspheres was being dragged down to the floor by the plummeting gantry that had just ploughed into it, but the underwater base had already beaten it to the bottom and had crashed through the ceiling.

Where it had broken through the roof another cascade of water was rushing in to add to the growing floodwater boiling beneath it. That wild white water now covered the entire floor and the tall crystal pillars just peeked up over the top. There was certainly no sign of any survivors from the Overseers' people, who'd rushed for the bathyspheres but hadn't made it in time.

'Why the hell are we back here?' Ruby said, spinning round to confront me. 'We're all going to be drowned at any damned moment!'

'We're here because that's where we need to be to protect that micro mind when she launches,' I replied. 'Several squadrons of TR-3Bs are about to arrive, not to mention that bloody Zumwalt that's bound to open fire the moment it spots her.'

'Her? Did you meet the AI when you vanished just now?' Jack asked.

'Yes, and Lucy too; we put together a plan.'

Their expressions grew wider, especially Mike who threw me a *what the heck* look.

'Look, I haven't got time to explain all the details, you're just going to have to trust me,' I said.

Jack gave me a sharp nod. 'We always do, don't we Lauren?'

Ruby and Mike nodded too, which brought a lump to my throat and I so didn't have time for that right now. But yes, we were definitely a tight knit team even when we were caught in the middle of an unfolding disaster.

Far above us the domed roof had finished opening to reveal a massive round hole that was easily a kilometre wide. Far above that, on the distance surface of the ocean the tiny speck of the Zumwalt was still visible. Getting Eranos past that ship intact was going to be a major problem, let alone whatever was waiting for us in the air above it by the time we reached it. But I also needed to remind myself that help was on the way in the form of the Pangolin squadron and Lucy herself. We just needed to keep Eranos alive long enough for her to merge with the AI. Everything else was secondary to that, including our own lives.

I could see just one bathysphere rising fast towards the

surface. Knowing the nine lives that a certain Overseer colonel had, I fully expected Alvarez to be onboard it.

The water was rising faster now, pushing *Artemis* towards what remained of the glass ceiling. To make matters worse, our ride was also starting to list to one side as the water rushed in through the large missing section of the hull beneath the waterline. She was probably only floating at all because of the pockets of air still trapped inside the broken cockpit.

With a roar of steam, the last of the fireball was extinguished by the waterfall thundering down into what remained of the quarry. But despite the detonation of the C4 charges that had wiped out the forcefield, Eranos's tetrahedron crystal was still glowing fiercely blue even as its protection started to fail. The crystal began to rise up towards the top of the shield as the seawater smashed down onto it.

Lucy had been right that the timing would be down to the millisecond. At the last moment, as the shield completely failed, Eranos accelerated fast, straight up into the waterfall and for a moment we lost sight of her in the maelstrom.

I knew that everything that happened next depended on her pulling off this very precise manoeuvre and I didn't even realise that I was crushing Jack's hand until he squeezed mine back.

But then a surge of relief passed through me as I spotted Eranos again, a glowing gemstone rising quickly through the water and out into the main cavern.

My tense shoulders relaxed a fraction. 'Oh thank God, she's made it. Now all the lives of the people in her stasis field in E8, including Raúl, will be safe.'

'Not wanting to doubt you, but what about saving our lives too in this cunning plan of yours?' Mike said, starting to look more than a little bit apprehensive as *Artemis* began to slowly sink into the frothing water.

'Hopefully, any moment now,' I said, my eyes searching the ocean directly above us for another critical part of this plan.

Then I saw something speeding straight down into the chamber through the vast hole in the ceiling. The identity of the craft was given away by bubbles trailing off the surface of its saucer shape.

Jack, who'd spotted it too, stared at me. 'Is that *Ariel?*'

'I bloody hope so because a huge part of this plan depends on it, and Erin's flying skills,' I said. 'So get ready for a fast boarding everyone. Lucy is going to extend a gravity bubble and we need to get onboard fast when *Ariel* arrives. Then we need to get clear of the chamber before the earthquake hits.

Everyone stared at me.

'Earthquake?' Ruby said, even her professional calm looking visibly shaken.

'Another detail for the debriefing later,' I said.

'Right...' Jack said, shaking his head.

Ariel tore down towards one of the large blast holes in the glass ceiling to the west of our position. Her chameleon cloak flickered off just before she entered the chamber, something that I'd already agreed with Lucy, as it was going to make this manoeuvre a hell of a lot easier if we could actually see what we were leaping onto.

The X103's thrusters were fighting hard to maintain *Ariel's* course as she tore down through the column of water and into the flood. Then in one of the near impossible right hand turns that our craft was capable of, she switched direction and came surging underwater straight towards *Artemis*.

It felt like an eternity but was probably just a few seconds by the time *Ariel* slowed to a stop to one side of the other craft. The water had risen to our knees and a tentacle of clear air was extending up from *Ariel's* top hatch like a giant, transparent, elephant's trunk. It broke the surface of the frothing water less than a few metres from our sinking craft and expanded into a vertical air corridor.

'Okay, go, go, go!' I shouted.

Without hesitating, Ruby leapt first, dropping down through the air tunnel and landing cleanly next to *Ariel's* hatch.

Mike went next but slipped on the surface of the hull as he landed. Ruby reacted with lightning reflexes, grabbing onto him before he fell through the gravity shield.

Two down and two to go. Now it was our turn.

The water surged as *Artemis* submerged beneath Jack and I. As the boiling flood rose to our hips it began pummelling into my legs, threatening to sweep me away into the torrent. As the smell of brine filled my nostrils, Jack grabbed my hand. Together we half-jumped, half-swam through the freezing water and dropped in through the gravity corridor to land next to *Ariel's* hatch, Ruby and Mike grabbing on to steady us. At that same moment, *Artemis* started to tip towards *Ariel* as the craft sank, carried towards our own ship by the current.

But Erin was obviously on the case, deftly moving *Ariel* out of the way. The hull shifted beneath us as the water surged past the gravity passageway, starting to break through it. We all dived for the hatch and began to clamber down the ladder into the safety of the cockpit. Jack slammed the hatch shut behind him just as the gravity tunnel collapsed and water surged over the hull.

The others were already in their flight seats as we rushed to ours and strapped in. Even with the protection of the gravity shield *Ariel* seemed to be buffeted from every side, making the self-levelling gimbal mechanism for the flight deck whine as it fought to keep it level.

My gaze snapped to the virtual cockpit screen. On it I could see Eranos's micro mind still rising up through the main Resonancy Generator chamber as the giant tree structures pulsed faster around her with increasingly strong bursts of rippling light.

'Get after that micro mind and stick to it like glue, Erin,' I said, locking my harness into its buckle.

'You can count on me, Commander,' she replied.

Erin pushed the throttle lever far forward and *Ariel* shook as her thrusters fought to drive us through the surging current towards the hole in the roof after the micro mind.

'Jesus, are our thrusters going to be powerful enough to get us out of here?' Jack asked.

'They just need to get us to an opening in the glass roof, then I'll use the main REV drive to lift us out,' Erin said, chewing her lip.

'You've got this,' I said.

'All I know is that is no end of flying experience can quite prepare you for something this crazy,' she replied.

'You mean the part where your flying saucer is turned into a submarine trapped in an underwater cavern?' Jack asked with a wry smile.

'Along with everything else they never mention in the job description,' Mike added.

'Yeah precisely that,' Erin replied, but at least the banter had raised a smile from her, hopefully enough to ease some of the panic she was no doubt feeling, just as I would be in her shoes.

The hole in the roof was crawling towards us way too slowly for my liking as we were buffeted from every side by the surging water.

'Come on, baby, you can do this,' Erin murmured.

The drumming sound of the waterfall slamming onto the hull echoed throughout the cockpit as we entered the wild vortex of water pouring through the roof. But despite everything it was throwing at her, with fine corrections on the controls Erin brought us into precise alignment with the ragged hole roof in the roof.

'Here goes nothing,' she said as she pushed the throttle forward.

Ariel shot straight upwards and it was then that I realised not only just how good our new pilot was, but the updated REV drive too. With not so much of a punch of G-force, *Ariel* cleared the blast hole in the roof with barely a metre to clear, up into a fountain of bubbles. We could all see the micro mind, now a shining beacon of light in the main chamber and rising fast through the roof.

'Nice flying, Erin, although technically I guess that isn't quite the right description for what you just pulled off,' Jack said.

'Oh, thanks for the compliment.'

But suddenly a vibration ran through the ship and I shot Erin a questioning look. 'Please don't tell me we've developed a problem?'

'That's nothing to do with *Ariel*, Commander,' she replied. 'According to our sensors that vibration is coming from outside.'

Mike, who'd been peering at his Sky Wire, which had become active again thanks to *Ariel's* quantum radio system, nodded. 'Yes, I'm seeing seismic monowave readings right across Cuba. According to the data, we're sitting right at the epicentre of it.'

'Sound like that earthquake you mentioned, Lauren?' Jack asked.

'Yes, but this is just the opening act,' I said. 'Eranos, the micro mind, said the quake was literally going to tear this place apart.'

'Now you tell us,' Jack said.

'As I said, there is a lot to talk about and not a lot of time to do it in,' I replied.

The tree structures were strobing with an almost constant brilliance now as a humming sound grew stronger from beyond the hull of our ship.

'Bloody hell, the quake has already got a reading of a constant two on the Richter scale,' Mike said, looking at his screen.

'I think it's going to get much worse,' I replied. 'Time to get us out of this chamber, Erin.'

'On it, increasing power to REV drive.'

We hurtled straight up towards Eranos, who'd come to a dead stop about a thousand metres above the Angelus megastructure in the open sea.

As *Ariel* cleared the chamber we rose past the pyramid structures that were now all blazing with intense light, casting sharp elongated shadows across the surrounding seabed. Every so often one of the tall towers let out a whip line of superheated plasma that instantly boiled the water around it into bubbles, marking the underwater lightning's zigzag passage before fading away.

Much to my relief I noticed that the whale pods that had been circling the facility had obviously got the memo that something bad was about to kick off and were nowhere to be seen.

Tremors rippled across the seabed in increasingly rapid succession, making the surface undulate as though it had been turned to jelly. But even more significant than that, I could see spinning columns of water around the edges of the chamber beneath us, beginning to merge in the middle.

'Crap, a torpedo has just launched from that damned Zumwalt destroyer and they seem to be targeting the micro mind,' Ruby said.

'Then take it out now!' I shouted.

Ruby nodded and grabbed hold of her weapon system's joystick. With a whine we heard the miniguns spool up and then a torrent of flechette rounds tore away from *Ariel*. Like a swarm of silver fish they sped past the micro mind straight into the path of the torpedo streaking down towards it. The torpedo smashed into the flechettes and instantly detonated. A moment later its stern section, propeller still spinning, corkscrewed past the micro mind, which had remained stationary in the water during the whole engagement.

I pressed the comms button on my seat arm. 'Niki, we need air support urgently!'

'Roger that, coming in with weapons hot.'

Above the surface of the sea, I saw something streaking through the sky before glancing off the invisible ship.

At once an answering laser lanced out from it into the sky.

'Taking incoming fire and our shields are down to twenty percent. We can't handle more of this,' Niki said. 'Oh shit...'

'What's wrong?' I asked.

'Sixteen TR-3Bs are just two minutes out and according to our sensors three of them have those damned new laser turrets too. This is going to get messy fast.'

'ETA on our reinforcements, Niki?' Jack asked.

'Five minutes out. Lucy is gaining fast and is about another minute behind them.'

'We just need to keep the micro mind alive long enough to merge with Lucy,' I said.

I turned to Erin. 'Get us in front of that micro mind to protect her. If it comes to it we sacrifice ourselves to protect that AI.'

I caught the look that she and the others gave me.

But then Jack nodded. 'Right call, Lauren.'

'It is, but I'm not sure how long we can survive this either.'

'So let's improve things in our favour and use the Overseers' weapons against them,' Ruby said.

'How can we do that exactly?' I asked.

'Like this.' Ruby pressed an icon on her screen and suddenly, around the edges of what had been the square of the underwater structure, dozens of torpedoes burst from the Overseer launchers stationed there. The missiles sped past us towards the surface.

'Oh you absolute beauty, Ruby,' Mike said as we watched torpedoes converge on the destroyer.

'Why thank you, kind sir,' she said, grinning.

The detonations lit up the surface of the ocean like the Fourth of July and New Year's Day fireworks all rolled into one. But as the explosions faded, I wasn't surprised to see the destroyer still sitting there. However, there was one key difference now, the destroyer was no longer invisible and its black angled sides were now clear for anyone to see.

'Okay, not a kill shot but it shows that damned thing is actually vulnerable,' Ruby said. 'Are you seeing this too, Niki?'

'Roger that. It suggests that if you hit that ship's shield hard enough, we can get through it. But it will have to be one hell of a missile to pull that off.'

An idea immediately burst into my mind and I sat up straighter. 'What about the X103 that you have slaved to you, Niki? There's no one on it; could it be large enough to break through their shield?'

There was a momentary pause and then a laugh. 'I like your thinking, Lauren. Let's give it a go and see what happens.'

'Just to make sure we have maximum impact, we're going to fire all our Spearfish missiles at the same time in a coordinated attack,' I said.

Ruby grinned at me. 'Twisted thinking! I like it, Commander.'

'Okay, we've just ordered Delphi onboard that X103 to begin a one-way attack run,' Niki said. 'Sending you the live feed that we are receiving from her so you can coordinate your own attack.'

Another video popped up on our virtual cockpit. In the far

distance the angular shape of the Zumwalt destroyer was clearly visible and growing larger fast. An intense beam of green light burst from it and the X103 just had time to jink sideways out of its path as the light beam sped past.

My guts rose to my chest as the X103 sped straight towards it.

'All Spearfish torpedoes are away!' Ruby shouted.

Ariel shuddered as our cockpit display showed five cylindrical shapes bursting from us, heading straight towards the destroyer.

The prow of the Zumwalt filled the video feed as the automated anti-aircraft systems desperately fired tracing rounds towards the X103. But the AI piloting the ship was faultless in its execution of the kamikaze manoeuvre and Troy, Eden's most skilled pilot, would have been proud. Delphi spun the craft in every direction in its last seconds. The video showed the Zumwalt's rear deck growing larger fast. In the last few frames it was close enough to see the individual rivets in the superstructure. Then static filled the window.

A series of massive explosions rocked the craft in a shocking display of raw power, ripping through the stern as the X103 scythed straight through it. That was followed by secondary explosions as our Spearfish torpedoes reached the Zumwalt's hull, detonating along its length as the gravity shield failed. As waves erupted around the destroyer, it started to list heavily to one side, fires sweeping along its upper decks.

Ruby whooped and fist-thumped the air. 'One serious take down – take that, bitches!'

But despite our victory part of me found it hard to share her joy. How many people had we just killed up there?

Suddenly a blinding light burst from below us and for an awful moment I thought the Overseers had left us a present in the form of a tactical nuke set to detonate if they lost control of the site. But when that wasn't followed by a massive explosion that ripped *Ariel* apart, I looked down to see that beams of light were now shooting out of the chamber to converge on Eranos. And that wasn't all. A large, spinning column of water had begun to rise up towards her just as she'd told me. The Resonancy Chamber was getting to ready to transmit the critical broadcast.

'Quick, back us up to safe distance, Erin,' I said.

'Affirmative, Commander.' She pulled the joystick and we shot backwards. About two klicks out she brought us to a stop as the column of water enveloped Eranos, who was starting to shine like a tiny star.

'What the hell is going on? It looks like that Angelus megastructure is trying to destroy that micro mind?' Jack said.

I shook my head. 'No, Eranos told me that she needed to act as a transmitter for the megastructure when it sends out a high power broadcast. This has to be part of that process.'

'To do what exactly?' Mike asked.

Of course, I still hadn't had time to tell them what this was all about.

I beamed at the team. 'To wake every micro mind on the planet, that's bloody what.'

They all stared back at me, gobsmacked.

'You're shitting me,' Ruby finally said.

'I promise you that I'm not; I'll tell you everything in that debriefing later.'

'I'm increasingly looking forward to it,' Jack said, raising his eyebrows.

'Damn it, we've got company,' Niki said. 'Those reinforcement TR-3Bs are here and have already locked weapons onto us. Our shields are glowing right across the thermal spectrum thanks to all the punishment *Thor's* been getting. Not sure we can survive much more until our own reinforcements get here. Shielding is down to twelve percent.'

'Just hang in there, we're on our way,' I said. I glanced at Erin. 'Time to get up there and get into that fight.'

'With pleasure. It'll be good to see the sky again,' she replied with a wide smile.

She pushed the throttle forward and with a surge of bubbles in our wake, we began to rise rapidly towards the surface.

CHAPTER TWENTY-SEVEN

WITHIN SECONDS *ARIEL* had reached the surface and burst through it like the flying sub from the old sci-fi series *20,000 Leagues Under the Sea.* To our port side the Zumwalt destroyer was well and truly alight. Fires were everywhere over its superstructure and clouds of black smoke billowed from the ship as it listed heavily over at a forty-five degree angle.

Much to my relief I caught a brief glimpse of lifeboats speeding away. Then they and even the sinking destroyer became dwindling specks as we shot up towards the aerial battle, where laser shots and railgun rounds were carving up the sky with light and vapour trails.

'Ruby, give them hell,' I said.

'Oh I intend to. Switching our miniguns over to armour-piercing rounds.'

Darting black enemy TR-3Bs seemed to be everywhere, swarming Niki's single disc ship *Thor* that had been made visible with our virtual cockpit display. I took in the considerable scarring in its ablative armoured hull, some parts of which were literally glowing red hot from the incoming laser rounds that its gravity shielding had no effect in stopping, unlike a projectile.

Erin slammed the joystick sideways as a *welcome to the fight* railgun round came barrelling out of the sky straight towards us. It hurtled past *Ariel* with a sonic boom that rattled the ship.

'Time to return the compliment,' Ruby said.

A lock box appeared on the cockpit around the triangular-shaped TR-3B and Ruby opened fire as Erin raced us straight towards it.

Impacts exploded all over the other craft's hull and then detonations began to ripple beneath its plating, buckling in several places. As the TR-3B began corkscrewing down towards the ocean, its crew compartment ejected along with its reactor in separate pods. Parachutes burst from both a moment later.

We sped through the stricken craft's trail of smoke as Erin spun our cockpit three-sixty to engage the next target. Then warning alarms were shrieking at us all at once.

'We have multiple locks on us,' Ruby said, her forehead furrowing as she stared at her screens.

Three railgun rounds came tearing towards us. Erin dodged two, but the third was too close to avoid. The deadly projectile sped straight towards us but suddenly veered off as it hit a Pangolin that had put itself in the way, its gravity shielding throwing it off. For a moment I thought it was *Thor,* but then five other Pangolins blinked into existence around us.

'Did someone just order the cavalry?' Alice's voice said over the comm.

'God damn it woman, talk about great timing!' Niki replied.

Immediately the fresh ships started to engage the TR-3B craft.

'Not that we aren't grateful, Alice, but I thought you promised that you wouldn't be involved in combat missions again,' Jack said as Erin spun us away into a fresh dogfight.

'I think to maybe paraphrase what my six-year-old self might say to you right now, no one's the boss of me.'

Jack chuckled. 'Fair enough.'

The shift in the battle with the extra craft was instantaneous, even despite the fact that our fleet was still heavily outnumbered by three to one.

Already the TR-3Bs were reacting to the new threats, firing lasers and railgun rounds at the new arrivals. But the skill of our pilots in this battle was breathtaking, especially Alice, who'd lost none of her stunt pilot's edge. Rendered in its full glory on our virtual cockpit, I watched her Pangolin spin and dive, avoiding every attempt to hit her craft.

Erin was also proving more than able in combat. Our X103 might have been smaller than the Pangolins, but *Ariel* was faster and certainly more manoeuvrable as skilfully demonstrated by our new pilot. She weaved the craft through a squadron of TR-3Bs like a whirling dervish.

And Ruby was every bit a perfect match for our pilot with her weapon skills. Our miniguns continuously clattered away as she locked onto target after target. A TR-3B made the mistake of lingering a moment too long as it poured laser fire into Niki's craft and was duly given some instant karma.

With an extraordinary corkscrew role, Erin threw off a TR-3B that had been chasing us. Then our hulls practically kissed the cockpit of the craft attacking *Thor* as we sped over it. Our missile lock indicator immediately flashed up and Ruby's gunslinger instincts had already responded.

'ASSAM missile away,' she said with icy calmness despite the beads of sweat that had broken out all over her forehead.

Before the enemy craft had a chance to manoeuvre away, Niki's Pangolin cut off its escape route with an intense four-way stream of minigun fire.

As our ASSAM raced towards the hemmed-in enemy ship,

puffs of silver chaff exploded around it as it tried desperately to jink around the sky, trying to evade our incoming missile. But Ruby kept the laser locked on to the enemy craft.

The missile flew straight through the clouds of foil, curving up into the triangular craft's belly. With a loud *whump* it exploded, hull cracking open, then suddenly it was plummeting towards the ocean as its anti-grav drive died.

It was as I tracked its death spiral that I saw what was happening on the ocean surface.

A huge whirlpool at least a kilometre wide had opened up in the ocean, the surface churning around it with white water waves, the funnel extending all the way down to the Resonancy Chamber that was blazing burning white light. The crystal trees were crackling with energy discharges that lanced down and struck the parabolic dish of the curved glass floor. And just as Lovell did with radio waves back at Jodrell Bank, the dish focused that capture energy straight back upwards towards a focal point – Eranos's micro mind. She hung like some sort of luminous spider at the epicentre of this maelstrom of energy as the whirlpool swirled around her.

'Goodness, will you look at all the fun that you've had without me,' Lucy said, popping up in a video window. At the same moment her merged micro mind craft blurred to a stop in the sky, high over the battle.

'You know us, it's just one big party when we're out on a mission,' I said as Erin exercised a high-speed manoeuvre to avoid two incoming railgun rounds.

Lucy laughed and then her face grew more serious. 'Okay, Eranos isn't responding to my messages, but that's hardly surprising as it looks like she has her hands full. But I'm reading a rapid increase in the power output that—'

She didn't get a chance to finish her sentence because several huge beams of light suddenly burst from the underwater chamber, converging on Eranos. The micro mind blazed with brilliance and then with a blinding flash at least fifty light beams burst out from her, speeding away beneath the ocean towards the horizon. A number of them shot past us up into the sky.

'Everyone avoid those energy beams whatever you do!' Lucy shouted over our fleet's comm channel.

At once Erin spun us away, along with our other battling pilots, from the beams blazing past. But one TR-3B, while being harried by Alice's Pangolin, was struck directly by one of the white lances of energy and it passed straight through the ship. Rather than being instantly ripped apart as I thought it would, the ship stopped dead in the air, trapped like it was in some sort of tractor beam. Then the craft began to vibrate faster and faster until it seemed to expand, plates buckling, before blowing apart in a fireball of shrapnel.

'Is that micro mind firing off some sort of energy weapon?' Jack asked, staring at the light lines beaming straight into not just the sky but by the look of it, straight into space.

'No, they're intensely high-powered communication bursts across every available frequency,' Lucy said.

Before I could ask where the beams might be aimed at, our cockpit was flooded with the sound of intense, whale-like song that echoed around the ship so loudly that we had to cover our ears. Then suddenly the sound stopped dead, leaving my ears ringing.

Now visible through the shaft of the whirlpool, the light in the chamber had died to nothing. Then the Resonancy Chamber began to shake, the crystal columns of the tree structures splintering apart and beginning to topple onto the glass bowl collector and crashing through it. Eranos, far above the destruction, was beginning to rise away from where she'd been hovering.

The Zumwalt destroyer wasn't so lucky. The currents of the whirlpool had dragged it towards the edge and the ship had begun to tip over it. As it did so a series of explosions detonated across its hull as its back was broken. Then it tipped into the funnel, kicking up spray as it crashed towards the chamber. The whirlpool began to close up on it like a giant throat swallowing a piece of food whole. I caught a last glimpse of the Zumwalt being torn into fragments as it crashed straight into the Resonancy Chamber. Then the ocean rushed back in to claim the site and the destroyer for its own, leaving nothing but a cauldron of white water boiling on the surface.

'Incoming railgun round!' Ruby shouted.

Erin just had time to shift us sideways to avoid it.

I gazed out at the six remaining TR-3Bs coming back in for an attack run.

'Okay, time to wrap this up,' I said.

Lucy nodded from the video window. 'You'll need to cover both Eranos and me because our gravity shields will be down during the merging process, which by the way has just kicked in so we can't stop it now.'

'You've got it,' I said. I pressed the comms button. 'All ships, protect the merging micro minds at all costs.'

Lots of affirmatives came back over the channel.

Erin was already on the case, tucking us in tightly behind Eranos as she rose past.

Niki and Alice's ship had done a similar manoeuvre around Lucy, forming up around her to shield her from the TR-3Bs, which unfortunately included two laser-turreted variants, currently being engaged by the rest of our fleet.

I spotted one of the TR-3Bs dive towards the rising micro mind, lining up for a railgun shot.

'Ruby!' I shouted, gesturing to the threat.

She shook her head. 'I'm out of ASSAMs and its too far away to hit with our miniguns.'

'Then allow me,' Erin said.

With a rotation of the joystick she manoeuvred us straight into a position between the TR-3B and the micro mind.

A shape blurred towards us from the enemy ship and slammed into our gravity shield, deflecting it but making the whole craft rattle. But the job was done because the railgun projectile arced harmlessly towards the ocean.

Things didn't go so well for the TR-3B that had taken the shot, as it had left itself as something of a sitting duck. A Pangolin was already speeding towards it, miniguns blazing and slicing through the crew compartment. The enemy ship exploded into a cloud of shrapnel.

'Oh crap, I have more incoming radar signatures – at least thirty more craft travelling in at hypersonic speeds,' Ruby said.

'Jesus, that's going to be more than enough to overwhelm us,' Jack said.

'Don't be so sure,' Lucy replied.

Then all around the aerial battle were white pill-shaped craft coming to a dead-stop. I recognised them instantly. These weren't Overseer reinforcements but craft I hadn't seen since a mission that had ended up taking me to Area 51 in pursuit of one of these craft's pilots, namely an alien Grey.

'Well paint me surprised, those are Tic Tac craft,' Ruby said, swinging her targeting reticule away. But her hand twitched the sight back towards them as blue energy beams lanced out from each and every one of the alien ships.

However, rather than our craft being the target, they struck the remaining TR-3Bs. Each one dropped out of the sky like a stone, tumbling end over end until they hit the ocean far below, sending up great plumes of water.

The others in the cockpit stared at me.

'Was this all part of the plan too?' Jack asked.

'Not as far as I know,' I replied.

Lucy's voice cut in. 'The Greys piloting those ships picked up

Eranos's radio broadcast. It seems they decided to turn up on their own volition to help out, not that we necessarily needed any by that point. Anyway, I'll talk to you on the other side of the merger. My systems will be offline during the procedure.'

'See you on the other side, Lucy,' I said.

'Looking forward to it.' She beamed at me as her video window closed.

Our fleet and the Tic Tacs came to a stop about two klicks out from Eranos and Lucy, as they headed towards each other, our squadrons bearing witness to what was about to happen.

The Angelus AIs closed to within a few metres of each other and as we'd seen on previous occasions, they slowed at the last millisecond. Then Eranos's crystal tetrahedron slid into Lucy's micro minds craft, sparks flying from both AIs as they merged.

A huge pulse of light burst from each craft, making our virtual cockpit blink off for a moment as the light washed over us.

Erin stared at *Ariel's* readouts and then her face relaxed. 'Don't panic, we're all good.'

Ruby nodded. 'Yes, that was just an energy spike, but the cockpit display is already rebooting.'

The hexagonal display panels lining the cabin flickered back into life. Before us, hanging in the sky, was a star-shaped, merged micro mind craft, now with an extra three points.

Whoops and claps were coming over the comm channel.

But rather than looking at the micro minds, I noticed Jack was gazing down towards the ocean.

'Well will you look at that?' he said, a sense of wonder in his voice.

The whale pods had returned. Hundreds of the beautiful creatures had converged on the spot where only a few minutes ago had been a spinning whirlpool of death. The sunlight glistened off their backs and they swam towards the centre of it. I was pretty sure that if we had still been down in that sea we would have heard the ocean filled with the sound of their songs as they called out to each other.

Mike sat back in his seat. 'After that huge firework display, can someone please tell me what happens now this signal has been sent?'

A video window opened up and Lucy appeared on it. 'Oh, I'd be delighted to after what I just learned from Eranos and trust me, it's seriously going to blow your minds!'

CHAPTER TWENTY-EIGHT

I SAT WITH JACK, Mike and Ruby in Leon's quarters onboard *Venus* a week later. We were in the sea off Cuba, at the site where *Hercules* had been sunk. Carlos had made a personal request via Glenn, saying he would very much like us to attend. So here we were, all dressed in our finest and waiting for the ceremony to begin.

It also marked the end of what had been a gruelling emotional week after funerals had taken place for Tom and Daryl, who'd both been buried in the jungle back at Eden. Erin had stayed behind to work out the arrangements to visit Daryl's family and share her condolences with them.

If those burials hadn't been enough to break my heart, there'd also been the memorial service where their names, along with Maricela's, had been added to the memorial wall in hangar bay one. Oh how I'd wept at that one, my soul splintering into tiny pieces. And now the last part of this emotional marathon was about to conclude with Maricela's burial at sea. Carlos and Raúl felt it was exactly what she would have wanted rather than the more traditional Cuban funeral.

But it had also been a frantic week as events had unfolded after the Resonancy Chamber broadcast and so Lucy had just rung in via my Sky Wire to get us up to speed with the latest developments.

She gazed at us from the screen that I had propped up on Leon's desk.

'I've just finished correlating all the data from radio telescopes around the world,' Lucy said. 'We finally now know where those fast radio bursts that were aimed up into the sky, were targeted.'

I cradled my hands together; that topic had really been bugging me, and even Eranos had no idea of the answer when I'd asked her about it.

'Which was where exactly?' I asked Lucy.

'It turns out they were headed for all of your solar system's rocky core planets: Mercury, Venus and Mars. Quite a few moons were also targeted including Earth's own, Jupiter's Ganymede and Callisto, and Saturn's Dione and Mimas.'

'And has any activity been detected on them?'

'Radio telescopes registered brief pulses of return data, suggesting that if micro minds are buried on them they certainly received the message.'

Jack shook his head. 'It never occurred to me that the Angelus might have hidden micro minds across the whole solar system and not just here on Earth.'

'In fairness, none of us did,' Ruby replied with a shrug.

'Which only adds extra weight to the fact that my creators went to extreme lengths to hide whatever secret it is that we have buried in our collective consciousness,' Lucy said.

Mike pulled at his shirt collar, which was clearly a few sizes too small for him. 'I think that whatever is capable of stopping a Kimprak invasion must be off the scale compared to anything that humanity can currently get their hands on.'

But that was the thing that had kept us all guessing. If our species already had nukes, what could pose even *more* of a threat to the Kimprak scavenger race heading towards the planet?

'Has any activity been detected on Earth yet, Lucy?' I asked.

'The quick answer is yes and to give you a fuller answer, I'm going to patch Jodie in to our call as there's been a major development in the last hour,' Lucy said.

Jodie's face appeared on the screen. 'Hi guys. I didn't want to disturb you until the ceremony was finished but yes, Lucy's right. It's been a full eight days since that broadcast was sent and our TREENO CubeSats network has registered over fifty neutrino bursts right round the Earth.'

'That's the good news,' Lucy said. 'The bad news is that the micro minds still need to be excavated from their hidden locations even if they have become active.'

'Hang on, logistically there is no way that we're going to be able to get to that many sites ahead of the Overseers, let alone the ones on the other planets and moons,' I said.

'Ah, that's the other bit of news,' Jodie said. 'There have been multiple sightings of Tic Tac craft guarding the sites where the neutrino bursts have come from.'

'Seriously, you mean we're going to have plenty of time to get to them?' Jack said.

'Well if it were just your team, I'd say no. But Alice is already briefing other flight crews to begin the retrieval process. She has even sent Pangolins out to begin the recovery of the micro minds across the solar system.'

'That's great news,' Ruby said.

I leaned forward. 'It is, but is there any more news on all those people who returned from Eranos's E8 stasis field yet?'

'Alice has been flat out doing what she can to set up what's turned out to be a major reorientation exercise, as you can probably imagine,' Jodie replied. 'In some cases they have to get up to speed with the several centuries of history they missed whilst they were away. Those with living relatives can be reunited with them. They have already expressed a desire to make a go of creating a new life in a very changed world. They'll need new identities too, for obvious reasons. But many, especially those who disappeared centuries ago, will need far greater levels of support. They will of course get everything they need. A few of the returnees, as they've become known around Eden, have even volunteered to come and work for Sky Dreamer Corp.'

'It's great to hear that things have been progressing so well, and so quickly,' Jack said.

Jodie smiled at him. 'You know Alice. She doesn't slow down for anyone or anything.'

'Just like us,' Mike replied.

'I for one am looking forward to getting back to work and heading out with the others to recover the rest of the awoken micro minds,' I said.

But Jodie was already shaking her head. 'Alice said you'd say that. But she's insisting that you all have a bit of proper R&R and just kick back for a few days. I mean, God, you must need it after everything that you've all been through.'

Jack met my gaze. 'You can say that again. I could sleep for a week after all this.'

Mike nodded. 'You're not wrong, I feel completely shattered as well.'

'But it doesn't feel right to be sitting on our hands when there are all those micro minds waiting for us out there,' I said.

'I think on this one occasion we can let someone else take the strain because this is what delegation looks like,' Jack said. 'We can't do it all by ourselves, Lauren.'

I knew he had a point. As the person in charge there was a

compulsion within me to try and do everything myself, perhaps even more so since the awful loss of Tom, something that I was still trying to come to terms with. To make matters worse, I kept reliving his death in my dreams, often waking in a cold sweat, my brain constantly coming up with a hundred other strategies where he might have survived. But every scenario I came up with, somebody still died in it. And constantly reliving that awful moment had left me hollowed out. Yes, maybe my body and even my soul, needed a moment to recover.

I slowly nodded. 'Okay, I give in. A bit of R&R sounds like something we could all do with right now.'

'Good, because Alice has a suggestion for you,' Jack said.

'Hey, have you been talking to her behind my back?' I asked.

'Maybe,' he replied, smiling at me. 'Anyway, how about spending some time kicking back in Cuba with Glenn at his place? It's all sorted if that appeals?'

I exchanged a look with Ruby and Mike, who were now both smiling too. 'You two were in on this?'

Mike shrugged, grinning at me. 'Whatever makes you think that?'

I shook my head. 'But let's be clear here. You mean actually have a real holiday where we're not on a mission and nobody is trying to kill us?'

'Exactly,' Alice said.

'I could catch up with some surfing,' Mike said, his grin widening.

'I would certainly love to do some diving with you that doesn't involve any secret underwater bases, Lauren,' Jack said.

The thought of spending some quality time with him was instantly appealing. If nothing else, having a holiday in such a special location would help remind me just how precious the world we were all fighting for actually was.

'Sounds like we have a plan,' I replied. 'But how about you, Ruby? Are you really okay with this?'

She shrugged. 'Hey my idea of kicking back is time on the firing range, but set me up with a sniper rifle and a few tin cans on a beach and I'll be a happy camper... and I do mean that in the first-person shooter sense.'

I smiled at her. 'Then it sounds like we have our vacation booked.'

A knock came from the door and my smile faded as Glenn, his face drawn, entered the room.

'They're ready to begin Maricela's funeral, guys.'

'Okay, we'll be straight there,' I said. I glanced back at the screen. 'Catch you guys later.'

Jodie nodded. 'Good luck, I'll be thinking of you all.' The screen went dark as she ended the call.

As we stood up, I straightened my black dress for the third time in a week. Then I took a large physical and mental breath. 'Okay, let's go and give Carlos and Raúl the moral support they need.'

Jack patted my shoulder as we headed towards the door, but already the feeling of dread was filling my stomach. I was emotionally wrung out, but I wouldn't be able to relax until this last ceremony was behind us. My head lowered, a heaviness in my step, I followed the others out onto the deck under a bright blue sky that seemed completely incongruous to how I was feeling at that precise moment.

Jack and I swung gently together on one of the twin hammocks in front of Glenn's crumbling mansion as we gazed at the sunset over the Caribbean sea.

I breathed in the salt-filled air, noticing that the tension in my neck had finally relaxed. It had taken a while, but at last the trauma that I'd been carrying inside me had begun to loosen its hold on my soul.

Out on the sparkling water, Mike was riding the waves on a surfboard that he'd borrowed from Glenn. He zipped back and forth, turning on a dime as he crouched low, riding what he had already told us was great surf. He might be a long way away but everything about his movement was joyful and I could just about see the huge smile on his face as sliced up those waves.

Further along the beach, Ruby had been true to her word and had set up a tin can firing range. She was currently giving Antonio some weapons training with her Accuracy International sniper rifle. Glenn was with them too, taking a very active interest in his son's performance. Every so often the gentle sighing of the waves was punctuated by Glenn's applause when the teenager managed to hit one of the cans.

'Ah, I could seriously get used to this lifestyle,' Jack said, sipping on the ice cold beer that our host had furnished him with along with a seriously good mojito for me.

I reached across and squeezed his hand. 'Me too. Life has been so non-stop over the last few years that I'd sort of forgotten what a holiday even feels like.'

'Absolutely. I certainly know that I needed this time away from the coal face if I wasn't going to flame out.'

I grinned at him. 'Yes, all work and no play makes Jack a very dull boy.'

Jack snorted. 'And just how long have you been waiting to hit me with that particular line?'

I grinned at him. 'Forever.'

'Yeah, I thought so.' He kissed the side of my head. 'I so needed this, Lauren.'

'What all the sun, sea and sex?' I said, giving him my best attempt at an innocent look.

He laughed. 'Yes that, but just as importantly, some quality us time. We get so little time to just hang out and be a normal couple.'

I rested my head on his chest and nodded. 'I know normal doesn't really come into it. But hopefully it won't always be this crazy.'

'If we manage to retrieve all those micro minds out there waiting for us, you mean?'

'Yes, but *when* we recover them all, not if.'

He kissed the side of my head. 'Absolutely.'

A gull on the beach squawked and took off as a nearby tin can went flying when a bullet whistled through it. Ruby gave Antonio a high five as she beamed at her prodigy.

'If he keeps that up, Ruby will be recruiting him into our team next,' I said, smiling.

'Yeah probably,' Jack said, suddenly sounding distracted.

My spidey sense immediately told me he had something on his mind. I drummed my fingers on his chest. 'Okay, out with it, what are you thinking about, Jack?'

'Am I that transparent?' he said.

I sat up and looked at him, a lot more concerned that I had been only a few seconds ago. 'Apparently so.'

'Damn it, you know me way too well. I didn't want to spoil the holiday mood so I was going to delay showing you it.'

'Oh God you've got me properly worried now. Showing me *what* exactly?'

He sighed. 'It's Tom's last message. He recorded it onboard *Artemis* before he passed.'

Any sense of peace was instantly wiped away as the ache in my chest throbbed. My feelings were obviously written in large letters across my face as Jack took my hands in his.

'This is exactly what I was worried about; I didn't want to spoil things for you.'

'Just tell me what he said, Jack,' I said in a small voice.

He sighed and nodded. 'Okay, Lucy recorded Tom's video via the QEC radio system. Although it's to you, she asked me to be the one to show it to you and only when I thought you were ready to see it.'

My heart twisted. 'Oh God, this sounds really bad.'

'It's not and it may actually help you in a small way.'

He took a Sky Wire from his bag, pressed play, and handed the device to me.

As I took it, Tom's face had already appeared on the screen. He looked exactly as he did the last time I'd seen him, his face calm, not a hint of fear in his expression, just utter certainty. But the moment I saw him, a huge lump filled my throat and tears began to flow as Jack rubbed my back.

'This message is for you, Lauren,' Tom said, as water hissed into Artemis's cockpit around him. 'Please believe in yourself as much as I and all the others always have. You're the mission commander that Eden needs whether you realise it or not. And I for one am so bloody proud of you. All I ask of you is to continue to be the extraordinary woman that you are.' And then, so uncharacteristically for Tom, he blew a kiss towards the camera. 'Goodbye, Lauren, and good luck. The world needs heroes like you.' A second later the video was filled with static.

'We think that's the moment that the self-destruct sequence detonated,' Jack said gently.

Then I was sobbing so hard that it felt like my very being was breaking in two. But even as Jack enveloped me in his arms, I made a silent vow to myself as complete and utter grief took hold of me.

I would never stop fighting against the evil that had stolen Tom and so many others away before their time. And I would do whatever it took to save this big beautiful world of ours against the threat that was coming for us from the stars. I would do it for all the people I loved, for Aunt Lucy, for all the friends I lost along the way and now for Tom, too. I would be that woman, the hero that the world needed me to be just like all the incredible people I was lucky enough to call friends.

Then, as I rested my chin on Jack's shoulder, my anchor in this storm of grief, I gazed out towards the horizon.

Mike was waving frantically at us and for an awful moment I thought he was in trouble. But then I heard him whooping and pointing further out to sea, where a spout of water was shooting up from the surface. Then a whale's back broke the ocean's surface and a moment later its giant tail was propelling back down again.

I'd never been one for taking omens – good or bad – seriously. But right then, in my emotional state, I interpreted that as a sign from Tom, because how could I not?

I breathed out as some of the tension flowed out of me and I hugged Jack harder, knowing his love and support would help get me through whatever lay ahead. And the other thing that would keep me going, in no small part thanks to Tom's sacrifice, was knowing that right now, fifty very awake micro minds were out there waiting for us. That changed everything.

Whatever it took, I was determined that we'd recover each and every one of them because I couldn't think of a better way to honour the memory of a man who had become my mentor and friend.

Another whoop came from Mike as the whale broke the surface again. This time it was heading directly towards the sunset.

Okay, Tom, I get the message, I thought, smiling to myself.

I pulled away from Jack and stood, wiping my tears away with my towel. Then I picked up my snorkel and mask.

'Fancy a quick swim?' I said.

Jack looked at me, his head tilted to one side, and then a smile filled his face. 'With you? Always.'

Then hand in hand we headed towards the lapping waves as the whale flicked its tail again and disappeared once more into the depths of that golden ocean.

LINKS

Do please leave that all important review for **Earth Yell** here:
https://geni.us/EarthYell
So now you've finished **Earth Yell,** are you ready to preorder
the next page-turning instalment in the series?

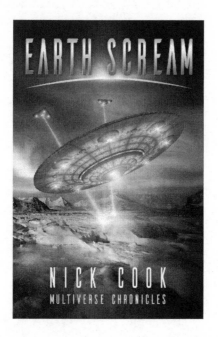

Ever since Lauren and the rest of the team activated the Resonancy Generator near Cuba, the radio signature of our planet,
known as Earth Song, has been changed forever. But it's raised as
many questions as it answered, including why the signal didn't
revert back to normal after nearly all the micro minds were
awoken. Could it be there is something else coded into the Earth
Song signal, whose purpose hasn't yet been fulfilled? Can Lauren
and the team piece together the final clues to discover the whereabouts of an alien artefact from before the dawn of human history
that will change the fate of our world forever? You can preorder
Earth Scream here: https://geni.us/EarthScream

    Meanwhile, whilst you are waiting for the next book, if you
haven't already you may want to consider reading the **Fractured Light** trilogy which is also part of the Multiverse Chronicles. This continues the story of the AI *Sentinel* six years after the
events covered in **The Signal.** A secret hidden in human DNA

is about to be unlocked, but can college students Jake and his underground hacker friend Chloe solve the mystery before reality itself starts to break down?

The **Fractured Light** trilogy is available here: https://geni.us/FracturedLightTrilogy

OTHER BOOKS BY NICK COOK

Prequel to the Multiverse Chronicles

The Earth Song Series (The Multiverse Chronicles)

The Fractured Light Trilogy (The Multiverse Chronicles)

AUTHOR NOTES

As I write this it's almost the start of March 2021 and the UK is still stuck in the midst of the COVID 19 pandemic. As someone who falls squarely into the extremely vulnerable category, I have been stuck in the house for over a year now, only able to go out for exercise when no one else is around. However, I've been extremely lucky to have just had my first dose of the AstraZeneca vaccine and I'm feeling incredibly grateful to the huge effort around the world that has made that possible. My heart certainly goes out to everyone who is anxiously waiting to get the vaccine. There is light at the end of the tunnel and one day we will be able to catch up with all those friends and family that we haven't been able to physically see for such a long time.

Anyway, throughout this enforced homestay period, I've poured my energies into writing the Earth Song series, so it's been an incredibly productive period creatively for me. Along with my wife and son, Lauren and the rest of the team have been my constant companions and have become like part of my extended family.

As always I had a great time doing the background research

for this book. Yes, the Cuban underwater structure really exists and is crying out for a fresh expedition to confirm one way or the other whether it's just some sort of natural formation or is in fact something far more interesting. This video, although not the best quality, and the creators do put their own interpretations about the structures found, does have a good summary of the acoustic and photographic evidence that has been found. When you watch it you'll quickly see why my imagination triggered when I was writing this book.

https://www.youtube.com/watch?v=pdCG2gIu2fE

The pirate angle to this story is a great example of a moment when I was researching Cuba and my research threw up an expected gem in the form of the rich history of pirates who sailed the seas around that area. If you're interested in learning more you should check out the real buccaneer Bartolomeu Português here: https://www.atlaslisboa.com/bartolomeu-portugues/

Earth Yell probably has the most epic finale to any of the Earth Song books yet and it will only build from here to the end of the series in book seven.

I have always enjoyed the slow reveal of bigger plot lines that often lurk in the backgrounds of the best sci-fi series. To this day I think one of the best TV examples of this form of epic story-telling was best personified by *Babylon 5*, truly one of the great sci-fi series. Each episode often had its own complete storyline, but lurking behind it was a far bigger story arc that was gradually unfolding. And this story form goes right back to books such as *The Hobbit*, where we are introduced to their homely world and then grows through the *Lord of the Rings* into a far more epic and rich tale.

It was actually reading those books as a teenager that well and truly lit the match of my own love of writing and in many ways, the book you have just read is part of the journey that as an author I've been on ever since. I think that the best books do exactly that, they take you on a journey into the imagination and I hope that my own work has done exactly that for you.

So this is where I thank everyone involved. As always a huge thank you to my tirelessly working editors who help to make this all possible, namely Beverly Sanford and Catherine Coe, who have helped to make Earth Yell sparkle and shine with all their hard work. Thank you, guys! And yet again another big shout-out to my wife Karen who has supported me emotionally through every twist and turn of my writing career. I really wouldn't be where I am today without her love and support.

And this is where I thank you, the reader. No book, let alone a series can work for everyone. However the fact that you are reading Earth Yell, book five in the series, would suggest that you have been entertained by my twisted sci-fi imagination. The series has continued to climb up the charts and now shares shelf space with some of my all-time sci-fi heroes, some of which like Asimov, were big influencers on my own writing as I grew up. I certainly wouldn't be able to do what I am today if it wasn't for you buying this book and maybe even spreading the word about it. Thank you from the bottom of my heart for your continued support and belief.

And so here I will sign off and whilst I wait for the first set of edits to come back, next week I will be starting work on book 6, Earth Scream! As they say, the best is yet to come.

Take care and in the meantime, keep reading and dreaming!

Nick Cook, March 2021

Made in the USA
Columbia, SC
14 October 2021

47172016R00202